Pat is deeply in love with Vernon, her husband. And he, a popular academic and TV chat-show celebrity, loves her. But after three years of marriage, she has doubts about her compatibility – not so much with him as with marriage to him. For their love is not enough to sustain what she increasingly comes to regard as a kind of imprisonment. She used to be a good photographer, much in demand, but has virtually given up to look after Vernon's daughter and their house; she used to enjoy parties, lovers, the 'swinging' London of the late sixties, but is now often alone and always in the shadow of her brilliant husband, her opinions and needs no longer seem to count for anything.

Perhaps love is not enough to base a marriage upon, Pat muses. And she is left having to make an agonising decision: frustration with the man she loves or self-fulfilment and independence at the risk of wasting three years with the best man she is ever likely to have met . . .

The Pursuit of Happiness is a telling, moving story of contemporary marriage appealing to all those who were enthralled by the television series *Helen: A Woman of Today*.

Also by Mervyn Jones

Fiction
No Time to be Young
The New Town
The Last Barricade
Helen Blake
On the Last Day
A Set of Wives
John and Mary
A Survivor
Joseph
Mr Armitage Isn't Back Yet
The Revolving Door
Holding On
Strangers
Lord Richard's Passion

Non-fiction
Potbank: A Study of the Potteries
Big Two: Aspects of America and Russia
Two Ears of Corn: Oxfam in Action
Life on the Dole

THE PURSUIT OF HAPPINESS

MERVYN JONES

QUARTET BOOKS LONDON

First published by Quartet Books Limited 1975
27 Goodge Street, London W1P 1FD

Copyright © 1975 by Mervyn Jones

ISBN 0704 320983

Computer typeset by Input Typesetting Ltd.,
4 Valentine Place, London SE1

Printed in Great Britain by The Anchor Press Ltd
and bound by Wm Brendon & Son Ltd
both of Tiptree, Essex

THE PURSUIT OF
HAPPINESS

THE PURSUIT OF HAPPINESS

I have woken up in the morning, sometimes, and looked with surprise at my husband sleeping beside me. The surprise did not exclude familiarity. No, it was the familiarity that surprised me. Thus, I thought, you might wake up in hospital or in prison or in a foreign country, knowing that you'd been there for years but still feeling it to be strange. He was my husband, this man; this was our bed, our room, our house; and yet these facts seemed to explain nothing. I wasn't in bed with him because of anything that had happened last night – any decision or persuasion – as with other men earlier in my life. Time could pass, I could change, he could change, and we'd continue to go to bed together. In short, we were married.

I stared at the ceiling and wondered how many women had these thoughts. Then he woke up. We looked at each other and kissed and lay close together. Everything was all right, because I stopped thinking.

I want to write about my marriage. I must. It has become a necessity.

I came across an interesting fact. In 1870, seventy-something per cent of women were married. In 1970, it was ninety-something per cent. Victorian women, outnumbering

1

men in the population, needed desperately to find husbands; those who failed had little chance of interesting work or independence, had a shabby sex life or none at all, and were despised as old maids. Women nowadays can earn a living in all kinds of ways and have affairs as openly as they please (I don't think this is confined to my own slice of middle-class London). So what do we do, ninety-odd per cent of us? We celebrate our improved status by getting married.

To ask why women get married is like asking why a moth flies into a flame. Deeper than thought or will, deeper than self, is the need for absolute intimacy, absolute commitment. The danger is terrible; you can be enslaved, hurt beyond relief, consumed, only when you have entered that blinding zone of intimacy. But the need comes first, the awareness of danger later. When I read that women are still oppressed by men, I say: of course. As fast as some escape, others surrender themselves. Workers can get rid of capitalists, blacks can get rid of whites: women cannot live without men.

I came to London five years ago, glorying in my freedom and confidently determined to lead my own life. Two years later, I got married. I hoped to be happy. I wanted the lot, the three-card trick; life, liberty and happiness. That's an inaccurate quotation. The inalienable rights are listed, with a prudent reservation, as life, liberty and the pursuit of happiness. Anyone can pursue; not everyone can achieve.

My name is Pat Bell. After I got married I continued to think of myself as Pat Bell, partly because it's my working name and partly because I believe it suits me. It has a straightforward, no-nonsense sound and I don't think of myself as a complicated person. Besides, it's easy to sign and nobody can go wrong about spelling or pronouncing it, which is more than you can say about some names.

My father is a doctor. A year or so before I was born, he took a hospital appointment at a small town in Northern Ireland. He liked the place, so he settled down and gave up all thoughts of professional advancement – he's that kind of man. It gives him a comfortable feeling to be what's called a universally respected local figure, and since the troubles began he's felt it important to fill this role. We're neither Protestants nor Catholics; in Ulster a Protestant means an Ulster Protestant, and we're English, and anyway we don't go to church. But when I was growing up, a little town in County Tyrone was a very peaceful place.

I'm the middle one among five children, a secure if undistinguished position. I have two elder brothers, a younger brother, and a younger sister. I suppose we're a close-knit family, but the kind that can stay close-knit by means of hastily scribbled postcards and 'Yes, I'm fine' phone calls.

My life, when I look back on it, can be seen as a wayward and blundering journey towards my husband. It didn't seem like that at the time; I have often been taken by surprise. At the boarding-school which I attended from the age of twelve to eighteen, I thought often about men, like most girls, but seldom about marriage, thus differing from what was considered normal at that particular school. In tone and social bracket, the school wasn't exactly where I belonged. It was because we lived in Northern Ireland, and because we're English, that my parents reluctantly sent all their children to boarding-schools.

The school's first, and only durable, achievement was to knock my Ulster accent out of me. Manners and speech were in reality the most important subjects taught. Though I wasn't exactly unhappy at my boarding-school – merely bored, and impatient for real life to begin – I couldn't at any time accept its scale of values. My manners were adequate, apparently, at the homes of my parents' friends, so I saw no need for added refinements. I did care about being good at lessons, or at least the lessons I enjoyed, and was puzzled by the implicit assumption that this didn't matter so much. After O-levels I had a somewhat tense interview with the Head, in which I maintained my determination to take science A-levels, while the Head kept saying that I could do very well in English and French, obviously more desirable accomplishments to her mind, and implied (without actually saying so) that science

3

wasn't quite the thing for a nice girl. The science teaching was in fact pretty poor, as I realized even at the time, and I was lucky to pass my A-levels in biology and botany.

Here there was a basic divergence between my outlook, developed and supported at home, and that of the school. It was assumed in the Bell family that every young person, a girl just as much as a boy, should prepare for a career. My mother had been a nurse and continued – indeed, continues to this day – to work two and a half days a week; this, as she often says approvingly, takes her out of the home. All five of us received periodic hints that it would be splendid if we became doctors, which was my ambition for a time and which my eldest brother did. The idea at the school was that a few brainy girls would go on to a university, another bracket of the semi-brainy to a college of education, and as for the rest it didn't really matter because they would get married anyway. Very few girls dissented from this scheme of things. Indeed, even those who were aiming for university saw it primarily as a more favoured field for husband-hunting.

All the girls talked a great deal about the kind of man they hoped to marry. Physical characteristics were seldom mentioned, except between very close friends, and the discussions concentrated on character (reliable, considerate, keen to get ahead) and social status (barrister, diplomat, 'interesting job' or, at moments of candour, just rich). Your chances of making a good catch were taken to depend almost entirely on your looks, and there was plenty of desperate worrying on that score, since few girls could kid themselves that they were ever likely to look like Brigitte Bardot or Elizabeth Taylor. I worried a bit – what girl doesn't? – but I was saved from real anxiety by my amusement at the worrying of the other girls, and frankly by my confidence that I'd turn out all right, as I think I have. I've a sort of funny-face which no one could describe as beautiful, but men like it.

Even the dimmer and primmer girls were vaguely aware that this talk about marriage was a code for talk about sex. To

4

say that you wanted to get married before you were twenty-one, which was the prevalent view, meant that you wanted to 'do it' before you were twenty. For there were also long and earnest discussions about the circumstances in which one might, or should, do it. The old morality, according to which you mustn't do it until you were married, had yielded in general to newer conventions – but they were still conventions – which allowed you to do it if you were engaged, or if you were truly in love, or if you had 'a real relationship'.

I couldn't regard these conditions with proper gravity, and doubted whether I'd have the patience to observe them. When I was sixteen my mother gave me a straight talk about methods of contraception, on the clear assumption that I'd soon be needing them. I looked forward cheerfully to the loss of my viginity – a phrase, indeed, that I found absurd, since I saw the event as gain rather than loss and considered virginity no more worth preserving than illiteracy. It didn't seem to me to be of overwhelming importance who the man would be, though naturally he'd be someone I liked.

But for the other girls, I observed, the prospect of 'doing it' was placed in a context of responsibility. It was accepted that you were supposed to enjoy it, and would in fact be judged by your ability to do so. Magazines with articles about orgasms, adjustments to your partner, 'overcoming problems' and so forth circulated constantly and were read avidly. Yet in a sense it was all as much of a mystery, and a source of mingled anticipation and trepidation, as it had been for their grandmothers. It was something like the mystery of the Mass, in that what you had to do was obvious, but the inner experience was indescribable, incommunicable, unrelated to the world about you. For me, however, it belonged to the whole course of life, which I accepted as a mixture of pleasures and difficulties. My mother grumbled about her menopause as readily as she explained to me about periods; my father answered questions about hysterectomies, Caesarian births, defective children and venereal diseases. I wasn't daunted by any of this, but I was thankful that one could begin with something nice.

I couldn't see this something as a mystery, for I linked it with the friendships between men and women – more vibrant and eager because the two sexes met, but firmly set in the everyday world – which I'd been aware of all my life and which began between boys and girls. I had two older brothers and had grown up with the constant presence of their friends; it was the boarding-school that made an unnatural interlude. It seemed reasonable to expect that the first man to make love to me would be someone like Bob Curran. He was a few years older than me, and very thick with my brothers. As children, Bob and I had gone hiking and picnicking in summer and skating in winter; so we still did, in my school holidays. It happened, also, that we were both keen on photography. I used to spend long afternoons on the top floor of the big Curran house, where Bob had fixed up a darkroom in what used to be an extra lavatory and taught me how to develop my pictures. Naturally, as I saw it, we spent part of the time like this and part of it in his bedroom (also on the top floor) kissing and cuddling. One rainy afternoon, when his parents had gone to Belfast for their regular big shopping spree, he paused in this activity to say: 'You know what I'd like to do, Pat?'

I indicated that I could guess.

'Would it be your first time?'

'Well, yes.'

'I'll be gentle with you. I know about it.'

'So I've heard,' I said. Bob had a certain reputation in the town; when he smiled at a girl she felt his easy confidence, as I felt it now. I asked him later which of my friends he'd had, to which he replied that it was against his principles to talk, and assured me that he wouldn't talk about me.

I undressed, feeling rather as though I were in for some unusual but beneficial kind of medical treatment. As the action began, my mood was one of curiosity heightened by a certain larky gaiety. He was gentle, as he'd promised, and

6

hurt me hardly at all. It was less of a whirl than I'd hoped, but enjoyable. Then we lay and talked. Naked in the warm room, with the coal fire blazing and the rain pattering quietly on the windows, I felt dreamily pleased with what I now shared with my friend Bob.

'How do you feel, Pat?' he asked.

I said: 'Fine. Can we do it again before they get back?'

He wasn't so scrupulously gentle the second time, so I enjoyed it more, and said so. He assured me that it could be better still; you got more out of it as you progressed, like anything else. 'We'll stick at it then, shall we?' I said.

This happened in the Easter holidays; I was just seventeen. When term began, the other girls guessed. Maybe I let something slip during one of the endless discussions, and maybe this thing just shows. Of course, it was all round the school in no time.

The achievement increased my prestige, since few other girls had matched it, but not my popularity. When I said that it had been fun, but failed to describe it as inexpressibly beautiful or deliriously exciting, it was generally felt that I'd let the side down. By the highest standards, I was offering the impatient virgins a disappointment. I also offended by not being in love with Bob. It was unsuitable, they clearly considered, to dedicate the precious gift to a friend whom you'd know since childhood, and altogether wrong to go on thinking of him in the same way as before. Did I want to marry Bob? It hadn't occurred to me. Was he my boy-friend? Not exactly. Was it a real relationship? Sort of, I replied lamely. I emerged with the reputation, not so much of being immoral and 'cheap' – though some girls undoubtedly thought that – as of being excessively matter-of-fact in a sphere that ought to be purely emotional. In self-defence, I adopted and stoutly maintained the theory that sexual experience should come first and love afterwards. That was Bob's line, the girls said cattily, was it? More out of tune with the bloody school than ever, I was glad that I had only one more year there.

7

I went through that last year writing long letters to Bob (who replied affectionately but more briefly), mulling over memories of sessions in his room in the holidays, and not working for my A-levels so hard as I might have. Then I finished school, we went for our usual family holiday in County Kerry, and I came home to find that the A-level results, as I'd feared, weren't good enough for university. They would have done for a college of education, but I didn't fancy becoming a teacher. I wasn't unduly cast down, for I'd made up my mind about the profession I wanted to take up if I couldn't become a doctor. Bob and I had been developing photographs as often as making love, or rather more often, since the former activity could be carried on when the Curran family was at home. In the Christmas holiday, I'd devoted a great deal of time to studies of trees in snow, a perfect subject in the hard clear light of that winter, and one of my results had won a newspaper competition. I told my parents that I wanted to be a photographer, and they thought it was an excellent idea. There was a suitable course at the polytechnic in Belfast. I had no difficulty in being accepted.

Here I may say that I am permanently in love with my profession. What's great about photography is that it has so many satisfactions to offer. If you're scientifically minded, you can go on enlarging your knowledge; it's a miracle, like all the arts, but a miracle that can be explained. If you enjoy using your hands, there's plenty of scope for skill and precision. If you have an urge to create the unique and the beautiful, that delight is waiting for you; I insist that photography is a creative art, whatever some people may say. On top of all this, you're always dealing with people, and usually on the most amiable terms. For some reason, people expect a raw deal when reported or described in words, but assume that when they're being photographed the result will bring joy to their hearts.

I was given digs, through the poly's lodgings bureau, in a part of Belfast that was lower-middle-class, forbiddingly respectable, and solidly Protestant. My landlady, Mrs

Lauchlan, was a widow and might have been any age between forty and sixty. She began by laying down a set of rules: use of the kitchen at stated hours only, no radio or records after eight o'clock or on Sundays, no visitors after ten o'clock. I said hastily that I expected to go home at weekends. Sunday in this house, and indeed in this neighbourhood, was no enticing prospect.

It was about three months before I exchanged any more words with Mrs Lauchlan, except for muttered greetings on the stairs. She had, I think, a natural disposition to think the worse of anyone who came her way, especially anyone young. By degrees, however, she evidently made up her mind that I was an acceptable, rule-obeying girl and no trouble. I had no visitors at all, I had most of my meals out, and I even did my washing and ironing at home so far as possible. Whether because I'd completed my probation, or perhaps because of the approach of Christmas, she took the major step of offering me a cup of tea in her sitting-room, or lounge as she called it. This became a recurrent event, though never frequent, and we got on to terms of civility – considerably short of friendship – rather like neighbours. I was to stay at Mrs Lauchlan's for the whole three years of my course. It was as good as any other digs, and it was on a direct bus route to the poly.

It was only for the money that Mrs Lauchlan had a student lodger, as she didn't hesitate to make clear to me, and she preferred being alone. I don't think she ever left the house for a single night, and I felt that she enjoyed (so far as she could enjoy anything) the spells at Christmas and in the holidays when nothing mitigated her isolation. It struck me that there wasn't a picture of her late husband on the mantelpiece, which I should have expected a widow of her degree of respectability to consider obligatory. Once I ventured to ask whether she had been a widow for a long time. 'Yes,' she replied. (Conversation with Mrs Lauchlan was always heavy going; my questions got such terse replies that they were made to seem intrusive, while she put no questions at all.) I

9

wondered if Mr Lauchlan had really died or had decided to gratify her preference for living alone. Having gone so far, I asked whether she had any children. Not surprisingly, she replied 'No.' I got the impression that her marriage was a regrettable interruption to what was otherwise a life of contented solitude. It was clear, anyhow, that she didn't wish to be reminded of it, perhaps because it had been unhappy or unsuccessful, perhaps because it revealed that she had indulged in – I ought to say, had been subjected to – the act of sex, something which you could barely imagine when you looked at her. If she expressed an opinion it was in terms of disapproval (generally of Catholics) and among those of whom she disapproved where 'young women who only thought about chasing men'. I gathered that this covered young women who were seeking husbands as well as those who had other ideas. As for children, her implicit view was that the fewer of them that got born, the better; her main objection to Catholics was their glaring failure to share this attitude.

Now it seems to me extraordinary that I shared a house for three years with this human iceberg. But the digs were convenient, as I've said, and a big point in Mrs Lauchlan's favour was her total lack of curiosity about what I did elsewhere so long as I kept the household rules. I found myself disliking Belfast people in general – they are colder, more defensively suspicious, and in a curious way more provincial and peasant-like than people in the countryside – and Mrs Lauchlan was no more than an embodiment of these qualities. Long before my three years were up, I was utterly bored with both Belfast and the poly, and as impatient to get away as I'd been impatient to get out of school.

I didn't see then, and I don't see now, why a course in photography should last for three years. I suppose the three year course and the diploma represent a pathetic attempt by the poly to show that it's in the same line of business as a university. Photography, being an art, has things in common with the other arts. The basic process can be mastered quickly,

10

and most students have in fact mastered it before they become students at all. All the rest is experience, and that isn't completed by a diploma; perfection is for ever out of reach and you're going to be learning all your life. Last but not least, in any bunch of students you can soon tell who has talent and who hasn't. Those who haven't got it won't develop it if they study till they're drawing the pension; those who have got it are chafing after one year. I was among the chafers.

Spread over those three years, the work wasn't demanding, and I had a good deal of time to myself. Huddled in my room in the long dark evenings, I got through a lot of reading. When I gathered from the Sunday papers that someone had ideas which were causing excitement in distant London – like Robert Ardrey or R. D. Laing – I got hold of his books, either from the library or in paperback. I also read quantities of novels, some of them new and recommended by reviewers, some that had been around for years but would have been considered modern at my school. When I latched on to a writer, I couldn't get enough of him. At one time it was Lawrence, at another it was Moravia. My reading was utterly random, since there was nobody to guide me, but I had an urge to grab at everything within reach. There were then, and there are now, thousands of young people like me in Belfast and Dublin, Manchester and Leeds – reading by the hour in digs, queueing for concerts, seeking out Japanese and Swedish films, aching from a hunger that, in most cases, they never satisfy and gradually cease to feel.

However, there weren't many such types in the photography course at the poly, nor were there many to whom photography itself meant what it meant to me. Most of the students didn't aspire to anything more than a meal-ticket. Their future would be a routine of weddings and school groups or, at most, photo-journalism on some boring paper. I unwisely let it be known that I had wider ambitions, and this – combined with a degree of favouritism from teachers who found me an exceptional pupil – made me rather unpopular. I made some friends, of course, and the boys were keen enough

11

to take me out, but the general view was that Pat Bell was pretentious and stuck-up. My family background and my English accent didn't help to make me acceptable, since the students came mainly from the Mrs Lauchlan class. Most were Protestants, a minority were Catholics, and the two didn't mix; my inclination to make friends regardless of religion was another count against me. The feeling was that I didn't belong in the poly and my proper social mileu was the university, divided from the poly by a rigid caste barrier. I was aware, in fact, that I'd be likely to find more kindred spirits among university students, and I made an innocent attempt to get acquainted with them, the link being a girl from my home town who was one. But I didn't rate admission to the university caste, while my blunder stamped me as a snob from the poly viewpoint as soon as I was observed entering certain bars and cafés, so I gave up.

I spent the weekends and holidays at home ostensibly to be with my family, actually to be with Bob. Simply as friends, we had a lot to give each other. I offered him fun and high spirits, and a certain spontaneity which isn't common among small-town people, and he liked to hear me talk about books and ideas although – or because – they didn't belong to what he regarded as the real business of life. He gave me the feeling that I was with a man, not a mere boy; for Bob, though he didn't lack a sense of humour, was serious and responsible, and gave the impression of being older than his years. (Mr Curran, who owned a building and decorating business, was in poor health, so Bob took most of the work on his shoulders.) We went for country walks, we drove about in his father's car and Bob gave me driving lessons, we kept up the photography, and we kept up making love, which did indeed get better all the time. Bob, enjoying the role of senior partner and instructor, said that I was coming along marvellously. I had effortless orgasms, of which I was smugly proud, for Bob said that lots of women never managed it in their lives. I must be quite passionate, I decided. But I gave him most of the credit; I was sure, though I hadn't any basis for comparison, that he

12

was an outstanding performer. I've come across better since, and I can see now that his technique was rather limited, and not what I'd settle for to last a lifetime, although Mary (his wife) is probably quite content. Still, looking back, I'd say that he was a cut above what you might expect in a small town.

The only trouble was that I didn't get so much of it as I should have liked. The Currans were Catholics and highly respectable – not that the Protestants of the locality weren't equally so – and were supposed to believe that only photography accounted for my visits to the house. Bob was very careful about not taking the slightest risk that anyone might walk in on us, and this made things difficult. Houses in Ireland are seldom empty, especially in winter, and there aren't many other places where you can disappear – we might just as well have screwed in the street as taken a room at Flynn's Hotel. I was inclined to argue that the younger generation were indulging pretty extensively, as Bob well knew, and the older generation were too shrewd not to guess. To this Bob answered that guessing was one thing and knowing the time and place was another, and maintaining the decencies (or 'dacencies' – Bob's accent tended to thicken when such questions came up) saved trouble for all concerned.

It was my father's custom to announce, every three or four years, that he thought we could afford a more ambitious holiday than the usual spell in County Kerry, and this he did at the end of my first year as a student. We had a week in London complete with theatre and Prom tickets, three days in Paris, and a fortnight on the French Mediterranean coast. We stayed at one of those places between Marseilles and Toulon which my father, whose ideas were based on his own youth, imagined to be off the beaten track. In fact, of course, there's one damn great track nowadays from Portugal to Turkey, and in August it's beaten harder than a copper plate by innumerable cars, tents and bodies. But I've never minded crowds, whether in Oxford Street or on a beach. I like to mingle – to float among the human race to which I'm

13

delighted to belong.

With this crowd, I should have liked to mingle more closely. I'd have liked to be staying in one of the cities of tents, with people of my own age, rather than in a hotel among staid married couples, irritating small children, and elderly folk who complained about the heat and the noise. I used to wander round these tent cities, which I saw indeed as cities of a new kind, insubstantial and temporary, yet in another sense everlasting, since they would be renewed year after year and would never, like other cities, show signs of shabbiness and decay. Cities of brilliant colour, mostly blue and orange; cities that woke and slept amid the endless sound of pop music; cities in which intimacy was everywhere and privacy nowhere; cities without centres of authority or formality, without police stations, without Council offices, without churches; cities composed of a single element – people, people, people.

And what people! They were all so much at home that they seemed to have no other life; they could no more be imagined in an ordinary city than could the tents. They were all tanned to a deep gold (nobody seemed to have just arrived), they went about almost naked, and they were all beautiful. This wasn't so, of course, but they did all move with the confident frankness that comes from beauty. They were all young – this too wasn't literally so, but they assumed youth as they assumed beauty, and even an occasionally glimpsed grey head made the effect of being an amusing oddity, not of diminishing its owner's youth. They were independent of the outer world of houses and hotels; some were obviously younger than me, but it was impossible to picture them going on holiday with their parents, and an effort to imagine that they had parents at all. And they belonged to a sort of composite nationality, whatever part of Europe or America they came from. Regardless of language, I noticed, everybody managed to understand everybody else. I was discovering a new world; the English were as alien to me as the French or the Swedes.

14

During my second year at the poly, I lost Bob. There were two or three weekends on which he had no time to spend with me, even on Saturday evening when we'd been in the habit of going to the local dance-hall, and I'd just made up my mind to ask him what this meant when he forestalled me by telling me that he would like a serious talk. I must have known what this meant, though I didn't admit it to myself. We drove into the country on a freezing March day and sat in a deserted, cheerless bar. He told me, without beating about the bush, that he was engaged to Mary.

'I see,' I said.

'It's no pleasure to be telling you this,' he said, and I knew that it wasn't. 'But there was never any understanding between us, was there?'

'Oh no. No, there wasn't.'

'And you'd never see yourself spending your life in a place like this with a man in the building and decorating business, would you now?'

'I suppose not.'

'So let's say we've made each other happy, and remember it like that, shall we?'

'Yes.' I made an effort, and said: 'And I hope you'll be happy with Mary, too.' I hadn't much doubt of it. I had known Mary since we were kids; she was a pleasant, sensible girl, by no means stupid but easily contented with narrow horizons.

'You're a sweet girl, Pat,' Bob said with evident relief. 'Give us a kiss now. A good one, because it's the last.'

When I got home I said I didn't want any supper, and went up to my room and cried, but knowing that this was a means of adjusting myself rather than a sign of deep sorrow. My mother came in with a cup of tea and two of my favourite scones; I ate them gratefully and smiled when my mother remarked that I was hungry after all. She went on to say that Bob was twenty-five, and it was natural for him to want to marry, and a Catholic in a town like this, wild oats or no wild oats, was bound in the end to marry a Catholic girl and bring up his children in the faith. All of which was so clearly true that in a quarter of an hour I was chalking the whole thing up to experience.

Under Mrs Lauchlan's chilly roof, however, I went through some gloomy evenings with no man in my life and no weekends of fun and friendship to look forward to. I had never responded with more than civility to the advances of the poly students; carrying on with more than one man at a time seemed to me, at that period, vaguely dishonest and in any case unnecessary, and besides they were a pretty dim lot. I now made up my mind to give them a chance, since I had to spend another year and some months in Belfast and was well aware of my needs, or at all events inclinations. To my annoyance, my bright smiles and ready chit-chat in the cafeteria didn't bring me a rush of requests for dates. I had to pay for being unavailable hitherto, and by this time I was firmly classed as an alien element. Such dates as were forthcoming led to a series of stiff and boring evenings, eating tasteless chow mein in bad Chinese restaurants; if it was a matter of scintillating conversation, I'd have been almost as well off with Mrs Lauchlan. Nor did these evenings lead to anything else. Though none of these lads appeared likely to be in Bob's class, there were two or three with whom I wouldn't have declined to go to bed, where it was reasonable to hope that they'd put up a better performance than in the conversational sphere, and altogether the time would be devoted to more rewarding use. But I couldn't actually suggest it, and they didn't try to go beyond a bit of squeezing and stroking in the cinema and kisses in the bus-shelter. Perhaps they thought that a nice girl of my class wasn't open to further demands. Perhaps they simply had nowhere to take me to. The Belfast boys lived with their families in small and constantly occupied houses, while those from the country had landladies like Mrs Lauchlan. So I languished in enforced chastity until the autumn – six long months, quite a spell for a girl like me.

I found a man, eventually, through pursuing a different

16

interest. About this time, the artistic vacuity of Belfast was modified by a revival of Irish music. It was connected, though this wasn't clear at the time, with the political revival that first simmered and then boiled over soon after I moved on to London. I sing passably, at least in a chorus, so I joined a group and stated going to the ceili every Thursday night. My English accent caused raised eyebrows, the atmosphere being fervently patriotic, but I got myself generally accepted. Everybody except me, of course, was Catholic. The Protestants have their own songs and their own culture, if I may use the word in at least the anthropological sense.

The artistic level of the group was really quite high, and the acknowledged star was a young man called Kevin O'Hagan. He played the harp and sang in a high Irish tenor, and did both very well indeed as a result of natural talent and sustained practice. Indeed, he had nothing else to do, being unemployed like many other young men in what's now called the Catholic ghetto. When launched into a ballad, he appeared to be in the true line of descent from the minstrels who did their stuff in Tara's halls in bygone days. This effect was greatly aided by his flaming red hair and almost theatrically Irish looks. He was quite tall, but so slender that he made an impression of breathtaking grace and delicacy. In short, Kevin was one of those men for whom the word 'handsome' is inadequate and who can only be called beautiful. I gazed at him while he sang with a kind of awestruck passion, which could be prosaically rendered by the words: 'That's for me.'

Kevin took a gratifying interest in me, though at first for more impersonal reasons. He was profoundly absorbed in his Irish culture, and I think he was flattered – unselfishly, for he was modest on his own account – to find it appreciated by someone bred outside it. It proved, I suppose, that Irish culture was as good as any other and maybe better. At all events, he took it as his mission to teach and encourage me. After a few weeks he told me that there was another group, with rather different specialities, meeting on Fridays, and I might find it

17

interesting. Of course, I said I'd go.

Most people in this other group knew Kevin but no one knew me, so he was my sponsor and in a sense my host. When the evening broke up and the pub closed (the group met over a pub) he thanked me gravely for coming.

'I'm glad I did. Thank you for bringing me.'

'I'll see you home, then.'

'See me home? I wouldn't dream of it. I live miles away.'

He insisted, however, and of course I was really delighted. We had to take two buses. The first was crowded, but on the second we were alone on the top deck, and I slipped my hand into his. This produced a remarkable effect; he fidgeted on the seat, as though a pulsation of energy prevented him from sitting still, and rearranged his coat to conceal what I guessed to be an erection. I was still more delighted. It hadn't struck me before that he was the randy type, but evidently he was – I hadn't been alone with him until now, after all – and I made a guess that he had chalked up the same kind of score among the girls who went to the ceilis as Bob in my home town. I drew the further conclusion that he fancied me, and this was why he'd asked me to the Friday group and was now seeing me home.

'What d'you do when you're not at ceilis, Kevin?' I asked.

'Well, I practice a lot.'

'Go to the films much?'

'Not much.'

'There's a film I'm awfully keen to see.'

He said he would take me to it. He didn't sound very keen, but I took this to mean either that he wasn't interested in films or that the expense was a difficulty for him, since the film was on at a first-run cinema. I made a mental note to suggest Dutch treat as soon as we got things on a regular basis, which I trusted would be soon.

He hadn't cooled off physically, however, and I counted on a delectable kiss at Mrs Lauchlan's door. To my surprise, he said goodnight and 'See you on Tuesday', swung round with his usual lithe grace, and walked quickly away. I was disappointed, but didn't think much about it. There were certain conventions, and this was our first date, if it counted as a date at all.

At the cinema we ran into Kate and her husband. Kate was the girl from my town who went to university in Belfast; she had graduated a year ahead of me and was married. Since it was raining and they lived in my direction, she and her husband offered to drive me home, and there didn't seem to be much sense in Kevin coming too and then making his way back to the Falls Road.

When I saw Kevin at the ceili, I said: 'You can see me home tonight.'

'Oh, I will.'

'You'll be able to kiss me goodnight. You got done out of that on Tuesday, didn't you?'

He smiled, but I could see that he wasn't amused. When he did kiss me goodnight, I was sorry that I'd made my little joke. I had robbed the kiss of its spontaneity, almost imposed it on him. He would have kissed me anyway, I told myself. Curiously, I wasn't quite sure.

At all events, Kevin was now my boy-friend, in the traditional sense that we were keeping company. I saw him almost every day, and gave up going home at weekends to see him more often. We had meals together (back to the chow mein), we went to the dingy Odeon in my neighbourhood, and I persuaded him to be a visitor at my digs. He wouldn't let me pay for myself when we went out, so this was a suitable way to be together and spend no money.

We didn't progress, however, beyond the mildest kind of kissing and fondling. I was puzzled. Whereas Bob had never become aroused except in promising circumstances, Kevin was liable at any moment to intense spasms of desire. When we kissed, when we held hands in the cinema, even when he touched me accidentally, he was seized by impulses that could have been called uncontrollable, had they not been controlled. He had these astonishing erections, swift and sudden like the release of a coiled spring. I waited for him to say; 'You know

19

what I'd like to do, Pat?' But at these moments, he never said a word. If I looked at him, he blushed in the fiery way that went with his pale Irish colouring.

I realized that I'd got the wrong idea about Kevin. He wasn't trying to seduce me; I faced the task of seducing him. He was going through an inner struggle against me and against his imperious sexual drive. What I represented for him was a temptation, in a sense of the word to which his whole background gave a fearful power. He belonged to a type that I'd had no dealings with: a good Catholic boy.

I was somewhat daunted by this unexpected problem, but it was beyond my power to give up. Holding hands with Kevin had the same effect on me as on him. I wasn't in love with him – there must be more to love, I believed, than this narrow elemental passion – but I lusted for him as I'd never thought it possible to lust for a man. Besides, had anything been needed to concentrate my desire, there was also the fact that I had no other reason to seek Kevin's company. I'd always enjoyed talking with Bob, but I rather preferred Kevin to keep quiet so that nothing distracted me from his beauty. His only interest was in Irish folk-music, a subject that palled on me beyond a certain point. Except in this field, Kevin was quite uneducated – he had left school at fourteen – and, what was more his fault, devoid of curiosity. He read no books except thrillers, was bored when I dragged him into the art gallery, and never had an opinion about what film we should see. He had little or no sense of humour, which matters a lot to me; yet, though he was serious-minded, I had to admit that he wasn't intelligent. I was crazy for him – but it was just that, crazy.

So we went on for a while, meeting to make laboured conversation, achieving no ease or intimacy, aware of how little we had in common, yet both of us burning with a need of which we never spoke.

But if Kevin could only burn, I could make plans. I sometimes told myself, though I knew it wasn't true, that he was held back only by the usual Belfast problem – finding a place. This at least could be overcome. True, I shouldn't have dreamed of getting down to business under Mrs Lauchlan's roof, being convinced that the old bag had X-ray eyes. I asked Kevin to my room simply to build up a habit of domesticity – I used to make tea or supper – which, as every girl knows, is half the battle. But Kate and her husband spent most weekends in Derry, where he had an invalid mother. They had a flat in a modern, anonymous block. Kate had some experience of the Belfast problem, and readily gave me a key.

I told Kevin about the flat, pointing out that we'd be able to play records and sing without protest from Mrs Lauchlan. He couldn't believe at first that Kate had agreed to the arrangement; it was quite alien to his way of life, in which people came into your home as guests or not at all. I over-came these scruples, and we spent a cosy Saturday afternoon and evening together, featuring the most ambitious meal I'd ever cooked and some tormentingly passionate embraces. At eleven o'clock, however, he said that he ought to go, or his mother would wonder where he was. I hadn't reckoned with this, but could see on reflection that it was going to be a permanent aspect of life with Kevin, and I'd have to advance the timetable.

He returned next day after Mass and the family Sunday dinner. When darkness fell I drew the curtains, lay down on a handily placed divan, and patted it invitingly. He approached as though magnetized and lay beside me. We did some of what I'd been doing a few years back with Bob. I was soon in such a state that it would have been positively bad for my health not to follow through, and I knew that he was too. I unhooked my skirt and whispered: 'I'm all yours, Kevin darling.'

He stiffened – I mean his whole body stiffened, not what had happened quite a while earlier – and muttered in a sort of dry croak: 'Oh, Pat, Pat.'

I thought it was plain sailing at last, but he jumped off the divan and stumbled to a chair, where he covered his face with both hands.

'Kevin, come here,' I said in a tone that I meant to be

21

pleading but perhaps betrayed some annoyance.

'Don't Pat, don't,' he croaked. 'I'll go – I must.'

I didn't say anything more. I turned off the lights – this would suit him, I thought – and stripped. Then I knelt in front of him and coaxed his hands away from his face. He shuddered as if his soul were on the brink of hell, and that phrase is no joke. However, I wasn't giving the old faith any chance now, and we were soon in the bedroom.

He fucked me savagely, blindly – his eyes were closed – and very quickly. I didn't have time to come. He rolled off me, and when I touched his body I found it trembling. Then he got dressed.

Well, I thought, it was a start. We'd get used to each other, and it would get better as we went on. But, although we went to the flat almost every weekend for months, it was always more or less like this. This frantic release was all he knew of making love, and I found after one attempt that it was impossible to discuss the subject with him. I've no doubt he thought he was doing very well. You couldn't fault him on the score of potency, and he could do his act – the phrase seems inevitable – with impressive frequency. But the key to it was guilt, whether he knew it or not. It was as though he were strangling me, appalled by the deed and yet driven to it, getting it over and done with so that his thinking mind scarcely had to reckon with it. You could explain it all by his attachment to his mother, and the sociology of the Falls Road, and St Paul, but that didn't help me much.

Kevin's attitude to me – remember, he wasn't very bright – was a tangle of contradictions. He believed that he was in a state of mortal sin, but he also thought that as a non-Catholic I couldn't be expected to understand. My carefree habits – walking about the flat naked, for instance – shocked him deeply; but he was also in awe of me for reasons of class and education and influenced by me despite himself. He'd never met anyone before who took sex as sheer pleasure and seemed to be none the worse for it. He asked me time and again, in tones of bewildered fascination, if I really believed in going to bed with anyone who attracted me, and was envious as well as reproving when I laughed and said: 'Sure'. And after all, he was a man and he had a woman. On the principle of being hanged for a sheep rather than a lamb, he was as keen on going to the flat and getting into bed as I was.

I adjusted myself to his technique, if you could call it that. The storm of assault was exciting in a way, and I could usually manage to get a kick out of it. But the best times for me were the pauses, when I lay caressing and admiring his beautiful body. After that, the actual fuck was an anti-climax, if that's the word I want.

This weird affair couldn't have lasted very long, but I wanted – for fear of hurting Kevin – to keep it going as long as I was in Belfast. I wasn't prepared for it to end, as it did, in disaster. I might have had a premonition when Mrs Lauchlan summoned me to her lounge with the formula: 'May I have a word with you, Miss Bell?', which indicated that no cups of tea were to be offered and, as a rule, that I'd offended by going upstairs in muddy shoes or something like that.

'I'm afraid,' she said, 'I can't allow any more visits from that young man.'

In the course of an acrimonious few minutes, I couldn't get clear whether she objected to Kevin as a young man or specifically as a Catholic. The latter, I think; there were several references to 'this kind of neighbourhood'. Protestants like Mrs Lauchlan can detect a Catholic as infallibly as the Gestapo could detect a Jew. I pointed out that I had a right to visitors under the rules and Kevin had never stayed a minute past closing-time, but she was unrelenting.

I didn't like to tell Kevin about this. I wasn't seeing him so much during the week, because I was working hard on my photos for the diploma show, in which I was determined to do well. When we did go out together and he saw me home, I made sure that I reached the Lauchlan fortress after ten o'clock, when the rules forbade his crossing the threshold anyway.

I'm sorry now that I wasn't at the flat with Kevin for what

would have been our last weekend together. However, my twenty-first birthday fell on the Saturday and I went to my home town, where my parents gave a big party and I danced sentimentally with Bob Curran. I met Kevin on the Tuesday evening. He gave me a brooch in the form of a harp, which I still have and occasionally wear. We went to the cinema and he saw me home as usual. On the bus, he told me that he wanted to give me a birthday treat as well as the brooch, and proposed to take me to the dinner-dance at the leading hotel. I protested about the expense, but he was set on it.

I appeared at the hotel wearing my best long dress and waited in the foyer for Kevin. After about ten minutes I began to get worried; he was normally very punctual. I looked in the dining-room itself and all the bars and lounges, thinking that I might have got mixed up over the arrangements, but there was no sign of him and eventually I went back to my digs. I couldn't figure it out. Kevin had never missed a date and certainly wouldn't forget such a special occasion. Probably, I thought, he'd been unable to raise the money or to borrow evening clothes, and was ashamed to face me.

The O'Hagans were not on the phone, and I thought it wiser not to go round and see them because Kevin had never told them that he was going out with a Prot. Luckily I hadn't long to wait before I saw him, or at least got news of him, at the ceili.

When I arrived, everyone stopped talking and looked at me as if I ought not to be there. I went up to a girl called Maureen, who was more or less a friend, and asked; 'Where's Kevin?'

'Oh, Pat – you don't know?'

'Don't know what?'

She steered me into the refuge of the ladies' loo and told me. Walking to the bus stop on Tuesday night, Kevin was stopped and hemmed in by a group of Protestant youths who made clear their disapproval of his presence in 'their' territory and his connection with one of 'their' girls. Before they let him go, one of them carved a cut down his cheek with a

24

razorblade. They also took his watch and all his money; he walked for about a mile, dripping blood through his handkerchief, until he was seen by a police patrol and taken to hospital.

I gathered that he was now at home after being stitched up, and I asked Maureen to take him a note. She met me a couple of days later, embarrassed and shaken. Kevin didn't want to see me again, she said. His mother knew the whole story and had spoken bitterly about 'that wicked girl', adding that Kevin had now made a full confession to the priest. Maureen said, too, that the bandages had just been taken off and the scar was horrible – he would carry it to his dying day. I should have burst into tears if Maureen hadn't laid her head on my shoulder and burst into tears first. I suppose she was in love with Kevin; most of the girls were.

I had never been so miserable in my life. The fact that I'd never really been in love with Kevin, that I'd often been bored in his company and we'd given each other so little happiness of any kind, somehow made it worse. Then there was the cruelty of it, the ugly sneer of deliberate violence. Northern Ireland was peaceful in those days, but I glimpsed all at once the quicksands under the smooth surface of civilization. And the injustice, for Kevin was innocence itself and it was impossible to imagine him doing anyone an injury. Or it was impossible then. I've little doubt that he's in the Provisionals now.

I was fed up, fed up to the back teeth with this bloody little country, or province or whatever they called it, with its prejudices and hatreds, and its blind resistance to reason, and its obsessions that put the future in the grip of the past, and its sheer coldness of heart. I didn't belong to it, and I had an almost physical feeling that I could no longer breathe its thin dank air. I counted the days to the end of term as a prisoner counts the days to his release.

I went home at weekends, went nowhere on weekday evenings – certainly not to the ceilis – and tried to think of nothing but work. I did very well in the diploma show and

25

got a special award. I immediately applied for a job in London, answering an ad placed by a photographic agency. It said: 'fashion, portraits, general' which sounded varied enough. I cautioned myself that I must expect several rejections before I clicked, and I was delirious when I got a letter, signed 'Joan Baldwin (Mrs)', saying that the agency would give me a three-month trial on 75% salary and a permanent position if I suited. I ascribed this to my award, but found later that Mrs Baldwin couldn't care less about an award from a poly in Belfast; she judged me solely on the examples of my work that went with the application.

I was at home at the time, for I hadn't stayed under Mrs Lauchlan's roof a day longer than necessary. I packed as soon as I got the letter, took a train to Belfast, passed through it virtually with my eyes shut, and caught an afternoon plane. I figured that I'd need a week to find somewhere to live before starting the job.

I knew that there were lots of hotels near West London Air Terminal, and set out hopefully along Gloucester Road with my suitcase in one hand and my camera-bag in the other. Two hours later I was a sadder and wiser girl. I'd taken no account at all of its being the peak of the tourist season. I returned to the air terminal, had a meal, and settled down on a bench. Around midnight I was approached by a man who said he represented an organization called 'Friends in Need' and dealt in emergency accommodation. I told him I wasn't so dim as I looked, and spent the night on my bench.

In the morning I set out again. Stopping to buy fags and a paper, I noticed some cards offering furnished rooms. There was no point in going to a hotel after all, I decided – I wasn't a tourist. I copied down the addresses and soon got a room. It was tiny and distinctly grotty, and cost exactly four times what I'd been paying Mrs Lauchlan, but it would do while I looked for a flat.

On that first day, however, I just strolled around London. I didn't consider myself a complete stranger, having been there several times. I wore Marks and Spencer sort of clothes and spoke what's called standard English; twice that day, when Americans asked me for directions, I was delighted to see that they took me for a Londoner. And somehow, although I once got lost myself, I didn't feel that I was a stranger at all. I was already sure, as I've been sure ever since, that London is where I belong.

My pay was going to be quite decent, even at the 75% rate, and my father had given me something pretty generous to start me off. But I soon realized, reading the ads, that a flat of my own was beyond my means. There were a lot of ads seeking 'girl to share' or 'third girl' or 'fourth girl'. The more of a crowd the better, I thought. One ad said: 'sixth girl wanted'. That seemed to be the jackpot, so I rang the number.

The phone rang for a long time. Then a sleepy voice answered — it was about eleven in the morning — and said: 'Oh yes, we do want somebody. Come round now if you like.' The address was in Kensington, where I was already.

I thought at first that I'd copied it down wrong, for I found myself in front of the broad steps and dignified portico of what looked like the town residence of the Duke of Grousemoor. Later, when I knew London better, I grasped that houses of this size are a teeming womb of furnished tenancies, while the rich actually live in smaller houses in Chelsea or Hampstead. In this case, the house hadn't been a single unit since 1939. First it had been converted into five flats, each itself an ample family home, and at a later stage these flats had been either sub-divided or shared. The flat I was going to occupied the first floor. There was an enormous communal living-room, where probably deb dances had once been held, a big bedroom which had been some kind of reception-room too, and five other bedrooms created by cunning work with partition walls. The rent was steep, but feasible when divided by six. By this means, hundreds of girls in London are living in houses which their parents would never have dreamed of entering.

The sleepy girl opened the door, wearing nothing but a bath-robe. She had long golden hair and the kind of figure for

27

which the girls at my school had yearned in vain.

'Come in,' she said. 'I'm Stella.'

'I'm Pat.'

'I'll be a bit more with you in a minute. It was one of those nights, I'm afraid. I ought to make some coffee.'

She didn't seem up to the required co-ordination, however, so I said: 'I'll make it if I can find things.'

'Oh, bless you. There's the kitchen. You'll see everything.'

I almost cried out in delight at the kitchen, which Mrs Lauchlan would have regarded as something out of science fiction. The disorder was considerable, but I found what I needed and got the coffee started. Stella ambled in.

'You're wonderful, Pat. Have you got a ciggy?'

'Here you are.'

'Have you had breakfast? I only have coffee, but there's eggs and things.'

'No, thanks, I had breakfast hours ago.'

'Oh, you're really one of those capable girls, I wish I was. What do you do?'

'I'm a photographer,' I said proudly.

'Is that right? Any photographer's a friend of mine, because I'm a model.'

At this point a young man came into the kitchen, also wearing nothing but a bath-robe, and at a glance quite worthy of Stella.

'This is Hugh,' she said. 'This is Pat.'

'Are you going to be the new girl?' he asked.

I said: 'Well, we haven't discussed it yet.'

'I hope you are. I'm so bored with Stella, I can't tell you.'

'Bastard,' Stella said lazily.

'Tell me about yourself, Pat.'

I told him about my job, and that I'd just arrived in London and needed somewhere to live.

'Oh well, it's very comfortable here,' he said.

'And one meets such a nice polite class of man,' Stella added.

I poured the coffee, and Stella made the effort to explain

28

about the rent and so forth. After that, I went off to fetch my belongings. When I returned, Hugh had gone.

'I liked your boy-friend,' I said.

'You mean Hugh? There are things to be said in favour of Hugh, actually. He's got money, really loaded, and though you mightn't think so he's quite brilliant. He makes films for TV, he's got his own company.'

'You're a lucky girl, then.'

'Oh well, you know, there's nothing between us really.'

I burst out laughing.

'No, I mean, we just end up here sometimes when we've been at the same party.' Stella eyed me more alertly than before. 'Did you say you'd just arrived in London, Pat?'

'Yes.'

'Where from?'

'Northern Ireland.'

'Oh. I hope you're going to like it.'

'I'm going to love it,' I said with conviction.

Next Monday morning, I started work. Mrs Baldwin didn't waste time on chatting, but sent me out on an assignment at once. She was a woman of about fifty, divorced, and she lived for the agency. She had never been a photographer herself; she was just a good organizer and studied the market as a general studies a battlefield. She seldom moved from behind her desk, perhaps because she was no more that five feet tall and nearly everyone who came into the office was likely to be bigger than her. I picture her, while I write, as I often saw her, holding the phone to her ear with a hunched shoulder, talking to me over it, scribbling on a pad with one hand and flicking over prints with the other. To look at, she was like one of those rare birds you see at the Zoo. Her silver-grey hair stood up like a crest and her spectacles, with bright green frames, seemed to be part of her colouring. Like many small people, she had a peremptory and rather defiant manner, as though to indicate that she didn't intend to be put down because she lacked inches. Clearly, she was hard as nails. I realized that she wouldn't hesitate to get rid of me if she wasn't satisfied after

29

my trial period, so it was a real boost when she put me on the permanent staff. I can't say that I liked Mrs Baldwin, nor did she wish to be liked, but she was exactly the kind of boss I wanted. I was setting out to make my way by my own efforts and it wouldn't have suited me to have a boss who 'made allowances', still less a kind of substitute mother. Mrs Baldwin was exacting, efficient and reliable; you didn't need to think about catching her in a good mood or avoiding a bad mood, because she had no moods, and she judged her staff entirely on their work without favouritism or friendship.

The agency was on the top floor of a building in Mayfair, once a house and now offices. There were two rooms, one for Mrs Baldwin and another where the photographers could write letters and make phone calls. If we had any time to spare, we spent it at a nearby sandwich bar called Angelo's, away from Mrs Baldwin's vigilant eye. However, we were on the go without much respite. I sometimes began the day by going to the office, but my first job could quite well be in Kensington or points west, so it saved time to get my instructions on the phone. Mrs Baldwin didn't care whether she actually set eyes on me for days together.

There were four other photographers, all years older than me – three men, and a woman called Eileen Hurst. The men might have been taken for computer technicians if you'd seen them on the tube. Mrs Baldwin didn't favour photographers who came on like David Bailey, calculating that they were likely to follow their own bent and eventually leave the agency to go freelance. I didn't see much of these men but I liked them, as I liked Mrs Baldwin, the way they were. I was a professional among other professionals. Friends I could find elsewhere. I did, however, establish quite a friendship with Eileen, and a chat with her at Angelo's or in the pub was a welcome break in the day. She was an intelligent woman with a caustic sense of humour, who gave the impression that life hadn't offered her quite what she deserved. Her husband was news editor on one of the papers and worked most evenings, which Eileen didn't mind; he wasn't quite what she deserved

30

either, I gathered. Their children were teenagers and ran their own lives to a great extent. Sometimes Eileen came back to the flat with me for a snack, or we had dinner together in Soho.

As for the work, general was the word for it. I photographed models who posed as though born to wealth and idleness, then cadged a smoke from me and hurried off to queue for a bus. I did close-ups of hair sleek with shampoo, necks adorned with diamonds, arms gracefully displaying costly watches, and breasts held in Holborn escalator bras. Also men in rugged sweaters, men in Savile Row suits, men in exiguous swimming trunks. Alcoholics beaming over mugs of cocoa, non-smokers with pipes in their mouths, homosexuals gazing into the eyes of girls. I photographed on top of the Post Office Tower, on a launch speeding down the Thames, and in Covent Garden at dawn. I sat through rehearsals of plays and took pictures for programmes and publicity. I went into factories and photographed lathe-operators, fork-lift drivers and analytical chemists, all destined to demonstrate their concentration, devotion and contentment in the pages of company reports. To make the occasion immortal, I went to society dances, City banquets, learned conferences, publishers' parties, the opening of a hospital and a centenarian's birthday celebration. For a road safety campaign, I sped along the North Circular Road in a police car to photograph a crash. For a conscience campaign about the homeless, I waited three hours for a rat to come out of its hole and triumphantly snapped it. I made portraits of people who were famous, people who wanted to be famous, people who were just vain, and people who were just rich. I trailed out to places like Sunningdale or Rickmansworth to photograph wives, children, babies, houses, rose-gardens, dogs, cats and ponies. I photographed a countess in her robes and, after a quiet word with her husband, his girl-friend in a bikini.

It was hard work. I was always hurrying about London and the outskirts, standing in the tube, running to catch buses, and of course carrying my heavy camera-bag. Mrs Baldwin was

31

reluctant to pay for taxis and at first I couldn't afford them. Later, I took them without worrying so much, and after a year I bought a car, which made life much easier. I needn't have worked so hard, for Mrs Baldwin wasn't a slave-driver and understood that too much haste meant bad results. But we were allowed to take on jobs privately so long as we got through the agency work, and I jumped at them. I did them partly to make more money, partly because the subjects interested me, partly because I couldn't say no to a friend – but above all because I love using the camera. With my salary, once it was at the full rate, and these private commissions, I did very nicely. At the age of twenty-two I was making more money than I knew how to spend. The money didn't matter to me, however, nearly so much as the happiness of succeeding in my chosen career.

That, and being in London. Every day in London was a joy; I grudged the week I spent with my family at Christmas and didn't really care about having a summer holiday. The most exciting thing about London was simply the people. First of all their variety – I found it wonderful to be among all these Italians and Cypriots and Jews and Irish and West Indians and Pakis and Indians and Australians, and wonderful to see how they managed to be Londoners and still be themselves. And then, it's a fact for better or worse that the brightest people in a country make their way to the capital. After this spontaneous selection has been going on for centuries, as it has in London, you get a population that's more alert and quick-minded and independent than people elsewhere. I was happy to think that I was part of the process.

Through my work, I was meeting Londoners all the time and getting to know quite a lot of them. A photographer has to chat the customers up to put them at their ease, and my natural curiosity is considerable, so I was always asking people about their jobs, their homes, and their lives in general. Most people are more willing to give out to a stranger than to someone they know, which accounts for the astonishing frankness with which they confide the most intimate details to

TV cameras. I was a camera too; after a few weeks in the business, it no longer surprised me to be told about the marriage being kept up only for the sake of the kids, or the old Mum who was an intolerable pest, or the boy who was on acid. Quite often I was even asked for advice, as a person who doubtless knew her way around.

I passed in and out of these lives, generally, pretty much as when you meet someone on a journey. But, out of the dozens of people who said 'I hope we'll keep in touch', a few of them meant it and asked me to tea or dinner or a party. There I met more people, and within three months I made more friends – and a vastly more varied selection of friends – than I could have made in a lifetime in Belfast. Some were friends and some were men, if the distinction is clear. But about men, more later.

I'd have found plenty of friends and plenty of men even without the job, because I'd answered the right ad when I was looking for somewhere to live. It was a while before I met all five of the girls, though. They worked different hours and some of them went away for varying periods. One wall of the kitchen was used as a notice-board, on which you could read such appeals as: 'Stella – phone Denis NOW – crisis he says.' Empty, however, the flat never was. It was more like coming into a club or a pub than a home. You never knew whom you might find there. Men, though their appearances were irregular and unpredictable, tended to behave as if they lived in the place, especially when it came to demanding large breakfasts.

Stella's sex life was wide-ranging and motivated by impulse or, as with Hugh, by friendship; she was too wary to have permanent affections and too cool, or too lazy, to get emotionally involved. She was merely amused when a man who had spent a night with her chose to spend the next night with someone else, and she was baffled by any hard feelings if it was the other way round. She worked just enough to keep herself in funds. She posed for fashion when she was in a position to choose, for nude girlie when necessary, and for

33

porn when she was really hard up. She soon asked me if I'd like to take the nude pictures, explaining that she found it unnatural to strip for a man and just get dressed again. She knew where to sell them and we split the proceeds.

Claudine (whose name had originally been Doris) was one degree more promiscuous than Stella, in that she wasn't averse to taking money. She worked for a fairly dubious escort agency and went out with American businessmen or Arab oil sheikhs, sometimes accompanying them to their hotels or bringing them back to the flat. For the rest of us, the advantage of Claudine's line of work was that the flat was always full of expensive chocolates. She had certain principles, however; she never slept with a man who didn't attract her, and when off duty she often brought home a man who was just a friend.

Janet was the oldest of the girls – almost thirty – and had the big bedroom because she had originally found the flat and was the legal tenant. A Scot with a good head for business, she managed and partly owned a successful night-club and was never home until four in the morning. Though I soon got used to seeing non-resident men at breakfast, I was puzzled to see non-resident girls until I grasped that Janet was gay (as I learned to call it) and they were hostesses at her club. She didn't bring them in often, because they teased her by flirting with the men. Stella, out of her casual good nature, slept with Janet from time to time. I was approached, but Janet didn't take it amiss when I said that I wasn't interested.

Peggy worked as a secretary for a man whom we called the Tycoon and was often away, going on trips with him to New York, Latin America or Australia. He depended on her both as secretary and girl-friend; his wife disliked London and was usually at his country place in Gloucestershire. The Tycoon, a nice man with a quiet voice and diffident manners, didn't much like coming to the flat and was ill at ease when involved in sociable breakfasts, but Peggy was loyal to the other girls and used to bring him along by saying that there was to be a party, ordering cases of champagne and quantities of smoked

34

salmon and charging them to the firm. We all liked the Tycoon and Stella made quite a play for him. Peggy bet Stella that it wouldn't come off and won a pound.

Erica too was away periodically. She was a film continuity girl and went on location when necessary. Otherwise, I saw more of her than of the others, because she had to be on the set early in the morning and was normally in the flat in the evening. Erica was Jewish (her parents had been refugees from Hitler), dark and intense-looking, and had a fatal tendency to fall passionately in love with men whose inclinations ran to no more than easy-going enjoyment. We took turns to stem her tears and to offer her comfort and advice. In the dominant atmosphere of what the Pope describes as sinful hedonism, Erica supplied the element of serious drama.

Erica it was, in fact, who answered the phone a few days after my arrival and said: 'Pat, it's for you.'

'For me?'

'Yes,' Erica said with a brave smile. It was her fate to pick up the phone hopefully and find that it was ringing for someone else.

A male voice, vaguely familiar, said: 'Well, my dear, how do you like London?'

'Who's this?' I asked.

'It's Hugh,' the voice said, apparently surprised at not being recognized. I did a quick think and grasped that it must be the man who was bored with Stella. He wanted me to have dinner with him. I didn't see why not.

He took me to an extremely expensive restaurant, where the food was excellent and I wasn't called upon to make great conversational efforts, for Hugh recognized some friends and got the waiters to shift the tables so that we could make up a party. I was to find, as I got to know him, that Hugh preferred not to be alone with a girl, except in bed, and even there you had the feeling that he would have preferred two or three other couples to share the fun; I have never met a more gregarious man. We stayed at the restaurant for about six hours. The meal took ages, and you could also dance, which I did, with Hugh and several of his friends. When the crowd thinned out and the place showed signs of closing, I thought it correct to look at my watch and say: 'Well, I've had a simply wonderful time.'

'I'm so glad,' Hugh said. 'But I've had practically no chance to talk to you. Shall we go to the flat?'

'My flat?'

'The atmosphere is always congenial there, wouldn't you say?'

The big room was empty, surprisingly enough. I made coffee and we settled down on the couch, Hugh with his arm round me and stroking my breast with an engagingly casual air, rather like a man stroking a dog. We talked, or rather he told me scandalous and entertaining stories about the people we'd met at the restaurant. I wondered for quite a while whether he was going to kiss me, and had got quite impatient when at last he did, with the same casual air, but very pleasantly.

'That was nice,' I said.

'Yes, wasn't it? I rather think we could become good friends. Would you say that's a reasonable idea?'

'Very reasonable.'

'Do you find this room rather large, I mean for two people?'

I was charmed; I had always supposed that people in London used some such phrase to indicate their wish to go to bed with you. We went into my bedroom. 'Ah, this is very cosy,' Hugh said.

Hugh's knack, so far as girls were concerned, was that you were always impatient by the time that anything happened. After we got undressed he spent a long time admiring me, as he put it, and praising my attractions; then a long time touching and fondling me, still standing up; then a long time caressing me on the bed; and when he finally made love to me, Kevin could have gone through his act three times while Hugh did so once. All this delighted me. I had never been treated like this by a man before. I saw that what had always been exciting (as a matter of fact, it wasn't very exciting with Hugh) could also be delicate, subtle and luxurious. It was with Hugh, during my first months in London, that I became acquainted with sexual good taste, sexual skill, and sexual ingenuity.

It would be inappropriate to say that Hugh was my boy-friend, or my lover (certainly neither of us was in love), but we did become good friends and we often made love, always in the same leisurely and amiable style. I soon saw what Stella had meant by saying that there was nothing between them really, they just ended up together at times; I was now on exactly those terms with him.

When I slept with Hugh ... this, by the way, is an inappropriate phrase ... we always went to bed very late, coming on from a night-club or a party, the activities took a long time, and when they were over he liked to talk, often resuming a conversation where we'd left it hours before. I liked talking in bed too, but there were limits, and I made it clear that he mustn't take offence if I dropped off. I had work to do in the morning, whereas it could hardly be said that Hugh ever actually worked.

When I slept with Hugh, to resume, it was always at the flat. He lived with his parents. They were very rich, his father being a merchant banker, and they had a luxurious house with servants — very central too, in fact one of the few remaining private houses in Mayfair — so it had never occurred to him to move out although he was in his late twenties. The parents, I gathered, made jokes about his 'strings of girls' but didn't press him to get married. They probably realized, as I did after a time, that he had a childish streak.

He wasn't interested in making love more than once a week or so, partly because he wasn't highly sexed — the prolonged foreplay was for his benefit rather than mine — but mainly because his sexual life was really an aspect of his social life. If there were other people in the living-room when we came back to the flat, he settled down for a good gossip and eventually I had to say: 'Come on, Hugh, let's go to bed.'

37

When he came across a new girl he always wanted to sleep with her, but chiefly in order to get to know her better. I sometimes thought, perhaps exaggerating but not all that much, that what he sought from me – in bed as well as around town – was the pleasure of my company. He was happiest at lunches and dinners, ideally of at least a dozen people, and at crowded parties, from which it was almost impossible to drag him away. Once he asked me to go to an orgy with him. I agreed, I suppose out of curiosity, but I had to admit that I didn't really enjoy being fucked in the midst of a circle of commentators. Hugh enjoyed every minute – as a commentator more than as a participant, I noticed.

Everyone liked Hugh, and not only because of his money. He was unfailingly good-tempered and charming, a good talker in his easy, superficial way, and often very amusing. The money helped, however. If I expressed an interest in a new book, he bought me a copy (though reading was too solitary an occupation for him); if a play came up in conversation, he organized a party of four or six to see it; and he always paid at restaurants and night-clubs, or rather signed his name and showed one of his numerous credit cards. Stella was mistaken, I discovered, when she said that he was brilliant as well as rich. His films were brilliant and his company successful because he had the flair to employ the best directors and cameramen. Then, out of a mixture of good sense, amiability and laziness, he let them get on with it.

Like Stella, Hugh was incapable of possessiveness or jealousy. He used to ask – I suppose to find something new to talk about – whether I'd slept with anyone else since our last time together. If I had in fact slept with a man he knew, he listened contentedly while I told him all about it. It was like telling one of the other girls, and despite my innocence at this time I was more or less aware that Hugh was bisexual by nature. But I had to be careful what I told him. He was very cross, instead of amused as I'd hoped, about an incident when I had a quick bash with a hire-car driver on my way back from a job in the suburbs. That was deplorably bad taste,

Hugh told me.

If I'd been in love with Hugh, or if he'd been a knockout in bed, I might not have slept with anyone else. As things were, it was more or less inevitable, because of the atmosphere around the flat and, quite simply, because I met so many men. I met them at the flat, I met them through my work, I met them at parties. Whether escorted by Hugh, towed along by Stella, or invited on my own account, I went to a party practically every Friday and Saturday night. I don't suppose I ever got through a party without at least one man trying to pick me up. I said no far more often than I said yes, for I didn't fancy myself as a girl who said yes whenever she was asked, still less as a reliable name and phone number to be handed on from one man to another. Also, I reserved the right to treat men as friends. Because a man interested me and I was willing to drink coffee or Scotch and chat with him until a late hour, it didn't follow to my mind that I was bound to go to bed with him. Still, I did go to bed with quite a few. Keeping score is detestable, and I couldn't get the number right after this lapse of time, but it may have been ten or a dozen during my first winter in London.

I was young and free; I wasn't always going to be young and free. I was curious about men, especially men so different from any I'd known hitherto. You really did get to know more about a man – his character, his real self – in bed. I was curious about sex, too: about actions and sensations that brought discoveries about the resources of the male and the female body. It didn't seem to me wrong to find out what my body was capable of, as well as my mind.

This makes it all sound planned, which of course it wasn't. Particularly after a good party, I used to find myself rather dreamily allowing a man to get me beyond the point of no return, while saying to myself – or occasionally aloud – 'I honestly don't know why I'm doing this, but what the hell.' It was a pleasure (after Belfast) to follow an impulse without guilt, secrecy or complications. There were men whom I liked so much that it was the friendly thing to do. There were men

39

who got so insistent that it was easier to give in than fight. And there were men who were just so attractive that I needed no other reason.

But after six months or so of this kind of thing, I was able to take a cool look at the way we lived in and around that flat in Kensington. It was lavish with easy gaiety, and free from malice and suspicion, and honest in its open candour, and to be sure it was fun. But there was something hard about it; there was a cold core within the friendly warmth, a selfishness within the ready generosity. Men and girls gave freely in several kinds of coinage, yet gave nothing that cost them very much. There was something shallow about it too, an airy flitting over depths that we seemed to fear. It was good for a span of youth, so long as you knew how not to get hurt. I was willing, indeed eager, to get what I could out of it. But I began to foresee a time when it wouldn't suffice me.

I began to think of how good it would be to settle down in contentment and security with one man, and one man only. 'A real relationship', they had said at school. Not a bad idea, after all. There was certainly something unreal about my relationship with Hugh. I wasn't yet tired of the non-stop comedy-drama that went on at the flat, but I thought sometimes of the calmer pleasures of living with a man: counting on his presence at the end of a long difficult day, the whole steady intimacy contained in the words 'living together'. However, I didn't want to live with Hugh and he definitely didn't want to live with me. Nor had any other man made the suggestion, though plenty fancied me as a regular partner when they were in the mood. I decided not to worry about it. Life was pretty good on the whole, and I had a lot of it ahead of me.

I was almost always late to bed – doing an evening job, or at a party, or being taken to dinner or the theatre by one man or another, or just chatting till all hours with Stella and Claudine. I had to plan to get an evening to myself and early to bed, something that would have seemed incredible in Belfast. On one of these evenings, I came in from work to find

Erica pacing about the big room and puffing at a Gauloise. In periods of yearning, she used to smoke so many Gauloises that the room would have smelt like a Foreign Legion barracks if the ceiling hadn't been so high.

'Hasn't he phoned?' I asked.

'No,' she said miserably. 'I know he isn't going to, but that doesn't help.'

'Perhaps there's some reason why he can't.'

'I know why he can't. He's with his bloody wife.' This was said with such venom that it gave me the creeps; if I have one prayer, it is that I'll never be driven to hate another woman.

I sighed and said: 'Oh, Erica, why do you keep picking on the married men?'

'I do, don't I?' She stubbed out her cigarette, sat down and stared at the blank television screen, then absently lit another. 'Desirable men tend to be married. You can see that, can't you?'

I sighed again. Listening to Erica's sad stories, I had begun to see in her a perverse desire for unequal contest and defeat. Out of every ten husbands who play around with girls, only one will contemplate leaving his wife and two or three, at most, will consent to put her into second place. The girl bears the burden of the deceits and contrivances, the repeated disappointments of the kind that Erica was enduring now, the necessity of being part of a 'situation' that clouds happiness and limits freedom. It could work in certain circumstances, as it did for Peggy. But Peggy made it work by armouring herself in a hard cynicism which Erica could never have mustered, and which I hoped to get through life without acquiring.

I saw what Erica meant, all the same. I was attracted, more often than not, by what girls call 'older men'; they offered a share of experience, both of sexual knowledge and of life in general. Of the men who had taken me out to dinner or drawn me into long conversations at parties, quite a number were married, either to my knowledge or probably. They were married because they were desirable, because they were

41

free from the hang-ups that kept a man like Hugh single, because they knew how to give and sustain affection.

One bright spring day, I went out to Blackheath at the request of a Mrs Bartram to photograph her children. They were spoiled little brats, and sulky over being made to give up a Saturday afternoon, so it all took a lot of time and cunning, but in the end I said that I thought I'd got the pictures and I'd come again if Mrs Bartram wasn't satisfied. She said I'd done wonders, she'd had no idea it would be so much trouble, and she was sure I could do with a drink. I accepted gratefully. Mrs Bartram was a beautiful olive-skinned creature – Greek, though she spoke flawless English – and so exquisitely turned out that I couldn't help asking where she got her clothes. She must have been about thirty-five, and was the kind of woman who looks her best at that age.

The children dashed off to a neighbour's house, and after a while Mr Bartram came in from playing golf. He was roughly the same age as his wife, and presented a striking contrast or perhaps complement to her, as he had the Nordic good looks and clear blue eyes attributed to Gerald Crich in *Women in Love* (the book, not the film). He spoke in an upper-class accent through which unsuitable vowels were faintly perceptible, and I guessed that he had swiftly and efficiently made scads of money with which he had acquired the large elegant house and Mrs Bartram.

He wasn't the ordinary kind of businessman, however, for as soon as he'd shaken hands with me he plunged into a conversation about photography – Cartier-Bresson, Bourke-White and so forth. I found later that this was typical of him. He wasn't an educated man, but he had boundless curiosity and a sort of surprising information on all kinds of subjects. It was always fun talking with him.

About a week later, I was at the agency office when a call came in for me. After a bit of clucking from switchboard girls and secretaries, one of them said: 'Miss Bell? Mr Bartram for you.'

He came on and said in his loud, confident voice: 'Those

pictures have turned out jolly well. My wife and I are delighted.'

'Oh, good,' I said.

'I might be able to put some more work in your way. Come and have lunch.'

It would have been more normal to hear from Mrs Bartram, and I wondered briefly what he was up to, but I accepted anyway. We lunched at the Café Royal. The question of 'more work' – three phone numbers for me to ring – was quickly disposed of, and he got me talking about the various jobs I did. After I'd told some anecdote or other, he said: 'I'll show you where you could take some remarkable photos.'

'Where?'

'From my office. I've got the best view in London.'

A few days later I turned up there with my cameras and telescopic lenses. It was on the top floor of one of those huge buildings near Victoria. I had to wait a little while before being conducted to Mr Bartram's presence. He had an enormous desk with a variety of the latest gadgets.

'Hullo,' he said. 'Have you got your things? Come this way.'

I followed him through a door behind the desk and up a flight of stairs. It led to a room built as a sort of extra on top of the office block, with picture windows looking out in all four directions. It was indeed a photographer's dream. You could see Westminster, the river, Piccadilly Circus, Hyde Park, the lot.

The room was furnished in the same way as the drawing-room at Blackheath – that is, with Swedish furniture which had evidently been bought as a unit, or probably the job had been handed over to a designer. There was a divan-bed, the sort that could be described as a wide single bed or a narrow double bed, covered with a mohair rug.

'Is this your home from home?' I asked.

'It's where I sleep when I work late,' he said, omitting the roguish grin that most men would have put on. 'How's the view? All right?'

43

'Fantastic.'

'I'll leave you to it, then. Take all the time you like. See you before you go.'

When I'd finished, he walked to the lift with me. I expressed my thanks.

'Not a bit of it. I like you, you're a bright girl. I say, d'you think you could get good pictures of London in the dark from up there?'

'That's not a very original line for a bright girl,' I said smiling.

He didn't smile back. 'If and when I make that kind of suggestion I shan't leave you in any doubt about it,' he said. 'Come at six-thirty. Shall we say Thursday? You take your pictures, I'll finish my work and we'll have some dinner.'

He fixed me with his blue eyes, which had a curious cold luminosity, like ice over clear water. They didn't convey much except that he expected people to do what he told them. He had a plan all right, but perhaps the pictures were going to be publicity for his business in some way or other. Anyway, they'd be marvellous pictures if they panned out and it would be silly to turn down the opportunity.

'All right,' I said. 'Thursday, six-thirty.'

This time I went straight into his office, as the staff had left. He was on the phone; he gestured to the door to the stairs, and I went up. He joined me after I'd been working for about twenty minutes. Taking panoramic shots at night is one of the trickiest jobs you can imagine, and I was determined not to hurry and to get good results. I took the yellow-white face of Big Ben, and the dark pool of St James's Park, and the dense traffic of Victoria Street, and the gleaming snakes that were trains going in and out of the station. He poured himself a drink – I said I wouldn't have one while I was working – and sat watching me, asking an intelligent question from time to time. I had the impression that he liked the air of activity, which matched his own character. Probably he liked being with a girl who did something; his wife, I guessed, was purely decorative.

44

Eventually I packed my cameras away and said: 'OK, I'd like a drink now, Mr Bartram.'

'Roger. You're having dinner with me.'

'My name's Pat.'

'I know it is. Campari soda?'

'That's fine.'

He looked at his watch. 'I ordered dinner for eight o'clock.'

'Where are we going?'

'They're bringing it. I didn't know how long you'd need for the pictures.'

Sure enough, two men appeared and set up one of those portable cookers. We had avocados, veal in marsala, and peach melba. Roger saw to the wine, Chablis and then Pommard.

When the men had packed everything up and gone, he said: 'I hope you enjoyed that.'

'Very much indeed.'

'I'd rather have dinner here than at any restaurant you care to name. We're in the middle of London, and as much alone as if we were on the top of Mount Everest. That's something, isn't it?'

'Is that your aim in life – having this kind of set-up?'

He stared at me and gave me a slow smile, an admission that I'd seen him as he was. 'Yes, I think it is,' he said.

I stared back. It was one of those moments that sometimes come about between a man and a woman, a moment not primarily of attraction (though he did attract me) so much as of intense expectation. I'd already reckoned that I'd have to make love with him if he insisted – after all, it was an impossible place to get away from – but now I saw that it was absolutely inevitable.

I walked to one of the windows, the one looking toward darkness. He followed, not at once but with leisurely confidence, and put both arms round my waist.

'Hullo, hullo,' I said.

He kissed me expertly on the back of the neck and said: 'You're a very attractive girl, Pat. In my experience, bright

45

girls are generally attractive.'

'I'm sure your experience is considerable.'

'Yes, it is. I also like bright girls because they know what they want. If you'd like to go, I'll drive you home.'

I didn't move.

He turned me to face him and said: 'You'd be disappointed, wouldn't you?'

'You're pretty bright yourself, Roger, aren't you?' I said.

We didn't get into bed that first time, but lay on the mohair rug. Roger, I wasn't surprised to find, was virile, sure of himself, and unsubtle. I'm sure it had never occurred to him to set a woman's satisfaction above his own; he wasn't that sort of man. And yet there was a high excitement in the direct, purposeful driving-power that thrust into me.

Just at this time, Hugh was going off me. He had started to pursue one of Janet's night-club girls, who set him a new problem because she preferred Janet. So I became Roger's mistress – that would be the correct term. I didn't go out with him; I assumed that he wished to be discreet, though it wasn't in his character to be anxiously secretive. Once he offered me a weekend in Paris – 'or Rome or somewhere', he added casually – but I normally worked on Saturdays and even sometimes on Sundays, so I told him I couldn't spare the time. I used to go to his office about once a week, arriving not before seven-thirty, as he sometimes kept his secretary late. (She was also bright and attractive, but he told me that he didn't sleep with her – 'it's a mistake, they slack off'.) We had dinner, and then as likely as not we drank brandy and talked for hours. When he was tired of talking he said abruptly: 'Right, let's go to bed.' After making love he went straight to sleep, which was a nice change after Hugh. He slept soundly and had his own built-in alarm-clock; he never failed to get me out of the building before any of the staff arrived. He used to walk across to the station with me, to put me in a taxi and to buy the papers he considered essential – *The Times*, the *Daily Telegraph* and the *Financial Times*.

I loved going to Roger's place. (It was always Roger's place

46

in my mind, not our place.) We never drew the curtains, and it was marvellous to stroll about naked in this island among the stars. Like Roger, I was fascinated by the luxurious combination of absolute freedom and being in the midst of the London that I loved. We were sometimes woken by the sun pouring in from the east, and we used to stand by the windows and watch the great city stirring: the mist swirling in the park, the dazzling red splashes on the glass squares of office blocks, the first buses, the speeding newspaper vans.

I didn't believe that there was much future in the affair, though Roger said that he'd never had a girl who suited him so well as I did. I didn't altogether fancy myself in the role of the Tycoon's Mistress, with which Peggy was so contented, and could accept it only by reminding myself that I was essentially Pat Bell, the up-and-coming photographer, and I could manage without Roger any time I chose. I was still sleeping with other men from time to time: it had nothing to do with Roger and it maintained my independence.

Roger's marriage was a worry to me, though not to him. It jarred on me a little when I suggested a certain evening for our next meeting and he said: 'No, that's no good, I'm taking Melissa to the theatre that night.' As affairs with married men go, it was plain sailing. I assumed that Melissa had her own life, based on Blackheath, and preferred not to make guesses. Still, there was always the chance that she would find out through some mishap and cut up rough or even threaten divorce, and I wanted no part of that kind of unpleasantness.

Since I declined the trip to Paris, Roger made a plan to spend a Sunday with me. We were to drive to Suffolk, where he had the key to a cottage belonging to a friend, stay the night, and be back by ten on the Monday morning. It was lovely spring weather, so it seemed like a good idea. I left it to him what he would tell Melissa; he would think of something, no doubt.

On Saturday evening, as I was ironing a dress in the kitchen and listening to Erica's tribulations, the phone rang. I answered.

47

'May I speak to Pat Bell?' a woman's voice asked.

'Speaking.'

'Oh, Pat, how are you? This is Melissa Bartram.'

First I thought: this is it. Then I thought: don't be silly, she wants some more pictures of the kids. I was wrong both times.

'Roger asked me to call you. He had to go to New York unexpectedly, so he's sorry but the trip tomorrow is off.'

I don't know what I answered.

On the Tuesday, I got home rather late after taking pictures at a City livery company dinner. Stella and Peggy were playing draughts, a game which was just within Stella's capacity but at which she never won.

'Your Roger just called,' she said. 'He sounds super, I must say. He said will you either go round or call him. You'll know where, he said.'

Tired as I was, I went straight round. Roger was still in his pffice. I could hear his voice as I approached and wondered if his secretary was there too, but he was dictating into a machine. He switched off and kissed me.

'How are you, darling? I've missed you. Sweet of you to come.'

'I'm fine. When did you get back?'

'Not long ago.'

'You look worn out.'

'No, no, it's just this bloody jet lag. Now look, I'll get this finished and then we'll go upstairs.'

'Roger,' I said, 'you know Melissa phoned me?'

'Yes. I asked her to.'

'I was surprised.'

'Why, who else could phone you? My secretary went to New York with me.'

'Was Melissa under the impression that we were going to Suffolk to photograph wild geese?'

He started to laugh. 'My dear child,' he said (he was in the habit of calling me this), 'd'you think I'm the sort of man who deceives his wife?' He made the word sound ridiculous.

'How am I to know? You don't explain anything to me.'

48

'Well, stop worrying. You remember that time you came to the house? Melissa said to me: "She's just your cup of tea, Roger." '

It may sound foolish, but I felt like crying.

Roger stared at me and asked: 'Would it interest you to know who Melissa's lover is?'

'If you want to tell me.'

It was quite interesting. It was a prominent member of the Government.

'So this is swinging London,' I said.

'Whatever you want to call it. I call it grown-up behaviour. Now you just trot upstairs and have a nice little Campari, and I'll be with you in five minutes.'

When we made love that night, I put more into it than ever before. But it was no good. I couldn't feel free or happy with Melissa smiling ironically over my shoulder.

The routine continued, but every time I came home in the taxi from Victoria Station I asked myself whether I really wanted to keep it up. Also, I met Alan. (I'll come to Alan shortly.) The final scene was at the beginning of June.

I went to Roger's office, as usual, at about a quarter to eight. Greatly to my surprise, it was a hive of activity. The word 'hive', indeed, was a good one, with junior executives flitting to and fro on errands that were mysterious and faintly absurd to me but evidently urgent and serious to them, just like bees. I considered beating a retreat, but the receptionist said: 'Miss Bell, is it? Mr Bartram says to go straight in,' so I had no option.

Roger, in short-sleeves but with his tie impeccably in place as usual, was dictating to his secretary. He looked surprised to see me. Obviously, after giving orders that I was to be admitted, he had forgotten all about me. Then he said: 'Sit down for a bit, Pat, would you? We're in rather a flap. Shan't be long, I hope.'

He went on dictating, interrupted every minute by muttered queries from the subordinate Bartrams or by calls on his black, red and white phones. In a way it was an intriguing

49

spectacle. I'd never before witnessed a crisis in the citadels of capitalism. The secretary (I did know her name, but I've forgotten it) looked at me from time to time with a smile of mingled amusement, sympathy and condescension, as though to say: 'You can't understand all this, but do stick around, the great man's going to need you when he rests from his labours.' I realized that she knew all about me, after all.

Then Roger picked up the white phone and said: 'Hullo? . . . Yes, dear.' Melissa.

'Oh, not too bad . . . Well, the market's crazy, but it's not going to do us any harm . . . Bearing up, don't worry . . . Yes, she is.' (Is Pat there, Melissa must have asked.) 'Yes, indeed . . . Right . . . See you tomorrow, dear.'

I got up and walked out. Either they thought I was going to the loo or they were too busy to bother; anyway, no one took any notice. I had a panicky feeling that I'd be captured and brought back while I waited for the lift, but most of the building was empty and it came quickly. I went to the movies in case Roger phoned the flat, but when I got home there was no message.

The next morning I wrote: 'Dear Roger, thanks for everything. It was fun but it's over now. Love, Pat.'

I sent it to his home and used a postcard so that they could both read it.

Now, about Alan. I met him through Eileen Hurst. Although the Hursts didn't have much home life, they gave a party now and again at their ugly but surprisingly roomy semi-detached house in Dulwich. One of these parties came up at a time when I was feeling a bit low, having just found out that my affair with Roger was by courtesy of Melissa.

The guests were a mixed lot – some friends of Eileen, some journalists from Tony Hurst's paper, some teenagers invited by their son and daughter, and a few neighbours who'd been asked to stop them complaining of the noise. Tony bustled about offering red or white plonk, and Eileen bravely introduced people who had nothing in common, but the occasion failed to get off the ground. I arrived late, because I'd just bought my car and navigating in south London was a new problem for me. Eileen greeted me with that anxious hostess look which conveys: 'Ah, thank God you've come, maybe you'll get things moving.'

I scanned the men, as one does at parties. They were a poor selection, and I soon got stuck with one who struck me as exceptionally hopeless. He wore a blue suit — pretty depressing for a start — and was big in the fashion of a schoolboy who has grown out of his clothes. He loomed over me clumsily and began our relationship (I was to tease him about this later) by spilling some wine on my dress and failing to notice.

'Are you on the paper?' he asked me.

I explained that I worked with Eileen.

'Oh, I see.'

This brought us to a halt, so I could only ask: 'You're on the paper, are you?'

'Yes. I'm on the sports desk.'

Fat stock prices are about the only subject that interests me less than organized sport, so I resolved to escape. This was easier said than done. When I needed another drink, he fetched it for me; when I helped Eileen hand round food, he helped too, following in my wake; when I talked to other people, he stood beside me, apparently quite content to listen if no one addressed him.

A pretty deadly evening, in fact, but I owed it to Eileen to stay the course. Between twelve and one the party began to dwindle, and I decided that I'd done my duty. I thanked Tony and Eileen, trying not to make it too effusive lest Eileen should detect irony, and fetched my coat.

Alan (not that I could have recalled his name at that point) was at the door saying: 'Can I drive you home?'

'I've got my car, thanks.'

'Oh.' He hesitated, then visibly mustered his courage. 'I did enjoy talking to you. I hope we'll see each other again.'

'I hope so,' I said with an automatic smile.

Two nights later there was a phone call for me.

51

'This is Alan.'

'Oh, yes.' I went rapidly through all the men I'd met recently, but couldn't remember one called Alan.

'Alan Carter. We met at the Hursts' party. I work on the paper.'

'Oh, sure.' The deep voice, with a Midland accent more marked on the phone, was now unmistakable.

'I remembered you saying you'd like to see Harold Pinter's new play. I've got some tickets. I do hope you're free, it's for Friday.'

I hesitated. It seemed dishonest to be indebted to this man, since I obviously shouldn't want to see him again. But I very much wanted to see the Pinter, there was a big demand for tickets, and I hadn't got time to queue for them, which he'd doubtless done.

'It's very thoughful of you,' I said.

Despite my enjoyment of the play, I stole a few looks at Alan as he sat beside me. He was working hard at it. He stared at the actors as though afraid to miss a single movement that might offer him a clue to a difficult but fascinating problem.

'I've never seen a play quite like this,' he said in the interval. 'There's some things I don't get.'

'We'll talk it over afterwards,' I said.

I suggested a place for dinner. He didn't eat much, which surprised me, as he looked like a hearty feeder; so he normally was, and he confessed that he'd had a meal already, not realizing that having dinner after the theatre was the thing to do. I advanced my theories about the play, and I could see that he took them not as theories but as an authoritative guide. All the time I knew him, Alan was convinced that I was far more intelligent than he was. In reality, I'm better with words and better informed. Well, I'm more intelligent too, actually, but not so much as he thought.

He took me home in a taxi. On the doorstep, he said: 'Thanks so much for coming. I won't forget this evening with you.'

'I enjoyed it too.'

'Well, you see . . .' He mustered his courage again. 'I've never known a girl quite like you – Pat.'

Then he kissed me: and I hadn't been kisssed like this – clumsily, earnestly, respectfully but also fondly – since Belfast.

The next time he phoned, I was perfectly happy to see him again. I had found myself thinking about him, much to my surprise, and seeing something in him that my smart friends would have found ridiculous, but that was worthy of respect. We had an early dinner and saw a film: I chose one that was for laughs, to give him a break and also to indicate that I wasn't an intimidating intellectual. He laughed a lot – it was a joy to hear him.

'Come back to my place for some coffee,' I said. Peggy and Erica were both abroad, and there was a fair chance that the others would be out. They were. I had no intentions except to get Alan talking and find out more about him. I didn't ask myself whether it would be a pleasure to sleep with him or not, for I was sure that he wouldn't try to make me at this early stage of our acquaintanceship.

He was awed by the huge flat, but I explained the economics of sharing it between six. He talked about himself readily, as though he didn't often have a listener. His father was a tool-maker in Coventry; the bracket was the well-paid, solidly established working-class. Alan had done well at school and his A-levels were good enough to get him into a university. This would have amazed me after the Hursts' party but now only mildly surprised me. My own A-levels hadn't been good enough, I told him; this he found hard to believe.

'I suppose it shows that exams are a lottery.'

'Perhaps. Go on about yourself.'

'Well, I missed my chance. It was stupid of me, I can see that now. But when I was eighteen I was just football crazy.'

So he had become a footballer, and played three seasons for a team which apparently had considerable status. But he recognized coolly that he would never be an outstanding player. As he explained it, if you're good but not that good, you can find yourself dropped after half a dozen years and unequipped to do anything else. He had enjoyed writing at school – 'essays and that' – so he had the idea of going into sports journalism. He worked on a Birmingham paper for two years, and came to London at about the same time as me. He shared a flat with a friend, also from the Midlands and also a sports journalist. Alan didn't know many people in London, and being invited to the news editor's party was an event for him.

'Haven't you got a girl?' I asked.

'I wouldn't be here with you if I had a girl, would I?'

I was charmed by this. I cleared away the coffee-tray and poured some drinks, and casually sat down beside him on the couch. He put his arm round me, in his clumsy way which I now found rather endearing, and said: 'I'm surprised you haven't got a boy-friend, Pat.'

'I've got various men I go out with.'

'You'll go out with me again, won't you?'

'Sure.'

He engaged in some back row at the movies stuff while we went on talking, and kissed me several times, but it was all perfectly respectful. I felt that he attached a value to my feelings and took nothing for granted, and I was grateful to be treated like this, considering that Roger Bartram was taking me very much for granted at the time. Eventually, as I'd expected, he thanked me for the evening and said goodnight.

My next two dates with Alan weren't a great success. The first time, unfortunately, I couldn't stop yawning.

'You look whacked,' he said as we came out of the cinema. 'Sure you're not sickening for something?'

'No, I'm just tired. I've been working hard.' I had been with Roger the night before, as a matter of fact.

'I'll see you home, then.' And he did, with another kiss on the doorstep.

The other time, I asked him in and there was quite a crowd at the flat – about a dozen people who had come on from one of Hugh's dinner-parties. Alan couldn't join in the conversation, which was a mixture of insiders' film talk and sexual gossip. When one of the girls said (referring to an absent friend): 'Oh, he's kinky, he's got rubber sheets on his bed and you have to pee on him,' Alan decided that he'd had enough and left.

This glimpse of my environment, however, did show him that I was no innocent, and I think he had made up his mind to see where he could get with me on our next evening. After all, it was our fifth date. But as it turned out, little effort on his part was required, because I'd just broken up with Roger. I was shaken and humiliated, and in need of sincere affection, to use the phrase with no irony at all. When my notebook reminded me that I was due to see Alan, I felt that he was just the right medicine.

We met, as usual, by the phone boxes at Leicester Square tube station.

'Where would you like to go?' he asked.

'I don't know.' I didn't really want to go anywhere. 'Come to my place. I'll cook you a meal.'

'Will there be a lot of your friends there?' he inquired cautiously.

'I don't expect so, at this time. You'll have to take a chance.'

There was no one in except Claudine, who was hurriedly changing to go along to the Hilton, and Erica, who retired to her room with a noble air of refusing to intrude on the happiness of others. As soon as her door had closed, Alan put his arms round me and kissed me. I subsided on to the couch, one thing led rapidly to another, and I said: 'Let's go to my room.'

So we went to bed in the sunlight of a summer evening. He began a bit tentatively, as though he ought somehow to treat me differently from girls acquired at football supporters' club dances. But he soon got into his stride, and gave me a good old-fashioned bashing, to which I've never been averse.

'Happy?' he said afterwards.

'Mm. I could just lie here for ever. Couldn't you?'

'Oh yes,' he said. He didn't sound quite convinced, though,

and a thought struck me.

'Christ, I was going to make a meal. Are you hungry, Alan?'

'Well, I wasn't going to mention it . . .'

'You stay here, I won't be long.'

I brought the food on a tray. I liked the look of him, sitting up naked and munching a steak with his powerful jaws. He grinned at me and said: 'This is the life.'

Later, we heard Stella and a man come in. We lay still, breathing each other. The phone rang and Stella knocked at my door, calling: 'Are you there, Pat?' We froze; I had to put my hand over Alan's mouth to stop him laughing.

In the morning, he asked: 'When can I see you again?'

'Tonight, why not? This is going to get better as it goes on, I know it.'

'I didn't think you'd be free.'

'I'll make myself free. You've got a girl-friend now.'

'I still can't believe my luck.'

He eyed me dubiously, as though the situation (like Pinter's play) contained hidden traps beneath its apparent simplicity. Probably he was thinking that my mood had favoured him and wondering whether it would last through the day. Another night with me reassured him, but he never did take me for granted. Even when we made love several nights running – which I was glad to do, for no other man had been so regularly at my disposal – he regarded each of these nights as a special and fortunate occasion. And there were evenings, months later, when we went out together and parted with a kiss.

But if Alan thought that I was doing him a favour by being his girl-friend, it had rewards for me that neither Hugh nor Roger had offered. I'd had some varied experiences in London, which I didn't regret, but I hadn't, in the simple and normal way, had a boy-friend before: that is, a man whom I met at Leicester Square tube station. Alan had come into my life at a time when the novelty of mixing with the rich was wearing thin for me. The lobsters and the Rémy-Martin were very pleasant in their way, but the more you had of them the less fun they were. My work – photographing fashion displays one day and condemned housing the next – kept reminding me that girls like Stella and Claudine and Peggy had a limited, even an unreal, notion of the London in which we lived. Besides, when I went to roulette rooms or champagne parties, I bore in mind that we girls hadn't got the price of entry. We were beholden to the men with whom we trailed along and repaid them by adorning the scene; and, in the not so ultimate analysis, by opening our legs. These men, when you took a cool look at them, had never done much in the world except to inherit, make or spend money. Alan was working at something he had chosen to do for its own sake, as I was. We were equals, in that neither of us had any money beyond what we earned by our skills and energies. Once we were on a regular footing, we shared the bills. We were both earning pretty well, and both ready to spend, but we tacitly kept an eye on the prices. I liked to hear Alan say: 'That's just ridiculous, love, isn't it?' There were certain restaurants and certain bars to which we simply didn't go, and I never missed them. Alan took a canny pleasure in getting good value, and I was happy with him discovering cheap Cypriot restaurants in Camden Town, coffee-stalls with satisfying meat pies, jumble sales, street markets, second-hand bookshops. The best of treats was to spend no money at all, to be freed from bothering with it. After a walk in Epping Forest, or an organ recital at St Paul's, or an afternoon at the British Museum, he would squeeze my hand and say: 'There you are, we haven't spent a single penny and we've had a great time, haven't we?' He was right; we had.

Then, most of the men I'd known since coming to London indicated pretty clearly that they'd seen everything and done everything – not least in bed – and that all they looked forward to was more of the same. Alan had a sense of wonder, a capacity for discovery. I can still hear the tone of deep satisfaction, mingled with an astonished delight, in which he uttered his favourite phrase: 'That was great.' After a goal in

57

extra time at Highbury, after the Ninth Symphony at the Albert Hall, after eating paella for the first time, after a fuck in a new position . . . 'that was great'. It gave an extra dimension to being with him, the dimension of sharing his discoveries.

I won't deny too, that I got some pleasure out of his readiness to learn from me. When I met him, he really didn't know much about London outside the sporting world and Fleet Street, whereas I knew a good deal. And of course I had my middle-class cultural equipment relating to the arts, psychology and sociology, taste in clothes and food and wine. He had read quite a lot, but only books that he knew one ought to read, such as *War and Peace* and *David Copperfield*, so I introduced him to contemporary writing. Similarly, before he met me he'd been to Shakespeare productions at the Aldwych, but would never have found his way to the Open Space. He had a good brain, slow-working and unsubtle but persistent and retentive. It was wonderful to watch him reading poetry or listening to music, rubbing his forehead (a habit of his) as he worked to seize and follow the theme. I don't think this was, on my part, an ignoble pleasure; what is finer in life than to help in the expansion of human powers, the growth of a man?

He relied on me and looked up to me, as I've said, enormously. He over-estimated me, of course. But this I couldn't reject, for it was bound up with his love for me. Alan loved me as Hugh and Roger put together could never have loved. I say this without pride, even with shame. I often wished that I could love him half as much.

Also, he was faithful to me. I hadn't supposed that this could matter; when I used the word at all in gossip at the flat, it was in ironic quotation marks. But, in bed with Alan, I had a direct and physical sense of his devotion to me, as much as of his love. His loyalty — the sheer impossibility of his even having a date with anyone else so long as I was his girl — was integral to the contentment of these summer months. I decided that I would be faithful to him too, and with a very few lapses I actually was. Various men declared themselves baffled, especially men I'd slept with before, and in the atmosphere of the flat the consideration that I was having a long-running affair was irrelevant. I told them I was winning a bet with myself, and that was more or less how it felt to me.

The other girls hadn't come across a man like Alan before, and were distinctly intrigued. Since he didn't talk much (unless he was alone with me) and had no social graces, they deduced that he must be fabulous in bed. I recall one occasion when Stella rested her languorous eyes on him and said: 'You might be a pal and lend him to me some time, Pat.'

'It's up to Alan,' I said.

Alan tried to smile and said: 'Yes, and what would Pat be doing while she was out of my sight?' But I knew that he didn't like this kind of talk.

Alan was due for a holiday in August, before the football season started, and wanted me to come with him. We would go in his car, take a tent, and make for the Mediterranean. I didn't really want to leave London, but I saw that it meant a great deal to Alan. For three weeks, he would have me with him day and night. Besides, he had never been abroad before; it would be the greatest of his discoveries.

He drove; my job was to decide the route, read the map, talk French, and generally pilot him through this strange territory. His curiosity was insatiable, his gratitude for fresh experience was continual. Everything was great – a Roman amphitheatre, a big barge on a canal, French bread, vines, olive trees, the game of *boule*.

We stopped, for four or five days each, at three camp-sites on the coast: two in France and one in Spain where things were cheaper. I hadn't enjoyed the journey so much as Alan, but my spirits soared as soon as we put up our tent near the sea. Here I was at last, a citizen with full rights in the fantastic city of the European summer. I was at home before I'd unpacked, as I'd been at home as soon as I reached London a year ago. I loved the incessant noise, I loved the crowds, I loved the queues for coke and cigarettes, I loved the endless borrowing and lending, I loved the smell of paraffin and sun-tan oil. Time seemed to be halted, not in peace and quiet but in a uniqueness of sensation. The heat was scorching as it surely could be nowhere else, the news on the radio was no more serious than disc-jockey chatter, the rest of the world was unimaginable. You ate when you felt hungry, slept in the day more than at night, and forgot what it was to dress or undress; you slid a hook when you wanted to make love, and that was all. I never knew what day of the week it was, or how long we'd been away. I had Alan to tell me when we ought to be moving on.

For I was with my man — that was the best of it. He belonged, as I did, to the summer city. As I had noticed before, language barriers melted away in this jumble of nationalities. Alan threw off, along with his blue suits, the awkwardness and shyness that he showed in London; here, he made friends all the time. He organized football teams, playing on the sand with bare feet and a light rubber ball — a good fast game, he said. People invited him — and invited me, of course, but Alan usually knew them before I did — to go sailing and water-skiing and scuba-diving. He was always close to me, but we had no chance to get bored with each other.

We returned to London in a breathless dash, for we stayed by the magical sea until the last possible moment and drove round the clock, taking turns at the wheel. There was plenty of work waiting for me, and Alan plunged into the football season, going to a lot of matches even when he didn't have to report them, and watching them on TV if he didn't go. Sometimes his work took him away from London. But, now that we were past the stage of finding each other, we didn't need to meet every day. A phone call was enough to sustain the warm feeling of continuity. That autumn, my second in London, was an easy and settled time for me.

It wasn't quite without problems, however, including one that I thought I'd left behind in Belfast — the problem of where to go in order to be alone together. It was difficult to arrive at my flat, at any hour of the evening or night, without finding someone in the living-room, and it was regarded as unfriendly to go to bed without pausing for a drink and a chat. Alan never felt at his ease there. The conversation was either over his head or else what he called silly, by which he meant shallow and artificial. It tended to exclude him, and he tended to think this deliberate when it wasn't. 'I don't know why you stick with that crowd, love,' he used to say to me; he couldn't allow me a frivolous streak that conflicted with his picture of me. The sociable breakfasts – often with new faces and casual introductions – jarred on him particularly. Alan had had other girls and accepted that I'd had other men, but his innate respectability was offended by the thought that I had conducted myself like Stella until I became his girl-friend. He disliked Stella, and still more Claudine whom he saw simply as a tart; and unfortunately he also took a dislike to Erica, who was at home in the evening more often than anyone else. She paraded her emotions, something that he couldn't stand. This led to our first quarrel, when he concluded his disparaging remarks about her with: 'Well, it's what you'd expect.' I asked what he meant, and was outraged when I pinned down the allusion to Erica being Jewish. There followed an unseemly wrangle, with Alan denying charges of anti-semitism, insisting that different people had different ways of behaving, and withdrawing finallx into a sulky silence. I was angry, I realized later, because – for the first time on any subject except sport – he wouldn't take a lesson from me.

I brought him to my flat whenever I could, however, because I didn't like going to his. Everything about it depressed me: the neighbourhood (the outer reaches of Muswell Hill), the mean outlook from the windows, and the wallpaper and paintwork, which Alan couldn't defend but had got used to. My main objection was to Len, who shared with Alan, and who really was just as dreary as I had at first imagined Alan to be. A domesticated type, Len was almost always at home, and unlikely to be in bed unless we came in after midnight. One look at him, slumped in a chair with a fag stuck to his lower lip and dribbling ash on his invariable grey cardigan, made the most dubious of Stella's pick-ups seem like a combination of Fidel Castro and Mick Jagger. Len used to keep the TV on regardless of the programme and regardless of any conversation; if he himself talked, it was exclusively about football. The fact that he had no girl-friend (though it wasn't surprising) also made me uneasy, as though our happiness were in some way abnormal. It seemed natural to say, 'Let's get into bed, Alan,' in front of Stella, but not in front of Len.

Alan didn't dispute my opinion of Len; he simply said that Len was easy to get on with, he was an old friend, and anyway the flat was Len's as much as Alan's. When I was too outspoken, Alan said, 'Oh, you just won't see the good side of him, Pat,' and hinted that I was being a snob.

In November, Alan's parents spent a weekend in London, staying with relatives in Chigwell or some such place. It was a regular event, Alan said; his father went to an international football match, his mother had a shopping spree, and they took in a show. I found myself considerably involved. On the Friday, we all had dinner at an Italian restaurant which Alan and I patronized. On the Saturday, I trailed along Oxford Street with Mrs Carter while Mr Carter and Alan were at Wembley, and then we went to some witless musical. The Carters were nice people and it was pleasant to see them having a treat. However, I declined a pressing invitation to Sunday lunch in Chigwell. I did genuinely have an appointment to photograph some kids in Blackheath – on a recommendation from Melissa Bartram, funnily enough – but I'll admit that I shouldn't have gone anyway. Alan was annoyed; his father had to say to him: 'Give over, lad, Pat knows her own mind.'

It was obvious that I was being presented to Alan's parents and weighed up by them. I was amused by this, while attaching no great significance to it; if their son had a steady girl-friend, they had a right to take an interest. They asked a lot of questions – about my family, about Northern Ireland (which had begun by now to get into the headlines) and about my work. Alan had made me bring along a folder of my photographs, which were duly admired. It was clear – indeed, it was made clear – that I was approved of.

The next development was that Alan asked me to spend Christmas with him and his family in Coventry. Again, I had an honest excuse. I hadn't seen my own parents for a year and they were assuming that I'd be with them for Christmas. But again, Alan guessed that I shouldn't have taken up his offer in any case.

'Couldn't you go to your parents for New Year? Or to us for New Year, if you'd rather.'

'Well, actually, we're having a party at the flat on New Year's Eve.'

'I see. I can imagine what that'll be like.'

'You're very welcome. I was going to mention it to you.'

'Thanks, I think I'll skip it.'

The party at the flat, I'm afraid, was all that Alan could have imagined. Claudine invited her current escort (or escortee, I suppose) and he gave the address to three other men from Cosmopolitan Plastics or whatever it was. So at three o'clock or thereabouts we had these enormous juvenile Yanks, uttering college yells and yippees, coming on from the Playboy Club and amply liquored up. It was impossible to get the idea out of their heads that the address was a private brothel. I escaped to my room and had just got into bed when one of them barged in. I told him I had to go to the bathroom and made a dash for Erica's room. We barricaded the door and I slept, or attempted to sleep, on some cushions on the floor. Barely five minutes had elapsed, it seemed, since the fading of the last sounds of rape and revelry when the sound of the phone invaded my battered consciousness. I let it ring. It went on and on, convincing me through sheer persistence that it must be important. I dismantled the barricade and staggered across the living-room, which was littered with bodies.

'Happy New Year, darling!' Alan carolled.

'Oh. Yes. Happy New Year.'

'It's snowing here. All fresh and beautiful. Is it snowing in London?'

'I haven't a clue. Did you have to ring up at the crack of dawn?'

'It's ten o'clock,' he said in an injured tone.

'That's what I mean.'

'I see. Well, I won't keep you talking. I'm coming back this afternoon. See you in the evening?'

'No, I'm going to bed early.'

'When shall I see you, then?'

'I don't know. I'll call you.'

'Mum and Dad send their love.'

'OK. See you.'

When we got together, I apologized for my coldness and he apologized for being thoughtless. The trouble with mutual apologies is that something is still wrong if they're needed. We began, from then on, to watch what we said to each other; it's always the first danger sign.

One Sunday afternoon in January, Alan suggested going to Epping Forest. The expedition had a guise of spontaneity – 'it's not a bit cold, love, we could go for a drive' – but I guessed that it was premeditated. Epping Forest was a special place for us, with memories of summer walks when we were joyfully drawing closer together. It was in fact a lovely day, mild for January and serene under a pale blue sky. Among the trees there wasn't a breath of wind, and we sat down on the softness of the leaves that cover the ground from season to season. Alan took my face between his hands and gave me a long and loving kiss, the kind that is intended to create a mood.

'I missed you so much when you were away,' he said.

'I missed you too, darling.'

He looked at me steadily and with the sort of earnestness that he gave to puzzling out a poem or a serious article.

'Pat, don't you feel how great it would be if we were always together?'

'Very nice indeed,' I said lightly, but not without

64

uneasiness.

'You realize what I'm saying, love?'

'Well . . .' I began.

He said very firmly and deliberately: 'I'm asking you to marry me.'

'You what?' I said before I could stop myself.

Despite all that had led up to it, I simply hadn't imagined – of course, hadn't wanted to imagine – that this was coming. My face must have indicated astonishment and dismay, to be translated as: 'Oh Christ, how am I going to get out of this?' He was, I have no doubt, deeply hurt.

'What's so funny about that?' he asked.

'It's not funny, darling. It's very sweet.' As, honestly, I felt that it was.

'But?'

'But . . . well, I hadn't thought in those terms.'

'I love you, Pat. You do believe that, don't you?'

'Yes, sure.'

'We're always happy together. We've never had a cross word all the time we've known each other.' (This wasn't precisely true, but he probably believed it at the moment.) 'Those are pretty good reasons for getting married, aren't they?'

'I suppose so. I'm afraid I don't look at it by adding up reasons.'

'Well, what's against it? We're both earning well. We could put the money down on a house.'

I reflected on this. House prices in London weren't so appalling then as they became later, but any house we could afford would take me far from the parts of London where I felt at home. It struck me that Alan would settle down happily in a house like the Hursts'. It wasn't an alluring thought.

'You know what?' I said. 'I don't believe you really want to get married. I think you're trying to prove something. And I think your parents have put you up to this.'

'That's not true.' But at once he started to confirm it. 'Well, I don't mind saying they'd be very pleased.'

'There you are. They believe in a certain order of events: courting, maybe making love because it's OK nowadays, then marriage. I don't believe in that, and I wasn't aware that you did.'

'Don't you ever want to get married?'

'I want to do what feels right to me at the time when it feels right.'

'What does feel right, then?'

'Being your girl. I'm very contented. I wish you were.'

We threshed around in an increasingly miserable discussion, saying the same things over and again and making the failure of contact more and more obvious, until I said: 'Look, darling, this isn't a thing one can argue about. When we both feel we want to do it, we'll do it. That's all.' And we walked back to the car in silence, probably looking as if we'd had a violent quarrel.

I was badly shaken. I was sure I was right, but I knew that I'd handled the situation badly and wounded Alan needlessly. And I had to put some uncomfortable questions to myself. Why had I been so surprised by Alan's proposal? Why had I been so instantly certain that I didn't want to marry him? True, I was in no hurry to marry anybody. But I wasn't opposed to marriage on principle, I was nearly twenty-three, I'd had my share of screwing around, and Alan's reasons were quite as sound as he thought. The answer had to be that I'd always regarded our affair as just that – an affair, temporary. I had never admitted this to myself, and I certainly didn't want to break it up. I hated, quite honestly, to think of such a thing. But what I had been making clear to Alan, in reality, was that we had a limited future together. Things, I recognized sadly, could never be altogether the same again.

I wished that we'd started living together months ago. It wouldn't have been impossible to sort things out financially with Len and either take over the flat or set up in a new one. I hadn't suggested it, I suppose, because I'd been trying to draw Alan into the orbit of my life and my friendships. He hadn't suggested it, evidently, because marriage was what he was

66

planning for. And now I couldn't suggest it. Advanced as a counter-proposal, it would rub in the idea that I wanted to be free to split up at some future time. It was too late, anyway. You start living together to establish an affair, not to fortify it when difficulties appear. I realized that I wasn't willing to commit myself altogether to Alan. I hadn't yet begun to find being with him dull, but I was afraid that I might.

So, things were not the same. It was a gradual change, which we both tried to evade. It had begun even before Christmas; whether it might have been halted or a fresh adjustment reached, without what happened in Epping Forest, I shall never know. Things that hadn't mattered, or had been jokes, now became irritants and ultimately dangers.

In the first place, football. I hadn't grasped at the outset what a passion this was for Alan, because our affair had begun in summer when he was covering athletics and golf, with interest certainly but without total involvement. Come the autumn, he urged me to go to football matches with him. I went quite cheerfully. I wanted to please him; I had hopes of catching his enthusiasm, up to a point anyway; and the atmosphere of a big match, at least when it's new to you, is picturesque and entertaining. I used to take pictures of people in the crowd, thus missing the crucial moments of the game, which Alan deplored – at that time – in a good-humoured way. But after January I found it more and more of an ordeal. I'd got enough pictures of men in scarves yelling themselves hoarse, and I began to grudge the time that I could have used elsewhere. The weather in February and March was cold and nasty; we shivered even in the press box. And I knew by now that I would never make a football fan, and that for me it would always be a bloody silly game. Alan's passionate commitment, which had been entertaining when the game was entertaining, became absurd, tedious and indeed rather frightening. A man could be thus stirred, I thought, by a cause or an ideal or an ambition – but by a ball being kicked about, no, it didn't make sense. No doubt, my attitude changed along with the hidden decline in my feeling for Alan. It cut both ways; when you see your man's chief interest in life as childish and boring, it's bound to make a difference.

Meanwhile, Alan was losing interest in what I could share with him – books, plays, music. His striving for discovery, it seemed, had been a sudden spurt, not what the economists call sustained growth. I hadn't sought the role of tutor, but I couldn't help being piqued when my tutelage was no longer required. Maybe, without consciously intending it, he was paying me out for not following him into the lore of football. This change, too, was gradual; we still had good talks, we still shared stimulating experiences. But these were now on the margin of his life, while football was central. There were evenings when I wanted to see a film or watch a good TV play, and he absolutely had to take in Match of the Day. There had been such evenings in the autumn too, but one or other of us had given in cheerfully. After January, we argued. We still gave in by turns, more or less, but the one who gave in was left with a grievance.

All this time, things were going well for me professionally. One of the men at the agency left, and Mrs Baldwin decided to carry on with a staff of four instead of five. We all got salary increases, and mine – she told me privately – was bigger than for the others. 'Your work's better,' she said. 'Finding you was a real stroke of luck.' Praise came sparingly from Mrs Baldwin, so I valued it. I knew I deserved it, though. The handsome raise was to deter me from devoting my enthusiasm to private commissions and eventually going freelance. I had already cut down on the private jobs in order to spend more time with Alan, and now I took practically none, for Mrs Baldwin had stopped sending me out on routine stuff and reserved me for assignments that called for quality work. I was, in fact, the star photographer of the agency. I did a lot of portraits, often of people who were distinguished in various ways and were interesting to meet. This contributed, I suppose, to making me aware of Alan's limitations.

I didn't believe, all the same, that my affair with Alan was nearing its end. I did feel that it was narrowing. It had been

68

many-sided, filling and enriching our lives. Now it was sustained only by love. And so it had a dangerous imbalance, because I was – at most – only half in love with him.

This is hindsight, but it's through hindsight that one sees the truth, revealed by distance as faint footpaths are visible from the top of a hill. I had no thought of leaving Alan. I was happy with him far more often than not, and I cherished him. This was my first affair that held a real meaning, and I'd have been ashamed to think that I couldn't keep it going for so much as a year. I see, with hindsight, that a loyalty has to be weakened from within before it can be attacked from without. But when I broke up with Alan, I preferred to think that all had been going well until I chose – as I had a right to choose – to move on to a more exciting man.

One day in April, I was sent to take some publicity photos of an actress called Gabrielle Spencer. She was a tricky subject – a woman of forty-five and looking all of it, with a face that was 'interesting' rather than beautiful. I set myself to bring out her individuality and character; she was the kind of actress whom intellectuals admire, best known for her thoughtful interpretations. Talking to her, I found that she really was an intelligent and cultured woman, though vain and pernickety. She was married to a man called Arnold Black who produced poetry programmes on Radio 3.

I thought my pictures were pretty good, but Miss Spencer considered that they weren't quite her. Mrs Baldwin never argued with a customer, so back I went to do a repeat. This time, perhaps feeling rather guilty, Miss Spencer offered me a drink when I'd finished. Her husband came in and I stayed for about an hour. We talked about poetry, which I've always loved. Mr Black asked me what university I'd been to, and was flatteringly surprised when I said that I hadn't. I was sorry when I had to leave because Alan was waiting for me. An air of good taste, neither trendy nor snobbish but genuine, pervaded the house; I didn't see too much of that.

About a week later, I called in at the office and found a message: 'Ring Gabrielle Spencer.' The woman surely couldn't want another repeat, I thought. No, she was asking me to dinner the same night. 'Terribly short notice, I'm afraid — we've got some American friends who've suddenly arrived in London.' I was pretty sure that I was replacing somebody who had cried off, but I didn't care about that. I accepted at once. Only after I hung up did I remember that I was supposed to be seeing Alan. I phoned him at the paper and explained that I'd been unable to refuse, Gabrielle Spencer being an important customer. He was in the middle of writing about a big match and said that he quite understood.

I wore my best dress, and a good thing too, as this was a distinctly classy occasion. There was an American couple, whether or not they had suddenly arrived in London; they were academics, I gathered. There was a quite well-known actor, with his wife who wrote children's books. And there was another man — on his lonesome, hence my presence. How funny, I thought as I waited to be introduced, he looks just like Vernon Longuehaye.

Then Gabrielle (I'll call her that, as I was soon to know her well) said: 'This is Vernon Longuehaye.'

Vernon Longuehaye . . . practically everyone I'd ever met would know who he was, except perhaps Kevin O'Hagan. If this book were meant to be published, I'd have to change the name. But I'm writing for myself, with fanciful notions of being read by some daughter or granddaughter years hence, so I'll explain who he was. He existed in three concentric circles of fame. In the first place, he was a professor of philosophy, and no ordinary professor. His books were respected by the elect — other philosophers — and also sold well in paperback. He was the originator of relational analysis, which was acknowledged to be not only a new method of thinking about problems but a real extension of knowledge as well. You were expected to know the phrase, and have a general idea what it meant, if you sat at the class of dinner-table where I now found myself.

Secondly, he applied his mind to the social scene, politics, culture in the broadest sense, education. A philosopher — more than a historian or a psychologist, and perhaps by definition – is an intellectual who doesn't appear as a specialist, to whom people turn for depth of understanding and not for a particular slant. So Vernon was always being asked for articles and reviews. You found them in the weeklies, in the quality Sundays, in the more sophisticated women's mags, in the *Evening Standard*. He never turned down a request, wrote fast and easily, and maintained a consistent standard. Whether he wrote on 'Universities for Whom?' in the *New Statesman*, or on 'Flying Isn't Too Bad' in a travel supplement, he illuminated the subject as no one else could.

Thirdly, he was a familiar face on television, which extended his fame to people like Stella who had never read anything he'd written. I had been seeing him on the box ever since I was a schoolgirl, for TV producers had long ago discovered that he was a natural. He could talk about anything, just as he could write about anything; he was unfailingly fluent and never uttered an 'um' or a 'sort of' in his life; he was adequately 'controversial', but never lost his cool in the most heated discussion; he was impressively earnest on serious occasions, and elegantly witty when that was called for. He was especially good at destroying a fallacious argument with a few incisive words in a way that was effective but not unnecessarily crushing, as though he were dealing with a brash and conceited student who nevertheless mustn't be badly hurt because he showed promise. (Students, naturally, worshipped Vernon.) Producers also knew that he never refused to go on TV or radio, whether it was a minority programme on Radio 3 or a mass-entertainment like a panel game or the Frost Programme. This wasn't primarily out of vanity, but because he found it so easy. One couldn't refuse, he used to say, to be paid for doing what one did whenever one went out to dinner.

On top of all this, Vernon's fame gained an extra dimension from his being beyond dispute one of the best-looking men in London, and regularly named in women's mag features as 'The man I'd most like to ask me to dinner'. He was about forty, one would guess, and in mint condition. Tall and long-limbed, without an ounce of surplus fat, he looked remarkably athletic for a professor. Actually − to list these facts in the order in which I discovered them − he went for regular country walks, played a swift and energetic game of tennis, and did ten minutes of exercises when he got up in the morning. Coming now to his face, which was what you mostly saw on TV, he had a noble forehead, deepset dark eyes, and a firm, lean profile. He had been growing his hair fairly long since it became the thing to do, and the sweep on either side contrasted well with the early hint of receding above the said forehead. The effect was completed by an unusual style of beard, neat and pointed − trimmed at the barber's twice a week, as a matter of fact − which made an impression of civilized distinction. So he was not only handsome, but handsome in precisely the way that he ought to have been to suit his reputation. Just as some women − including Gabrielle when she was younger − are described as the thinking man's crumpet, Vernon was the bright girl's pin-up.

We went into dinner, and to my delight I was placed next to him. I made no attempt to join in the conversation, partly because everyone else (especially Vernon) had plenty to say and you had to be fairly assertive to get in, partly because I was decidedly out of my league. However, I could follow everything except for identifying some of the first names, and I enjoyed listening. That's putting it mildly − I'd have thought myself amply rewarded if I had queued for hours and paid Covent Garden prices. It wasn't so much a conversation, from my point of view, as a high-class entertainment. I've been to many such dinner-parties since, but at that time I wasn't prepared for the sheer range of subjects discussed: the shortcomings of the National Theatre, the psychology of chess masters, the link between music and mathematics, the rejected Palladian design for the Houses of Parliament, the relationship between Queen Victoria and John Brown, to name a few that I've heard Vernon discourse upon, though I forget which of them came up that evening at Arnold and Gabrielle's. All were handled with skill and authority, as if everyone had thought about them beforehand, and the whole performance was spiced with jokes, anecdotes and gossip. As at a really good cabaret, you'd never had enough of each turn before you were caught up in the next.

Between the coq au vin and the cheese, I began to feel that I ought to contribute something, if only to earn my keep, and just then the conversation turned to Northern Ireland, where things were boiling up in a big way. A mistake by the American, who thought that Catholics were in a majority in Belfast, gave me my opportunity. When I explained that I'd lived in Northern Ireland most of my life, I was encouraged to describe what it was like in normal times, and I scored a hit with a funny story which everyone in my home town would have heard before, but which was new here. The next subject was Buñuel – anyone who has been at this kind of dinner knows that it's no trick at all to get from Northern Ireland to Buñuel – and as I'm crazy about his films I was able to come in on this too. Finding that I was going over well, Gabrielle informed the company that I'd taken the best photos she'd had done for years, and I was quite the centre of attention until a transition was effected (photos, portraits, *Portrait of a Lady*) to Henry James.

I had nothing to say on this subject and retired from the limelight, but Vernon turned to me and asked whether I was a Jamesian. I thought it was wiser to tell the truth than to be led out of my depth, and anyway someone else was talking at the time, so I said quietly that I'd tried to read James but found him the most unbearable bore.

'Ah. Some people do. What have you tried?'

'*The Ambassadors*.'

'That was probably a mistake, certainly on your part and it could be argued on his. You might get along better with one of the earlier novels. Try *The Princess Casamassima*.'

'All right, I'll do that.'

'In point of fact it's not so easy to get hold of. I could lend it

73

to you if you like.'

'I'd be most grateful.'

'Ring me up and remind me, would you? I'm in the book.'

'Aren't you ex-directory?'

'No, no, my dear, that's a vulgarity of which I'm not guilty.'

I wasn't able to sit near Vernon when we adjourned for coffee, and I can't claim that he spoke to me or glanced at me for the rest of the evening. I spent most of the time wondering whether I really ought to ring him up, and whether he would remember who I was. Hopefully, I thought, he's one of those great men who give equal attention to a student and to a Prime Minister. This was indeed true of Vernon; only with time did I grasp that it was because he felt superior to both.

I rang up the following day so that he wouldn't have time to forget.

'This is Pat Bell. I was at the Blacks, if you . . .'

'Of course. I'm going to lend you *The Princess Casamassima*. Could you come here for a cup of tea on Saturday?'

'I'd love to.'

'I'm afraid it's rather out of the way. Have you a car?'

'Oh yes.'

'Let me explain how to find me.'

This he did with great precision, doubtless having had to do it often before. It would have been hard to convince Stella or Hugh that I was going to visit anyone who lived in Plumstead, and they'd have flatly refused to believe that Vernon Longuehaye lived there. Plumstead is part of Woolwich, and frankly the least credible part. I know London better than most people, but here I was exploring, and I couldn't have found my way without Vernon's directions and frequent recourse to the A to Z. The streets were mostly very short, involving me in constant left and right turns, and all looked alike. The houses, with bay windows and minute front gardens, were depressing; I felt that they were inhabited by elderly people who did the pools, lived on tinned spaghetti and baked beans, and grumbled about students and immigrants.

I guessed, however, that Professor Longuehaye had found some fantastic hideaway in this sad neighbourhood. I was excited about this, and still more excited because I was going to the home of a man whom I recognized to be irresistibly attractive. I told myself not to start thinking – and above all not to behave – like a fantasy-struck schoolgirl. No doubt he was happily married to some gorgeous creature, although she hadn't been at the dinner; indeed, now I thought of it, I vaguely recalled his wife being mentioned in a profile of him that I'd read. Married or not, he was sure to be fixed up all right. I should be humbly grateful that he was giving me tea and lending me a book.

Eventually I found the street. On one side there were eight houses of the usual grotty kind. On the other, there was a space where a bomb had fallen and nothing had been built since, and a large house set back behind a wall. I went through an ironwork gate, crossed a paved courtyard, and stopped to gaze at the house. As I learned later, it was described in its conservation order as the Manor House, and this was what it had been since the reign of Queen Anne, though Vernon considered it vulgar to use the name on his writing-paper.

I knocked – there was a heavy knocker, no bell – and Vernon opened the door. I said, inevitably: 'What a fabulous house!' He asked if I'd like to have a look round, and we embarked on a tour which, no doubt, was a routine for him.

It's difficult, looking back, to recapture my first impressions of my future home. I'll get nearer the truth by mingling those impressions with later ones and describing what the Manor House was like to live in. It was beautiful – one has to start with that, for its beauty was an atmosphere, never entirely out of mind, like heat in the Mediterranean summer. It wasn't huge, certainly not grandiose, but the way it was built – the ample entrance hall, the broad curving staircase which rose

75

out of this hall, the proportions of the rooms (all very nearly square), the tall windows – created a wonderful sense of space. And it was full of beautiful things. Vernon lived up to William Morris's rule: 'Have nothing in your house that you do not know to be useful or believe to be beautiful.' Everything you saw – a chair, a painting, a reading-lamp – looked as though it had been carefully chosen, both for its own quality and for its place, as indeed it had.

Then, it was very quiet and secluded. The street was a cul-de-sac and you never heard any traffic. The people who lived opposite seemed to have no children, or incredibly well-behaved children. Noise, in any case, could scarcely penetrate the walls that enclosed the house on all sides. There was a wall in front, as I've said, and the garden at the back – very big for London – was surrounded by an old brick wall ten feet high. The house was on the steep escarpment rising from the Thames, and the ground dropped away almost sheer beyond the garden, so it was impossible for anyone to see in except a helicopter pilot (I used to sunbathe in the nude, though I don't think Vernon altogether approved) and it was equally impossible to see out. I put a step-ladder in the garden, and by going up it you could get a splendid view of the Thames estuary. But the view included factories, power stations and council flats, so Vernon preferred not to look at it.

Unless you used the step-ladder, you could hardly believe that you were in London at all. Once inside the house, you didn't seem to be living in the modern world but in the home of an eighteenth-century gentleman, surrounded by woods and fields, as of course the house had been when it was built. I was never quite sure how Vernon achieved this effect. True, certain things were different from in other houses. The phone was in a little room called the telephone room, with an extension to Vernon's study; and the TV was in what was called the music-room, where we went to watch it or to listen to records on the hi-fi, since Vernon thought that a TV didn't belong in a room designed for conversation. But in most respects there was no deliberate archaism. There was central heating, and the kitchen and bathroom fittings were modern. Some of the furniture was antique, but some wasn't and there were abstract paintings and a Brancusi, which harmonized in the most unexpected way – at least, it was unexpected to me, though Vernon said that beautiful things always harmonized. And yet, the character of the house was that of a retreat from the world of new universities and conferences and controversies in which Vernon actually functioned. He himself, so long as he was at home, seemed to take on the air of a gentleman-scholar, collecting engravings and annotating Horace, if that's what they used to do.

That first time, I kept wondering who else lived there. Though the house was in Vernon's style of informed good taste, I had a feeling that he hadn't created it alone. The main rooms were all on the ground floor – living-room, dining-room, music-room and study – and he didn't take me upstairs. I couldn't see anything feminine lying about. Once, however, when I asked about a small marble vase, he said: 'We found it in Turkey.' If he didn't want to refer explicitly to his wife, or mistress as the case might be, I couldn't help it. I wondered if they had split up, either permanently or temporarily. It would have been natural for him to say: 'My wife is away just now,' but he didn't. He talked more quietly than when I'd met him before and didn't made any jokes. I detected, or thought I detected, a certain sadness or loneliness, restrained in a self-disciplined and civilized way. But I didn't trust myself to be sure that I wasn't romanticizing.

He made the tea, declining my offer to help, and we had it in the living-room. It was a good tea, with scones and jam and a ginger cake, but he hadn't done the things a woman would have done, such as cutting sandwiches. We talked mostly about the house. He knew all about the family who had owned it for most of its history, and somehow seemed to identify with them. It had been virtually derelict when he discovered it, he said – 'I should be ashamed to tell you how little I paid for it.'

'You never come to an end of the things you find in

London,' I said.

'That's true. Have you lived in London long?'

'It'll be two years this summer.'

'You come from Belfast, I think you said?'

I explained that I had been a student in Belfast, but I really
came from a small town.

'So you're a country girl. Do you like walking?'

I said yes, wondering what was coming.

'I walk in the country almost every Sunday with some of
my friends. You'd be welcome to join us tomorrow.'

I was tied up with Alan; in fact, we always spent Sundays
together. But I said that I could manage the following
Sunday. Vernon seemed disappointed at my putting it off,
which was flattering.

Soon after this I said I had to go, and I was sure he had lots
of things to do.

'Well, I have a review to write. But one can always
postpone writing when one has such a charming guest.'

I liked this. I didn't build anything on it, but it was genuine
courtesy rather than the standard kind of chatting up. I left,
taking the book with me. It was an early edition, printed on
thick paper and distinctly bulky — awkward to read in bed,
which was about the only place where I found time to read.

During the week, Arnold rang up and said: 'I hear you're
coming on our walk.' He was the walk organizer, it appeared.
I was instructed to be at Westerham station at eleven o'clock.

I made my way there in a dubious mood. Alan had been
baffled, if not resentful, at this project of a day out 'with
friends' and clearly didn't grasp why he couldn't come along.
And I was only up to about page twenty of *The Princess
Casamassima*, which didn't turn me on any more than *The
Ambassadors*.

The party included five men, of whom I knew only Vernon
and Arnold, and one other woman. She was about thirty,
attractive in a long-lashes sort of way, and managed to look
smart and elegant in spite of being dressed for the country. I
disliked her at once.

'How are you getting on with the Master?' Vernon asked me.

I didn't know that Henry James was called the Master, but it seemed right for him.

'About halfway,' I lied. 'I've had a busy week.'

Vernon nodded, and didn't pay much more attention to me. The long-lashes woman kept by his side, and I drew the obvious conclusion and felt unreasonably that he might have told me.

'How's your wife?' I asked Arnold. 'Doesn't she come on these walks?'

'No, it's not exactly her style. And wives don't, on the whole. Laura never did.'

'Who?'

'Vernon's wife. You don't know?'

Arnold halted to fill and light a pipe, or to avoid catching up with the others.

'Laura died about six months ago. The most awful thing — cancer. She was only about thirty-seven, thirty-eight perhaps. It was a ghastly blow for Vernon. They were married young — Laura had just left school, as a matter of fact — and they were always idyllically happy.'

'How dreadful. Are there any children?'

'Yes, three. Two are grown-up, fortunately. The youngest is at boarding-school, she's only ten.'

'I'm afraid I had no idea,' I said. 'Actually I thought that must be Vernon's wife, or . . . you know.'

'Who, Helen? No, she's merely one of the many hopefuls. I don't rate her chances very high. Between ourselves, she's made a fatal blunder by inviting herself today.'

I smiled, and hoped that I didn't look too pleased.

'And I doubt,' Arnold continued, 'whether anyone could take Laura's place. Laura was a very rare human being — it's hard to describe, she had a certain uniqueness. And incidentally she was the most beautiful woman I've ever seen.'

I took this, no doubt correctly, as a friendly warning, and was careful not to try to get Vernon to myself as we walked

79

on. Conversation, as a matter of fact, was general and incessant; the whole thing was virtually a mobile dinner-party, and not always mobile, as we made a long stop to eat our picnic lunches. I suspected that Vernon would have liked to put on more mileage, but Helen wasn't the athletic type, and when she suggested turning back nobody argued.

We had all left cars at Westerham, and I drove home – or rather to Alan's – alone. I was annoyed at having scarcely spoken to Vernon, and wondered whether I'd see him again. I still had the book, but it might be tactful to return it by post.

A few nights later, when I came in very late from a party, I found a message in Stella's sprawling handwriting: 'Pat! Vernon Longhay called!!!' Vernon's surname was frequently misspelled, apart from the fact that it was as much as Stella could do to spell Pat. The exclamation marks were her comment.

I rang his number at intervals during the next day, but got no answer. In the evening, as Alan was away from London, I came home as soon as I'd finished work. I was still putting my cameras away when the phone rang. I dashed.

'Is that Patricia?'

I didn't recognize myself, but I said: 'Speaking.'

'This is Vernon Longuehaye. I wonder if you would care to have dinner with me next Tuesday.'

Alas, Tuesday was the night when Alan and I had tickets for the National, and he'd queued. There now ensued one of those maddening conversations, familiar to all Londoners, in which diaries are frantically consulted and each suggestion is met by a counter-proposal. Vernon, not surprisingly, had a great many commitments. Whenever he was free, I was either tied up with Alan, or doing an evening job, or going out with someone else (my fidelity to Alan stopped short of refusing dinner invitations). I tried to convey that I was honestly keen to have dinner with Vernon, but he sounded distinctly miffed at my non-availabilty. Getting desperate, I said I'd made a mistake about a date he'd suggested and decided to ditch a man whom I quite liked, but who was dispensable if something had to give. Vernon said he would book a table at a restaurant in Soho, which was roughly midway between Alan's financial bracket and Hugh's.

I spent the interval doggedly reading Henry James and wondering what this was all about. For a man who could take his pick among numerous females, and indeed was warding off quite a few, Vernon was unbelievably keen on my company. But perhaps he wanted just that – the company of a girl with whom it would amuse him to relax and chat because there was no question of anything more. Humility isn't my outstanding quality, but I didn't kid myself that I qualified for Vernon Longuehaye, either in intellectual calibre or (remembering what Arnold had said about his late wife) in beauty. Still, no girl in my position could have kept her mind from lingering on the possibilities. I avoided thinking about Alan; it seemed foolish to puzzle over a dilemma which in all likelihood would never present itself.

It was a Friday, and the restaurant was crowded. I got there five minutes early, a record for me. When I uttered the magic name I was conducted to a table in an upstairs room, of whose existence I was unaware although I knew the restaurant. Some other tables were occupied or labelled 'Reserved', but it was quiet and I had the feeling that admittance was at the management's discretion. Vernon arrived at exactly eight o'clock and apologized with his usual courtesy for keeping me waiting.

'I've brought your book,' I told him.

'Ah. Has Henry James risen at all in your estimation?'

'Well,' I said, 'it does seem he's going to be one of my blind spots, I'm afraid.'

'You didn't finish it?'

'Sure I finished it,' I said indignantly.

'That was a mistake. You shouldn't finish a book that you don't enjoy.'

'But you told me to read it,' I blurted out.

He smiled and rested his hand lightly on mine.

'No, Patricia, I didn't tell you to do anything. I advised you

81

to try it.'

'Yes, you did say try it,' I admitted, contrite.

'No more of Henry James, then. Now I advise you to try the chicken cacciatore. Remember, it's only a recommendation.'

What did Vernon talk about that evening? I can remember quite well – much of the time, it was the history of Soho and the home life of Karl Marx, commemorated by a plaque across the street from where we were sitting – but the important thing was how he talked. It made no difference to him whether he had an audience of one, or a group of friends, or a lecture-hall, or the cameras. The style was the same: polished, rich in ideas and illustrations, and yet always spontaneous and intimate, so that you had only to be within range to feel that it was all specially for you. Naturally, when this was literally so, the effect was enhanced. We sat there until after midnight, until we had the room to ourselves. We drank wine, and then coffee, and then more wine (Vernon never went in much for spirits). I was endlessly fascinated, and it would be impossible to work out how much of the fascination was intellectual. You missed the point about Vernon if you tried to disentangle the elements: the glittering display of his mind and his words, the pleasure of receiving his attention, and the excitement of being physically close to him. All were fused into a compelling whole. A girl could only feel – what a man!

In the later stages the conversation became more personal. I realized afterwards that Vernon didn't tell me anything at all revealing about himself, but at the time it felt as though he did. He talked at some length about students, comparing those he taught to his own generation, and about the difficulty of learning to think and learning to live at the same time. He had a theory – Vernon always had a theory – that it would be better if young people set up a home and family first and studied after that. I said that I'd certainly hated living alone in digs when I was a student.

'And how do you live now?' he asked.

82

I gave an account (somewhat tidied up) of my flat and the other girls. Vernon wasn't what is usually called a good listener; what you said to him soon reminded him of an idea or an experience of his own, and he interrupted shamelessly. But he was an appreciative listener – I mean, he was helped along and stimulated by what the other person said. Although he did most of the talking, you felt that you had taken part in an exchange.

I thought, as on the tea occasion, that it would be wise to say I had to go before he showed any sign of having had enough of me.

'Must you?' he asked.

'Well, it's quite late. I can't tell you how much I've enjoyed it.'

'Not more than I have. Please believe that.'

This time, it sounded like more than courtesy. I had a queer, sudden lift of the heart. I told myself that it must be just the effect of the good time I'd had, and the wine.

'I'll drive you home,' he said when we left the restaurant. 'I'm afraid I had to park rather far away.'

'I shouldn't dream of it,' I said. 'You're going in just the opposite direction. I'll easily find a taxi.'

He stood there, his hand light on my arm – he had a way of touching you just enough to establish a contact – and seemed to be hesitating. Roger, in these circumstances, would simply have got me into his car and headed for his own territory. And Vernon could have done that, so far as I was concerned. I didn't know what he wanted.

'You're sure you'll be all right?' he asked.

'Sure. Really.'

He said suddenly, and in a tone so unlike what I'd heard so far that it was almost a different voice: 'I must see you again, Patricia. Soon.'

I was startled by his manner, urgent and almost clumsy, in utter contrast with his normal confidence and charm. It was the manner of a lonely man; and it came to me that, after midnight, this was what he was. I almost said: 'Don't go alone. I'll stay with you.' But I checked myself, with a curious feeling that to say this would be to take advantage of him.

'Yes. Soon,' I answered.

He found me a taxi. I felt unexpectedly tired; perhaps it was from sitting on an upright chair for four hours. No, I was tired as though I'd been making love.

A surprising thought occurred to me. One would assume that Vernon Longuehaye was experienced with women, that he handled a sexual approach as easily as any social situation. But if it was true that he had married young and been happy with his wife, perhaps he was a beginner at the business of securing a girl. It made me feel strangely tender toward him.

Stella and Peggy were waiting for me. Everyone in the flat had been vicariously looking forward to my date with Vernon.

'How was it? Tell all,' Stella demanded.

'It was fabulous.'

'You're back early.'

'We've just been having dinner. And talking.'

'What did you talk about?'

'Relational analysis,' I said unkindly.

'All right, be like that. Are you seeing him again?'

'Yes.'

'When are you going to bring him here?'

'I don't know. I don't know anything. I need to sort myself out.'

The next day was Saturday. I was working in town in the morning and doing road safety pictures on the suitably named Death Hill in the afternoon. For the evening I was invited to a party, but it didn't matter much whether I went or not. Alan was going to the Cup Final – by now I seldom went to matches with him – and spending the evening with football friends. As I was driving across the Serpentine bridge during the morning, one of these 'up for the Cup' morons from Scunthorpe or somewhere stepped blindly in front of my car. 'You're in London now!' I yelled as I braked.

I had a quick lunch with Eileen and drove out to Death

Hill, which is south-east of London on the Maidstone road. I didn't catch any actual crashes but I got some good shots of motor-bike cowboys seeking to reduce the average life expectancy. At about six o'clock I packed in and drove to Plumstead.

I can't define my state of mind. I was in a dream, one of those dreams when you do something that would normally be illogical, and in the framework of the dream it's wholly reasonable and indeed inevitable. I didn't even think about where to go; it was as though I were going home. I was going to Vernon because Vernon wanted me, and to be wanted by Vernon was the most wonderful thing in the world.

I walked through the gate, into his secluded domain, and knocked. (It didn't occur to me that he might not be in, nor that someone else might be there.) He opened the door.

'You wanted to see me soon,' I said.

He said: 'Patricia', put his arms round me, and kissed me. It didn't seem in the least that he was kissing me for the first time; it was more as though I were returning after an absence.

I went into the living-room, walking with the same sort of dream-like certainty.

'What were you doing?' I asked.

'Letters. They accumulate – I generally do them on Saturdays. And thinking about you.'

I smiled contentedly.

'And you, what have you been doing?'

'Well.' I launched into an account of my day, the kind that I'd often given to Alan. Vernon listened with interruptions. He had a theory that there ought to be roads reserved for people who wanted to take risks, with alternative routes for those who wanted to arrive. We went on talking of this and that, as we had the night before.

After a time – I don't know how much time, I wasn't noticing – he asked: 'Shall we go out to dinner?'

'We could. What is there round here?'

'Oh, there's nothing round here. We'd have to go into town.'

'It'll be frightful. Saturday night, and Cup Final too.'

'Cup Final? How well-informed you are, Patricia.' This made me think of Alan, but not for long.

'We'll have dinner here, then,' he said. 'I have a piece of veal. What would you suggest doing with it?'

We discussed this, or rather I accepted his ideas.

'I'll start it now,' he said.

I wasn't at all surprised that he was able to cook. It was in the order of things that he should be an excellent cook, as indeed he was. However, I said: 'No, I'll do it.'

'We'll do it together.'

This we did. I had cooked for men before, but I'd never cooked with a man. It was a new intimacy, a new pleasure. I didn't have much chance to reflect on this, because everything had to be done with great care and precision, so it was demanding work.

We went down to the cellar – the first real wine-cellar I'd ever seen – to choose a wine. I endorsed Vernon's choice, needless to say. Then we had the dinner: 'a simple dinner', he called it (the veal, cheese and fruit) but we ate slowly and it seemed like a feast. Vernon talked all the time. I can remember what he talked about, but it mattered even less than the night before. I was with him – that was what mattered.

I was wondering whether we'd go back to the living-room, when he said: 'Would you like to listen to some music? I've just bought a Sibelius recording that's really rather beautiful.'

So we went to the music-room. Here I found another level of intimacy, another happiness – being quiet together with Vernon. I got up to turn over the record, and sat down on his lap instead of where I'd been sitting before; he kissed me, only once, but it made everything absolutely certain.

He put the record away (wiping it clean, which he never failed to do) and stood waiting for me to go to him. I expected him to embrace me, but he only took my hand. We walked upstairs.

He undressed me, taking off all my clothes before he removed any of his own, and kissing what he laid bare. I found this sweet, and very gracious, and altogether in his style. When he made love to me, I felt that he was taking me – the phrase, which I disliked in books, seemed right. I was giving myself to him. I was making a ritual surrender, like the surrender of a temple maiden to a priest. I entered a state of exalted anticipation, charged with wonder more than with passion. It seemed that I was in love. But to be in love with some other man would not have been quite like this. Simply, I worshipped him.

But he did bring me – many times, and certainly that first time – to the high peak of ecstasy, gasping and trembling and threshing in the bed. I woke early in the morning and thought about this. It hadn't happened for the same directly physical reasons as with some other men. Considered in that way, Vernon was good but not extraordinary – you might even say not quite what a girl would expect, in view of his distinction in other respects. I must be in love, I said to myself. And I knew that I was, deeply and helplessly and gloriously in love, for the first time in my life, in a way that I not only hadn't experienced but had been unable to imagine before. And there could be no going back, even if I'd wanted it; I had begun a new life.

It was a fine morning, clean and fresh as you only get it in May. Birds were twittering in a tree that grew close to the bedroom window. I had a tremendous sense of the beauty and richness of the world, not as a spectacle – as I had seen it from Roger's penthouse – but as something I was in the midst of.

Vernon woke up and smiled at me.

'Please take me again,' I said, like a child asking for one more treat.

I should have liked to stay in bed all day, but I guessed that Vernon wouldn't do this even on such an exceptional occasion. So I made breakfast and took it up to him with the Sunday papers. He at once started talking, commenting on the news and the book reviews, as though it were the usual thing to have me to talk to on a Sunday morning. Then he said: 'I must get up. I'm going walking. Are you coming?'

'I don't know.' I had remembered that Alan was expecting me.

'Helen won't be there.'

'Oh, I don't care about Helen.'

'Nor do I, needless to say.'

'Needless to say. No, the thing is, I ought to . . .' I made up my mind. 'I'll go and phone.'

I rang Alan and said that I had to see a friend in hospital. It was the first outright lie I'd ever told him; I'm afraid it left me quite unmoved. Alan said that he would be working on his Cup Final story, so he would expect me in the evening. I couldn't pretend that I'd be spending the evening at a hospital. 'All right,' I said.

'We're going to Beaconsfield,' Vernon told me. 'We'll take my car; there's no point in taking both.'

'Look, Vernon,' I said (it may have been the first time I called him Vernon), 'I can't come back here after the walk.'

'You must.'

'I want to, but I just can't.'

'Well, you'll come back some time tonight, won't you?'

'I'll try.'

'You see, I have to fly to Paris tomorrow for a Unesco meeting and stay the night, and I'm always out of London Tuesdays and Wednesdays. I shouldn't see you till Thursday. That's unthinkable.'

'I'd better explain,' I said. 'I've got a boy-friend.'

He stared at me. Obviously, the possibility had never crossed his mind.

'Girls do have boy-friends, you know,' I said.

'Well, you'll have to deal with that problem.'

'I know. It's going to take a bit of sorting out.'

He shrugged; to him, it was an irritating complication, like his having to be out of London.

Arnold was on the walk, two other men whom I'd met when we went to Westerham, and two whom I didn't know (except by name – most of Vernon's friends were well-known names). It was a mobile *conversazione* once more. But when we were on the home stretch Vernon walked hand in hand with me, a little ahead of the group. I was very proud.

I went to Alan's flat, feeling awful. I knew perfectly well that I was going to break up with him. It wasn't even a decision; it was an obvious consequence of the change in my life. Len was present, as usual, and the two of them spent the evening reviewing and debating every moment of the Cup Final. This made me feel even worse. I didn't want to see Alan again as the drip I'd thought him at first, even if that made things simpler for me. It seemed unjust, pitiable, that he should be so unequal to Vernon. I didn't feel up to speaking to him that evening. Anyway, Len showed no signs of leaving us alone.

About eleven o'clock, I said that I felt tired, so I'd be going.

'You don't look quite yourself, that's a fact,' Alan said.

He came downstairs and kissed me as usual.

'See you soon, love.'

'See you.'

I drove slowly across London. I was longing for Vernon. But I didn't want to go to him like this, depressed and anxious. I went back to my flat and phoned him.

'I can't come tonight. Please forgive me.'

He said nothing for a moment. Then: 'Where are you?'

'At home. You do believe that, don't you, Vernon?'

'Yes, yes. Well, I'm disappointed, but I shan't press you. I'll count the days until Thursday.'

'I'll come to your place, shall I? As soon as I've finished work.'

'Please do.'

'I love you very much,' I said quickly, and hung up. It was strange, but I hadn't said that to him before.

On Tuesday morning I got a letter from Vernon. I would quote it if I still had it. Considering that it was written in the departure lounge at London airport, it was a masterpiece. It was phrased with as much style and care as any of Vernon's articles; actually, I don't think he ever wrote anything without remembering in a corner of his mind that it had to be suitable for eventual publication. But its sincerity – 'the voice of true feeling', to use a phrase he was fond of – was unmistakable. The gist was that he didn't use the word 'love' without a full sense of its meaning, he had loved only one other woman in his life, and he was in love with me – this bit I'm sure I recall correctly – 'with as much devotion as passion, with as much certainty as joyous amazement'. And he cursed Unesco, and cursed the University of East Anglia – that was where he went in the middle of the week – and had nothing in his heart but longing for his sweetest, dearest Patricia.

I had never received a love-letter before (a penalty of the telephone age) let alone a classic of the genre. I carried it everywhere I went, and couldn't resist showing it to Stella.

I still flinched from breaking the news to Alan, and I'm ashamed to say that I slept with him that night. I felt that I was being doubly disloyal – to Vernon, and to Alan himself because every kiss was a falsehood. I didn't enjoy it at all, and Alan's pleasure made me want to weep.

On Thursday I drove to Plumstead, and went over a zebra crossing when somebody had started to cross (which I'd never done before) and was flagged down by a cop and subsequently fined for driving without due care and attention. Vernon told the story at dinner-parties and maintained that I should have defended myself on the plea that I was in love.

'Have you seen your boy-friend?' he asked in the course of the evening. He used the word as though he were quoting it from some badly written book.

'Well, I've seen him,' I answered. 'I haven't actually told him yet.'

Vernon took a sip of coffee and said: 'You know that I love you, Patricia. And you've said you love me.'

'Oh, I do.'

'I think we'd both be happier without any loose ends.'

'You're absolutely right. Only, it isn't so easy as it seems. Can't you give me a little time?'

'I don't think time will make it easier.'

'I suppose not.'

'Is your boy-friend also a photographer? You haven't told me anything about him.'

'He's a football reporter.'

As soon as I'd said this I wished that I'd made something up, or at least said more vaguely that Alan was a journalist. Vernon said: 'You must be joking, my sweet.'

'He's really an intelligent person.' I felt a need to defend Alan, partly for his sake and partly for my own. 'He's interested in books, and the theatre, and ... all that,' I concluded lamely.

'Well, of course I haven't met him.'

'You know, darling, you mustn't have any glorified ideas about me. I'm quite an ordinary girl. And I'm only twenty-three.'

'Twenty-three is a delightful age. And since I am in love with you, I can't agree that you're an ordinary girl.'

'I'm seeing him again tomorrow,' I offered.

'Will you speak to him then? Surely it's only fair.'

'I'll try.'

We went to the music-room, and had a delightful time. Vernon had a collection of 78 records which had belonged to his parents – Caruso, Tauber, all sorts – and we played one after another of them. Then we went to bed, which was as good as before.

The next day, I rang up Alan at his office and asked him to meet me as soon as he could get clear. He said he could manage six o'clock. I said I'd meet him at Hyde Park Corner and we could go for a walk in the park. I had decided that it would be easier in a public place.

In fact, it was ghastly. Alan had never been sure of me; but losing me was a disaster so long averted that it had become unreal, so he was as amazed as though he had never dreaded it. And it seemed, apparently, that he had thought only of my leaving him to return to the non-attached state in which (to the best of his knowledge) he had found me. It was incredible to him that I'd fallen for another man while I was still his girl-friend. He could see nothing but an outrageous betrayal of his trust.

'How long has this been going on?' he demanded.

'What does that matter? It's quite definite.'

'What does it matter?' Alan pointed out with cold fury that I'd spent the night with him 'just this Tuesday'.

'It wasn't easy to tell you, Alan.'

'I suppose you haven't told this chap about me, either.'

'Yes, I have actually.'

'Who is he, anyway?'

'Vernon Longuehaye. I expect you've . . .'

'What? The TV personality?'

I was irritated, of course, by this description of Vernon.

'Oh well,' Alan said with ponderous sarcasm, 'I can't compete, can I?'

'If you imagine it's because he's a famous man, that shows what you think of me, I suppose.' My tone wasn't improved by the knowledge that this was indeed part of Vernon's attraction, though in a more complex way than I could explain.

'How did you meet him?'

I went into this. It was news to Alan that I considered myself free to have dinner with another man. Admittedly, I had never gone out of my way to inform him of such events.

'Have you had sex with him?'

I particularly dislike the phrase 'to have sex', as though it were a disease. I said: 'Naturally.'

I thought Alan was going to hit me; perhaps he would have, if we hadn't been sitting on a park bench. He clenched his fist and the knuckles went white – I'm sorry that moments of emotion so often have to be described in clichés, but it's a fact.

'I don't know how you can sit there and tell me that,' he said.

'Look, Alan, I'm trying to tell you the truth. It's not much fun for me – I hope you'll believe that. We've been very happy together, and I hate to hurt you. But everything has changed since I've met Vernon. I don't think there's anything more to say.'

'You mean you just want to say goodbye – just like this!'

It was emphatically what I did mean; I couldn't take any more. The end of the scene was as painful and humiliating as it could possibly have been. I walked – at the end, literally ran – to my car, with Alan shouting, pleading, threatening. When I got in and started the engine, he dashed round to the passenger door, which was fortunately locked, and rattled the handle. I drove off, almost into the side of a bus. All the way to my flat I was blinking to keep back the tears, and if I didn't have an accident it must have been because everyone gave me a wide berth. Then I rushed inside and poured myself a large Scotch. I wanted desperately to be with Vernon or at least to phone him, but I knew that he was at the Television Centre.

By a strange chance – it seldom happened – all six of us girls were in the flat when Vernon came on the screen. We sat and gazed like fans at a pop concert. Stella and Claudine came on with remarks like 'Jesus, isn't he dishy!' and 'Take him away, I can't bear it!' Erica, who was in a state of unrequited yearning as usual, reached for my hand and said tremulously: 'I'm so happy for you, Pat.'

Vernon rang me from the hospitality room after the programme. I suppose he wanted to know if I'd got back from seeing Alan, and perhaps also whether I'd been watching.

'I want to be with you tonight,' I said.

'I'll collect you. I'll leave now.'

I knew the girls were longing to have him in their midst, and very likely he would find them entertaining, but I wanted to be alone with him. I told him that I'd meet him at the Goat in Kensington High Street.

On the way to Plumstead, I said: 'I talked to Alan.'

'Yes?'

'Well, he knows now.'

'Bless you, my darling. I can understand that it wasn't pleasant for you. Still, it's over now.'

But it wasn't. Alan kept pursuing me – phoning the flat and the agency, demanding to see me, once turning up at the flat

93

at a late hour. On that occasion he didn't find me, but twice I weakly agreed to see him, first for lunch and then at Angelo's café one evening. Both these meetings were disastrous, inevitably. Alan declared that he couldn't sleep, he couldn't work, he didn't know what would become of him. (He looked his usual healthy self, which rather spoiled the effect.) In an effort to finish the wretched business, I was driven to say things that wounded him badly. I was angry with him for eclipsing our happy memories, for abandoning his dignity as a man, for forcing me to despise him. Meanwhile, Vernon knew that I was still seeing Alan; I couldn't help telling him everything I did, and he could see when I'd been upset. 'Oh, not again, darling,' he said. One would almost have said that he was jealous; at least, he didn't like the idea that I had been fond of Alan, and still cared about him enough to have trouble in breaking away. Altogether, it was messy. I had never been involved in anything like this before, and I loathed it.

The worst part of it was that the men felt obliged to denigrate each other. Alan's line was that Vernon was fooling with me, as he doubtless fooled with lots of girls, and I could expect no mercy when he'd had enough of me. Vernon's rather more subtle ploy was a total refusal to take Alan (whom he called 'your football chap') seriously. 'It's extraordinary enough that he's occupied your time for a year, but now, really ...' Neither attitude was exactly complimentary to me. To both, I retorted indignantly: 'You don't know anything about him. He isn't like what you imagine.'

'I seem to spend all my time defending them,' I complained to Eileen. She had known all about my affair with Alan, naturally, and I was quite vain enough to tell her about Vernon. Besides, now that I was being seen around with Vernon, the gossip columns were taking an interest.

'Are you surprised?' she asked. 'Men are much more bitchy than women.'

'Well, Vernon knows I'm crazy about him. I don't see what,

more he can want.'

'He wants you to think of him, and nothing but him, all day and all night. Also typical of a man.'

'But Tony isn't like that, is he?'

'Ah, well, we've been married a long time. When he was a young reporter he used to dash home between stories and I always had to be there, jumping for joy. Now he has girl-friends, I can get on with my own life.'

'You're a cynic, Eileen.'

'No, it's just that I'm not in love and nobody's in love with me. I envy you, really.'

I was indeed to be envied. Except for the mess with Alan – and that couldn't last much longer, I trusted – I was utterly happy. Happiness was complete when I went to live with Vernon.

This happened by degrees. It began when he said – he was phoning me on a Friday morning – 'I want to take you to a party tonight, and I've got some rather interesting Italian friends coming here on Saturday. Then there's the walk on Sunday. Why don't you bring the clothes you'll need and stay here?'

So I did that, and did it again, and the effect was that I was living at the Manor House about half the time. There was no sense in being there in the middle of the week, when he was in Norwich. He had a flat on the campus.

'You don't spend much time at that university,' I remarked.

'As little as possible,' he replied cheerfully. 'How can it compete with my Patricia?'

'But you're a professor, after all.'

'I do two lectures and a seminar, and I get through the departmental office work. You can waste a lot of time at a university if you've nothing else to do.'

I still found it curious; he was actually in Norwich for about forty-eight hours, from mid-day Tuesday to mid-day Thursday. I had always thought of a professor as a fixture. I learned, however, that it was quite the done thing to be a commuting professor. The university just had to put up with it, especially when he was a celebrity. As for me, I wasn't grumbling.

I was all in favour of living with Vernon permanently and, so to speak, officially, if only because it might cause Alan to give up hope. (He did give up, in fact, when the girls were able to answer his phone calls with: 'Pat doesn't live here any more.') But I was careful not to hurry Vernon. I was sure that he was genuinely in love with me and wanted all he could get of me – in bed and as a companion – but I also knew that only one other woman had ever lived at the Manor House: Laura, his wife. He had loved her, and that love remained as a feeling which one would have to define as piety. I respected this feeling. It was for him to decide whether he wanted his mistress to live in the house that he had shared with his wife.

We went on like this until the university term ended and he didn't have to go to Norwich any more. One evening, when he was finishing an article and I was cooking dinner, I turned round to see him standing in the doorway of the kitchen and watching me.

'Finished work, darling?' I asked in a domesticated way.

'Finished work. Oh, Patricia, I love to see you like this.'

'Like what? Getting your grub?'

'Living with me.'

'Well,' I said, 'that does seem to be what it amounts to.'

'I want you here, Patricia, now and for ever.'

So I moved in. When I finished packing and saw my room at the flat bare and anonymous, I felt sad for a few minutes. But the flat had been a phase in my life and I'd got the best out of it. I'd had more than enough of affairs that took the form of visits, from Bob Curran all the way to Alan. For quite some time I had been ready to live with a man, in need of the emotional security and the full commitment. But I was glad now that I hadn't lived with Alan (apart from the extra trouble that would have been involved in leaving him). It was with the man I loved that I was making my home.

On the practical side, it was convenient to have all my clothes and things in one place, and I'd be saving in rent. The only drawback was living in Plumstead. It took at least an hour to drive into town in the morning rush, and no possible combination of public transport was much better, especially as the house wasn't close to a station or even a bus stop. These considerations didn't mean much to Vernon; if he went into central London it was mostly in the evening, or perhaps for an afternoon appointment.

The girls gave me a going-away party, of course on condition that Vernon would be there. He was in good form, throwing off witticisms, telling funny stories, and amused by Stella's efforts to flirt with him. We drove off to Plumstead in the bright splendour of a June morning, dazzled by the rising sun. I felt that the world had just been created for me.

I had that day, a Saturday, all to myself. Vernon was speaking at a conference at Kent University, but would be home by the evening. I sorted out my possessions in an orderly and durable manner. After this I made a tour of the local shops, asking questions about what they stocked and whether they delivered, and conveying the idea that I was around for keeps. I could guess that the shopkeepers already knew who I was. They were all very pleasant to me, whether naturally or by calculation. Vernon's custom was valuable, no doubt. I dawdled in the shops, listening to 'Lovely day again' and 'We've got your cucumbers in, love' and 'How's your Mum, better is she?' People in Plumstead seemed to know one another, to have lived there for a long time. It was like shopping in my home town more than in Kensington.

I had a light lunch and settled down to some household jobs. Vernon employed a capable daily help, whom I'd already met, but some repairs had been waiting – I had to assume – since Laura's death. One bedroom curtain was unstitched at the seam, so I took it down. I had to wipe the dust off the sewing-machine before I could use it; this gave me a rather creepy feeling.

A knock at the door. It was Gabrielle.

'I was in the district,' she said, 'so I thought I'd pop in.'

I didn't believe the bit about being in the district, but I was glad to see her. She came in and looked round the living-room, which of course she knew well, as though she half expected it to be different. Then she looked at me with a friendly but appraising air. I did look different, no doubt, from the agency photographer and the emergency dinner guest. I wasn't wearing any make-up, and I'd stacked my hair and stuck a comb in it. I didn't mind; I looked as I wanted to look, in my home.

'Well,' she said, 'little did I think.'

'If you ask a girl to dinner and sit her next to Vernon, anything can happen.'

'Yes, indeed. I'm very glad it has happened, Pat. The best of luck to you.'

'Thank you. Would you like some tea?'

'Oh no, I won't stop. You're busy. What were you doing?'

'I'm just mending this curtain. But now I look at it, I don't think it'll last much longer. It's faded, too, isn't it? Those curtains upstairs get a lot of sun.'

Gabrielle didn't answer at once. Then she said: 'You know, Pat, if I were you I wouldn't change things too much. Vernon's a rather conservative man, although people don't realize it. This house is — well, it indicates that, don't you think?'

'I suppose it does.'

'I hope you don't mind what I said.'

'Of course not. You must have known Vernon for a long time.'

'Quite a long time.'

'And Laura.'

'And Laura. Yes.'

I said: 'Arnold told me something soon after I first met Vernon. He said that Vernon and Laura were idyllically happy together. I haven't forgotten.'

'You're a very sensible girl, Pat, aren't you?'

'I'm in love with Vernon. I think that goes a long way, or does it sound naive?'

'No,' she answered, 'it's what counts, when the chips are

down.'

When she left, she kissed me and said: 'I really am glad about this. We must celebrate – I'll ring you.'

In the evening, I said to Vernon: 'I want to ask you something, darling. Haven't you got any pictures of Laura?'

He made a curious sort of fidgeting movement in his chair, as if he'd sat on a pin. Then he said: 'I have several photographs, also a painting. I took them all down.'

'You could put them up again. I mean – don't not because of me.'

'Don't not because of me. Really, what a sentence.'

'Let me see them, please, Vernon. It's no good her being a mystery to me.'

He fetched them. The photos were all studio portraits; none had been taken, or none kept, which caught her unawares or showed her doing anything. She was very beautiful. It made sense for a man like Arnold, who hadn't lived in a monastery, to say that she was the most beautiful woman he'd ever seen. The face didn't express any strong character or any lively intelligence. Perhaps this was because the photos were posed, but I didn't think so. It was a face that could have been called vapid – vapid on a very high level, if I can use that expression. Yet it made a great impression of sweetness; you felt that this was a woman who had never spoken a harsh word or had a malicious thought, whom a man could love, and (more remarkable) whom other and less beautiful women would like. The painting, though it was by an artist who was far from being a chocolate-box decorator, bore out this impression and told nothing more.

'My God, she was a beauty,' I said.

'That was the general opinion. When one is in love with a woman, the general opinion doesn't matter. I'm in love with you, Patricia.'

'I know. But just now I want to know about Laura.'

'What do you want to know?'

'Well, for instance, is it true you married her straight from school? Arnold said so.'

'Yes, that's true. I fall in love quickly and decisively, as you're aware. Her family put up a certain amount of resistance. Her uncle was an earl, and none of your political titles either. You observe the aristocratic jaw-line.'

'Is that what it is? Where did you meet her?'

'At Aix-en-Provence. I was on a walking trip, which I brought to an abrupt stop, and she was staying with a French family to learn the language. I met her — came face to face with her — at a certain place in the pinewoods. You can imagine the immediate impression. And we used to meet there, in this secluded place, every afternoon. The stillness of pinewoods made the perfect setting for her. Laura was always a very quiet person.'

'Tell me more.'

'Tell you what?' Vernon smiled, but a little uneasily. 'We were married as soon as possible. She was my wife. We were happy. Happiness is uneventful.'

'What did she do? Did she have a job, a profession, whatever?'

'No.' The question seemed to surprise him; I could see, indeed, that it wouldn't have been like Laura.

I was about to ask about the children, but he said: 'I could tell you about her death. It would probably be good for me to tell you.'

The cancer, he said, was hopeless as soon as it was diagnosed, because Laura had concealed the onset of pain. She had great courage, even later when the pain became bad. She couldn't bear to distress other people, especially Vernon. While in hospital, she insisted on his doing his usual work and going to Norwich in mid-week.

'Did she know she was dying?'

'Only right at the end. She thought the treatment was doing her good, or she made an effort to reward the doctors. When the state of affairs was obvious, she wouldn't stay in hospital. It was wrong to make useless demands on other people's time and skill, she said.'

'Did she die here?' I asked, shivering a little.

100

'No, she wanted to go back with me to Aix, where we'd met. I rented a house as near as I could to the one where she'd stayed as a girl. There was a view of the pinewoods, and the mountains beyond them. She used to lie on the verandah all day. I think she was not only calm, but even happy. At that stage, one is taken beyond pain by sheer weakness. She died one afternoon while I was reading aloud to her. I closed her eyes and went on sitting there. I had a sense of still being with her, so long as it was possible.'

'What were you reading?'

'*Alice in Wonderland*. She practically knew it by heart. Well, one wouldn't read Henry James in such circumstances.'

Vernon wouldn't, either that evening or when I tried again, say any more about his life with Laura. It seemed that their courtship and her death were, so to speak, the pictures that he was willing to keep. The painting showed her as a young girl, or else she didn't change much. I hung it in the music-room, where it had been before.

Vernon's children were called John, Cressida and Aethra. I had to ask him to spell Aethra, and I felt sorry for the poor girl having it spelled and pronounced wrong all her life. I didn't say this to Vernon, who was very proud of his choice of names.

'It means the sky, or the air,' he explained. 'To my mind, it's a charming concept. In the Greek myth, Aethra was loved by Poseidon.'

'Who?'

'The god of the sea.'

'I thought that was Neptune.'

'Neptune to the Romans.'

As for Cressida, it meant golden-haired; Vernon had been sure that Cressida would have golden hair, like Laura, and luckily she did. He considered that names ought to be distinctive and ought to have a meaning. According to his theory, people who had unusual names tended to develop exceptional qualities, while those who had commonplace names tended to settle for a commonplace future. He was

101

particularly against the reduction of names to what he called 'meaningless monosyllables', like Bill and Tom. This was why he persisted in calling me Patricia. The Patricia habit did say something special about Vernon, if not about me, so I didn't mind, so long as other people called me Pat. It did strike me as odd that his eldest child was called John. Either he hadn't yet evolved his theory, or else John was Laura's choice – perhaps a tradition in her family.

John was at Cambridge, Vernon told me, and Cressida was at Oxford. John had gone in for science.

'What science?' I asked.

'Biochemistry.'

I mentioned that I had taken biology for A-levels.

'Really? I see you distinctly as an arts person.'

'Well, I am now, I suppose. When I was at school I wanted to be a doctor, but my As weren't good enough.'

'You wanted to be a doctor?' It seemed to take him aback.

'Yes, I did actually. I think being a photographer suits me better, though, doesn't it? What's Cressida doing?'

'She's reading Modern Greats.'

'What are they?'

Vernon was amused at my not knowing this, but explained. He was always ready to explain things to me. Discovering that I didn't know this or that put him in a good mood, rather than the reverse. He had a real zest for adding to a younger person's knowledge; I could well believe that he was good with students, and I felt sure that he was a wonderful father.

Aethra was at a boarding-school in Sussex. She was a sensitive child, Vernon said, and went into her shell if she didn't get encouragement. The local primary schools were crowded and of a pretty low standard, so she had been sent to a private school in Blackheath, and then to the boarding-school when Laura fell ill. It was a small school, concentrating on individual attention.

Vernon himself was an only child, and his parents were dead. But, to my surprise, he had a clannish feeling about the Longuehaye family and was on moderately close terms with various cousins. He had even been to the small town in Normandy where the Longuehayes came from, and was delighted to find one there. The original Longuehaye, so far as this country was concerned, was a prisoner of war in Napoleonic times. Under the civilized rules of that period, he was allowed to live on parole, married an English girl, and stayed on. The Longuehayes were an intellectual dynasty, in the style of the Huxleys, although Vernon was the first famous one. They produced a public school headmaster, a historian who wrote about the Byzantine Empire, and a judge (Vernon's father). Vernon talked about these traditions in a tone of amusement, but in reality he was a bit snobbish about families that could be traced back, and I guessed that he'd got a kick out of marrying into Laura's family, though they weren't a brainy lot and had produced only generals and colonial governors. He in turn found it surprising that I didn't care about ancestors and couldn't even tell him what my grandfather had done in life.

What between his family pride and his concern about names, Vernon was particular about his own surname. He seldom failed to make a remark, or at least put on an irritated frown, when a letter came with the wrong spelling, which was pretty often. Another point was that it had to be pronounced correctly – that is, with a hard 'g'. I was taken up on this at an early stage, when he overheard me saying on the phone: 'I'm afraid Professor Long-haye is busy.'

'How do you mean, a hard "g"?' I asked.

'Say in French: *la route est longue*.'

'*La route est longue*. Yes, I see. It's a losing battle, though, isn't it?'

'One has a name, or one doesn't,' he said firmly.

But Vernon's quirks only made him more fascinating. I had never known a man before who had white sugar in tea but brown sugar in coffee, and had his beard trimmed twice a week, and had a hard 'g' in his name.

Life with Vernon was an intricate, perplexing, demanding, exciting mixture of the regulated and the impulsive. Meals

103

had to be planned, with the right vegetables for the right meat. He selected the next day's clothes before he went to bed, claiming that it saved thought in the morning. He gave me presents which were a provision for future needs, such as warm gloves in summer. On the other hand, he would suddenly decide to play tennis, or go to Sotheby's, or visit a friend. If we were at home in the evening, he might put down the book he was reading and suggest – in fact, order – a game. He taught me several talk-games, sophisticated variations on Twenty Questions; he improved my chess until I could sometimes beat him if he gave me a knight; and sometimes he was in the mood for a childish game, such as beggar-my-neighbour, in which he could get as absorbed as in anything else. I was aware that the one common factor in all these activities was that he did – we did – what he wanted. I didn't mind. It was impossible to be bored with him. There was never enough time for all the things we could do together.

Then there were his friends. I didn't meet all of them; sometimes he was invited to dinner alone and explained to me, half apologetic and half amused: 'They're a bit stuffy, you know how it is.' I was glad of the opportunity to drop in at my old flat; the girls had begged me not to lose touch and wanted to know all about living with Vernon. Few of Vernon's friends were stuffy, however, and most of them were eager to meet me, no doubt to give me the once-over. We went out to dinner two or three times a week, and it could have been more if Vernon hadn't insisted on setting aside some time to be alone with me. For one reason or another – because the friends were glad to see Vernon fixed up, or because they really liked me, or because I had a profession and therefore some status in my own right – I was quickly accepted. I was soon getting phone calls that began: 'Pat? This is . . .' and *this* was someone whose books I had read as a humble poly student. It was splendid to know that Vernon's friends were now my friends.

Before I met Vernon, I considered myself a reasonably

well-informed person. Well-educated I was not, having been
to a backwoods school and no university, but I read widely, I
saw the right films and plays, I'd talked with a great variety of
people. But when I listened to Vernon and his friends, I saw
that picking up impressions was one thing and understanding
was another. A casual remark would reveal, without any
deliberate showing off, its roots in reflection and solid
knowledge. It was the difference between knowing *The
Ancient Mariner* and having digested Coleridge's aesthetics, or
between having read *Kon-Tiki* and having debated
diffusionism. I blushed to remember that I had offered Alan
my tutelage. But I never felt, even when I was out of my
depth for an hour at a time, that I was doomed to inferiority. I
was extending my reach as Alan had, though on a far higher
plane. There was nothing, Vernon assured me, that one
intelligent person couldn't explain to another. I didn't doubt
that I was intelligent, and anyway I must be, since Vernon was
living with me.

I knew now what I'd been missing since I came to London,
and indeed all my life. It was the world of the intellect, the
world in which purposeful thought and discussion were part
of the atmosphere. Perhaps I was a snob, perhaps I was a
culture-vulture – no, I didn't believe it; there was something
real here. To sneer at these people was like using the sneering
name of do-gooder for those who do good. I compared
Vernon's friends with Hugh's party-going set, who were
mostly 'involved in the media' and imagined themselves to be
clever and sophisticated. Simple souls they were, really; they
didn't know how to talk except in imitative catch-phrases,
they didn't know how to think except in fashionable
assumptions, and they didn't – it came down to this – know
anything very much. Even when it was a matter of being up
to date, Vernon's friends had the edge on them. The talk to
which I now listened wasn't academic in the sense of being
remote; it was easy and entertaining, it had a brisk flavour of
gossip, and it often had to do with the current scene – indeed,
the future. It was about forthcoming novels which someone

had read in proof, and films that might be made if the money could be raised, and reports that the Government was trying to suppress, and unfinished research projects, and sometimes the probable divorce of a Vice-Chancellor. At the flat, I had regularly heard people talk about 'the inside track', about 'where it's at', about 'where the action is'. Vernon's friends had no need to make such claims. I had been fluttering on the outside; the inside was here, where I had come to live. This is putting it cheaply, in the terms that I had brought with me and could now discard. I had a sense of liberation, of calm and profound satisfaction.

In short, I had not the least doubt that I was a very lucky girl.

I was living, that summer, at a tremendous pace. We never went to bed before midnight, even when we were at home, and sometimes it was much later. I sometimes left the house before eight in the morning, in the hope of beating the rush, and never later than nine. Vernon also got up early, and I knew that he did a good day's work; still, when I left him reading the paper over his second cup of coffee, I couldn't help feeling that he had it easy. It was no concern of Mrs Baldwin's, of course, if I chose to live in Plumstead, manage a house, and go out to dinner-parties. I tried to dodge work one morning a week in order to do the household shopping in Plumstead, and also to have some contact with Mrs Wall, our daily help. But mostly I shopped by sweeping like a cyclone through a supermarket in whatever part of London I was when I remembered it, and hurling the things into my illegally parked car. Sometimes I did a couple of errands for Vernon – delivering an article if he was too near the deadline to rely on the post, or getting a book from the London Library. After work I struggled through the rush hour again, had a cold shower – it was an exceptionally hot summer – and as likely as not went out again. I could save some time, if we were asked to dinner in Hampstead or Holland Park, by meeting Vernon there instead of going home first. He liked me to be attractively dressed, so I used to put my glad rags in the car and change in a public lavatory, or with some contortions in the car itself in a quiet side-street. However, this required a degree of advance planning of which I wasn't always capable.

One problem was that the wives or mistresses of Vernon's friends, who were even more curious about me than the men, invited me to tea or six o'clock drinks. They were educated women, most of them, but either they didn't work or they worked part-time, doing a bit of lecturing or reviewing or reading for publishers. I used to arrive hot and grubby and with my hair all over the place, to be confronted by some elegant creature who had just done her eye-shadow and her nail-varnish. Laura could never have turned up looking like me, it occurred to me.

I felt most at my ease with Dido Jackson. We had things in common: we weren't wives (it does make a difference even in this day and age), we were recent arrivals in intellectual high society, with equally shaky qualifications, and Dido wasn't much older than me. She was a coffee-coloured West Indian – black or brown girl-friends were just coming into fashion – and lived with a sociologist called Michael Glover, who had left his wife for her, in a pretty little house in NW1. Michael's name was familiar to me from paperback reading in Belfast, and the name of Dido Jackson seemed to ring a bell too, but I couldn't place it. So my first time in the house, prefacing my question with an apology, I asked her what she did.

'I sing,' she replied. 'Folk and blues.'

'Oh, sure. I've seen you on the box.'

'Not any more. I cut loose at parties sometimes, that's all.'

I must have looked surprised. She gave me a grin and said. 'Well, the rent's taken care of, isn't it?'

'But what do you do all day?' I asked.

She narrowed her eyes.

'You shack up with this class of man, a nice pair of legs helps, but it isn't everything. I read all those books.' She waved her hand: they covered the whole of one wall.

'Yes, I see.'

'I didn't go to no university. Shit . . . see what I mean? I didn't go to any university.' Evidently she assumed that I had. 'I've got a long way to catch up.'

I assured her that I was in the same position. There was something valiant and touching about Dido, as I got to know her; she used to ask me the meanings of long words and put them down in a notebook. Nevertheless, if I'd been a singer I'd have gone on singing.

With the university term over, I wondered whether John or Cressida — or both — would come to stay. Vernon said: 'They have their own plans, no doubt. They tend to visit rather than stay.' But one morning, as he was going through his letters, he told me: 'Cressida's coming this weekend.'

'She does know about me, doesn't she?' I asked.

'Naturally she knows about you.'

Cressida was there when I got home from work on the Friday. I hadn't seen a photograph of her. It sometimes happens that features are inherited with a slight change in the proportions that makes a fatal difference. Cressida was unmistakably Laura's child, with some resemblance to Vernon too, and yet she wasn't even good-looking. Both Laura and Vernon had rather long faces and fair-sized noses; exaggerated in Cressida, these gave her a frankly horsey appearance. The effect was of a sketch of Laura by an unkind cartoonist. Her one asset was the golden hair, but she had stressed the length of her face by having it cut short. In fact, she seemed to have resolved to make the worst of herself, including her figure which wasn't at all bad. She was dressed — despite the warm weather — in a tweed skirt and a sweater which was tight at the shoulders and baggy at the waist.

Vernon said: 'This is Patricia.'

I don't know if it is etiquette to give your lover's daughter a kiss, but in this case it certainly wasn't possible. Cressida said 'Hullo' and went on with the conversation with Vernon, which was about the inadequacies of her philosophy tutor.

'So if logical positivism is the only thing he knows about, that's his funeral, but he doesn't have to pretend he

108

invented it.'

'It's galling to know that one is second-rate,' Vernon said. 'Especially at Oxford.'

'What he's doing at Oxford is what I'd like to know.'

Vernon said to me: 'Cressida finds it difficult to shed her illusions about the academic profession, despite my warnings. Have you had a good day, Patricia?'

'Galling,' I said. 'I'm going to use that, galling. I'm dying for a drink. What will you have, Cressida?'

'I don't drink much,' Cressida said.

I can get along with people who don't drink, but people who don't drink 'much' are difficult, because you never know whether to offer or not. Cressida's practice at dinner was to drink one glass of wine quicker than anyone else and then refuse a second glass. She never did anything to put other people at their ease, but this was all too clearly because she wasn't at her ease herself.

Things improved in the course of the evening, but not much. Seeing that the atmosphere was edgy, Vernon did all the talking, which of course presented him with no difficulty. He chose subjects that ought to have brought Cressida in, such as the seminar he was planning to give next year. I contributed occasional questions; every time I did, Cressida looked at me as though I were trying to put Vernon off his stroke. She herself said practically nothing.

Vernon didn't make love to me that night. There was nothing in this, I told myself; we didn't make love every night. It was a fact, however, that Cressida slept in the adjoining room.

We usually got up rather late at weekends. But about nine o'clock I could hear Cressida going downstairs, so I dressed quickly and went down too.

'I don't know what you like for breakfast,' I said brightly.

'I'll make my own, thanks.'

I kept out of the way until she'd finished. After feeding myself and Vernon, I did some housework while she read a book. Lunch was mostly silent; even Vernon didn't seem up to much. Then I decided to try again. I said: 'I'm going to do the shopping. I wonder if you'd care to come with me, Cressida.'

'I'm afraid I've got a lot of reading to do.'

Vernon and I were due to go out to dinner. He explained to Cressida that we'd accepted before we knew she was coming, but we could easily ring up and make an excuse.

'No, go on. I don't mind.'

'I'll put some dinner on for you,' I said. 'There's some lamb, it would make a nice casserole.'

'I'll get something myself if I'm hungry.'

In the car, Vernon said: 'You mustn't attach too much importance to Cressida's manner. She's a particularly self-contained person. It's not her way to show affection.'

'It certainly isn't.'

'I meant, to me as well as to others. I've grown used to it. I'm sorry, darling, I ought to have prepared you.'

I gave him a quick kiss at a traffic light. We had a more than usually lively and enjoyable evening; Dido was there and was persuaded to sing. We stayed until half past one and I must confess that I never gave a thought to Cressida, even driving home. But in the house, I suddenly remembered her and we went upstairs quietly. Again, we didn't make love.

Vernon wanted Cressida to go on the Sunday walk, and she agreed. I decided that a bit of tact might improve my rating, so I said I'd stay at home and take some pictures in the neighbourhood. I roamed about and took some kids playing hopscotch in a nearby street, but I knew that the pictures weren't going to turn out right. Eating a scratch lunch alone, I felt unreasonably depressed. I rang up the flat to see who was there. Peggy was, so we went to a film together.

When I got home, I could hear the typewriter in Vernon's study. I went in.

'What are you doing, darling?' I asked.

'My contribution to this American symposium. I'm in good time, but a few ideas struck me.'

'Where's Cressida?'

110

'She went back to Oxford,' he said, not looking at me.

'Vernon, you might have told me she was going today.'

'I didn't know.'

I thought for a moment.

'Could you come and talk to me, please?'

'I'm working, Patricia.'

'You said you're in good time with that thing. Please, Vernon.'

'I'll be with you in a couple of minutes,' he said reluctantly.

I went into the living-room, started to pour out a drink, and changed my mind. Vernon came in and said: 'I know you think this has been disastrous. I don't take that view, and I know Cressida. She would find it difficult to form a new relationship at the first meeting.'

'I was so sure it would be all right.'

'It is all right. That is, it will be.'

'Perhaps you'd better prepare me for meeting John.'

'Oh, John's a much easier proposition. He'll be charmed with you, don't worry about that.'

'Well, what am I to do about Cressida?'

'Nothing. Be yourself. In any case, it's my problem.'

'So there is a problem.'

'Yes,' he admitted, 'there is a problem.'

I put my arms round him and rested my head on his shoulder.

'I hate being a problem.'

'My darling, to say that a problem exists isn't to say that you are one. My children are my responsibility. You are my happiness. You'll always be that, always and always.'

So we were together, as usual; we cooked dinner together, and talked about all kinds of things, and listened to music, and ended up by making love. Everything was all right, after all. Or rather, it wasn't, but it was possible to pretend.

Ten days or so later, I came in from work (earlier than usual because of a cancelled appointment) to find Cressida with Vernon.

'Hullo,' I said. 'This is a pleasant surprise.'

111

'Hullo,' Cressida said glumly.

'I didn't know you were coming. I'll see to your room.'

'I'm not staying.' She looked at her watch and said, with no attempt at plausibility: 'I ought to be going now.'

There was a silence. Vernon hadn't said anything at all and looked more disturbed than I had ever seen him. It was obvious that they had been talking about me.

I walked to the gate with Cressida.

'Look,' I said, 'I don't think it should be impossible for us to talk to each other. I want to be friends.'

She looked at the ground.

'I haven't said anything, have I?'

'I'd rather you did. I mean, we can't get anywhere without being frank. You resent me. I don't blame you in the least, I think it's absolutely natural. But I'm only here because Vernon wants me here – these things do happen. And I'm not trying to take Laura's place.'

Cressida winced, and I saw that I'd made a bad blunder: what could have led me to say 'Laura' instead of 'your mother'? I tailed off hopelessly: 'You do see that, don't you?'

'I don't think it's any use continuing this conversation.'

When I returned to the house, Vernon asked: 'What did you say to her?'

I told him.

'I think it would be best if you let me handle this, you know.'

'All right. You can imagine how I feel, though, can't you? It's getting fantastic if she can't even stay here. I'm put in the position of driving her out of her home.'

'That's over-dramatic. Cressida has a very close friend – another girl, I mean – and she likes to stay with her. It's right the other side of London, in Highgate.'

'That's not what it's all about, though, is it?'

Vernon thought for a moment, and then said: 'Patricia, I have to ask for some understanding on your part. Cressida is younger than you, and very different. She's intellectually advanced but emotionally immature – she's had no relationships with men, unfortunately – and she's finding it hard to cope with this situation. She's making a demonstration. If we allow her to do so, I'm confident that she'll come to see that her attitude is irrational. In the end, Cressida has a great respect for rationality.'

I had to be content with that. I wasn't so confident that Cressida would come round, but I could do nothing more. If she didn't – well, she wasn't a child, she was in her second year at Oxford, and she'd have to manage her own life. I could hope for better luck with John, and maybe with Aethra, although I didn't know how to deal with a sensitive child of ten. John, however, didn't appear, despite the university vacation. He was staying with somebody in the country, Vernon said.

I had something else to think about – our holiday plans. (That is to say, as usual, Vernon's plans in which I was involved.) His holidays were among the regulated aspects of his life. A friend of his, a wealthy Italian publisher with offices in Milan, owned a villa on Lake Como. Vernon showed me a picture of it and it certainly was a place of extraordinary beauty, perched on a headland with a terraced garden going straight down to the lake. As the publisher had a Swedish wife and always went to Sweden in August, he had been lending the villa to Vernon for the last six years. Vernon had everything worked out, including what to do with Aethra. One of the Longuehaye cousins had a farm only a dozen miles from her school and would be delighted to have her to stay.

I said: 'It sounds lovely. Of course, I'll have to talk to Mrs Baldwin.'

Mrs Baldwin was annoyed, quite justifiably, since it was the second year running that I'd announced in the middle of July that I wanted time off in August. Vernon couldn't understand the difficulty.

'How can this blasted woman stop you having a holiday? You're not her slave.'

'I'm her employee.'

'More's the pity. Perhaps you could think about finding a

more considerate employer.'

'Look, Vernon, she's got a business to run, she can't have all her staff away at the same time. I'll try to fix something.'

I appealed to Eileen, who was due for her holiday in August, and she agreed to put it off to September. Even so, I could only get a fortnight.

'Better than nothing,' Vernon said. 'But I've always spent a month in Italy. I dislike London in August.'

'Spend a month in Italy, then. You don't have to come back when I do.'

'That's out of the question. Can you imagine that I want to be parted from you? All the same, it's exasperating.'

We flew to Milan and collected a Hertz car at the airport. It was about eighty kilometres to the villa, part of it on the autostrada and the rest on a winding road by the shore of the lake. The traffic was thick and very slow, with thousands of people taking the motorized equivalent of an afternoon stroll. Evening came, dark and soft and mysterious. Tiny lights gleamed on the vague outlines of the mountains, and the water was like the smooth gleaming coat of an immense black panther. 'Blast this traffic, we'll never get there,' Vernon said. But I loved the drive, including the hold-ups in the little towns with their crowded cafés and lively streets, and I didn't care how long it lasted.

At last we turned off the road into the drive to the villa, which took two sharp bends as it climbed the headland. Then we stopped at the porch of the villa. So there we were, alone together – or so I thought for about ten seconds. I'd forgotten that the place belonged to a rich man and, this being Italy and not England, he had a domestic staff. As I sorted them out later, there was a butler, a cook, three maids, a gardener, and a chauffeur-boatman. They all came pouring out of the side-entrances (they never used the main door) like the cast of a play coming on for the curtain-call. They greeted Signor Longuehaye – pronouncing it Long-guy – rapturously, and bowed or curtsied to me, not forgetting to eye me in that special Italian way and form a quick estimate of my qualifications as Signor Longuehaye's bed-mate.

Vernon went upstairs, while I was detained by the cook, who asked me – through the butler, who spoke English – whether I approved of her plans for dinner. I said *'Bene, bene'* and followed Vernon as soon as possible. He was in the bedroom, which contained practically nothing but an enormous bed and a lot of floor-space, suitable for the spectators at one of Hugh's orgies. There were no cupboards, and no sign of our suitcases. Vernon explained that we each had our own dresing-room, with bathroom attached.

I went into my dressing-room. It had a single bed, presumably in case of marital discord or sexual exhaustion. One of the maids was there. She introduced herself as Maria-Grazia, and I gathered that she was my personal bit of the staff. She asked for the key to my case and unpacked energetically, putting my things where I was sure I'd never be able to find them. It was nice, however, to find that she'd already run a bath for me. I lazed in it for a while. When I got out, I found that Maria-Grazia was still hovering and wanted to dry me. I drew the line at this, but I showed her which dress I wanted to put on and allowed her to zip me up.

Dinner was a very formal affair, served by the butler and one of the maids, who stood by the wall while we ate. We proceeded solemnly through soup, antipasto, veal, salad, and cheese soufflé. I tucked in heartily, partly because I was ready for it after the plastic lunch on the plane and partly because the butler made reproachful noises if I didn't empty my plate.

We had coffee and liqueurs on the loggia, gazing over the calm dark lake. The butler hovered within observation range and strode off purposefully when we showed signs of making a move. Could he, I wondered, be going to alert Maria-Grazia to undress me? I hoped it couldn't be true, but it was. As I discovered later, if I stayed up until two o'clock Maria-Grazia stayed up too, and there was just no way of preventing her.

She conveyed in fragmentary English and with considerable anxiety that she hadn't been able to find a night-dress. I took

115

my pyjamas off a shelf; she looked at them incredulously. 'OK,' I said, reaching for my dressing-gown which I'd luckily brought, '*Niente. Stanotte, niente.*' At this her eyes misted with tears. The butler, the cook and Maria-Grazia had all addressed me as Signora – apparently Vernon and I were supposed to be on our honeymoon. I knew that if I caught Maria-Grazia's eye I'd get either the giggles or the weepies, so I looked down at the floor, which was doubtless the proper thing. Maria-Grazia, I learned later, had been engaged for two years to a young man who was working as a waiter and saving up to start his own restaurant.

It took me quite a time to reach the bedroom. Maria-Grazia drenched me with scent, powdered me, and rubbed me with a mysterious oil which she produced from the pocket of her apron. The oil was really quite sexy, and Vernon commented on it favourably.

In the morning, my faithful maid divined by some sixth sense that I was awake and came to dress me. It was the beginning of a long and tedious fortnight. Poised between the serene blue sky and the serene blue lake, the villa was a paradise; and, like paradise, it was boring. Vernon regarded the idea of venturing outside the gate with aversion. We kept the Hertz car, but we used it only twice, and then because I insisted. His attitude was logical: the road was one long traffic-jam, the whole district was swarming with tourists, we had the servants to do the shopping, and since we had the advantages of the villa – peace, comfort, seclusion – it was absurd to deprive ourselves of them. Whenever I suggested going somewhere – that is, to a place that looked inviting from the loggia – his invariable response was that it would be terribly crowded.

Goaded, I said at last: 'I like crowds.'

He looked at me, half amused and half shocked, as if I'd confessed to a taste for tinned spaghetti or Nescafé.

'Well,' I said, 'there's not much to do here, is there?'

'That, my dear, is the whole point of this place.'

It certainly was. A maid came dashing up if I attempted

even to move a chair a yard along the loggia. Besides, everything was in such perfect order that activity could only have been a disturbance. The first sound in the morning, as a rule, was the gardener raking over the gravel of a path where we had walked.

What could one do? One could swim; there were concrete steps descending between rocks to the lake. The water was wonderful, always sharp even on the hottest day, and we were so secluded that I could have bathed naked but for the servants. One could go out on the lake, either in a very super cabin-cruiser with a striped awning or in a rowing-boat. I persuaded Vernon to steal the rowing-boat when the boatman wasn't looking, so that we could do the rowing, which was clearly against the rules. One could laze in a reclining chair, calling occasionally for an iced drink, and this was really the only correct behaviour for the Signor and the Signora. Or one could read. Vernon used his holidays to catch up on reading and had brought the year's output of philosophy. I had brought nothing except the latest Muriel Spark, which I finished the first day. There were some English books scattered about the house – crime thrillers and porn. They helped to pass the time, but got monotonous. My greatest regret was that, out of a feeling that anything like work would spoil Vernon's idea of a holiday, I hadn't brought a camera.

One morning, I dressed in jeans and an old shirt and told Vernon firmly that I was going out for a walk. I tramped along to the nearest town, which was about three kilometres, getting a perverse kick out of being almost mown down by the cars and covered in dust. The town was what you'd expect: souvenir shops, ice-cream stalls, currency-changing offices, and people, people, people. I mooched about happily for a while and then followed a sign to the camp-site. And here, amid the garish colours and the pop music and the suntanned bodies, I was where I belonged. Or had belonged. It was a holiday, at all events, even if it was only for a few hours.

I ambled toward the shore of the lake and was nearly hit on

the head by a big rubber ball. I caught it and threw it back, to a girl in a bikini who looked so much like me the year before that we both smiled in recognition. I was in the game at once, of course.

We – four or five of us – queued for coke, then for scampi. There was a boy who hadn't any money with him, so I staked him. We communicated in a mixture of languages, as usual; as a matter of fact, he was Dutch. While we sat on the ground and ate our scampi, he said there was a rather good disco in the town, and what was I doing in the evening?

I thought: why the hell not? I didn't ask Vernon's permission if I went out without him in London, after all. But in London I was tied to Vernon only by the voluntary link of love, and here there was the discipline of the villa. So, with a sad feeling that the game was over, I said I was staying at a house and I was expected for dinner. As I uttered these distancing words : 'house' and, still worse, 'dinner' – the boy looked at me as much as to say: 'You've got to be joking.'

I didn't go to the camp-site again.

The fact that I'd been out to lunch, it turned out, was enough of a lapse. There was such a thing as consideration for the servants, Vernon said. I retorted that it had been quite a treat to get away from the servants for a bit.

For me, the whole servant business was a constant irritation: the feeling of being always watched and followed, the implied denial of my ability to look after myself, and not least the fact that I was never indisputably alone with Vernon except in bed (even then, it wouldn't have surprised me to see one of them trotting in with an iced drink). They were certainly very good servants – efficient, willing, perpetually smiling and polite. This meant that, if I complained about them, I was the one who was being unreasonable, while they were just doing their job. What I couldn't take was that they obviously liked being servants. Actually, northern Italians don't rush to become servants any more than English people, and the staff of the villa was recruited from the deep south, where a lady is still a creature of another species from her maid. And, whereas

118

Maria-Grazia was an impeccable maid, I knew that I was a pretty inadequate lady.

However, I suspected that having servants suited Vernon very nicely, and that he would have lived in this style at home if it had been feasible and not patently ridiculous for a progressive-minded intellectual. I wondered why I minded about the servants so much — they ought to have been just an odd experience, and indeed a joke — until it dawned on me that I sensed a shadowy presence whenever Maria-Grazia hovered to receive my commands. It wasn't the presence of the publisher's wife (though I could see why she used the villa only for weekends and scooted off to Sweden in August); it was the presence of Laura, the genuine Signora.

I had felt this presence, admittedly, at the Manor House. If you have any sensitivity at all, you're bound to have a peculiar feeling about eating at the table and sleeping in the bed that have belonged to another woman, especially a dead woman. But I took this feeling to be natural and it hadn't worried me greatly. It was much more persistent, and much more disturbing, at the villa. I was sure that Laura had fitted in at the villa perfectly, just as Vernon did. It followed that Laura had satisfied a side of Vernon's nature which I was now discovering, and to which I was never likely to adjust.

I tried not to look too happy when we said goodbye to the servants and made our way to Milan. We flew back late on a Sunday night, stretching the fortnight to its utmost, and it really did feel like a homecoming when I opened the door of the Manor House and scooped a pile of post off the mat. It was marvellous to make coffee in my own kitchen and put clean sheets on the bed with my own fair hands. But the next morning, an odd thing happened.

I made breakfast, got my cameras together while Vernon was reading the paper, put on my coat — it was raining — and said: 'See you tonight, darling.'

'Where are you going?' he asked.

'To work, of course.'

He stared at me for a few seconds. Then he said: 'I should

119

have thought you'd have taken a day off, or at least a morning, to get the house straight.'

'Mrs Wall's coming. Don't you touch anything. Bye — I must run.'

Very funny, I thought as I hurried off, the way he'd looked at me. It was as though he had forgotten all about my job. I felt ashamed of being happy. Happy I was, all the same, as I won the race for a seat in the Southern Region train, marched into the office, and went through my programme with Mrs Baldwin. It was my work that I was glad to get back to. I didn't venture to say this to Vernon, who kept up a fair imitation of being still on holiday. He did some writing — I didn't know how much, as I was out all day — but assumed the personality of the gentleman of leisure with intellectual interests.

Some days after we had come home, he said to me: 'You know, I must make some arrangement about Aethra. My cousin agreed to have her for the month of August, and her school doesn't start until the middle of September.'

'She'll be coming here, then, won't she?'

He looked relieved. 'Will that be all right, from your point of view?'

'Christ, this is her home, isn't it? I only hope she won't be bored. I'll try and do things with her at weekends. You must tell me what she's interested in.'

I went with Vernon to meet Aethra at Victoria. I'd have recognized her without his help; she looked strikingly like Laura — golden hair, jaw-line and all. As she walked toward us, I turned to look at Vernon. I knew, from the tone of his voice when he spoke of her rather than from anything he said, that he was very fond of Aethra. Now his face was alight with pleasure, as it was when I came to meet him in some public place. I was always gratified when he looked at me like this, with open and irrepressible love. There was love too in the look he gave Aethra, and there was something else: the pride of a man who contemplates something of rare distinction — a painting or a jewel — and remembers happily that it is his.

Thus, I suppose, he had looked at Laura. She had deserved it, and so did Aethra. I had never seen such a beautiful child.

Myself, I was a bit nervous. After the fiasco with Cressida, I very much wanted Aethra to like me. I remembered that, with a child particularly, first impressions are vital. I decided to be friendly but not effusive, like a new acquaintance rather than a new member of the family, and on no account to hold Vernon's arm or do anything to stress the terms we were on.

'This is Patricia, my dear,' Vernon said. He had gone to see her at her school just before the end of term and explained about me. Aethra shook hands, very courteously as she must have been taught at school. We went home (it was a Sunday afternoon). I helped her to unpack and made tea. She behaved calmly and demurely and didn't seem shy of me, nor particularly curious about me. She addressed me, correctly, as Patricia.

After tea, she said that she wanted to go through her collection of picture postcards. Vernon used to drop a hint to his friends to send Aethra a card when they travelled; this had been going on since she was five, and the cards had poured in from everywhere between Vancouver and Kyoto, particularly from the sort of places where conferences are held, so it was a remarkable collection. Vernon kept up a running commentary of supplementary information, and I had no difficulty in entering into the spirit of the thing. Then I made dinner (Aethra hadn't been brought up to have supper) and at nine o'clock she went to bed without having to be told.

'D'you think that went off all right?' I asked Vernon.

'Of course. Perfectly all right.'

I couldn't draw any conclusions yet, except that Aethra was well-behaved and distinctly grown up for ten years old. Considering that she had lived mostly in an adult world, with no brothers or sisters anywhere near her own age, this was what one would expect.

Having Aethra with us was certainly no trouble We took her once to the theatre and once to the opera – grown-up stuff which we were glad to go to anyway, and which she fully appreciated. In the daytime she went to museums and exhibitions, either with Vernon who was still not working at full pressure, or with Cressida, who was staying with her friend at Highgate and evidently got on well with her sister. Also, Aethra had friends from the school she'd gone to in Blackheath, so the mothers asked her to tea or included her in outings. If she was left alone, she settled down contentedly with a book or her paint-box.

I was working, of course, and after the difficulty over my holiday I couldn't very well ask Mrs Baldwin for time off to take my lover's daughter around town. I volunteered to look after Aethra on Sundays while Vernon went walking. Once I took her swimming at the Charlton lido, and once riding, hiring the horses from a stables out near Sevenoaks. I took it for granted that a girl of ten would be wild about horses, as I had been at that age, and a matter of fact I was delighted to get on a horse myself for the first time for years. These Sundays passed off well, but I had an awkward feeling that I was the one who got most of the enjoyment out of both the swimming and the riding. Aethra's manner implied that such activities weren't quite her scene, but if they were mine she was prepared to fit in with my plans. Polite she always was. And a very grown-up child.

When she went back to school, I was left with a vague sense of dissatisfaction. I didn't feel that I'd been able to get anywhere near Aethra. Perhaps I had hoped for too much; perhaps I ought to be content with the absence of antagonism. But there was something strange about Aethra's attitude to me, which was scarcely an attitude at all, so devoid was it of any apparent emotion, even curiosity. She seemed to be saying that, if Vernon chose to live with me, it was nothing to do with her. Shyness, shrinking, even violent resentment, would have been more natural.

There was no sign, anyway, of the sensitive child of whom Vernon had spoken. Either he was mistaken – it occurred to me that, like many intellectuals, he wasn't very perceptive about people – or else the sensitivity was firmly battened down. Aethra's self-control and poise were so unfailingly complete that they made me somewhat uneasy. Had her emotions been anaesthetized, I wondered, by what she had been through in the past year? She gave no obvious proof even of affection for Vernon.

But I didn't think that I needed to worry much about Aethra, even if she had been my responsibility. She had a lot going for her. From the way she kept up with Vernon when he explained some adult subject to her, it was clear that she had inherited the Longuehaye brains. And it never did a girl any harm to look as Aethra was undoubtedly going to look in a few years' time.

The end of September was warm and beautiful. When I could get home from work in time, Vernon and I used to sit on a teak bench in the garden, enjoying the fading sunlight.

'It's good here, isn't it?' he said on one of these evenings.

'Sure it's good.'

'How much I love you, my dearest! Love has that special quality, among all its other qualities, of bringing perfection to what is already good. I could sit here happily alone in a fine September, but that happiness would be only the light on the wall of the cave' – he had explained to me about this bit in Plato – 'the suggestion of the reality of being here with you and loving you. Each moment I love you more, as another moment of love adds to what already seemed complete, and yet can always grow.'

'Go on,' I said dreamily. 'Tell me more. It's marvellous to be loved by you. I mean, most men say "I love you" once and sort of put it on record, and that's it.'

'Most men miss one of the pleasures of love, then. To renew it in thought and in words is to increase it. That's another of its qualities – really, they're infinite – that it's always fresh, always a repeated experience of the first falling in love, but also enriched by memories. Already we have memories, Patricia. I count them over while we create another. How long is it since I began to love you? A very short time, this delightful freshness tells me. A very long time, I could believe

123

from all the accumulating joys of loving you.'

'I'm confused too,' I said. 'It isn't six months yet, is it? It does seem more, it's so established, it's so part of me. Anyway, it's been a success, hasn't it?'

'A triumphant success. And established – you're right.'

'It's for ever.'

'It's for ever.' We kissed.

'And since it's for ever,' he said, 'we'll be married, shall we?'

I was taken completely by surprise. He had spoken of love many times, and of marriage never. I thought of Alan for a moment; why was I always surprised when a man asked me to marry him? This time, at least I didn't give words to my surprise. Vernon would have been as hurt as Alan.

I said: 'Do you suppose we could be more sure of each other if we were married? We certainly couldn't be happier.'

'How do you know? Happiness, like love, is capable of infinite growth.'

'Yes, but it's being in love and living together that make for happiness, not being married. Frankly, darling, I hadn't the slightest idea that it mattered to you. Or were you under the impression that it mattered to me?'

'No, no. The legal position and the official morality don't matter : of course not. To be married would be a symbol and an expression of our love. Another way of saying that it's for ever; there can't be too many ways of saying that, can there? I commit to you my whole life, my whole self. Marriage can have that meaning, at least for me.'

'Yes, I see. It's rather a beautiful idea.'

'I seem to be winning your acceptance. You haven't any rooted objection to marriage, I hope?'

'Me? Oh no. It's the icing on the cake, but why not?' I looked at him thoughtfully. 'When did you get this idea, Vernon?'

'Gradually rather than suddenly. It has grown from love, and from our being what you accurately call established.' He paused. 'The reason I've given you is far and away my first

124

and greatest motive. But there is a second reason, not entirely unimportant to me. It's Aethra. I don't ask you to be Aethra's mother, but what I do affects her since I'm her only parent. She did ask me how long you'd be living here.'

'Oh, did she?' From a child of six, I thought, this would be charmingly naive; from a precocious child of ten, it struck me as a bit sly.

'Well, you know, children like things neat and tidy, with a familiar label. Marriage would define for her what it means for us to be living together. It could even give her a sense of security, which she needs. At the most practical level, it enables her to explain you when she talks about you at school, perhaps to more conventionally-minded children or teachers.'

'Yes, I see that, too.'

It crossed my mind that there was a third reason. Once we were married, Cressida would have to accept me. It was possible that she had been pressing Vernon to give me up, and he wanted to put an end to the argument by a *fait accompli*. If so, that was a reason for me to be in favour of getting married; the cold war with Cressida hadn't been much on my mind, but I'd be glad of peace. However, I didn't need reasons. I was more than willing to do anything that made Vernon happy.

'All right, fine, we'll get married,' I said. 'Only one thing. If we're just going to sneak down to the registry office in a spare half hour, we might as well not bother. Let's do it in style.'

So we talked about this, with a great deal of enjoyment and laughter. Then I ran indoors to start telling people. The more I thought about the whole business, the more I looked forward to it.

Dido said: 'Hey, you clever girl.'

Stella said: 'Pat, how absolutely fabulous – are we invited?'

Erica said in a quivering voice: 'I'm so happy for you.'

Eileen said: 'He seems to be a man of decisions.'

Mrs Baldwin said: 'I hear you're getting married,' with the faint smile of the divorced woman implying that everyone has to make her own mistakes. Then she asked: 'Do you plan to

125

go on working?'

I stared at her. The question hadn't occurred to me.

'Of course,' I said.

'I'm relieved to hear that. I'd find it difficult to replace you.'

She went on to say that, in the event of my needing an extended period of leave, I would always be welcome to return. I stared again; this time I couldn't even see what she meant. Then I caught on, and told her that I'd bear it in mind if the situation ever arose.

I was beginning to regret that I'd suggested making the wedding a big occasion, as I couldn't possibly cope with the preparations while also working at full stretch to give Mrs Baldwin no cause for complaint. I sent an SOS to my mother, and she came over and took charge. We were to be married at the Kensington registry office, which was feasible because I was still in theory a Kensington resident, and to have the reception – the lunch, or wedding breakfast as Vernon insisted on calling it – at a big hotel nearby.

Vernon also insisted on observing the tradition that the bridegroom shouldn't see the bride on the wedding day until the ceremony. This seemed fairly ludicrous to me, since even my parents knew that we were living together, but he said that it was a charming old custom and anyhow I was the one who'd wanted to do things in style. So I moved out the night before and stayed with the Bell clan at their hotel. And I must say that, with my mother and my sister titivating my dress and brushing my hair, I did get a delicious sense of the occasion, and imagined with a touch of wistfulness what the wedding day would be like for a girl like Maria-Grazia.

The ceremony itself was family only, but this meant quite a party. My parents were there, two of my brothers, my sister, and my grandmother. Aethra had been given the day off from school and collected at the station by Cressida, who was inevitably wearing the wrong sort of dress, but at least it was a dress. Aethra looked delectable, of course, and all the Bells warmed to her. She behaved with her usual demure politeness. Cressida looked a bit martyred, but brought herself to give me a peck on the cheek.

Just when the proceedings were about to begin, a young man hurried in and said: 'Sorry – am I late?'

'No, you have made a well-timed appearance,' Vernon said. 'Patricia, this is my son John.'

He gave me a hearty kiss and said loudly: 'I've been longing to meet you.' I felt at once that I was going to like him. He was big and rather burly, running slightly to fat, and didn't look much like either Vernon or Laura; he had a chubby, amiable face, with no pretensions to intellectual forehead or aristocratic jaw-line. But I couldn't get more than a quick impression, as I was swiftly shunted up to the registrar's table to play my part in the formalities.

These followed the routine, naturally, but in an atmosphere of unexpected drama contributed by the weather. After a sunny morning, a sudden storm had broken just as we reached the office, and an ear-splitting crack of thunder made everyone jump at the moment when I was saying 'I do.' Once the ceremony was over, the drama turned into farce. Nobody had an umbrella, and the rain was falling in a tropical downpour. My brothers raced off to hunt for taxis, while the rest of us stood on the steps, jostling people who were next in line for their weddings, and then dashed frantically across the pavement. John gallantly assisted my grandmother, who walked with a stick, and I could see that she regarded the storm as an evil omen. The rest of us were pleasurably excited. Vernon said; 'The elements are paying their tribute to you, my darling.'

The reception list had been discussed at great length and considerably pruned, but it still amounted to about two hundred people. I had invited the girls from the flat and a number of friends from that environment, and also Mrs Baldwin and my colleagues. Vernon was responsible for most of the guests. In addition to a lot of our friends, such as Arnold and Gabrielle, there were all sorts of people whom I didn't know. The Longuehaye relatives were there in force, including the Sussex farming cousin, who turned up in full morning-dress, looking – a wry thought – as though he'd been left over from Vernon and Laura's wedding. There was a delegation from Vernon's university, ranging from the Vice-Chancellor through a bunch of professors to some favoured students. Also some men who had been at Oxford with Vernon, and an ancient wizened character who had been Vernon's tutor. Finally there were people who testified to Vernon's importance, such as the Director-General of the BBC, the Editor of *The Times*, and the Minister for the Arts Council. I thought myself that it was a bit pompous to invite these dignitaries, with whom Vernon was admittedly acquainted but who were not exactly personal friends; however, I could see that he was gratified by their presence.

A big wedding reception is always rather a bizarre affair, because so many miscellaneous people are mixed up together. I noted Hugh attempting to make conversation with my grandmother, an anthropologist of notorious fame chatting up my kid sister, Claudine describing her professional life to a bemused Longuehaye who was something in the Treasury, and Dido causing palpitations in a student from East Anglia. It's in the nature of the event, too, that things get pretty relaxed. Everyone drinks a lot, largely champagne; often, and certainly on this occasion, the company includes a good sprinkling of handsome men and attractive women; and minds turn increasingly to what, when you think of it, being married is all about. To add to these predictable circumstances, all the guests had to shout because the storm continued throughout the meal, and the dining-room had a glass roof on which the rain made a noise like (to use a simile of which Stella was fond) skeletons fucking. What with the flashes of lightning and the claps and rolls of thunder, the atmosphere induced a reckless – Bacchanalian, I think you could say – sort of mood.

By the time we got to the speeches, you could see that anything could happen. When my father rose to propose the health of the bride and groom, I noticed that, while not exactly tight, he had drunk more than is wise for a man who has to make a speech. The effect of drink on my father is to enhance his somewhat owlish manner, also to lead him into prolix sentences and an esoteric choice of words. He began quite suitably by saying that a father-in-law normally had to make an effort to get to know his daughter's intended, but I had been considerate enough to marry a man whose fame had reached even the remote regions of County Tyrone, and whose very features had been 'reproduced by the televisual process of transmission'. Vernon beamed, my father beamed, some people applauded, my father went on beaming, and I realized that he had completely forgotten what he'd intended to say next. However, the word 'reproduced' must have worked in his fuddled unconscious, for he now told us that he cherished 'patriarchal aspirations' – not without justification, he hoped, since he was one of six children, I was one of five, and the Longuehaye line was evidently 'capable of impressive ramification', judging by the number of them present 'on this auspicious occasion'. Should professional assistance ever be required, he went on, the mother of the bride was qualified in obstetrics – a word which gave him even more trouble than 'auspicious'. My mother gave me a helpless look, but my father ploughed on, to the delight of the guests who were now fairly steeped in a fertility rite. Eventually, a truly inspiring phrase came to his mind: that Vernon would prove himself not only philosophical but philoprogenitive. Alas, it was quite beyond him to get his tongue round this, and after several attempts he wound up with a gesture of amiable resignation and raised his glass amid sympathetic cheers.

Vernon, sober but a little rattled, deflected these pointed good wishes by saying that he was overwhelmed, while of course delighted, to be acquiring so many new relatives at a stroke. He then observed that there were unmarried Bells as well as unmarried Longuehayes – 'and since you all seem to be enjoying this celebration, you must apply to them to give you the pleasure of what, I believe, is called in sporting circles a return match.' John smiled wryly; my sister giggled. Next,

129

Vernon assumed an air midway between the serious and the sentimental and continued: 'Much has been said and written on the subject of matrimony by theologians, by legislators and indeed by philosophers. You will be relieved to hear that I propose to offer you no new thoughts on this theme. The one thought in my mind, as I stand here amid my friends and with my dear Patricia by my side, is the oldest of all: that marriage at its best is but the open proclamation of love. That love in our case, was as immediate as it was irresistible.' He put in a gracious phrase of thanks to Arnold and Gabrielle for making the introduction, and said: 'I suspect them of knowing, as I knew very soon, that Patricia and I were likely – risking the charge of determinism, I will even say destined – to come together. And come together, as you see, we have.'

Here he was startled by a shriek of laughter, emanating from Stella. The room was soon in an uproar, with about two thirds of the guests falling about and the rest asking what the joke was. Even the waiters couldn't keep a straight face. Vernon caught on after a bit of puzzlement, and recovered neatly by saying, when he could make himself heard, that he didn't deny any construction which might be put on his phrase (cheers). But he was distinctly put out and curtailed the rest of his speech.

The rain had stopped, and the sun was shining as we posed for press photographers outside the hotel. Vernon's car was adorned with two placards, thanks probably to the students. One of them read: 'Just married, no hand signals', and the other: 'Yea, yea, it's Longuehaie'. Vernon grimaced and said to me that he'd have been glad to have his name spelled right on his wedding day.

The Manor House seemed unbelievably peaceful and more beautiful than ever. Vernon carried me over the threshold, keeping up another old custom. Then he said that he had arranged a private concert, and we went to the music-room to listen to records which he'd chosen for the occasion. Laura's portrait looked down like a remote but beneficent household goddess.

130

In bed, I said to him: 'You know, it sounds silly, but I do feel different.'

'You see? I knew you would,' he answered.

Talking about the wedding next day I said: 'I'm sorry I never got a chance to talk to John. He looks nice. When can I really meet him?'

Vernon promised to arrange this, and a couple of weeks later John came to stay for a weekend. When he arrived on the Friday evening, Vernon was out for some reason, so John and I had a couple of drinks and got acquainted. I was relieved to find that he was the least brainy of the family. Philosophy was beyond him, he said : he could understand how things worked when you could observe them. I got the impression that he would always manage capably with work that was within his reach; he wouldn't excel, and it wouldn't bother him.

He asked me about my work, and I saw that he was genuinely interested, not just being polite. He did a bit of photography himself, he told me, and had once got into a college exhibition.

'Biochemistry's your subject, isn't it?'

'That's right. Dad says you did biology.'

'Well, only up to A-levels and I've practically forgotten it now. When are you taking your degree?' He looked older than Cressida, though I'd assumed before meeting him that he must be younger.

'What degree?' He looked at me with surprise, then laughed. 'Did you think I was a student? I'm flattered, I must say. I'm a lecturer.'

'Oh, I'm sorry.'

'Nothing to be sorry about. I wasn't sure what you meant, that's all. I ought to be trying for a Ph.D., but I'm too lazy.'

I started to work out dates and ages in my head, but Vernon soon came in and I didn't get a chance. But later on I tackled the problem and the more I thought about it the more puzzled I was. To have a son of John's age, Vernon and Laura must have been married incredibly young. If Laura had died at the age of thirty-eight, as Arnold had told me, it was a legal and damn nearly a biological impossibility.

It was a funny thing, but I didn't know exactly how old Vernon was. I could ask him now, of course. I can only say that it's awkward to put this question to a man when you've been living with him for months and have just married him. What I did was to go into a library and look him up in *Who's Who*.

The entry began: 'Longuehaye, Vernon, philosopher and author, b. 15 Feb 1921.' It was 1970, so this made Vernon forty-nine.

I read on. There was a bit about his parents, then his education (Winchester and Balliol), and then: 'm. Laura Alexandra Brackley, 1949'. *Who's Who* doesn't identify children or tell you when they were born, and on this subject it simply said: 'one s., two d'. After that came the details of Vernon's career and the titles of his books.

Munching crisps and drinking a glass of plonk in a pub near the library, I told myself doggedly that it didn't matter. I was in love with Vernon. He was my ideal of a man who had attained maturity while keeping the best of youthfulness, and if that was what I'd seen in him when I fell in love, it was still just as true. And if he looked ten years younger than his age, that was my good luck. All the same, when I used to think of the attractions of 'older men', I'd always had in mind the age bracket to which Roger Bartram belonged. And here I was, married to a man of nearly fifty. It seems quite a lot, to a girl of twenty-three. I found myself working out how old I'd be when Vernon was seventy. Few men fuck at seventy, I reflected.

Most of all, I felt cheated. I had never asked Vernon his age, but there had been opportunities for him to tell me – to take an obvious instance, when I told him mine. I remembered a dinner when other men had talked about their war experiences, and Vernon had deflected the conversation. According to *Who's Who*, he had been a captain in (naturally) the Intelligence Corps.

132

Besides, there was still a mystery. Cressida had done two years at Oxford, so it made sense for her to have been born in 1950. But this left John completely unaccounted for. Could he have been adopted? But, if Vernon and Laura swiftly had a baby, what for? Could he be a bastard of Vernon's? By this time, I felt like a heroine of Victorian fiction on the track of a family secret.

It may seem curious that I felt able to seek an explanation from John, and not from Vernon. But understandable, I think.

John wasn't the type for country walks, so I said I'd stay with him on Sunday and Vernon went off by himself. We settled comfortably in the living-room with the Sunday papers.

'John,' I said, rousing him from one of the colour mags, 'd'you mind if I ask how old you are?'

'How old I am? Twenty-five.'

'D'you know I'm only twenty-three? You're my stepson, officially. Sort of wild, isn't it?'

He grinned and said: 'If we were in a novel we'd be fatally attracted, and Dad would slaughter us and kill himself in the last chapter. I'd better restrain myself.'

'You could be married. You're not, by any chance?'

'No, I'm no good at making these things definite. You see . . .' He told me with complete frankness and a touch of self-mocking humour that he was involved with (though not living with) a girl who was starting to make pointed remarks about the practical advantages of marriage. John was fond of her, but reluctant to commit himself; I guessed that, unlike his father, he was one of nature's bachelors. However, I couldn't give my mind at the moment to this aspect of his character.

'I still can't get used to your being twenty-five,' I said. 'You see, your mother . . . that is, Laura . . .'

'Did you think Laura was my mother?' he asked.

'I did, until I met you. I'm thoroughly confused now. She's the only predecessor of mine that I'm aware of.'

'How peculiar. Laura was Dad's second wife.'

I said: 'Let's have a drink.'

We had a drink. I continued: 'Do you also think it's peculiar that Laura is the only wife of Vernon's listed in *Who's Who*?'

'Is that so? I didn't know.' He reflected. 'Peculiar, yes, but not astonishing. You see, Dad's first marriage didn't work out. It was one of those wartime romances. Handsome captain blows in between Africa and Normandy and sweeps girl off feet – that kind of thing. One child, unsuccessful attempt to live together after the war, divorce. Very common pattern at the time, I believe.'

'Vernon seems to rush into marriage rather impulsively.'

'Well he's had a fifty-per-cent success rate, which I'm sure he's now raising to two-thirds.'

'Is your mother still alive, John?'

'Alive and well and living in Sheffield. I spend most of the vacations with her.'

'Did she marry again?'

'No, I think she was put off it. She goes in for discreet affairs, at the moment with one of the city architects. She's still a decidedly good-looking woman. Well, she's only forty-five.'

'Vernon likes them young, too.'

John didn't take this up.

'You were just a small kid when they were divorced, then?'

'A baby. I grew up accepting the situation. In my opinion there's a lot of cock talked about broken homes. I always felt that I was one up on the other kids. I spent a month every year with Dad and Laura. It was a tremendous treat for me – another world, you can imagine – but I was always ready to come home.'

'How did you get on with Laura?'

'Smoothly. Also with Cressy. Laura was kind to me, and I ... well, I adored her. It was like staying with the Queen for a month – a fairy-tale queen, I mean. She wasn't quite real to me. I couldn't imagine her swearing because she'd missed a bus or arguing because she was overcharged in a shop. My Mum was reality. Reality's a very good thing for eleven months in the year.'

'A lot of people seem to have adored Laura,' I said. 'It's a bit daunting for me. Perhaps what they're saying is what you've said – she wasn't quite real to them.'

John looked uncomfortable. 'I don't know. I was talking about how I saw her as a child. I'm not sure that it tells you much about Laura.'

'That's a pity. I don't see Laura at all clearly.'

He didn't take this up either. Instead, he said. 'You know, I don't think you'd better talk to Dad about my mother. They've never met since the divorce. Dad didn't want to give me up altogether, having only one son, so they corresponded in a civilized way about my education and my holidays, but if I hadn't existed I think they'd both have preferred to forget about each other. That's why the *Who's Who* thing didn't surprise me.'

It was October or November by this time, and life was as busy as before the summer. Vernon had a lot of work, not to mention going on TV and lecturing here and there, and the dinner invitations showed no sign of slacking off; there were more of them, in fact, now that I was actually his wife, I wasn't often alone with him, but I didn't mind. We always looked forward to seeing each other and valued our quiet evenings, which is more than every married couple can honestly say. I even found that there were some advantages in his spending two nights a week in Norwich. I missed him of course. But I could take on an evening job if necessary, or just sit in a pub chatting with Eileen.

When parted from Vernon by the demands of his work or mine, I was still Pat Bell. But I was also Mrs Longuehaye now, and it was no sinecure. For instance, we gave dinner-parties. Since Laura's death, Vernon had received a great deal of hospitality which he'd been unable to return, and the time had come to redress the balance. As a hostess, I had everything to learn. I usually got in a muddle when telling people where to sit, and a couple of times I was guilty of putting a husband next to his own wife; it tells you a lot about

British marriage, I think, that this is the one thing you mustn't do. And I was always in danger of dropping bricks with guests whom I didn't know much about. Once I said that *Private Eye* was my favourite paper, unaware that the man I was addressing had been savagely attacked in it; another time, I defended militant students in the presence of a Director of Studies who had been besieged in his office.

I had trouble with the food, too. Vernon liked to do the cooking when we were alone, but he assumed that a dinner for guests was entirely my responsibility. Managing for myself at the old flat, or dishing up a straightforward supper for Alan, was one thing; making moussaka or coq au vin for eight or ten people was something else again. Vernon could always see exactly where I'd fallen down, and didn't neglect to tell me as the door closed on the last guest.

Time was my great enemy. If I had the car, some vile official would choose that day to have the Lower Road dug up. If I relied on trains, the Southern Region would be paralysed by a signal failure or a skirmish in its endless class war. Arriving home in frayed condition at seven, with guests due at eight, I was required to adorn myself like a lady of leisure, cook a dinner to my husband's exacting standards, and be on hand for the greetings and the gracious chatter over the sherry. We entertained on Saturdays and Sundays so far as possible, but this wasn't enough to meet the demand, to say nothing of the friends from Edinburgh and Perugia and Wisconsin who had to be fitted in during their brief visits to London. Any attempt to cut corners was mercilessly detected.

'Patricia, I strongly suspect that the mayonnaise was out of a bottle.'

'Patricia, you must be aware that if Brie is straight from a shop it's bound to be immature.'

'Patricia, even a libation of kirsch cannot disguise tinned pineapples.'

Disaster really struck one day when I'd gaily promised a pilaff, reckoning that I had ample time to shop and cook, only to find that Eileen was off work with a sudden onset of gastric flu and I had to take on her appointments as well as my own. I knew a good Greek take-away place which I'd patronized when living at the flat, so I dashed in there and bought pilaff for eight, drove home like a lunatic, and shoved the stuff in the oven. Unluckily, a historian from North Carolina got into a Bromley instead of a Woolwich train, so we didn't eat until nearly ten, by which time the rice was soggy and the whole thing utterly tasteless.

'Really, Patricia, what can have happened to your cooking?'

'I didn't cook it,' I confessed.

'Whatever do you mean?'

Take-away food, for Vernon, was on a par with package holidays, the *Reader's Digest*, and two-year degree courses. He was too appalled even to be indignant, and simply said: 'Let this remain a secret.'

I could see his point of view. He had lived for twenty years with a wife who not only gave ample time and consideration to dinner, but also made his lunch when he was working at home. This must have been a symbol of a calm and sustaining companionship which I didn't supply. He told me once: 'It's strange, but when you're not with me I sometimes feel more alone than before you were here at all.'

One Tuesday morning, when he was about to set off for Norwich, he said: 'I do hate leaving you, darling.'

'You know I miss you too,' I said.

'I wish you could come with me. I think you'd find it interesting, too.'

'Did Laura go with you?'

'Oh yes.' The question surprised him. 'Not invariably, but as a rule.'

Then he said: 'You have the rest of your leave still owing to you. If you took it, you could come to Norwich.'

I didn't feel in need of any more holiday, but I couldn't refuse, and I liked the idea of seeing a university from the inside, never having been to one. The campus was what I'd expected a new university to look like: very spick and span, and in no way related either to the countryside which could be seen from upper windows or to the 1930-ish suburbs which connected it to the city. I had the feeling of walking round some sort of exhibition, arranged to show foreigners that Britain wasn't finished yet. Vernon's flat had all the things we didn't have at the Manor House – fitted cupboards, recessed bookshelves, and ventilators which emitted a discreet hum. I could see that he enjoyed the contrast. In an odd way, this was his town flat and the Manor House was his secluded country home.

Jumping ahead (since I was to make several trips to Norwich) I'll say that the way Vernon spent his time there illustrated the best side of his character. Though he could have dined every evening with other professors, he chose to invite students to his flat for beer and sandwiches. I made the sandwiches, obviously, but it was a lot easier than making coq au vin. The students called him 'Vernon' and he talked, joked and told stories exactly as if he were with friends of his own age.

No, not exactly: he avoided the falsity of pretending to be a student. While he asked for no deference, it was accepted that he had a longer experience, a broader knowledge of the world, and – when they talked philosophy – a deeper understanding than anyone else in the room. He was first among equals; that, it struck me, was the position he liked to hold, in London or here. But here, he could be sure of it.

My position was quite different. When I strolled about the campus, I was taken to be a student. Sometimes I was urged to attend a meeting or asked to sign a petition. In the flat, I sat on the floor and kept quiet most of the time. My intellectual ranking – and no other ranking mattered – was in fact the humblest. The students whom Vernon favoured with his invitations were not just any students, but the brightest in the place, most of them post-grads. The talk was just as likely to be over my head as it was when we dined out in London. And our London friends knew that I had my own career, whereas the students didn't know and didn't seem to envisage the

138

possibility. So it was at Norwich that I was most unequivocally Professor Longuehaye's wife.

It was because of the students, I think, that I embarked on a serious attempt to grasp Vernon's philosophical system. It was all in a big book, called simply *Relational Analysis*, which had been published eight years ago and had established his prestige once and for all. Actually reading it was in itself a distinction; the number of Longuehaye fans could honestly claim to have read *Relational Analysis* was probably equal to the number of Marxists who have read *Capital*. Vernon was amused by my determination. 'Since you have regular access to the author,' he said, 'you can have the gist of it verbally in a tenth of the time.' I was sure, without needing to ask, that Laura had never read it. But I chose to set myself this test.

I passed the test in the sense that I read every word of the book. It took me about six months; life was always busy, it obviously wasn't the kind of book you could read in the train, and I used to slog at it with the aid of black coffee on nights when Vernon was working late in his study. My trouble was that a philosophical argument didn't seem to tell me anything, compared with a slide in the biology lab at school, or a picture in my view-finder, or a human experience like being loved by Vernon and hated by Cressida. I could understand every sentence as I read it because Vernon's style was beautifully clear – deceptively clear, I found myself thinking. But I didn't remember what I had read before. When I was in Chapter Five I couldn't possibly have answered the simplest questions about Chapter One, so that pressing on was more or less cheating. At the end, I had learned less about relational analysis than about Vernon's way of writing: a mixture of intellectual brilliance, instinct for the telling phrase, and sheer charm, like his way of talking.

Sometimes I put the book down and tried to connect it with the man who played tennis, walked in the country on Sundays, and made love to me. What did he actually do when he was being a philosopher? This analysis of abstract ideas was, I had to suppose, the reality of his life; they were to him what plans are to an architect, plants to a gardener, photographs to me. I saw that there was a Vernon whom I should never know. Laura hadn't minded, perhaps. I did mind.

The approach of Christmas was marked, so far as I was concerned, by monstrous morning and evening traffic-jams and by a hail of party invitations. Our friends celebrated Christmas in a spirit of ironic sentimentality. The attitude was that it was a crashing bore and a commercial racket, but since you couldn't ignore it you might as well take the plunge and do it properly. Women like Gabrielle decorated their houses with streamers and Chinese lanterns, made bowls of punch and mulled wine, cooked hundreds of mince-pies, and even made their guests sing carols. We couldn't possibly have gone to all the parties, and in the final week I said to Vernon that we absolutely must cut down. Aethra was at home, and I was uneasy about leaving her alone night after night, especially as a lonely and affluent house like ours was an obvious target for burglars. Vernon agreed, but we were rung up every day with insistent appeals: 'You are coming, aren't you? Oh, but you must!' We usually decided that we'd just drop in for a short time – which, having driven across most of London, we never did.

Christmas Day itself was an interval of astounding peace. The silence of the phone, in itself, was uncanny. We exchanged presents; I gave Vernon a rare book, secured with Arnold's help, and he gave me a ridiculously expensive bracelet. The task ahead of me, of course, was the Christmas dinner. I knew that he would expect all the traditional trimmings to the turkey and I was prepared to do the thing in style. My mother's stuffing would be ready-made and her cranberry sauce bottled, but mine would not. Before making a start, I went out to the garden for a breath of fresh air. Vernon was kneeling on the carpet, at work on the immense jigsaw puzzle which was my present to Aethra.

It was a mild day, as Christmas usually is. I climbed the steps to look at London; it was shrouded in an extraordinary

140

stillness, even more profound than the quiet that was normal around our house. This stillness, it seemed to me, could last for ever. It was the stillness of my new life. More truly than the parties and the phone calls, it was the reality of living with Vernon.

I found myself thinking of Christmas Day at home – the word, meaning my parents' home, came involuntarily to my mind. This was the first Christmas that I'd ever spent anywhere else. We'd go out for a stroll in the morning, leaving the turkey in the oven. The streets would be full of people, returning from Mass or church or chapel, or the younger families on their way to dinner with the old folks. A few cars, some pony-traps which were kept out of sentiment and used on rare occasions, but mostly people walking. It would be: 'Merry Christmas, doctor ... Merry Christmas, Mrs Bell ... Merry Christmas, Pat' all the way. But if we went out for a walk in Plumstead – an idea that would never occur to Vernon – probably we'd meet nobody, and certainly receive no greetings, because we didn't live within miles of any of our friends.

Only a year ago, I had spent Christmas with my family.

Only a year ago, I had been one of the girls at the flat in Kensington.

Only a year ago, I had been Alan Carter's girl-friend.

In every marriage, I suppose, there comes a time when you understand that you have not only contracted a new relationship, but in some degree become a different person. In the silent garden of the Manor House on Christmas Day, I knew that this time had come for me. It was the end of a time in which the delight of living with Vernon could simply be added to my existing life; the end of being a lucky girl, and of being proud that I was seen around town with him, and indeed the end of falling in love. Now there was something else, something deep and powerful and also mysterious. I was happy about it – I mean, I should have incredulously and sincerely denied that I was anything other than happy. Yet I was somehow frightened, though I couldn't imagine why or

141

of what. I decided that 'frightened' was an absurdly wrong word for this feeling; I was overwhelmed by the solemn vastness of the change in my life; I was – that was it – awed. I went indoors, but for some reason I didn't want to talk to Vernon. I told him I would ring up my parents. But the lines were busy and I couldn't get through, so I cooked the dinner.

One evening in January, I said to Vernon: 'Darling, what would you like to do on your birthday?'

He was reading – he always read with full concentration, whether the book was a work of philosophy or a thriller – and didn't answer at once. I waited, knowing his habit of finishing a paragraph before allowing himself to be interrupted. Then he looked up and said: 'My birthday?'

'Yes, it's on the fifteenth of February.'

'Fancy your knowing that.'

I said: 'My birthday is on the twenty-first of April, and don't you forget it.'

'All right. But I don't want any celebration – of my birthday, I mean.'

'You must do something special, darling,' I told him. 'You'll be fifty.'

He looked at me – I can only say – defensively. This was such an unusual expression for Vernon that I didn't know how to react to it. I wanted to laugh, but he seemed to be in anything but a laughing mood. After an awkward pause, I said: 'We didn't give a party at Christmas-time, did we? I was thinking, why not give one on your birthday?'

'You can't be serious, Patricia,' he said at once.

'Why ever not?'

'Birthday parties are for children. For young people, at most.'

I dropped the subject and he returned to his book. I thought, all the same, that he would feel pretty let down if I took him at his word and let the birthday pass as though it didn't exist. So I brought it up again a few days later when he was in one of his cheerful and talkative moods.

'Ah well,' he said, 'you're not going to let me off, I see. What day of the week will it be?'

He looked at his diary, apparently in the hope that he would be in Norwich or else have some unbreakable engagement. However, the birthday fell on a Monday and was completely clear. I said that the least we could do would be to go out to dinner, and sentimentally suggested the restaurant where we had spent our first evening together. He agreed, though without enthusiasm.

'Shall we ask anybody else, Vernon?'

'Whom had you in mind?'

'Well, some special friends, like Arnold and Gabrielle. Or perhaps John and Cressida if they can come.'

'No, no. I'd rather not.'

The great day came, and I began it by completely forgetting that it wasn't just another Monday. I had a lot to do, and had planned to drive into town ahead of the rush, but I dozed off again after the alarm went. I leaped out of bed, leaving Vernon still asleep, dressed, and raced downstairs to heat up some coffee and munch a slice of bread and marmalade. As I dashed out of the house I shouted: 'I'm off, darling!' but got no reply. Vernon strongly disliked these hurried departures. Crawling behind a lorry in Charlton Park Lane, and now only slightly behind schedule, I mentally checked over the timetable for the day and evening. Suddenly it hit me – I was having dinner with Vernon, it was his birthday dinner, and my present to him was in a drawer in the bedroom.

I got into a side-street, turned the car, and drove home, desperately hoping that Vernon would be still in bed and wouldn't have realized that I'd gone out. But he was eating breakfast and reading the paper.

'Forgotten something?' he asked.

'Your present,' I gasped. He made no comment. I ran upstairs and fetched it. It was a pair of cuff-links; I had pondered at some length over what to give him, and decided that it would suit his low-key approach to choose something

143

not too lavish. Now, the cuff-links looked rather pathetic. He examined them as if they represented a whim of mine and said: 'Very nice, darling.'

'Well, happy birthday, anyway,' I said.

'Thank you.'

I was going to kiss him, but he didn't look at all as though he wanted to be kissed. I was suddenly aware that if I stayed another minute I might burst into tears – the worst sort of tears, the undignified tears of a girl who has made a mess of things. So I mumbled something about being late and went off again.

This time, inevitably, I hit the worst of the traffic. And, just as inevitably, I never caught up with myself all day. In fact, the whole day was ghastly. The weather was foul – bitterly cold and with a miserable kind of thin urban snow. Mrs Baldwin was in the nearest she ever came to a bad mood and took me up acidly on various points; she was right every time, naturally, and made me feel like a beginner – or, more woundingly, like a promising photographer who is getting casual about her work because she's picked up a rich husband. Being late for all my appointments, I worked hastily and, I was sure, badly. I ran out of film and three shops hadn't got what I wanted. Finally, about five o'clock, the cops took away my car – a flagrant injustice, for I'd parked in a great wide road south of the river where a Russian tank couldn't have caused any congestion. I couldn't find a taxi (of course!) and had to make my way to Earls Court in the rush-hour tube, annoying everybody with my camera-bag and fingered by some sexually deprived character between Charing Cross and Victoria. Having muddled through my last job, I found that I'd be late for dinner if I collected my car, but have time to kill if I didn't. I decided that I absolutely must not be late; besides, if I went for the car I'd be sure to scream at the cops and incur some ingenious extra penalty. So there I was, adrift in London, carless, hungry (I hadn't had any lunch) and frozen.

I went into a pub and asked for a large brandy. A glance at

144

a mirror confirmed that I looked as bad as I felt. Also, I was dressed most unsuitably for the class of restaurant I was going to; in the morning, I'd dived into the clothes that I'd worn at home on Sunday, an old sweater and a cheap pair of needlecord trousers. I'd hoped to buy a dress during the day but I hadn't got around to it, and now the shops were shut. Worse still, I hadn't made it clear to Vernon that I wasn't coming home before the evening.

A cheerful voice said: 'Hi there, Pat!'

I gave the man an automatic smile and said: 'Well, hullo', meanwhile trying to place him. He was tall, good-looking, and turned out in trendy style, and I connected him with parties to which I'd been taken by Hugh, but couldn't put a name to him.

'Still the working girl?' he asked, pointing to my camera-bag.

'Of course.'

'Looks as though you've had a hard day.'

'So-so.'

'What are you drinking?'

'I've just got this, thanks.'

'Dispose of it. Can I let it be said that I failed to buy my old friend Pat a drink?'

'OK, it's a brandy.'

The man chattered on, while I listened vaguely and tried in vain to recall who the hell he was. After a bit, he said how lucky it was that our paths had once more crossed, because he was intending to take in the new Buñuel, and knew that I dug Buñuel, and pleasure shared was pleasure doubled or, since it was me, multiplied.

'I'm sorry,' I said. 'I have a date. In fact, I've got to run.'

He looked me over, obviously thinking that I didn't look as though I had much of a date.

'Change your plans, love. You know it makes sense.'

It was quite a reasonable thing to say, I suppose, but it grated on me – the confident smile and the commanding tone of 'Change your plans', and the male complacency in general

145

– and I flared up.

'Look, if I say I've got to go, I mean it. And I came in here for a quiet drink, not to get picked up.'

He stared at me. 'Pat honey, take it easy. Tell me what's wrong.'

'Oh, fuck off,' I said, and marched out. A very unsuccessful march out, too. I got as far as the door and the man said: 'You forgot this' – handing me my camera-bag.

I wondered why I'd said that I had a date and not that my husband was expecting me, and why I'd behaved so abominably. For in fact there was nothing wrong with the man – quite the contrary. He was a most attractive and pleasant man, and in the old days it would have been natural to see the film with him, and go on to dinner, and shack up for the night or not, according to mood. And if what had rattled me was a suppressed desire to do just that, in preference to dining with Vernon on his fiftieth birthday, it was a pretty bad situation.

Once again I couldn't get a taxi, and the restaurant wasn't near a tube station, and I had to wait in the snow for ages for a bus, so I was late for dinner after all. Vernon accepted my apologies without concealing that they were due. He was drinking a Tio Pepe. I had a Campari.

I started to tell him that I'd had a lousy day, including being felt up by a kink in a District Line train. At this point I realized that the waiter was endeavouring to hand me the menu, that people at other tables registered amusement, that Vernon registered total lack of amusement, that my voice was unnaturally loud, and that I had consumed nothing since breakfast except two large brandies and a Campari. I hastened to order.

To put it briefly, the dinner was a disaster. For one thing, while I ate ravenously, Vernon practically declined to eat at all. He ordered an avocado and an escalope, but scarcely tasted them.

'Isn't that escalope good?' I asked.

He gave me a pained smile and said: 'I'm afraid I have an

upset stomach.'

'Well, Christ, why didn't you say? We could have called this off.'

'I couldn't communicate with you,' he pointed out.

What was much more unusual – Vernon did have upset stomachs from time to time – was that he didn't talk. Questions failed to stimulate him. What had he been working on? Lectures, as usual. Had anybody phoned? No one of interest. He just sat there, behaving as though dining out were against his customs or his principles, and indicating fairly clearly that the dinner was a treat for me and an obligation for him. I recognized that he had every right to be annoyed with me – for forcing the arrangement on him, for looking like a dropout, and for being ahead of him on the drinks. On other occasions, however, such offences had been treated as part of my youthful charm. The trouble, I realized, was the fiftieth birthday itself.

'Do cheer up, darling,' I said at last.

He did the pained smile again. 'I'm sorry, Patricia. I simply don't feel cheerful.'

'You hate being fifty, don't you?'

'I resent it, shall we say.'

'But it's only a number, isn't it? I mean, I know this is corny, but you really are as old as you feel.'

'That's just it. I don't feel fifty. And therefore I feel that it has been imposed on me.' He mused for a while, staring across the room; then he looked at me and asked: 'Do I look fifty? The truth, please.'

'Of course not,' I replied loyally, but thinking that at this moment he almost did.

'Very well then,' he said, relieved and petulant at the same time. 'In that case, why the devil should I have to be fifty?'

I started to laugh. 'Because you were born in 1921. Like I said, it's only a number.'

'As I said, Patricia.'

'No, I said that.'

'I mean, the usage is "as I said", not "like I said".'

147

'Oh, I see. Well, you sound about seventy when you pick me up like that.'

'I beg your pardon,' he said frostily.

I took his hand and kissed it, and said: 'That was horrid of me – I know. I love you very much. I do really, Vernon.'

This melted him somewhat, but the atmosphere was still strained. I asked myself why I'd made this declaration – as though reassurance were necessary, as though loving a man of fifty called for a special effort. And I guessed that he was thinking on similar lines.

'I was always young,' he said abruptly. 'I was the youngest in my form right through school. I went up to Oxford at seventeen and took my degree at twenty. I had a chair at thirty-six. Heavens, that's fourteen years ago. A man of fifty – I always regarded a man of fifty as old. That's what it means, Patricia. What can there be to look forward to? Only repetition, only staying in the same place. That – and decline.'

'Oh well,' I said brightly, 'if I'd thought of that in time, of course I wouldn't have married you.'

I can see that this wasn't a very good joke, but I was astonished when he refused to recognize it as a joke at all. He gave me what I can only call a terrible look: angry, and shocked, and defencelessly sad. I stared at him and saw a man whom I didn't know at all. I wondered how I could possibly make amends, and realized that I never could. He would always believe that, whether trying to joke or not, I had uttered an unforgivable truth.

While I hunted for words, he regained an icy self-control and said: 'I think we'd better change the subject.'

The only other thing to record about that dinner is that we drank quite a bit: a bottle of Volnay, and another half-bottle because I had cheese, and brandy afterwards. But it's a sad fact that alcohol makes things better when they're good, and worse when they're bad. We ended with a long silence, broken by Vernon saying: 'We may as well get the bill.'

'Where are you parked?' he asked when we got into the street.

I confessed about my car being towed away. It then turned out that, assuming my car to be available, he had come in by train. It had been awful of me not to think of this and phone him; but apologies now merely made things worse.

What with the cold air and my general misery, I was visibly tight by this time. Vernon too had drunk enough to show up positive on the breathalyser. Clearly, it wasn't advisable to try to collect the car from the police. And no amount of money would induce a taxi-driver to go to Plumstead on a winter night.

So we went to Charing Cross, with half an hour to spare till the train, and drank horrible coffee in the horrible buffet. Then we shivered on the platform while the train failed to appear, being delayed by frozen points, one of the devices dear to the heart of the Southern Region. It turned up at last, and we shivered all the way to Plumstead, and trudged in silence through the mean deserted streets, a million miles from each other.

Last of all, we made love. We both knew that we were doing it because we ought to do it, and it was forced and meaningless, and that was worse than anything.

That was how the famous, admired, envied Professor Longuehaye, with his attractive and loving young wife, celebrated his fiftieth birthday.

Things soon returned to normal. A couple of days with his students, a good dinner-party, and Vernon was himself again: cheerful, full of health and energy, and a man of forty to all outward appearance. When I asked him whether he felt better about being fifty, he laughed and said: 'I've adjusted to it.' After that, I believe, he didn't think about it. But I did.

When two people come together (in the sense intended by Vernon in his speech) the overt assumption is that they start from scratch. It is, however, a convenient white lie. To marry a man of Vernon's age is to marry a man shaped by his past. He may wish to wipe it out — that's why he wants a young wife — but it's there. Vernon's past included two previous marriages, one of which had lasted for twenty years and must

149

have represented his idea of what marriage ought to be like.

Certain conversations were like keys that unlocked cupboards to which I had a dubious right of access.

In April I decided to take a week off work, partly because Aethra was at home, partly so that I'd have only three weeks available to go to the villa in August. Vernon, in the particular week that suited Mrs Baldwin, was at a conference in Switzerland. Over cups of tea in the kitchen, I talked for the first time (other than on strictly practical matters) with Mrs Wall, our daily help. Her manner and accent were those of a stage Mrs Mop, but I discovered that she read serious books, mostly on politics, and went to evening classes. Her husband was a shop steward in one of the big factories in Woolwich; they were both active in the Labour Party, and she took a shrewd and disenchanted view of the kind of people for whom she worked. As a matter of fact, with a teenage son also working, the Walls were quite well off, and she drove herself to our house in a well-polished new car. She did domestic work because she found it easy and fairly congenial, and to finance the car and holidays abroad.

'I used to work in the factory,' she told me. 'I reckon to go back there when my youngest is a bit older. That day nursery, it packs up at three o'clock, see. But I can't see myself not working at all. Go round the bend, I would.'

'I'm the same,' I said.

She eyed me thoughtfully. 'Work pretty hard, Mrs Longuehaye, don't you?'

'I keep busy.'

'And what does the Professor think of that?'

'He knew I was a photographer when he married me.'

'Different from what he was used to, though,' Mrs Wall remarked.

I poured out more tea.

Mrs Wall chuckled. 'Know what I used to call her, to myself, like?' It was implicit that *her* meant Laura.

'No, what did you call her?'

'The Duchess. Not that she was stuck-up or anything like

that. But you could tell she'd been used to have things down for her.'

'She came from that sort of family, I think.'

'Must have. Mind you, she tried her best. She used to come to me and say: 'Oh, Mrs Wall, the Professor wants me to mend this hole in his coat, do please show me how.' Always very polite, as if I was doing her a big favour, and very grateful – not a bit stuck-up or bossy, like I say. More sort of timid she was. Made you feel life was a bit beyond her. It'd have done her a world of good to have a job she could do, like something in your line. But there you are, she wouldn't have known where to start.'

Mrs Wall paused, a faint smile on her face, seeing Laura as one sees someone for whom one has felt an unexpected and pitying affection. 'Still and all,' she said, 'she was lovely, the Duchess – really lovely.' A woman, sometimes, can feel the quality of another woman's beauty in a way that no man can feel it. I saw that, despite Mrs Wall's principles, she wouldn't have had Laura different from what she was.

My best friend, among the dozens of friends I had acquired, was still Gabrielle. At that time, after a longish spell of television work and 'resting', she had a juicy character part in a West End play. The play, a comedy with a sure-fire formula, starred a young actress who was that year's darling, as a scatter-brained girl in perpetual doubt between three men. Gabrielle was the girl's mother, who had the job of inventing stories and keeping the men apart. 'I've graduated to Mum parts at last,' she said philosophically. Actually the part was quite good fun, she could go through it while thinking about the next day's shopping once she'd settled into it, and the play was bound to run for ages.

Gabrielle kept a stock of liquor in her dressing-room and had an old-fashioned actressy habit of entertaining friends there after the curtain. She urged me to drop in whenever I liked, and I did; it made a nice way to round off an evening when Vernon was away. I learned two things about Gabrielle – that she couldn't go to sleep until two in the morning,

151

especially after being on the stage, and that she was quite a hard drinker. But she never got out of control, and drink merely made her remarks more candid than they were otherwise.

'You've been very good for Vernon,' she told me one night. 'You're just what he needed, everybody says so.'

'Am I? I sometimes wonder. It was Laura who was really the right kind of wife for him, wouldn't you say, quite honestly?'

'Even if that was true, it's better for him to have somebody different than a substitute Laura. But being really honest, I'm not sure it is true. I'll tell you something you probably don't know about. A few years ago, Vernon was passed over for a chair at Oxford.'

'No, I didn't know that.'

'I didn't think he'd have told you. It wasn't all that surprising – those crappy old dons love slapping down a man who goes on television. But Vernon took it very hard. He's more vulnerable than people think, as I daresay you've found out by now. Well, you'd have said what the hell, it's their bloody loss, a new university's more exciting, and so forth. Whereas Laura helped him to feel that it was a failure. In her world, the Army was the Guards and universities were Oxbridge.'

I told Gabrielle that Mrs Wall had nicknamed Laura the Duchess.

'That's not at all bad. Arnold used to call her the Snow-Queen.'

'He considered her the most beautiful woman he'd ever seen. I think I once told you about his telling me that.'

'Yes, I remember. But it's double-edged, isn't it, the Snow-Queen? Being as beautiful as Laura is a bit off-putting, I mean for men. A man would rather go to bed with you than with Laura. That's also Arnold's opinion.'

'I don't think I'll ask Vernon about that.'

'Oh, I'm sure you're very good for Vernon in that department too. I doubt if Laura gave him the "come on, how

152

about it?" stuff very often. Drink up, Pat.' Gabrielle replenished the glasses. 'No, you don't have to worry about comparisons with Laura.'

'I'd like to know more about her, though. And Vernon won't talk to me about her.'

'He wouldn't, would he? Well, in a lot of ways Laura was quite an ordinary person – that is, an ordinary English upper-class lady. She was charming and gracious, she never said anything very interesting, she hadn't got much sense of humour; we all loved her, but we didn't exactly look forward to seeing her as one looks forward to seeing Vernon. And yet, in another way she was rather extraordinary. How can I put it? I've never known anyone who was so absolutely self-sufficient. She lived her own inner life, quite happily, serenely, whatever anyone else did. For instance, if Vernon had had all kinds of affairs – which I'm sure he didn't – you felt that it wouldn't have affected Laura. She would just have sat at home and carried on, like a good child on a rainy day.

'And you know,' Gabrielle continued, rummaging vainly for a cigarette and accepting one of mine, 'it sounds heartless, but I really think even dying wasn't so bad for her as it would be for you or me. She was able to accept it, as she accepted everything. She didn't ask why it had to happen to her, she didn't need to understand. The doctor told me she never asked any questions. It was very weird, I can tell you. Morbid subject – sorry. Have some more of this, Pat, there's lots left.'

What stayed in my mind from all this was Gabrielle's use of the word 'self-sufficient'. It was a rare quality, I reflected. I thought of myself as independent, which Laura clearly hadn't been, but not as self-sufficient – that was something else. I wondered whether Vernon had ever understood this. Perhaps he had seen Laura simply as pliant and easily contented; the outward effect was the same.

Living at the Manor House, I thought, must have suited Laura very well. It was grotesquely inconvenient, but she didn't have a job and probably seldom went into central London except with Vernon in the evenings. The elegant

153

high-ceilinged rooms, the enclosed garden, the atmosphere of a country mansion – these would have made her feel at home. The silence, and the sense that the world was shut out when the front door was closed, would have bothered her not in the least. It was a perfect setting for a woman who lived her own inner life.

It didn't suit me at all. I was sometimes glad of the peace and quiet after a day of dashing around town, and I was still conscious of its beauty, but in the course of a year the magic had palled considerably. It was a good house for a dinner-party, but it was so remote that people tended to arrive late and sometimes leave early. My friends, as distinct from our friends, never came to see me. Single girls like Stella mostly don't have cars, and anyway they took the view that Plumstead just wasn't in London, and quite possibly didn't exist.

In a sense, Plumstead didn't exist for Vernon and me either, although we lived in the middle of it. He had bought the house because it attracted him as a house, and that was that. After about ten years in it, he regarded the neighbourhood simply as a tract of territory which had to be crossed to get into town. If I suggested going to the local Odeon or having a drink in a local pub, he dismissed the idea as absurd. One couldn't ascribe this attitude to straightforward snobbery; a recognition of Plumstead as his neighbourhood would have spoiled his conception of the Manor House as his retreat. Now, although the London I love is the great sprawling city, and I don't go much for the fashionable cult of the community, I do like being on nodding terms with the regulars in a pub and exchanging good-mornings in the street. There ought to have been some of this as compensation for living miles from my friends, I thought, and there wasn't. I was known in the shops but the other customers didn't chat with me. I was set apart not only for obvious class reasons, but also because of an attitude created by Vernon and, presumably, Laura.

Sometimes I could have screamed – angrily rather than

sorrowfully — at the thought of spending the rest of my life here. I had vague notions of suggesting a move to a less distinguished but more practical home. But it was easy to guess that Vernon's reaction would be one of dismay, and I hadn't got the nerve.

In any case, that summer it became clear that I was stuck in Plumstead at least for several years. Aethra was now eleven, and Vernon decided to send her to the local comprehensive school in the coming September. It was only because of Laura's illness that Aethra had been sent away from home; Cressida had been at a grammar school, with excellent results. Vernon's reasons for giving the comprehensive a chance, as he put it, were not unconnected with the fact that he had several times held forth in public — on TV, too — in favour of educational equality. A paragraph in *Private Eye* about his daughter going to Roedean wouldn't do him any good, and nowadays even grammar schools were in disrepute in progressive circles. Although of course this aspect of the matter was never mentioned, I could already hear Vernon's voice; 'I may say that my own child is at the local comprehensive, and . . .'

He had some doubts to overcome, nevertheless, about both the teaching and what was delicately called 'the atmosphere'. The first point didn't worry him much; Aethra was obviously bright enough to head unerringly for a university whatever school she attended. But he had qualms about hurling a sensitive child into an environment so very different from what she was used to. I reassured him that she would be able to take it. I had decided by now that little Aethra had quite a hard core.

Vernon then made inquiries in suitable quarters, which was never any problem for him, and the word was that our comprehensive was on the approved list of enlightened schools. The head had pioneered some innovations which got his name successfully into *New Society* and the *Times Ed Supp*. The next step was to invite the head for a drink and a chat, which established complete understanding. The man was

155

clearly straining every nerve to put his school on the map as a 'good social mix' and to seduce middle-class parents from the private sector, and getting Vernon Longuehaye's kid as a pupil was like a dream come true for him. She would be tested, he said, but he'd be greatly surprised if she didn't take her place in the A stream. As for 'problems of adjustment', these were his special concern. I got the impression that, should any rash D-streamer give a tug to Aethra's beautiful hair, the headmaster would be on the spot within seconds.

Vernon discussed the choice of school with me in a somewhat guarded manner. In theory, the decision was entirely his; in practice, next to Aethra herself, the person whose situation was to be changed was me. I had taken on Vernon simply as himself — a man with two grown-up children and one at boarding-school. I had got used to a certain kind of life: the intimacy of being alone in the house with him, the frequent evenings out, and the Tuesday-to-Thursday spells when I came and went as I pleased. Now, the Manor House would be a family home. It was still on record that I wasn't supposed to be a mother to Aethra, but I could see that it wouldn't be Vernon who would buy her new shoes when she needed them.

I couldn't argue in favour of sending Aethra to a school like the one I'd been to myself (having more than once told Vernon what a waste of time I had found it) and of course I wasn't the only woman in the world who had become a stepmother. So I looked on the bright side. Aethra was ahead of her years in most respects, and wasn't 'difficult' in any of the recognized ways. She shouldn't, in fact, need much looking after. And getting on closer terms with her, which had so far eluded me, would be a distinct satisfaction.

On the practical level, there were few difficulties. Vernon asked me whether we ought to get an au pair, but this seemed ridiculous for one child of eleven who was at school all day and inclined to be content with her own company. The school was just over a mile away; as usual in Plumstead, there was no convenient bus, but Vernon or I could drive her there in the morning and it wouldn't hurt her to walk home.

In June, it was a year since I'd gone to live at the Manor House, and the period of living there alone with Vernon was as good as over. Cressida had been coming for occasional weekends, and when she left Oxford she arrived with all her possessions. As Vernon had calculated, she had decided to accept me after we got married. In the Manor house, we were like two animals who have been put in the same cage at the Zoo, circling around and tacitly acquiring our own corners. I made a point of not sitting in a certain chair in the living-room, which I guessed had always been Cressida's, and she wasn't the sort to miss such points. We didn't pretend to like each other, but in a curious way we understood each other. A helpful factor was that she now had more confidence in herself, having taken a brilliant First.

Her friend Jane came to the house too, sometimes for the day and sometimes to stay, sleeping in John's room which was virtually a guest-room, for he seldom appeared. Jane was a delicate-looking girl who spoke very quietly and moved very gently, as though afraid of making a noise; she was deferentially polite to Vernon and me, and it was clear that she was at ease only with Cressida. Vernon tried to draw her out, using his technique which seldom failed with students, and her remarks on her own subject (medieval history) showed that she was very bright, but she said no more than courtesy required. I could see that Cressida and Jane were lovers, and Cressida could see that I could see, which made another strand of understanding. I was pretty certain that Vernon never suspected anything of the kind.

Amateur Freudians, however, would have been wrong in assuming a close emotional relationship between Vernon and Cressida. They spoke the same language and enjoyed matching their brains, and that was about all. I was increasingly sure that it was Laura who had counted with Cressida; she hadn't so much resented me as resented Vernon's betrayal of Laura. Something else occurred to me. Laura's great quality had been her tolerance — not Vernon's

157

outstanding trait : or more precisely her power of acceptance. She would have (perhaps she had) accepted having a Lesbian daughter. Putting it another way, Vernon was a strongly heterosexual man, while Laura had been a not very sexual woman.

One Sunday morning, I went into the living-room with the idea of clearing up — we'd had guests the night before — and found Cressida staring vacantly at a newspaper which she evidently wasn't reading. She was in a low mood, I knew, because Jane had been counted on to come for the weekend and had been nabbed by her parents for some family occasion. Vernon was out walking.

Cressida dropped the paper scornfully on the floor and said: 'Don't you hate Sundays, Pat?'

I said: 'We ought to have planned something. I could ring round and get somebody to come over for a drink.'

'No. There's no point. We had quite enough of that last night, don't you think so?'

'I suppose so,' I said. For me, it had been a very successful evening; the talk had been up to the highest standards and Vernon had complimented me on the food.

'Sorry,' Cressida said, reading my thoughts (she was good at this). 'It was what one would call a successful evening, wasn't it? You do that sort of thing very well. Better than my mother.'

'Oh, I'm sure that's not true. Judged by Vernon's expectations, she must have been the perfect hostess.'

Cressida gave a 'huh' sort of laugh and said: 'She met his expectations, oh yes. She always did that. But with you, one can see that you really enjoy it.'

'I do, as a matter of fact.'

'I thought so. Well, good luck to you. I wish I did. Everybody talking at once, and showing off, and making up bits to go into diaries to be published in 1990 — no thanks.'

'And is that what your mother thought?'

'Oh no, she wouldn't have allowed herself even to think anything so bitchy. It was just that dinners gave her a headache. She used to slink out and take a couple of Veganins when she got a chance. He didn't know. He wouldn't, of course.'

I said nothing. My curiosity was aroused, but I wasn't prepared to engage in a discussion of Vernon's defects with Cressida. She yawned and picked up the paper again, and I thought she wasn't going to say any more. However, she did.

'I was the one who made her see a doctor, you know.'

I wasn't sure for a moment whether this referred to the headaches or to the cancer of which Laura died. It was the latter, as Cressida went on to make clear.

'She didn't want to worry him. She was like that. And he hadn't noticed anything – of course. I made her promise to see the doctor, but then I went back to Oxford and she put it off, and when she did go it was too late. I'm sure she knew she was going to die weeks before he did. So she resigned herself to everything. Right at the end – you might not believe this – he decided to cart her off to France. And she went. She had to be practically lifted into the plane.'

'Vernon has told me about that,' I said carefully. 'I gathered that it was her wish to go, because it was where they'd first met.'

Cressida did her scornful laugh again.

'Oh no, it was all his idea. She'd rather have died here. In any case, she wouldn't have thought of anything so . . . you know, so like a bad movie. But she'd always done what pleased him, so she didn't object to providing him with a suitable scenario for her death.'

'You're very hard on your father, Cressida.'

'I'm not a very nice person, though, am I? As you're aware. But all I'm saying, really, is that he wrote the script and she played the part. Mind you, he always convinced himself that he was giving her what she wanted. And she didn't mind, as I say. So no harm was done. You could even say it's the formula for a satisfactory marriage.'

Soon after this, Cressida went away. Jane was going to spend part of the vacation at Oxford (she had another year to her degree) doing library work, and Cressida said awkwardly that she might as well go back to Oxford too, as she had no other plans.

So Vernon and I were alone in the house, just for a few days until Aethra finished school and came home. These days were precious to me. There would be no more.

The weather was very hot, setting up some kind of record. Vernon said that it would hardly be worth while going to Italy, though of course he was looking forward to it as much as ever. What was most unusual, for England, was that it stayed hot – or warm, anyway – late into the night. The last night before Aethra came home, we sat in the garden until after twelve. We were drinking white wine with ice, as if it were Scotch, which Vernon said was a cultural abomination, but a pleasant drink on a hot night, he had to admit. The thing about this is that you don't feel you're seriously drinking, so you go on and on, getting more and more relaxed and happy. Vernon was in excellent form, telling me about a philosophical congress he had once attended in Moscow. Apparently, after an argument lasting half the night, a Russian philosopher conceded that relational analysis was compatible with dialectical materialism, but came to Vernon's hotel in the morning to withdraw this, explaining that it was just the vodka; to which Vernon replied that if vodka altered the perception of knowledge, the whole basis of materialism was undermined.

Reluctantly, we decided that we really must go to bed. We opened all the windows in the bedroom, and a sort of cloud of beauty seemed to come in, visible or tangible or (as Vernon would say) perceptual, made up of silence and warm air and velvet-dark sky. We knew without speaking that it was one of those special times that come without being sought, and are unmistakable when they do come, every now and then for people who are in love. We undressed and stood for a while by the window, holding each other and kissing and gently stroking, not wanting to spoil things by haste. Then we made love, and it was indeed one of those special times when all

160

possible experience is brought together and fused: wild excitement and utter peace, keen reality and the wonder of a dream, the sharpness of the moment and the immensity of time.

We were both covered in sweat, so we had a shower and then went back to bed, lying without even a sheet as if we were in the tropics.

'We ought to sleep,' I said, 'only I don't feel sleepy.'

'Busy tomorrow?'

'About average. I want to start early, though, and get home early because of Aethra coming.'

Vernon said: 'Darling, you mustn't feel that having Aethra here makes a difference for you and me.'

'We'll still make love, will we?'

'We'll still make love. It'll always be like this.'

'That's nice to know. Only we mustn't have showers in the middle of the night.' The plumbing made haunted-house noises.

After a minute I said: 'I'm glad Aethra will be here, truly I am. But I have enjoyed this year, just living with you. And it will be different, let's face it.'

'I know,' he said. 'But you see, I've always had a child in the house.'

Then he asked: 'Patricia, do you think I'm too old to be a father?'

'What? Of course you're not. You're marvellous with Aethra.'

'That isn't what I meant, darling.'

'Oh – you mean you and me?'

'Yes, my sweetheart. I mean you and me, and our love, and our happiness. We've always known that it's infinite. I see our child already, yours and mine, another dimension of our love.'

He held me in his arms, and I felt his body strong and urgent, and mine yielding, as if we were making love again. And, his mouth to my ear, he went on talking about having a child.

161

We had talked about it only once, soon after we were married. I had said that I needed to think it over, and various things had to be taken into account; also that I couldn't cope with too many new experiences at once, it was the first time I was really in love, and the first time I was sharing my life with a man, and that was enough for the present. It had been left, as I understood it, that I would tell him when I came round to wanting it. But that had been a rational discussion, downstairs in the living-room. Now, my nakedness pressed to his, and still joined to him in transcendent happiness, it was something else. So, in the persuasion of his words and his touch, I did really feel that having a child was the one joy still in store for us, and flowed naturally from what we'd reached. I lay close to him, dreamy and contented, saying 'Yes ... oh yes ... darling, yes, sure ...' from time to time. Slowly this mounted in me to a thrill of longing – for him, for the promise I was giving him, I didn't know – and we made love again in the freshness of dawn.

The next day, or rather the same day, I remembered all this as I was having lunch by myself at a pavement table in Charlotte Street. I was a bit light-headed, what with the heat and an almost sleepless night, and events came back to me as though I'd been either dreaming or stoned. I hadn't been dreaming, that was for sure. Everyone (or everyone I know) is familiar with the sinking realization of having done something rash and irrevocable in a haze of emotion or alcohol or both. I was thankful that I was on the pill. I could see that this was how men got women to have babies, even women who'd had about six already and had sworn not to have any more.

I knew that Vernon wouldn't forget my lying there in his arms and saying 'Yes, yes'. I felt that he'd taken an unfair advantage : of a mood and an atmosphere, of my love itself. I could see his point of view, however. He believed that a child was an intrinsic part of a marriage, the embodiment of a complete union. In his other marriages (his first wife probably hadn't worked, Laura certainly hadn't) there would have been no hesitation, no need for persuasion. Besides, while delay didn't matter to me, he was a man of fifty. I ought to credit him with forbearance, I reflected, for having waited until now. And yet, this made me think that there was a strange deliberate progression about the way he had drawn me closer to himself, taking each step when he counted on me to follow. First we were having an affair, then I was living with him, then came the unexpected and apparently unnecessary proposal of marriage. And now this. I had a certain feeling of being trapped.

At the same time, even in the light of day and cold sober, something in me responded to the appeal. I had always thought of a pregnancy as an imposition on the freedom of my body, as well as of course a threat to my career and the life that I chose to lead. But that was before I had lived with a man, let alone married him. Perhaps the acceptance of motherhood did follow from the change in myself which I had recognized on Christmas Day. I'd have to say at the least that I wasn't against having a child, as I hadn't been against marriage, on principle. There was more than this. Vernon had said that he wanted to marry me as a sign that he committed to me his whole life and his whole self; I had made the same commitment to him. Could it be true that our love demanded, as its ultimate expression, the creation of a new life? I discovered in myself that mysterious emotion, somewhere between awe and excitement, springing from the primal link between mind and body, which – I suppose – possesses any woman when she thinks about having a child. I remembered my mother once saying that there was something extra to making love – an extra thrill? no, she corrected that, an extra depth of feeling – when this was the purpose.

I paid my bill, got my cameras together, and took a grip on myself. Having a baby meant about a year off work, and I hadn't been working long enough to want that. If I yielded to the instinctive urge as soon as I felt it, I might as well be a dumb breeder down in the Falls Road, or at best the kind of wife whom I'd been commissioned to photograph, with her

163

children tastefully arranged as adornments of the home, in Sevenoaks or Rickmansworth. I was myself before I was Vernon's woman, damn it. I decided that I would have a child at a time of my own clear-headed choosing, and not before. And it wouldn't be yet. And I would tell Vernon so.

I managed to get home soon after Aethra arrived. Vernon was delighted with her; she was more beautiful than ever, shooting fast out of childhood. She seemed to be looking forward to her new school, glad that she'd be living at home, and extremely pleased to be going to Italy with us. We had a week before we left. Vernon was so wrapped up in Aethra that he gave no sign of remembering his plea and my promise on our last night alone. I didn't imagine that he'd really forgotten, but it was shelved for the time being; and, what between having Aethra with us and going out, we were seldom alone. So I never put things straight, after all.

I was bored at the villa, as I expected, but not so much as the year before. I took a stack of long books that I'd never got around to reading – the sort of books that Alan had read, like *Middlemarch* and *The Moonstone*. I also took my cameras. It was a delight to get back to the kind of photography that I'd had no time for since college; I built up a portfolio of light and water studies, which were subsequently exhibited and won a prize. Aethra took a great deal of interest in what I was doing, so I drove her into Como and bought a camera for her, and showed her how to get pictures. She caught on quickly, and I congratulated myself on forging a bond.

Aethra was the pet of the villa, always being pressed by the servants to accept sweets or ice-cream or samples of a meal that was in preparation. I noticed that she found the servant business quite natural; she never hesitated to ring a bell and make a demand in a tone of calm authority, oblivious of having interrupted somebody's siesta. In fact, she was a far better Signora than I was. The servants played their role gratefully, they had less time to hover round me, and so everybody was happy.

Maria-Grazia, however, was a bit hard to take at times. She

164

disapproved of my clambering around the rocks and taking pictures, especially in the afternoon heat. She said (her English had improved) that I looked tired, and I was too thin, and I ought to be eating more and resting. I admitted that I'd been working quite hard and tried to explain that I enjoyed work. Maria-Grazia hadn't realized that I actually had a job, and was baffled when I told her about it – as well she might be, since the only professional photographers she knew about were the kind who snap you in the street and force a grubby card on you.

'But the Signora does not need to work,' she pointed out.

'I don't know what I'd do if I didn't work,' I said.

This left her still more baffled. I saw what was in her mind: I didn't seem to be aware that I was a lady – even that I was a woman.

'This work will finish when the Signora has a bambino,' she said.

'You can see I'm not having a bambino, Maria-Grazia,' I answered, a little too sharply.

'It will be soon, Signora. I am sure it will be soon.'

When my three weeks were up, I was more than ready to return to London. Vernon was staying another week at the villa, and then taking Aethra on an educational tour to Verona, Padua and Venice. The Manor House seemed very empty; it struck me that I'd already begun to think of it as a family home. I stayed in town most evenings, going to films or boozing with Stella, and once I had dinner with Hugh for old time's sake. But re-living the life of a single girl, though pleasant, was only a pretence.

I hadn't seen my parents for almost a year, so I decided to take this opportunity and fly over for a weekend. I was sure that I'd enjoy strolling round the little town, calling in at the shops and bars, gossiping with old friends. I did enjoy it, I think. And yet, it wasn't the same. Ulster's troubles were at their worst in this summer of 1971. The streets were empty after dark, British armoured cars patrolled, policemen eyed strangers suspiciously and one of them asked me for

165

identification. People whom I knew told me how lucky I'd been to get to England in time, and implied that there were experiences which couldn't be explained to someone who hadn't shared them. They took refuge, mostly, in talking about the past and trying to see me, and also themselves, as we had been in those innocent times. A pretence had to be kept up on both sides, because our peaceful little town no longer existed, and the young Pat whom they sought to revive didn't exist either. The composite person that I'd become – Pat Bell, photographer; Mrs Longuehaye; Patricia – had no place here.

On the Sunday, I had tea with Bob and Mary Curran. Bob had taken over the building business from his father and was as prosperous as anyone could be in the depressed state of the economy. They had a new house in one of those 'developments' which represent an attractive country town's striving to turn itself into a suburb of Belfast, or Birmingham or anywhere else.

Mary at least didn't try to see me as young Pat (perhaps because young Pat had been Bob's girl). 'Tell me about the grand life you're leading over there,' she said. She herself couldn't remember when she had last been to Belfast. You'd be crazy, she explained, to go to Belfast unless you had to. Besides, she had two children and another on the way.

'I don't know,' she said while I helped her with the washing up, 'I didn't set out to have a big family. But there it is, one ties you down enough and more don't make that much difference. And when all's said and done, it's the greatest thing in life. When you know another one's started, your mind says "Ah, be damned to you" and something else says "Ah, the darling." You any signs, Pat?'

'Not yet.'

' 'Tis on that dreadful pill you are, breaking God's holy law,' Mary said, grinning at me and putting on an exaggerated accent. Like many Catholics of this generation, Bob and Mary made fun of the dogma and maintained that they would use contraceptives if they chose, but when it came to the point they had the children.

Bob drove me home, and we stopped at a practically empty bar for a Paddy's. For want of a better topic, I asked him whether he kept up his interest in photography.

'I haven't the time now,' he said. 'Those were good times, though, weren't they?'

'Not just the photography,' I said.

'Ah, don't think I forget.' He lifted his glass. 'It's a strange thing, Pat, I can't think of you as married.'

'Why not? Mary's my age, and you've been married to her for four years.'

'That's different. Mary had her sights on marriage from the first moment I kissed her. You wouldn't have married me, would you, Pat?'

'No,' I answered, and we both laughed.

'You were always independent,' he said. 'You were never the one to care about catching a man, nor to be caught. It took the great Vernon Longuehaye to do it.'

'Well, I didn't intend to marry him, actually. I started living with him, and when he wanted us to be married I thought: if it pleases him, I've no objection.'

'He must have wanted to make sure you wouldn't up and move out the next week.'

'Oh, I don't see that being married would prevent that, if I wanted to.' Afraid of giving a wrong impression, I added: 'Mind, I'm very happy with him.'

'I'm sure you are, Pat.'

'You must come and see us if you're ever in London.'

'I might, at that.' Though it wasn't likely, of course, that anything would bring Bob to London.

Vernon and Aethra returned from Italy. The trip had been a great success, he said; she had a real appreciation of works of art and of the civilization they represented.

I settled down in the family home. It was different, as it was bound to be. For one thing, going out was awkward; Aethra was too old and too responsible for us to insult her by having baby-sitters, but Vernon disliked leaving her in the house alone in case of fire or burglars. (He had never worried about

167

fire or burglars before.) So he was reluctant to go out to dinner except with our best friends. Either genuinely or as an argument, he made out that most of the people who invited us weren't worth the effort. 'Frankly, darling, I've heard everything they've got to say.' But to me, these people were still exciting.

Moreover, it was assumed that I would generally be at home with Aethra when Vernon was out by himself, at meetings or appearing on TV, and when he was in Norwich. It was another deprivation for me; I had enjoyed staying in town after work, going to a pub with Eileen or dropping in at my old flat. Now, I was always making my way home in the rush hour.

But, as a matter of fact, I couldn't drop in at the flat any more. Two of the girls had left – Peggy to marry her tycoon, who had finally nerved himself to leave his wife, and Claudine to set up in a small flat of her own, where she was more or less frankly a call-girl. Janet started to fill up the flat with her dikey girls, so Stella and Erica decided that it was no longer quite their scene and they would leave her to it. Stella, in the course of a long phone talk, told me she was thinking of giving up modelling. She was putting on weight, and her style was going out of fashion. A man – 'no, you don't know him, he's not from the old crowd at all' – was very keen on her and they were living together. As the man was rolling in money, there seemed to be no further point in working. 'I never thought I'd tie myself down,' Stella said, 'but it's got its advantages, hasn't it? I might even marry him. It seems to have worked out nicely for you.'

It was absurd as well as selfish for me to feel depressed about Stella getting married, but I did. I realized that I had wanted Stella and the others to be girls for ever, just as people in my home town wanted me to be a girl for ever. The zany, youthful, irresponsible scene in which I'd lived for two hilarious years was fading away. There were other scenes like it all over London, but I didn't belong to them. I knew that I'd wanted it to remain so that I could return to it – not seriously, I hastened to remind myself, but for an occasional dip.

We didn't see any more of Cressida. She had taken a research job in Oxford and managed to get a lease of a cottage in some out-of-the-way village, where she presumably lived with Jane. John was spending a year with a UN project in Iran. Vernon didn't seem to miss his older children. Aethra, very clearly, held a central place in his life.

It was because he had Aethra at home – or so I could only suppose – that he didn't renew his urging for me to have a child. But that question nagged at me, as questions do when they haven't been properly settled. I wished that I'd explained myself instead of leaving my dreamy 'Yes' on record. Now there was a permanent misunderstanding; perhaps Vernon even thought that I'd stopped taking my pills. It was ridiculous that we couldn't talk about it. But if he was no longer thinking about it – if, possibly, his wish had been transient, produced by the emotions of that strange summer night – then it was wiser for me to say nothing.

Aethra was getting on very well at school. She was in the top stream (of course) and clearly a star pupil. In addition to her natural high intelligence, the private schools with their small classes had given her a head start, so she sometimes told us – tolerantly rather than indignantly – that she was being taught things she already knew. She positively liked homework and got down to it, using the music-room as a study, directly after tea. She was a fast worker, like her father, and nothing gave her any trouble. Toward the end of her first term I went along to the Open Day (Vernon was in Norwich and couldn't go, to the evident disappointment of the teachers) and heard glowing reports of her. It must have given these teachers quite a kick to talk to their friends about Vernon Longuehaye's kid. Besides, she was pretty and charming, she was well-behaved, and she grasped an explanation almost before it was out of the teacher's mouth. 'A delight to teach,' one of them said to me.

But I could see, if I hadn't known already, that the liberal theory about comprehensives mixing children of different social backgrounds was a myth. Aethra had a group of friends, all top stream and all middle-class. They viewed the rest of the school, not exactly with contempt, but with an assumption of having nothing in common. Aethra soon observed that the kids in the lower streams were not interested in the lessons, but only in chasing round the corridors. They were forfeiting what she saw as the pleasure of learning. 'There's no point in their being in school at all,' she remarked. Even if this didn't prove them to be inferior, it did reveal a divergence of outlook that could never be bridged. It was hard to criticize this attitude of Aethra's; Vernon shared it, so did I in the last resort, and so did the teachers, or at least those who taught the A stream. The school therefore functioned in the same manner as a colonial territory, in which the more advanced natives are destined to get educated and staff the administration, and the others to pursue a less demanding way of life.

However, it was a territory simmering with revolt, or rather with sporadic outbursts of resentment. These were aimed at the head and the teachers, at the A stream, and particularly at Aethra when she was identified as Professor Longuehaye's daughter. In the homes from which most of the kids came, Vernon's television image didn't command unmixed respect. He stood for everything conveyed by certain popular epithets: clever-dick, smart-alec, show-off, and indeed (used derisively, as the word mostly is in England) professor. From this angle, it was simply a con trick to earn large sums of money by airing your opinions instead of doing an honest job. Aethra found notes on her desk addressed to Professor Longsay or Professor Longpay; the contents, I've no doubt, were abusive, though she commented mainly on the low standard of handwriting and spelling.

Being called Longuehaye was bad; being called Aethra was a burden too. A bunch of kids once made a ring round her in the playground, chanting: 'Ether, Ether, get a sniff of Ether.' Aethra herself didn't tell me about this; I heard of it from another child's mother, and I was careful not to tell Vernon.

In fact, she was bound to be picked on. She paid for being beautiful and for being clever, for her unfair share of luck. She paid for her private-school manners and accent, and for our living in the Manor House and having two cars. And of course she paid for being the teachers' favourite.

I don't think she suffered greatly. She knew her own value, she was prized by her friends, and she didn't care about being universally popular, especially among boys and girls who didn't matter to her. Still, a problem arose.

The problem was that, although Aethra could seldom be cornered and teased on the school premises, she was fair game on her walk home. Her friends lived in the opposite direction, in the one solidly middle-class neighbourhood that came within the school's area. The surroundings of the Manor House being equally solidly working-class, the kids who went Aethra's way belonged to the hostile tribes. I doubt if they ever have done her any real harm; the neighbourhood was too stable and old-fashioned to be seriously classed as tough. But they used to tread on her heels, elbow her into the gutter, and sometimes give her a smart jerk on the arm so that she dropped her books. Another trick was to form a line which moved in front of her very slowly, so that her walk home took twice as long as necessary. It was petty persecution, but it was no joke for Aethra. She was only eleven, and brought up in a sheltered way. She was baffled – she'd done nothing that she knew of to deserve this – and frightened.

One day, she came home in tears. She had been carrying a portfolio of drawings, much praised in the art class, which she looked forward to showing to Vernon. One of her tormentors shouted 'Give us a look, Ether' and grabbed it. When he opened it, the drawings were snatched away by the wind; most of them fell in the roadway and were crushed by a passing lorry.

I was out working, but Vernon was at home. The whole story came out, doubtless heightened by the sense of drama that no child can resist: the story of the daily ordeal that she had braved throughout the term. By the time I came in Aethra had more or less got over it, but Vernon was still very shaken.

'Can you understand it?' he asked after Aethra had gone to bed. 'Wanton, motiveless, unprovoked cruelty — it's not easy to come to terms with it.'

I could understand it reasonably well — being a philosopher doesn't qualify you as a psychologist — but I thought it prudent to shake my head and look sorrowful.

'Poor little thing,' he went on. 'All these weeks, and she never said a word. I blame myself. She's often looked very subdued when she came in. I should have realized that something was wrong.'

He sighed. The thing had hit him just as it had hit Aethra; he had been brought up against a reality from which he was normally screened. I was keenly aware of the silence in our comfortable house, the spacious garden, the high walls. We were living in a fortress.

'Perhaps we should never have sent her to that school, Patricia,' he said. 'As a matter of principle, of course it was right. But human beings come first and principles afterwards.'

'Oh, come on,' I said. 'It's going to be good for her in the long run. Besides, nothing disastrous has happened. Kids get bullied worse than that at Winchester, don't they? — if you cast your mind back.'

'That's different. That's boys.'

'I expect Aethra'll find a boy to look after her before she's much older.'

Vernon looked surprised. He hadn't begun to envisage Aethra as more than a child.

'Well,' he said, 'what is obvious is that we'll have to collect her by car. She tells me that most of her friends are fetched by car after school.'

'I don't see how I could manage it. She comes out at four o'clock.'

'Oh, I'll go whenever I can. We can work it out.'

I almost burst out laughing. I'd heard this one before, in connection with driving Aethra to school in the mornings. The original idea had been that Vernon would do it except when he was in Norwich. This didn't last long; taking Aethra to school became my regular job, on the grounds that I was going out anyway. The fact that I set off in the wrong direction and couldn't get ahead of the rush hour escaped Vernon's notice.

Fetching her in the afternoon, however, was a far more serious proposition. It was out of the question for me to stop work at three. In Mrs Baldwin's eyes, it would simply have meant that I wasn't doing my job.

I explained this to Vernon.

'Your Mrs Baldwin gets her pound of flesh,' he said.

'What d'you mean? She pays me a full salary, she expects a full day's work.'

'Can't you make some other arrangement?'

'No. She doesn't want part-timers, it complicates things.'

'I should have thought you'd be tired of being bound hand and foot to her.'

'We can't all work two and a half days a week, ' I said tartly.

Vernon came and sat on the arm of my chair, resting his hand on my shoulder. I became apprehensive. He did this when he wanted to persuade me into something that I wasn't ready to accept.

'You know, darling,' he said, 'I've been turning this over in my mind, quite apart from the incident with Aethra. Is it necessary for you to work for the agency?'

I twisted round, shaking off his hand, and stared at him.

'That's it, is it? You want me to give up my job.'

'As a job, yes. I don't see why you need to depend on Mrs Baldwin, nor why she should profit from your work. There are independent photographers, aren't there?'

'Freelances? Yes, there are.'

'It's not my field of course, but I should think you could be very successful. You know that your work's good, you have a reputation. You needn't be afraid to take this step.'

'Who said anything about being afraid? The question is whether I want to, and I don't.'

'You're very much on edge, my dear. Can't we discuss it rationally?'

I was on edge, that was true. I didn't know why. I sensed an indefiable threat.

'Look, Vernon,' I said. 'When we got married, you said I didn't have to be Aethra's mother. Actually I get her meals, I see to her clothes, and all that kind of thing. I've said nothing about that. But when you ask me to give up my job so that I can fetch her from school, I draw the line.'

'That's not quite fair, darling. Not at all fair. I've already said that I've been considering this for some time. The business with Aethra has merely brought it to a head.'

'But if I say no, what are you going to do about Aethra? Send her to boarding-school again?'

'I might be forced into that.'

'Forced by me, of course. It's going to be my fault, whatever happens.'

'Please, darling.' He pressed me gently down into the depths of the chair and stroked my hair. 'I've never known you like this before. Try to look at my suggestion on its merits.'

'What are they?'

'It may surprise you, but I give more thought than you may imagine to the kind of work you have to do. I've often heard you say that a great deal of it is sheer routine. You're sent out on jobs that don't interest you, don't offer you anything new, don't make demands on your skill. Why should you be subjected to that when it isn't necessary?'

I said nothing. It was true that some of my work was uninteresting, although I had more than my share of the quality commissions. It was true that I'd come home, more times than I could count, and told Vernon: 'Christ, I've had a dead boring day.' The greater part of all professional work – a doctor's work, for instance – is undemanding routine. But you're not a professional unless you accept this, and even take pride in it: pride in maintaining your competence, in devoting yourself to the dull jobs with as much care and alertness as to the exciting ones. However, this answer only occurred to me afterwards. At the time, my mind didn't seem to be ticking over properly. The more he talked, and the more arguments he found – he was never short of them – the more he seemed to be pressing me down, ever so gently, into this helplessness.

'As long as you do that kind of work,' he continued, 'you are cheated of the recognition that you deserve. You exhibited and won a prize, but that was with pictures you took in Italy, not in the course of your ordinary work. I want you to have more opportunities of that kind – opportunities of which you deprive yourself for Mrs Baldwin's sake.'

'You keep talking about what you want. You haven't asked me what I want.'

'But you're not very clear about it, my sweet, are you? All this routine, all this rushing from appointment to appointment, has prevented you from thinking about it. And what I want – must I say it? – is on your behalf. I love you, after all. I want you to have a little leisure, and decent holidays, and above all the chance to make plans and choices. I know from my own experience that one can't give of one's best without that. I want to see you in control of your time : in control of your life. I want you to be free.'

And so on, and so forth. By degrees, my resistance melted. I began to feel that I had reacted too sharply – irrationally, as he had said – to a new idea. I had been ungracious and distrustful. Why shouldn't he want the best for me? I didn't doubt that he loved me. And why shouldn't he be right? Or why should I necessarily be right, just because I was the photographer? He had something to gain from my going freelance, of course : but what was wrong with that? We had a life in common, surely.

It struck me the next day that there was another solution. How about Vernon giving up his professorship, and thus making himself available to fetch Aethra from school five days a week? Not a bad idea, not bad at all. He didn't need a university position in order to be a philosopher. We could live perfectly well on his books, his articles and his TV fees

175

plus my salary if I kept my job.

But I knew that it was a non-starter. I knew how much he enjoyed teaching, what a kick he got out of his sessions with clever young men; he wouldn't sacrifice that side of his life. on't be ridiculous, I said to myself. Can you imagine a professor — Professor Longuehaye, moreover — going to the Vice-Chancellor to explain that he's resigning because he's needed at home? To iron the pillow-cases, maybe? Men don't do things like that.

Vernon didn't press me for a quick decision. We were within a couple of weeks of the end of Aethra's term, and his university term had already ended, so he fetched her from school almost every day, making clear that this was a makeshift arrangement, but without actually grumbling. Like that, we got through to Christmas.

Christmas was like the year before, on a more subdued note. We didn't go to so many parties. The family aspect of the occasion was more pronounced; Vernon came shopping with me (in Regent Street, of course, not in Plumstead), we took Aethra to see the lights in the West End, we took her to the theatre. On Christmas Day, I was again aware of the silence and seclusion, of·time standing still. But this time, it made me rather sad.

We gave a party ourselves. Aethra was allowed to stay up late and I bought her a new dress. 'What a lovely child!' everyone said as she handed round mince-pies. With her beauty, her quiet charm, and her rather old-fashioned good manners, she was very unlike the excited brats who are often so out of place at grown-up parties; Laura's inheritance was discernible in her, which for most of Vernon's friends gave an emotional colour to the impression she made. They hadn't seen her since before she went to boarding-school, and there's a big difference between nine years old and nearly twelve, especially with Aethra. In fact, she was the sensation of the evening and attracted the same kind of curiosity that I'd attracted eighteen months ago, when I was first seen with Vernon. By now, the friends had got used to me, I thought

176

wryly. Wryly, or bitterly? It wasn't possible, surely, that I was envious of Aethra? For a little while, I didn't like myself at all.

But when the party was at its height, in that delightful hour between eleven and twelve when a few latecomers are still arriving and nobody has gone yet, I was completely happy. (To be truthful, I must add that Aethra had gone to bed.) I was happy about the smiling faces, the fascinating men and attractive women. I was happy about the flow of good talk, the laughter, the friendly arguments, the gossip and the stories. Our party was a success – how could the Longuehayes' party be anything but a success? I was happy about Vernon, in his true element tonight, surrounded by friends whenever I looked toward him, smiling at me across the room as though neither of us had a care in the world – and really we hadn't, or nothing that could possibly spoil our happiness, it seemed at this moment.

A few days after New Year, Vernon said to me: 'Have you come to a decision about your job? We'll have to make some arrangement.'

I had come to no decision. The question had been constantly in my mind, and yet I'd been unable to deal with it in a logical way, the way that produces a decision. I mumbled that I'd had a lot to think about – the party, and so forth.

Vernon repeated some of the arguments he had used before.

'Yes, I know, I know,' I said. 'The thing is . . . I was proud of getting that job, you see. I've been proud of doing it well. So it's a bit of a wrench.'

'I understand, darling. I'm sorry this situation with Aethra has precipitated a decision. But after all, you'd be giving up the job in the fairly near future in any case, wouldn't you?'

'I would? Why?'

He started to laugh. 'We're going to have a child before I draw my pension, aren't we?'

I mumbled again. One thing at a time, for God's sake, I wanted to say, but didn't.

He went to his study. I sat down and thought hard – about

177

the job, I mean – forcing myself to list the considerations in orderly fashion and weigh their significance. When I did this, the case for going freelance was really quite strong.

Firstly: although I had cause to be grateful to Mrs Baldwin for giving me a start, there was no need to feel myself under an obligation three and a half years later. On balance, I had done more for her than she had for me.

Secondly: I ought to look at going freelance, surely, as a challenge and a new departure. There were risks, there would be difficulties – but was I afraid of leaving the shelter of the agency? At my age, I ought not to flinch from shaping my own future. If it didn't work out, I wasn't going to starve in the meantime and I could ultimately go back to agency work.

Thirdly: it really would be nice to make my own timetable. Work wasn't the whole of life, after all. I was living in Plumstead – that couldn't be helped – and I had voluntarily accepted certain tasks that were also pleasures, such as cooking good meals for Vernon and for our guests. I'd certainly be glad to get out of travelling in the rush hour, for one thing.

Fourthly: it was true – wasn't it? – that I was going to have a child sooner or later. When I was pregnant, and when the child was small, it would be handy to work as a freelance, fitting in appointments as they suited me. If I built up custom well in advance, this period would be nicely provided for. But if I worked at the agency until it happened, it could be a period of complete idleness.

So I was convinced, or I convinced myself. Yet an inner doubt remained, a feeling that I had been won over by the desire to please Vernon and avoid a dispute rather than by the arguments; that something had been put over on me, imposed on me. I struggled to crush this feeling. To cherish a grievance against the man I loved could do nothing but harm.

He was relieved and happy when I told him my decision, and generous into the bargain. 'This has cost you something, my sweetheart, don't imagine I'm unaware of that,' he said. The least I could do was to look on the bright side, and be happy too in his happiness.

Mrs Baldwin, predictably, was not at all pleased. 'I can't say I think you're being wise, Pat,' she told me. 'However, I'm not exactly surprised' – meaning that she'd seen it coming every since I got married. I had half-expected her to offer me a rise if I'd stay, or maybe a part-time arrangement, but she didn't. At one point in our brief interview she gave me a shrewd up-and-down look; I suppose she thought I was pregnant already. In the end, she made a big effort and wished me good luck.

Eileen, over sandwiches and coffee at Angelo's said: 'You don't look all that cheerful, for somebody who's chosen freedom. Not worrying about letting Mrs B down, are you? She'll survive.'

'No, I'm worrying about whether I'll make out.'

'Of course you will.'

'I don't see how, at the moment. I'm not sure where the customers are coming from.'

'Well, it could be slow going for a bit. Still, in your position that's no tragedy, is it?'

I didn't answer. Eileen looked at me sharply and said: 'You don't think you'll give up being a photographer, Pat, will you?'

'What? Where d'you get that idea?'

'OK, don't fly off the handle. But you know, I was a freelance for a few years. It's easy to let things slide when you haven't any external discipline. You think: oh, I won't bother to ring up So-and-so, it's a boring job even if I do get it. Maybe you're not earning a living wage, but if you don't need to, you soon decide that doesn't matter. Work becomes a thing you do when you've got nothing else you'd rather do. And finally, it's just a hobby, and then you aren't a photographer.'

'Thanks for warning me.'

'Oh well, it won't be like that with you, of course. I just hadn't got the energy and the self-discipline. That's why I had to go back to agency work.'

I gave Mrs Baldwin a month's notice, according to

contract. Vernon behaved admirably during this period. He fetched Aethra from school almost every afternoon, except when he was in Norwich, and then he said she'd have to walk home and hope for the best. This was just as well, because I was working hard. I'm not sure whether Mrs Baldwin loaded jobs on to me deliberately, or whether there simply happened to be a lot of work and the fact that I was leaving made no difference in her eyes. The effect was that I hadn't a minute to line up the contracts that I was going to need as a freelance.

The last day came, a Friday of course. I was busy up to the very end, reported back to the office at six o'clock to collect my gear and exchange a final unsentimental handshake with Mrs Baldwin, and went to the pub for farewell drinks with the rest of the staff. By the time I got home – Vernon was on TV – I was just about equal to making a meal for myself and Aethra and going to bed. On Saturday morning we set off, all three of us, for Norwich. There was a rather special party being given by a couple of Vernon's post-grads and we'd decided to spend the weekend in the flat.

On Monday I got up as usual and drove Aethra to school. On the way back, I got behind a car which ambled slowly along and stopped to let a traffic light turn red instead of jumping it. The driver was a woman. I guessed that she'd taken a child to school, the same as I had. No wonder she was ambling. I ambled too. I had no idea how to spend the day. I stopped at a supermarket, which was absolutely empty – for a moment I thought it was closed, never having seen it except on a busy Saturday – and made a long, musing tour of the shelves.

When I got home, Vernon had started work in his study. I read *The Times* and the *Guardian* (we took both) with great thoroughness. The front door startled me. It was Mrs Wall – I hadn't seen her for weeks.

'Nice to take it easy, Mrs Longuehaye, isn't it?' she said.

We had a cup of tea and talked about the miners' strike, which was on at the time. Mrs Wall was strongly for the miners, naturally, but said that things were going to be difficult and advised me to buy candles. Then she said: 'Well, can't sit here all morning', and started to clean the sink. I felt awkward about watching her work, but I couldn't think of anything to do. I went out to buy candles. This involved asking at four shops and filled the rest of the morning.

I made lunch. It was strange lunching at home with Vernon, as though it were Saturday or Sunday, but without Aethra. He ate quickly, his mind evidently on what he was writing, and went back to his study. I sat at the table for a long time, drinking coffee and thinking of nothing in particular.

At last I decided to write to my parents. I had phoned them at Christmas but I hadn't been in touch since, and they didn't yet know that I was giving up my job. The letter became long and chatty, and I nearly forgot to go and fetch Aethra. I did this, and then helped her with her homework (or rather showed an interest, since she didn't require any help). After that Vernon appeared, and the day merged into the evening.

This is what it's like, I said to myself.

But the next day was worse, because Vernon went to Norwich. After Mrs Wall had come and gone, I was alone in the silent house. I told myself that it was an ideal opportunity for planning my future work and making phone calls. But I did nothing. I sat and let the strange new feeling sink into me, the feeling of having no work and no obligations, of being simply a wife − not even that, since my husband was a hundred miles away, but simply a woman. I had worked (if you counted being a schoolgirl and a student) practically all my life; not to work seemed a fundamental change, a change even greater than marriage. Of course, I reminded myself, it wasn't really happening − I would do some work very soon, perhaps even today. But I discovered in myself a curious desire to attempt this other kind of life, like Laura. It occurred to me that I lacked the calmness, perhaps the courage, to be alone; I didn't want to know that much about myself. As the hours passed, it became more and more impossible to do anything, and finally not worth while, because I had to do some shopping, and if I didn't hurry (why should I?) it would soon be time to fetch Aethra.

I decided that I was genuinely tired. That was natural. Except for holidays, I'd been working for three and a half years, and a lot harder than most people. And I didn't feel very well; that was a reaction, no doubt. The upshot was that I did nothing – nothing in the line of being a freelance photographer – all that week. The weather was miserable and it was a luxury to stay in the house. Any sensible person relaxed for a week after leaving a job, I told myself. Vernon agreed.

That break lasted only a week. But, as I look back on it, it seems to set the tone for the year that followed; the year 1972, in which I struggled to be a photographer.

I don't find it easy to describe that year. There was something nebulous and uncertain about it, something that kept slipping between my fingers. In a sense, time didn't matter; if I had nothing to show for a day, or several days, there was nobody to hold me to account (no external discipline, as Eileen put it). In a larger sense, time mattered more than ever before. I was aware of its passing – aware, as I hadn't been until now, of not having an infinite quantity of it. Birthdays, all quite early in the year, stand out in my memory. Vernon was fifty-one. Aethra was twelve. I was twenty-five.

It's a bit of a landmark, twenty-five. It isn't quite the beginning of middle age, but it's the end of being really young. And I had several reasons for feeling middle-aged. I lived in a world of the mature and established; all my friends, except Dido, were years older than me. I lost touch, gradually but surely, with Stella and her crowd. I had a child of twelve. She wasn't my own child, but the mothers whom I got to know were women in their thirties or forties, and I was involved with adolescent problems and O-level choices, not with nursery schools and toys. Meanwhile, my parents were moving into the older generation. They saw themselves as grandparents – which they were; I now had four nephews or nieces – rather than parents. My younger brother and my sister got married during this year, which enabled my parents to feel that all their children were disposed of.

The confusing thing was that, just at this time, I was trying to make a start again. I was at square one, exactly as I'd been when I arrived in London and was on probation with Mrs Baldwin. The difference was that I had no job. I was on my own. And things didn't go my way.

For quite a long time, I had done practically no work except for the agency. I had lost my personal contacts, of which I'd had a fair number during my first year in London. I racked my brains to remember people I could ring up, without much result. I felt awkward about offering my services to the steady customers – advertising agencies, fashion houses, good cause campaigns – who knew me as one of Mrs Baldwin's staff. It seemed like doing the dirty on her; I understood now how she felt about employees who set up on their own. Eventually, I overcame my scruples and made the phone calls, adopting a brightly innocent tone: 'This is Pat Bell. I hope you remember me, I used to work for Mrs Baldwin. Well, I'm working independently now, and I thought perhaps . . .' I soon found that most of these outfits preferred to deal with an agency. It was more reliable; they could be sure of getting a photographer regardless of illness or holidays; and probably they were afraid of offending Mrs Baldwin by employing a freelance, especially one who had walked out on her. So I got very little work that was at all exciting, and had to make do mostly with portraits, kids, dogs, and that kind of caper. Even so, I was never busy enough. After years of incessant bustle, I grew acquainted with the strange, uncomfortable, worrying feeling of not having enough to do.

I got some help from friends – from Eileen and other photographers I knew, from Gabrielle who recommended me to actors and actresses, and from Dido who had useful contacts in showbiz. But I found it humiliating to exploit my friends and didn't do it so much as I might have. And they –

183

especially the photographers – weren't greatly inclined to put themselves out to help someone who was married to Vernon Longuehaye and clearly wasn't in dire need. I sensed a general assumption that I was 'keeping up' photography while being primarily a wife; that it was an 'interest' for me, rather than being my profession. Other wives started to invite me to coffee mornings. 'So much easier now you've stopped being a wage-slave, dear.'

Time was a major difficulty. I had time on my hands – too bloody much of it – but there were also large slabs of time when I wasn't available for work. As I'd foreseen, it was soon taken for granted that fetching Aethra from school was my chore. Vernon did it occasionally when I made a special request, but as a concession; he said that it interrupted the flow of his work, which by degrees became far more important than my work. So it was pretty hard for me to make any afternoon appointments. Since I was also driving Aethra to school, my working day was ridiculously short. Also, Vernon didn't like me to do evening jobs such as banquets and dances. He had grumbled about them even when I was still at the agency, and now assumed that they were a thing of the past, though in fact I needed them more than before. When I was offered an evening job, it always seemed to be a date when we were going out to dinner or having guests. Finally, Vernon didn't like me to work at weekends. He seldom went walking nowadays, and on Sundays we went for some kind of outing with Aethra.

When you have a job, you can stick more or less to normal working hours. When you're a freelance, the only way to make a go of it is to be prepared to work whenever you're needed – often at short notice, too. Otherwise, the customers soon lose interest. It's a contracting spiral; the less work you do, the less you get. I hadn't fully grasped this before I left the agency. Vernon was never willing to grasp it.

Then there was the irritating problem of the phone. When Vernon was in Norwich and I was out, I couldn't be reached. I thought of having an answering service, but quite honestly I wasn't out often enough to justify the expense. Still, whenever I left the house empty I was tormented by the thought that I was missing some juicy commission. I knew that people who couldn't get me on the phone took their business elsewhere; it was another contracting spiral. Vernon said that if someone really wants you, he'll ring again. This may have been true for him – it wasn't for me.

On the other hand, things were distinctly awkward when we were both at home. The phone seemed determined to play tricks on us; if he picked up the extension in his study it was sure to be a call for me, and if I picked up the other phone it was sure to be for him. Sometimes we let it go on ringing, each expecting the other to answer it.

When I was out and he was at home, it was worst of all. Prospective customers who had my number didn't realize that it was someone else's too – didn't, as a rule, know that I was married. They used to say briskly: 'Can I talk to Pat?' or 'Is Miss Bell there, please?' Vernon had never liked to think of me as Pat, certainly not as Miss Bell. Sometimes, surprised at hearing a male voice the caller asked: 'Who am I talking to, please?' On being told: 'This is Vernon Longuehaye', he naturally said: 'Sorry, wrong number.'

Vernon didn't exactly refuse to take messages for me, but he didn't help much. He limited himself to saying that I'd be in at half past four, or at the most noting a number. If the customer started to say: 'Could you tell her that we'll need her tomorrow at twelve-thirty, and the address is . . .', Vernon drew the line. 'I'll ask her to phone you,' he said firmly. This kind of thing, naturally, did me no good.

I can remember dashing into the house, Aethra in my wake, opening the door of the study (Vernon didn't like this either) and asking: 'Did anybody ring for me, darling?'

'Yes, someone did. He'll ring again.'

'Who was it?'

'He didn't give his name.'

'Didn't you find out?'

'I did not find out. It should be clear by now, Patricia, that

185

I've never asked you to be my secretary and I don't regard myself as yours.'

'You might have just . . .'

'Please, Patricia, I'm trying to work.'

By the summer – which is supposed to be the harvest-time for photographers – I was uneasily aware that I wasn't making the grade. The obvious yardstick of failure was financial. This was artificial in a way, because I'd been paying my salary cheques into our joint account since we got married, and I couldn't have said how much of the family budget they covered. But the fact that I was earning a proper wage had continued to be important to me. My freelance earnings for the month, after deducting expenses for processing and so forth which I now had to meet, usually came to fifty or sixty pounds. The thought that I couldn't have lived on them was depressing.

Failure was hard to face. I had always, so far, succeeded in my chosen career. I'd been a good student, I'd landed a job easily, and I'd done the job well. Once I'd made the decision to go freelance, I soon made myself believe that it would pan out, partly because of my natural self-confidence and partly because Vernon said so. Besides, I knew of other photographers who had made the switch and brought it off. I hadn't allowed for the care with which they had prepared the ground.

So my reaction to failure was to evade facing it. At the most, I admitted to disappointment. There couldn't, in any case, be a precise moment at which it was necessary to say 'This is a failure' – unless I found myself with no work at all, which didn't happen, or ran out of money, and I was cushioned against that. I could find all sorts of plausible excuses. I was handicapped by being tied down in the afternoons, but the childish teasing of Aethra was only a phase and I would get her to walk home in the next school year. It took more time than I'd bargained for to build up a clientele. Probably most freelances went through a period when they didn't break even; they dipped into savings, or were helped by their parents, so what was wrong with my depending on my husband? The grim thought of the contracting spiral came to mind in my gloomier moments, but I put it aside.

I had some low times, all the same. I used to wander about the house – from the living-room to the music-room, from the music-room to the kitchen – bewildered by idleness. I envied Vernon, contentedly busy in his study. I longed for the phone to ring, but I expected disappointment even from this; it would probably be someone wanting Vernon to write a review, or a friend asking us to dinner. (Phone calls from friends, usually prolonged and chatty, had become a reproach instead of a pleasure, because they implied that I must be at home with time to spare.) Questions stabbed at me: what am I doing here? What's happening to me?

Then I thought: there are lots of ways to fill the time if I haven't got a job today. I could have another go at *Relational Analysis,* tackling it like a student this time and making notes so that I wouldn't forget what I'd read. I could decorate the house; it hadn't been done for five years and looked a bit tatty in places, and it would be fun to make it more my own. I could do something creative with the garden. But no, I thought; this was what Eileen had warned me of, allowing my profession to become a mere hobby. I'm a working girl, I'm a photographer, I'm Pat Bell.

So, on some of these empty days, I took a camera and wandered about London, taking pictures as though I were in some foreign city. But I hadn't much idea what the pictures were for. I could have submitted them to various papers, but that meant putting myself on a par with amateurs – other amateurs, ought I to say? – and I knew that I'd feel dreadful if they were rejected. I decided after a while that this activity was pointless. Anyway, I might be missing phone calls. So I gave it up.

Time slid by: days, weeks, months. We didn't see much of Cressida, who was doubtless quite happy with Jane. However, John came and stayed for a fortnight when he returned from Iran. He soon grasped how I was placed, and helped as much as he could by volunteering to fetch Aethra from school.

I could talk to John, in some ways, more easily than to Vernon; this made me feel guilty, but it was a fact. Once – Vernon was on the box, and we went for a drink at the local, a rare pleasure for me – he made me laugh by telling me his own troubles. He had got involved in an affair with a Persian princess, which turned out to be more than he'd bargained for.

'She wanted to run away with me,' he said, making a wry face. 'I mean, it wasn't at all what I had in mind. When it was time for me to come home, she said it was just *au revoir*. She insisted on seeing me off at the airport. I didn't like the sound of that. So I changed my ticket and got out on a slow plane to Istanbul.'

'She must have been wild.'

'I don't feel safe even now,' John said, looking warily round the Prince Albert. 'Money means nothing to those women, you know. They go to Paris for a day's shopping.'

'Was she good in bed?' I asked.

'Oh yes, when I could get her there. She preferred watching blue movies.'

I burst out laughing; John's honest, puzzled face was a study.

'I shall have to get married,' he said. 'It's the only solution to my problems.'

Something made me say: 'Married people can have problems.'

He looked at me attentively, seriously.

'There's nothing really wrong,' I said quickly. 'I shouldn't have given up my job. I want to love Vernon, not to depend on him. As things are now, it isn't so easy to keep my end up.'

'You must have known that keeping your end up would require a bit of effort.'

'I suppose so. I didn't think about it. I was in love – I mean, I am.'

'I've never been in love,' John said humbly.

'That must simplify life.'

188

He got up to buy another round.

'What I don't figure,' I began again, 'is why he wanted to marry me. No, I'm not being modest. I mean, why he wanted to marry someone who would wish to keep her end up.'

'He was in love too.'

'Yes, yes, I believe that. But still . . .'

John considered the question.

'I should say that you offered him a challenge. Being married to Laura was too easy. Does that make sense?'

'It makes sense. I'm not sure exactly where it leaves me.'

John smiled, and took this as the end of the conversation. 'Aethra seems to be getting along very nicely,' he remarked. I wondered later why, despite his real sympathy and the understanding we had established, he chose to switch off at a certain point. Perhaps he was afraid of emotional depths. Perhaps, I thought sadly, he didn't like discontented women.

Was I a discontented woman, as distinct from a dissatisfied photographer? I didn't think so. Being married to Vernon, as a great constant factor in my life, still made me happy. He was very sweet to me, very tender and loving. I always found pleasure in going to bed with him – the whole process, walking upstairs and undressing and lying down together – whether we made love or not. We didn't make love so often as in our first year, but even that seemed right, seemed to show that we were rich in time. We lay in bed with one small light on and caressed each other; and these caresses, which many times helped us to sink gently into sleep, were the unfailing assurance of what we meant to each other. When we did make love, I was satisfied in far more than a physical sense – renewed in happiness, and deeply contented.

Even my enforced idleness had compensating pleasures – the pleasures of being with Vernon. I looked forward every day to six o'clock, when he stopped work. He would give me a kiss, give Aethra a kiss, glance at her homework, settle down with a glass of sherry, and pour out all the talk – all the ideas, all the good phrases – that he had been obliged to keep to himself all day and was now eager to share with me. I lay

189

back and enjoyed it, a suitable phrase since Vernon's way of talking to me was always a kind of love-making. There had been nothing like this when I had my job, when I dashed into the house all rushed and flustered, sweating in summer and shivering in winter, just in time to cook dinner or else to change and go out again.

So I was happy far more often than not. Yet I was uncertain and suspicious, distrusting my own happiness. Was I being lulled into accepting my failure as a photographer? Was happiness — was love itself — a trap that Vernon had set for me?

Soon after I gave up my job, he started talking again about having a child. I saw that, to his mind, an obstacle had been removed. This was enough to arouse my suspicions. It meant, surely, that his arguments about my succeeding as a freelance photographer were no more than a stratagem. It wasn't for my sake, to give me 'control over my life', that he had wanted me to quit the job; it was to make me a mother — Aethra's mother, and the mother of this baby, so clearly envisaged that I could almost see the proud smile with which Vernon would greet it.

'I'm trying to make out as a freelance,' I said. 'I really am — I'm serious about it. You've got to let me do it. Once I know I can, things will be different.'

That settled it, on the external or logical level. But of course this wasn't the only level. I could feel Vernon's longing when he made love to me. My response to him began to seem false, as if I were simulating; I was denying him what he really wanted. Because I loved him, this was a torment to me. It was his love for me — or, as he said, one dimension of it — that I was rejecting. Besides, what I was denying him was something that a deep urge within me wanted too — as a woman, as a woman in love and settled with her man.

I was afraid of my happiness for this reason too, afraid of Vernon's strength and persistence and indeed his love. He had made me do everything he wanted — be his mistress, be his wife, make a home for Aethra, give up my job — and surely he'd soon make me do this as well. I wondered what was in his mind when he asked me how my work was going. Was he waiting for me to reach a definable measure of success? Or waiting for me to resign myself to failure?

Dido became pregnant. Michael hadn't been at all keen on it; it was something she wanted for herself.

'Was it an accident?' I asked.

'Sort of.' She grinned. 'I forgot my pills when we went on holiday. I really did forget them. I always forget something, it was my bikini last time. Well, you can't buy them in Spain, can you? And it wouldn't be much of a holiday ... well, would it? So I didn't say anything.'

'And are you glad now?'

'Oh, sure. The old instincts are taking over.'

So if it was right for Dido, who wasn't married and whose man hadn't wanted a baby, why wasn't it right for me?

Dido at once flung herself into this new enthusiasm – buying baby-clothes, learning exercises, talking endlessly about names – as if the kid were to be born next week. She had prided herself on her twenty-one-inch waist; now she prided herself on thickening. 'D'you think it shows yet?' she asked me hopefully. Except for its sex, the baby was already a real person. On the basis of some complicated theory, she was convinced that it would be jet-black. 'That'll shake the old cow,' she remarked cheerfully – the old cow being Michael's mother, who made occasional constrained visits.

And so my own baby, who didn't exist, began to be a person too. I could see him as dark-haired, lively, a bit of a handful, very precocious of course. I thought of the baby as a boy because I was sure that Vernon wanted a boy. He had never exactly had a son, since John had been brought up elsewhere and wasn't essentially a true Longuehaye – lacking the Longuehaye distinction, the Longuehaye ambition,

It came to this, then: not only was I denying Vernon his wish, I was also denying this child – my child, our child – the right to life. I couldn't have felt worse if I'd had an abortion.

August rolled around. Vernon took it for granted, now that

I had no job, that we were going to stay a whole month at the villa. I was sure that I'd be bored out of my mind, but I didn't feel equal to arguing. We went by car this time, because Vernon had the idea that it would be interesting for Aethra, and good for her French, to spend a little time in France before coming home. I didn't argue about this either. I could fly back and let Vernon do the trip with Aethra, I thought.

Still not pregnant after two years of marriage, I was quite scared of confronting Maria-Grazia. It turned out, however, that she was at last married to her young man – and pregnant, needless to say. The new lady's maid was a sharp-faced, lively girl, who also came from the south but had put traditional ideas resolutely behind her. She would never marry an Italian, she told me. She was keen to go to England and asked me incessantly about possible jobs. She also noticed my pills and questioned me about them – did they really work, didn't they make you ill, did my husband know about them? Italian men hate a girl to use anything, she remarked.

I lazed in the sun, swam, ate huge meals and fell asleep after them, read thrillers, took pictures in a desultory way. I wasn't so very bored, after all. I was surrendering at last to the ease and luxury of the place. Something seemed to have left me: my energy, or my professional conscience, or my capacity for impatience. I said nothing about flying home, and went with Vernon and Aethra on a rambling tour of France – over to the Dordogne, where we called in to see friends who had houses there, up to the chateau country, and then a week in Paris. With his batteries recharged by the month at the villa, Vernon threw himself into tourism with considerable zest. He always knew more than the guides, and instructing Aethra in history and architecture was distinctly up his street. I chickened out of some of the chateaux and cathedrals. I was quite content ambling round the streets, or just sitting at a café.

We got home to find a pressing invitation to attend my sister's wedding. As I've said already, this was a major event in the Bell family, enabling my parents to sit back with all five of their children disposed of – the youngest of my three brothers had been married in the spring. Not having a job, I couldn't very well refuse to go, and Vernon rather unexpectedly said he would go too. Aethra had started school, but it was easy to arrange for her to stay with a friend's family.

My sister was marrying an Irishman and the wedding was to be in Dublin, a better scene for festivities than the suffering North. The celebrations lasted about a week, during which nobody was ever strictly sober and I was even less in touch with the real world than I'd been in Italy. Vernon, naturally, was a huge success; a wit and raconteur is the top thing to be in Dublin, and he was certainly that. In the end, a large delegation from the Republic's academic and literary circles accompanied him to the airport and he was barely able to foil a plot to detain him in the bar until his plane had left.

I stayed on. It was argued cogently that, since I was here, I must spend some time with my parents. Then I could go on to Belfast and stay with my brother, as I had barely met his wife. 'You must come, Pat, you haven't got a job now ...' All right, I said.

So I was 'home' again; as all daughters know, your mother will always call it home. And in a dream-like way it did feel like home – my old room, and my place round the fire, and the bit of the garden known as Pat's patch. My mother fussed over me, saying that I looked tired. I didn't tell her how little work I was doing, and that what she noticed was the lassitude of idleness.

Then I went to Belfast. I expected to find it sheer hell, was puzzled when I didn't, and couldn't bring myself to leave until I'd figured it out. My brother lived in a comfortable Protestant suburb where you never heard a shot or a bomb, but I wandered about the city revisiting my old haunts, and I'm sorry if this is a callous thing to say, but I found it somewhat improved. Mrs Lauchlan's house had been damaged and was boarded up, I was glad to see. Soldiers were everywhere, all looking years younger than me, some of them rather what I would have fancied when I was eighteen. The

193

barbed wire, the warning notices, and the rapidly gathering little crowds lent an air of significance to what had in the past been a place where nothing would ever happen, or matter much if it did. Exciting it was not, but the newspaper word 'tragic' seemed to fit and conferred a certain dignity. It suited my mood; I mooched about, feeling that nothing could be demanded of me in such an environment. I had no work to do, and somehow it never occurred to me to take photographs, though I suppose I was missing fascinating opportunities all the time. As in Italy, as in Dublin, as at my old home, I lost track of time. I was recalled to reality by Vernon's voice on the phone, asking – absurdly, it seemed to me – whether I was all right.

He met me at the airport. As we crossed London – and you really do cross London from Heathrow to Plumstead – I was aware of the excitement that always sets me tingling when I return to my chosen city. Yet I was contemplating the excitement, not experiencing it. Eight million people were working, earning, making plans, chasing after one another – but not me. I had done no work for more than two months, and it had made no difference to London.

The gate closed, then the door closed, admitting me to the beauty and stillness of the Manor House. Vernon went off to fetch Aethra. There were no letters for me. No one was waiting for me. No one needed me. I sat on the bed, knowing that I ought to unpack, but not wanting to. I reminded myself that I was happy – I was in my home again, back with my man. And this happiness weighed on me like a burden.

The following day, I pulled myself together and made some phone calls. I landed a few jobs, just enough to raise my hopes. But, as time passed, I saw that the spiral had contracted again. Vernon no longer asked me about my work, and looked surprised when I went out with my camera-bag – understandably, for it didn't often happen. Otherwise, I was back in the routine of running the house, chauffeuring Aethra (I had never taken a stand about making her walk home), seeing friends . . . and waiting, waiting, waiting.

194

I saw Dido several times; she looked splendidly pregnant. Gabrielle wasn't working now and used to drop in unexpectedly, sometimes in the daytime, sometimes ('to cheer you up, dear') in the evening when Vernon was in Norwich. We drank a fair amount on these occasions. I had never been much of a one for getting sloshed except at the odd party, but there was something beguiling about this business of imbibing in my own home and in old clothes while swapping yarns with a friend. However, it was rather frightening too.

Leaves fell in the garden and I swept them meticulously into little heaps. The weather was calm and golden for weeks; then it broke up into gales and rain. Autumn is a sad time when things are going badly.

Vernon made efforts to occupy my time in 'interesting' ways. I went with him to long, talkative lunches of the kind that I hadn't attended before: lunches with publishers or academic luminaries, the intellectual equivalent of business lunches. Twice, leaving Aethra with her friend's parents, I went to Norwich with Vernon. I might be missing phone calls, I knew. But what the hell – most likely there wouldn't be any.

I'm not sure whether anyone else noticed that I wasn't perfectly contented. It's natural for me to look cheerful when I see my friends. Gabrielle, from her own way of living, took it for granted that you worked for a while and then didn't work for a while. Dido was absorbed in her baby. There was no one else, although I had dozens of friends, to whom I was at all close.

One person who did notice was Mrs Wall. 'Not out working today?' she would ask when she arrived at the house. I made excuses, but they became increasingly hollow, so in the end I told her frankly that it was tough being a freelance and things weren't going well for me.

'That's bad,' she said in her forthright way. 'It don't suit you hanging round the house, I can see that. All right for the Duchess, it was, but it's not all right for you. Couldn't you find something else, like working in an office? Part-time, perhaps.'

I had thought of this, but it meant the final abandonment of my profession. Mrs Wall could see that point. I was grateful that she understood my problem, instead of assuming that I was glad to be a lady of leisure. All the same, now that I had explained things to her there was no more to say, and it became awkward to admit that I was having another empty day. I got into the habit of sneaking out – to the shops, for a walk, anywhere – when Mrs Wall was due. I missed phone calls . . . but what the hell.

Then an awful thing happened: a job was actually cancelled. I had been looking forward to it very much. The job itself – taking rehearsal pictures of a distinguished guest conductor at Covent Garden – would have been quite a high spot even in my busiest days, and it followed a long bad spell. I was supposed to be there at twelve o'clock, and I was just checking my cameras to go out, a little before eleven, when a secretary rang to say that the arrangements had been altered. 'We'll be in touch with you, Miss Bell.' I suspected at once that they'd ditched me to use someone else. Either I was right, or I was getting paranoid. I couldn't decide which was worse.

It was a wet, miserable November day. I stood by the window, watching raindrops drip from the trees, feeling like a child who has been stopped from going to a party as a punishment – an unjust punishment. I tried to read a book, but the words made no sense. I poured myself a big Scotch, but it tasted foul and scared me, so I emptied it into a flower-pot.

Vernon came out of his study at one o'clock. 'Hullo,' he said, 'I thought you were going to be out.'

I explained.

'Oh, that's a pity. Still, it's a beastly day for getting about London. Have you made lunch?'

'I don't want any lunch.'

'Well, I do, my dear.'

I stared at him across the room.

'In that case you'd better make your own fucking lunch,

hadn't you?'

He stared back. We both knew that it was a terrible moment. I had never spoken to him, nor he to me, like this before. Besides, he hated what he called ugly language.

'All right,' he said, and went into the kitchen. I could hear him doing something, frying eggs probably, and then the scrape of a chair as he sat down to eat. I poured myself another Scotch, and drank it this time.

When he came back — I knew that he would come back, and was strangely frightened of it — he said: 'Darling, I'm very sorry you've had a disappointment. But you mustn't make a tragedy of it.'

'It isn't just this,' I said dully.

'I realize that. We must talk about it, Patricia. Sit down.'

'Aren't you busy?'

'You're more important.'

I sat down obediently, and he sat down too.

'I've said to you before that work isn't the whole of life. I know that it has, for various reasons, bulked rather large in your life. You've had — I observed this when I first met you — a certain conception of yourself: a girl with a job, capable, always busy, coming up to scratch, meeting requirements. That these requirements were imposed on you by others, you perhaps weren't sufficently aware.' (This Henry James style grew on Vernon when he delivered a set-piece.) 'Be that as it may, to fulfil your conception of yourself was an achievement. But must that achievement be constantly repeated? Must it be your limit? There is something larger, my dear. You're more than a girl with a job; you are a woman.'

'And what should be my conception of myself as a woman? Or should I ask, what's your conception?'

Vernon smiled. 'Don't set that simple trap for me, Patricia. You know I don't mean a woman as opposed to a man. I mean a human being — a complete person.'

'But that's just what I'm trying to be.'

'You won't do it by driving yourself to despair because you haven't gone out to take photographs.'

'What's wrong with taking photographs?' I demanded, bristling.

'Nothing, as a job. I'll say more – as a means that you chose to establish yourself. But that purpose has been served. If you try to centre your life on this particular skill, then you load more on to it than it will bear. It can't be the full expression of yourself. After all, we're not speaking of one of the creative arts.'

I jumped up, furious.

'That's what you've always thought about photography, isn't it? Just what I'd expect from a bloody intellectual snob.'

'If you'll try not to be unnecessarily defensive, Patricia, I'll explain the distinction I'm making.'

So we got into the old, old argument about whether photography is an art. The maddening thing was that Vernon was in command of my weapons. He knew all about photographic insights into light and shape, and the influence of photography on painting, and Monet and so forth, and he brought all this out just a jump ahead of me. But it all went to show – 'logically' – that art has a debt to photography, not that they are the same. His distinction, if I got it right, was that photography is descriptive and at most exploratory, while art is both of these and creative too. But as a matter of fact I didn't, and couldn't, listen to what he said as an exposition. It was an attack on me – on what I do and what I am. It didn't matter, in this showdown, whether photography is an art or a skill or a profession (what was philosophy, come to that?); it was an essential of my life, and the best I had in me, and to hear it dissected and denigrated by the man I loved was unbearable. But I couldn't say this, I couldn't give any ground, I couldn't afford to confirm my inferiority by appealing to him on a personal instead of an objective level. So I went on insisting that photography is an art, and this did me no good either, for I wasn't doing much more than exclaiming: 'It is . . . I know it is . . . It bloody well is.' The more confused and bothered I got, the more easily he retained his effortless calm. And I hated him, I really hated him then, I

198

wanted to scream and swear at him, because it was so easy to be Vernon Longuehaye and so wretchedly difficult to be Pat Bell. But I hated hating him – I still loved him. Anyway, if I did scream and swear, that would crown his victory. In the end I started to cry, and he kissed me and consoled me, which crowned his victory too.

When you've had one scene like this, you're bound to have more. The next, pretty soon afterwards, was even nearer to the bone. For one thing, it was over the most intimate and emotional of questions – the child he wanted. For another thing, we were in bed. Quarrels in bed – arguing, hurting each other, drawing apart, yet held together all the time by the touch and the yearning of the body – are the most desolating of all.

'But, my darling,' he said (there's no point in recording this scene from the beginning), 'all I want, all I could possibly want, is your happiness.'

I grunted derisively at this. 'I should think I ought to know whether having a baby would make me happy. I'm the one who has to do it, not you.'

'Don't speak of it as an ordeal, please. We can leave that attitude to the medieval Church. It's an experience which is denied to a man. Patricia, I see you searching for something – something that's missing in your life. You've already had success in your work, and a man's devoted love, and sexual satisfaction. As a woman, only one thing is ahead of you.'

'I see. Last time you were on at me, I was a human being. A complete person, quote unquote. Now I'm just a woman. Or just a cunt, is that right?'

'My dearest, why must you say things like that? Is it to hurt me? At the lowest level, if I thought of you only in that way I shouldn't be urging something that will deprive me of making love to you for a time.'

'You'll survive. But that's typical, isn't it – deprive you? What about me? Don't you think I like making love?'

Vernon was silent for a little while. Then he said: 'When I asked you to marry me, I had to persuade you that there was a

199

difference between being my mistress and being my wife. Am I to take it that, after two years, you'd still prefer to be a mistress?'

'I don't know. It might have been better. You didn't nag at me then.'

'Is that what it means to you – all my concern for you – only nagging?'

'Oh, you're always just concerned for me, aren't you?' I yelled. 'It's all for my own good, everything you want. You must think I'm fucking stupid. But I know why you want me to have a baby. I'll be tied down then, won't I? Tied down for ever. And that's what you're really after, so don't kid yourself I haven't guessed.'

He said nothing for a long time, or it seemed very long. It was another terrible moment, but far more terrible. Something irrevocable and unforgettable had happened.

At last he said: 'That was very cruel, Patricia.'

I wept, and he held me in his arms, and we made it up after a fashion. But, although I said I was sorry for hurting him, I didn't say I was sorry for what I'd said – a distinction that doubtless wasn't lost on him. For it was the truth; at least, it was the truth for me, though a truth which he couldn't accept. From now on there would always be my truth and his truth, and a great divide between them. So we didn't really make it up at all.

After this, we were civil to each other. It sounds awful, and it was. We were considerate and courteous, and stopped snapping about minor things like phone messages, and avoided the least risk of hurting each other – which meant that we avoided talking about the things that mattered. At Christmas we went to lots of parties, almost as if we were afraid of staying at home. We were at our best, in fact, in other people's houses. We put on a tremendous performance. People were always delighted to see Vernon and Pat. 'That's really worked out well, hasn't it?' I could imagine them saying after we went home.

Had it worked out, in its essentials, or not? I don't think, at this time, I asked myself whether there was anything seriously wrong with my marriage. Three things held me back from facing the question. One was pride – I still thought of myself as able to manage my life, so it was unreasonable that I could be incapable of making a successful marriage. Another was fear – it couldn't be true that I was failing on every front. And above all, love. I was in love with Vernon as deeply as ever; I had to cling to that.

We were going through a sticky patch, I told myself. This couldn't very well be denied. Nothing was spontaneous any longer, nothing was free from care and effort. The obvious symptom was that we ran into sex problems.

I had accepted from the start – or at least from the time when I found out Vernon's real age – that I wasn't going to get screwed so often as I could ideally have wished. I hadn't minded much; there was pleasure in the mere contact of our bodies, in the simplest reminder of love. Anyway, he made it as often as most middle-aged intellectuals, according to Dido who had sampled them extensively. But from the time of our first quarrels, the intervals became far longer. And this did distress me. I have my needs, as this narrative has doubtless made clear, and they were sharpened by my anxieties and my desire for reassurance. It wouldn't have been so bad if Vernon had simply cut down on the fucking, but quite often I was also left without our usual kissing and fondling; he read a book until I gave up hope, or just gave me a routine peck on the cheek and went to sleep. I didn't know whether this was meant as a reproof, or whether he was afraid of arousing expectations that he was unable (unable? unwilling?) to fulfil. I slept badly, which was a new thing for me. Miserable questions tormented me as I lay awake, sometimes furtively touching myself off when I was sure that he was fast asleep. Vernon still loved me, surely, or didn't he? Had I hurt him so much by refusing to have a child that he couldn't feel any desire for me?

We had never talked much about what the books call the physical side of love. In Vernon, a deep-rooted puritanism was reinforced by an aesthetic revulsion against treating sex as a technique; in his good moods, he could be derisively amusing about people who made love with a set of instructions on the pillow. Now, we could talk about it less than ever.

One night – about three in the morning, I think – I woke him up. I had only just woken up myself, probably from a sexual dream. I flung myself on him with a desperation that truly came from love, but must have seemed like the crudest kind of lust. 'I want you, I want you!' I said – or shouted, I don't know.

'I was asleep, Patricia,' he said, peering up at me anxiously.

'I want you,' I repeated, and I started to work on him, but without any effect. I was astride him, a position which (I remembered too late) he had never much liked.

'Patricia,' he said in a deliberate, lecturing tone, 'this is not how we behave.'

We stared at each other. We were close to hatred then, if ever we were.

'Lie down and put the blankets back, please,' he said.

'Why, are you cold?'

'Yes.'

I felt cold too, all of a sudden. The heating had switched itself off, and it was a freezing night in February – just after his fifty-second birthday, as a matter of fact. I did as I was told.

'I'm sorry,' he said grudgingly.

'No, I'm sorry. I went a bit crazy.'

He tried to laugh. 'You could have made your approach rather more persuasive, I think.'

'Vernon, d'you know how long it is since you've made love to me?'

'I'm sure you're ready to give me that information.'

'Oh, never mind. What I mean is . . . what's happening to us? What's gone wrong?'

He was silent for so long that I almost wondered if he'd fallen asleep again. Then he said: 'I'm not a young man.' The words seemed to have been torn from him; I felt that he wouldn't forgive me for making him say them.

'My darling,' I said, cuddling close to him, 'it doesn't matter, it doesn't matter. I won't be like this again. Nothing matters, except I love you.'

His body remained unyielding.

'You're going through a difficult phase,' he said. 'I've told you why it is. If I haven't convinced you, I can't help it. Meanwhile, I admit my physical limitations. I was never a stallion, if you want to know, at any age. I daresay I compare badly with some men whom you could call to mind.'

'Don't talk like that, Vernon, please.'

'Very well, we'll say no more about this. And we'll make love soon, I promise you – but like man and wife, not like a couple of drunks at a wife-swapping party.'

The next night, we did make love – tenderly, as in our best times, and as successfully as could be wished. Things had changed, all the same. It became usual for me to take the initiative and arouse him. I was pretty good at it, having learned the tricks with Hugh, who was usually the sexual equivalent of two whiskies below par. But I knew that Vernon resented it. It offended his masculinity, it infringed his freedom, and it reminded him of his age. I simply couldn't see what else I could do.

It seemed to me, indeed, that Vernon really was getting older. He still did his exercises, so he kept his admirable figure, but he had given up the tennis and the Sunday walks. At the fag-end of winter, he went down with a bad attack of flu and took weeks to get over it – weeks of sexual abstinence, therefore. Sometimes when he was reading, or relaxing with his sherry after his day's work – which seemed to take more out of him than formerly – I took a careful look at him and thought sadly that he had changed. He didn't look old, far from that, but he no longer looked younger than his real age.

Coaxing him into making love was bad enough. Worse still were the times when he was forced to say: 'I'm sorry, darling, but it's no good tonight.' We tried to make a joke of it, but

203

that was never easy.

There was one night when I'd got myself into quite a lather and felt badly let down. So I said: 'How about trying a spot of oral?'

'What?'

'Oral. You know. I'll suck you off.'

He gave me a cold, angry look.

'That has never been among my habits,' he said.

I saw that I had reminded him of my life before we were married, of other men. I should have thought of that. There was so much now that I had to think of, so little scope for spontaneity.

I began to ask myself in sheer bewilderment: where had our happiness gone? It didn't seem possible that it had seeped away, like sand in an hour-glass, in so short a time. Everybody else was perfectly happy, so far as I could see. Dido had her baby; it was an adorable little girl, actually a bit darker than she was. Arnold had a sabbatical from the BBC and Gabrielle was making plans for a world tour – 'If we don't do it now we never shall.' Out of the dozens of people we knew, presumably there were some who were going through a rough time for one reason or another, but no signs disturbed the shimmering surface of life among the successful and fortunate of London. I felt irrationally that everything was lovely for everybody except me – which meant that it must be my fault.

Things were pretty damn good, anyhow, for one person at the Manor House – Aethra. She was top of her form in practically every subject and her only complaint was that you couldn't get moved up ahead of your age at a comprehensive. She had time for reading outside her school work (like Vernon, she read very fast). She had no use for anything that could remotely be described as a children's book, and ranged avidly round Vernon's books and the public library, except that she didn't care much for novels and not at all for poetry; imagination, I think was one faculty that didn't develop in Aethra. Vernon got her going on philosophy, starting with

Plato, and it gave her no trouble at all.

Like most men of his type, Vernon was a bit awkward and detached in dealing with children, but excellent with young people anywhere from Aethra's age — thirteen now — to students. (I mean, of course, young people who are keener on books than on pop or football.) Aethra's company was a joy to him. It made a change fom mine, I thought bitterly. They spent hours in long discussions, mostly based on books which she was reading and which I had read years ago and forgotten, or hadn't read at all. I sat silent or retreated to the kitchen. Somebody, after all, had to get dinner and do the washing-up. Vernon seldom cooked nowadays. Aethra helped in the house dutifully when she was asked, but didn't volunteer, and I found it simpler on the whole to do things myself.

I realized that I had no legitimate grievance, since it had been laid down all along that Aethra was Vernon's child and not mine. But, when so many other things were going wrong for me, I was hurt by the bond between them and by my exclusion. What made it more unfair was that, in other ways, I was in fact a Mum for Aethra. I drove her to and from school, I fed her, I kept her clothes in repair. Above this level, she hadn't much use for me; she had dropped her interest in photography and didn't expect me to know about books. She had a firm idea, presumably derived from Laura's role in the family, of the respective spheres of Mum and Dad — intelligent discussion was emphatically Dad's. I'm sure she never thought of how I felt about this. There was quite a streak of ruthlessness in sensitive little Aethra.

She still wasn't popular at school, I imagine, but this no longer bothered her at all. She had a confident vision of her future, she had her network of clever middle-class friends, and now she had Simon. Simon was fifteen, just right for Aethra. His father was an architect, his mother a buyer for a West End store; they were typical enough of the A-stream parents, and it was at their home that Aethra stayed when Vernon and I were away. Aethra was well aware that she had eclipsed numerous rivals by securing Simon as her boy-friend, while also assuming that a boy-friend of his calibre was her rightful due. He rated high in both looks and intelligence, and was gifted with a style of mordant wit which equipped him to put down most of the teachers without actually being insolent. Out of uniform, he looked almost like a student and was seldom challenged when he went into a pub or saw an X film. Simon was useful to Aethra in a number of ways. He took her to parties where everyone else was fifteen or more and the conversation was on what she regarded as her proper level. His parents gave him plenty of money and he spent it on her freely (I was responsible for her pocket-money and kept it down to what Mrs Wall told me was the standard Plumstead amount). Finally, his protection safeguarded her from any more teasing by kids of her own – now purely chronological – age.

What, I wondered, were my obligations as a Mum now that Aethra was growing up so fast? I had no idea what went on at the parties she was taken to by Simon. I resented the task of questioning her; besides, I didn't believe that she would tell me the truth. The questions remained – questions in which Vernon was unlikely to involve himself. How about alcohol? How about pot? And, inevitably, how about sex?

All of a sudden, Aethra was tremendously interested in sex. Simon had a library on the subject – apparently including some of the 'technique' books that Vernon so despised – which doubtless helped the pair of them to pass the rainy afternoons. Anything that she couldn't learn from her reading, she asked me about.

For this, apparently, was in Mum's sphere. I don't suppose it would have been in Laura's, but Aethra had picked up a bit about my life at the flat in Kensington. Once, when Vernon was puzzled by the signature on a Christmas card – it was from Hugh – I said casually: 'Oh, that's one of my old boy-friends,' and looked up to catch Aethra's intrigued expression.

So I was at the receiving end of this kind of thing:

'What actually happens to you when you have an orgasm?'

206

'It's hard to explain, in physical terms. It's a state of excitement. It's all in the mind, really.'

'Do you have one every time?'

'Me, or women in general?'

'You.'

'Mostly. I wouldn't say always.'

'What are multiple orgasms? How many is that?'

'Two or more.'

'How many could it be?'

'I don't know, Aethra. Try *The Guinness Book of Records*.'

And I remember a day when, feeling very low because I hadn't got a phone call on which I'd definitely counted, I went into the music-room and switched on a silly TV programme, only to have Aethra follow me and ask: 'I say, what is cunnilingus?'

'It must be Latin,' I said meanly. 'Your father knows Latin.'

Aethra put these questions without any sign of either embarrassment or excitement, precisely as though she were asking Vernon the meaning of solipsism or pragmatism. Hopefully, this indicated that her interest was purely theoretical. But how was I to know? It wasn't hard to imagine her and Simon combining abstract knowledge with experiment. She was well developed for thirteen and extremely attractive; Simon was strikingly mature in every way, as I've said, and he carried with him an aura of sexual confidence, reminding me in this respect of Bob Curran. He registered with me, and incidentally he was aware of it. Now and then he gave me a look to show that he'd read books about handsome youths having affairs with married women. I thought it unlikely that he was a virgin. And Aethra was his girl-friend. They were years younger than Bob and I had been, but this was London.

Aethra used to phone from school once or twice a week to say that I needn't fetch her, as she was going to have tea and do her homework at Simon's house. They'd have it to themselves for two hours or so before his parents came in from work. And sometimes, on evenings when Vernon and I were going out, she remarked that Simon was coming over (he travelled on an elegant high-speed bicycle). There were also the parties, usually occurring on Fridays and Saturdays when Vernon and I were also at a party or out to dinner. I had no idea what time Aethra came in, though she contrived – by good luck or skill – never to be later than us. All in all, she and Simon enjoyed ample opportunities for having it off. There was nothing to be done about it, short of forbidding her to be alone with her boy-friend, and this was out of the question for at least three reasons – it was against my principles; it wouldn't work, in view of Aethra's capacity for evasion; and I shouldn't have been supported either by Simon's parents or by Vernon.

It would be a big laugh, I thought, if Aethra got pregnant before I did. Not much of a laugh if it was for real, though. It was happening all the time in the most enlightened homes, when theoretical knowledge was forgotten in a burst of enthusiasm. So ought I to put Aethra on the pill? If she was in fact still a virgin, this was direct encouragement. She really was only thirteen, damn it. I vacillated and did nothing, waiting for her to ask questions about contraception, which she never did – either because she and Simon weren't screwing or because it was taken care of, but I didn't know which.

As I fretted over this problem, I kept wondering why I did fret so much, and whether my concern had more to do with myself than with Aethra. Was I prepared to have a child in the house, but not another woman? Was I stirred to envy by the possibility that Aethra was getting her oats more than, at this time, I was? Shameful, humiliating thoughts – I could have done without them just then.

The world of the London comprehensive, in which pregnancy comes readily to a teacher's mind as a possible explanation of sudden tears, was wholly alien to Vernon. He was delighted that Aethra was growing up, but he saw this development only in intellectual and trouble-free terms. He approved strongly of Simon, and talked to him as he would have talked to a bright student; but he always talked to young people without condescension, and Simon too was simply a clever school-child in his eyes. It was good for Aethra, he remarked from time to time, to have a friend who shared so many of her interests. ('Boy-friend' was a word he didn't use – Cressida hadn't had any at thirteen or for that matter at eighteen, presumably.) Had I suggested that Simon and Aethra might be making love, he would have been first incredulous; then desperately anxious, because he clung to the notion that she was sensitive and vulnerable; and then completely at a loss what to do, so that the problem would have landed on my plate in the end. So I didn't talk to him about it. There were fewer and fewer thing, these days, that I did talk to him about.

One afternoon in May, I came home in a cross mood. I had waited outside the school for two thousand kids to drift out; Aethra had presumably gone off with Simon without letting me know, a new trick.

'Where's Aethra?' Vernon asked when he emerged from his study.

'At Simon's.' I wasn't going to admit that I didn't know for sure.

'I see. I'll have to leave soon, I think.'

'OK.'

He was going to a Longuehaye family function, a dinner for the eightieth birthday of the oldest of the clan. I had refused to go with him.

'Well, just time for a sherry.'

I poured it.

'Oh, by the way, there was a phone call for you. Eileen Hurst.'

'Really?'

'She left a number. I wrote it down,' he said virtuously.

It was the same exchange as my old office but not the same number. I rang it. No answer, of course. It was just like Vernon, I thought, not to tell me until after working hours, but I decided not to make an issue of it.

209

In the evening, I reached Eileen at home.

'Oh, Pat, how lovely to hear your voice. It seems ages. How are things?'

'Not too good.'

'I'm not surprised, everybody's doing lousy business,' Eileen said tactfully. 'Well, the reason I rang you ... You heard about the agency folding up, didn't you?'

'No.'

'Oh, you didn't? Mrs Baldwin had a stroke. You didn't hear about that either? She's on her feet again, I gather, but it's always a warning, so she's wound up the business and retired to Worthing or somewhere like that. We got a very decent pay-off, I must say. Well, the thing is, Pat, we've decided — that is, three of us, Sam and Peter and me — to pool the money and set up shop together. We're calling it a co-operative, so nobody will be boss. I managed to find an office, at an appalling rent but that can't be helped, and I'm rushing round having cards printed and so forth. We want to get cracking while we can still scoop up Mrs B's customers. Now look, Pat, I know you're on your own now and of course that suits you, but is there any chance you might come in with us?'

I didn't say anything. I was absolutely unable to say anything.

'Pat? Hello — Pat?'

'I'm thinking.'

'We'd simply love to have you with us. You know, Sam and Peter do a reliable run-of-the-mill job, but that's all and they do realize it, so it would make all the difference to have somebody who can produce work in your class.'

'Thank you,' I said sadly.

'And' — Eileen hesitated — 'if you didn't feel able to put in regular hours, I'm sure that wouldn't be a problem.'

'I'll think it over. How does a co-operative work? I don't think I could put in any capital.'

'Oh.' Eileen hesitated again; I guessed that the others, at all events, had reckoned on Mrs Longuehaye having funds at her disposal. She rallied quickly, however, and said: 'Well, don't worry about that. I mean, your value as a photographer would be your contribution.'

'Well, we'll be in touch.'

'Yes, we'll be in touch.'

I paced about the house, unable to settle to anything, and drinking the special Armagnac as if it were Scotch. I didn't think about the offer itself – it was a dream come true, obviously – but only about how to present it to Vernon. I tried out one form of words after another, actually speaking them or at least moving my lips; nothing sounded quite right. Aethra came home, driven by Simon's mother, who joined me in a drink, not without registering the interesting fact that I drank when I was alone. After this, I went to bed. I didn't want to talk to Vernon that night.

Sam Archer (one of the co-operative) rang up the next day to say that they'd talked it over, and I'd be welcome to share in the profits without contributing to the capital, and they all felt that I'd be a tremendous asset and were just praying for me to say yes.

Inevitably, when I spoke to Vernon I made a mess of it. Had I been in a fit state to plan intelligently, I'd have seen that there were two possible strategies. One would have been to say persuasively that belonging to a co-operative wasn't exactly a job, there were no fixed hours, other people would see to the details and eliminate phone calls at home, etcetera. The other would have been to face him with a *fait accompli* – 'I've decided to take a new job, I just thought I'd let you know.' But what I did was to tell him, nervously and with every appearance of uncertainty and guilt, that I'd heard from my old colleagues, they were setting up a new outfit, they felt that having me in it would be an asset . . . Vernon listened with the expression of someone who is sure that he's being conned but can't quite see how. I realized (too late, as usual) that I'd blundered by stressing that I proposed to work with the same people as before.

'What do you expect me to say, Patricia?' he asked when I ground to a halt.

211

'Well . . . we do discuss things, don't we?'

'It's a step backward for you, that's clear enough, surely. You decided only about a year ago to free yourself from dependence on other people's requirements. If you want to revert to that kind of thing, I can only say that it's a great pity.'

'It's work,' I said. 'I'm getting hardly any work now, you know that.'

'I wasn't aware that you subscribed to the gospel of work for the mere sake of work.'

'I need to work, Vernon. I can't just sit around here.'

'You don't just sit around. Just look at our engagement book, my dear. You live a certain kind of life, which almost anyone else would consider remarkably full and many-sided. But we've been through that before.'

'Look, Vernon, I'm a photographer. At least, I used to be. They're asking me because they think I'm a good photographer. It gives me a lift being told that, the way things are.'

'Oh, their point of view is easy to understand. You represent an asset for them, as they put it with commendable frankness. They're thinking of their own interests; you should think of yours.'

'And yours, I suppose.'

'Mine? You know very well that if you lead the life that a job like this demands – coming in late and tired, virtually cut off from me for days at a time – I am affected. But I don't aspire to be taken into consideration.'

'I knew you wouldn't let me do it,' I said hopelessly.

'Let you – whatever does that mean? We discuss things, as you said. If I were to say: "Do as you please, it's no concern of mine", what would you think of me? What sort of marriage would that be?'

I said nothing. He came over to me and put his arms round me.

'My darling, I hate to see you like this. You worry so much, and so needlessly. Think of how much you're loved and valued, simply because you are yourself, and you won't feel that this kind of offer is any real compliment. Believe me, to go back in time to what you've achieved and outdistanced is never wise.'

Eileen rang up again.

'It's not on at present, I'm afraid,' I said as brightly as I could. 'I'm very grateful to you for asking me. But I can't commit myself as fully as one's got to in a co-operative set-up. So it wouldn't be fair to the rest of you, would it?'

'Oh dear,' Eileen said. 'Well, there it is. I do understand your position.'

I bet you do, I thought bitterly.

'If you change your mind any time, Pat, just let me know.'

'Oh, I will.'

There was a pause. Then Eileen said: 'How are things really, Pat? We've been so out of touch.'

'Oh, you know. No special news.'

'Well . . . see you around.'

'That's right, see you around.'

The next two months were the worst in my life. I met every day with despair; from the moment I woke up, I dreaded the prospect of enduring it. I hated getting up, for the first time in my life. Why did I have to get up, after all, except to make breakfast and drive Aethra to school? And then, what?

The house was like a prison to me. I sat in the kitchen for hours as if it were my cell, as if I were forbidden to leave it. But I didn't want to see anyone. When Mrs Wall was due, I often fled to the bedroom. Sometimes I walked round and round the garden – my exercise-yard – confined by the high wall. I hardly ever looked over the wall nowadays. I thought of London, the city in which people were working and travelling about and meeting one another, as prisoners must think of it: a place beyond my reach, which no longer had anything to do with me.

The weather was beautiful. I could have gone for long walks, or roamed around in my car, or taken photographs to my heart's content. But I needed all my courage to scurry out to the nearby shops. I bought what I needed, avoided chatting, and scurried back to the house. I hated the house by now, but I felt safer in it.

I no longer did any work at all. The spiral had dwindled almost to vanishing point and I scarcely got one phone call in a week. When I did get a call I said: 'I'm sorry, I'm not taking on any more commissions at present.' Or even: 'There's no Miss Bell here, you must have a wrong number.' I was destroying my old life, helping Vernon to make a clean sweep of it; it gave me a kind of ferocious, gloomy satisfaction.

The days were void of events, indistinguishable one from another, and yet somehow not empty. It took me ages to do anything. I applied myself with laborious concentration to tasks like weeding the flower-beds, cleaning the carpets, dusting all the books in Vernon's study while he was in Norwich. Thus I left myself with no time to think – for what did I have now to think about, or to what purpose?

But if I was trying to drug myself into insensitivity, I failed. I was acutely, painfully, resentfully aware of what had happened to me in the eighteen months since I'd given up my job – or (let's face it, I thought) in the three years of my life with Vernon. It struck me at unexpected moments, as though for the first time. Moments of incredulity: it couldn't have happened to me, no, not to Pat Bell. Moments of panic: I must break loose, now, at once, before it was too late. I swung dizzily between rebellion and hopelessness. Most of the time, I was hopeless. It seemed to me that I was lost; there was nothing I could do about it, and never would be.

I remember those months as a time of searching and confusion – a more baffling and intricate confusion than ever before. Once, I had been wary of being happy; now, I was ashamed of being unhappy. I tried to regain my balance by thinking: what about the homeless, or lonely old age pensioners, or just ordinary wives in their millions leading narrow and monotonous lives in boring small towns, and for that matter in Plumstead? Wouldn't they all, as Vernon had said, have considered my life to be remarkably full and many-sided? We saw lots of interesting people (it was the peak season for visiting intellectuals); we went to the theatre, we went out to dinner, we went to parties. I had an enviable and devoted husband, good friends, money, leisure . . . Lucky me!

So, if I couldn't be content, it must be my own fault. It must be my immaturity, demonstrated no doubt by my refusal to become a mother. That was why I wanted to take a step backward. (I was still deeply influenced by what Vernon said, even if I rejected it in the heat of an argument.) Had I really been better off before? I'd had work, and the achievement that went with it, true. But I'd had one room in a flat, and friends whom I'd even then found superficial and silly, and poor old Alan for a lover. Did I want to go back to that? Perhaps my discontent was nothing more than a foolish nostalgia, a refusal to grow. And Vernon, with the wisdom and patience that flowed from his love, was showing me the way. I had only to accept his guidance, and I could be perfectly happy again.

We didn't quarrel now. Vernon seemed to have forgotten our quarrels, indeed, and was gentle and affectionate to me. He could afford to be, I thought in my bitter moods, now that his triumph was complete. And yet it was hard to go on thinking this. I resented what he had done to me, but I needed him more than ever. We were happy together – at rest, quelling the inner turmoil – when we listened to music or sat in the garden in the warm evenings. At those times, I could make myself believe that nothing mattered except that I loved Vernon and he loved me.

The myth-makers and the artists were right, it seemed to me, when they depicted love as an onslaught directed by chance – an arrow aimed by a silly, impish child-god. We simply hadn't, given our personalities, fallen in love with the right person. It had taken me three years to realize this, and Vernon would never accept it, but I was clear in my mind that it was the truth. But what followed? That wasn't clear at all. One could, by a deliberate decision, put an end to a career, friendship, a marriage: but not to love.

215

Was our marriage breaking up? I knew by now that this was a possibility, though a possibility that obviously hadn't crossed Vernon's mind. For what was I seeking to do, in my moods of hope and rebellion? To take the job with Eileen, to break loose, to choose the direction that Vernon thought wrong and intolerable – and that must be the end of the marriage. But I tried to find a way round this cruel logic. I had muffed the discussion about the job, but I must try again. I must make Vernon see that we couldn't go on like that – I couldn't, at least – and that our marriage was at stake. Since he loved me he would give in. But while this solution appeared sensible, and would doubtless have been recommended by my mother or Mrs Wall or a marriage guidance counsellor, I had no faith in it. What I was asking contradicted Vernon's whole conception of marriage, of our commitment to each other, even of love; I couldn't see him conceding that. He lived by intellectual integrity, whose essence was to change your mind only when you were convinced. I hadn't the strength, now, to argue with any hope of convincing him.

That was how things stood, or rather drifted, when I realized with a jolt that in a week's time we'd be off to the villa. At this, I really panicked. I thought of what the villa had done to me last year; it had effectively put paid to my efforts to make out as a freelance. And I understood that if I went to the villa again I should be utterly and finally lost.

A spell of rainy, chilly weather interrupted the fine summer. Vernon drew the curtains one evening (we usually didn't in summer) and remarked: 'Ah well, this time next week we'll be having our coffee on the loggia.'

I said: 'I'm not going.' I was literally trembling and I knew that my voice was unsteady. But here, or nowhere ever again, I had to stand firm.

He stared at me. 'Patricia, what on earth do you mean?'

'I don't want to go. I'm sorry, but I don't.'

'It's our holiday, dear.'

'Your holiday. You never ask me if I want to go to the

villa. You know I'm not crazy about it.'

'Would you prefer to have a holiday somewhere else? I must say you might have suggested that before; it's awkward to change our plans now. I'm committed to that lecture.' He was planning to leave the villa briefly to hold forth at a philosophical jamboree in Florence. 'And you know how Aethra looks forward to staying at the villa.'

'OK. You go without me. You and Aethra.'

'I'd be very reluctant to do that. Tell me, where would you rather go?'

'Nowhere. Why should I want a holiday? I don't do any work. I'll stay here.'

'Patricia, you're not being entirely frank with me. It's not merely a question of disliking the villa, is it?'

'Christ, Vernon, what's so peculiar about wanting to be alone for a bit? Lots of men have holidays without their wives and vice versa. We live very close together – maybe you don't realize that.'

'I certainly don't regret it. I miss you, even when I'm in Norwich. It's very unlike you, too, this sudden desire to be alone. I wish you'd tell me what you mean by that.'

But I couldn't tell him, because I didn't know what I meant. He complained that my attitude was negative, and I said: 'OK, it's negative.' I didn't want to go to the villa. I was sure, of that, if of nothing else. The bit about wanting to be alone had occurred to me on the spur of the moment, and I wasn't certain that I believed it, although I was ready to clutch at anything that might bring a gleam of hope.

'What will you do all the time?' Vernon asked, as though my life were normally packed with activity. 'Will you go and see your parents, perhaps?'

'I might. I don't want to make plans.'

'Frankly, darling, I don't understand this in the least.'

'No. There are things I don't understand about you, too.'

'It's sad to be saying that after three years of marriage.'

'Did you understand everything about Laura after twenty years?'

217

He thought this over, perhaps for the first time. 'No,' he said. 'No, I couldn't claim that. It's galling to have to admit to limits to understanding, but . . . Well, if I say that the human soul is the ultimate mystery, you won't report me to the British Humanist Association, will you?'

I didn't go to see my parents (they were on holiday in August anyway). I didn't make any other plans. I stayed in the Manor House; curiously, my hatred for it seemed to be suspended. Perhaps, half-consciously, I was saying a wistful goodbye to it.

Michael and Dido had bought a cottage in Wales and were spending the summer there. Arnold and Gabrielle were halfway through their world tour, sending lyrical postcards from Peru. Some of our friends must have been in London, but nobody I wanted to see. The phone didn't ring, either with social calls or offers of work. Mrs Wall was in Majorca, so I was alone all day. I got up late and made myself a composite meal of whatever came to hand – eggs, liver sausage, coffee, Scotch – which did for breakfast and lunch. I took a long time to eat it, reading the papers with pointless thoroughness, and also reading Vernon's letters, which took the form of descriptive essays and concealed whatever he was thinking. As the letters piled up – he wrote almost every day – I made repeated resolutions to answer them, but didn't.

After about a fortnight, the phone did ring. It was John. He was spending a few days in London, he said.

'Any chance of seeing you, Pat? Would you like to have dinner with me tonight?'

'Sure.'

I took a train into town in the afternoon, for want of anything better to do, and mooched about the West End until it was time to meet him. I had forgotten what London was like in August. Hordes of tourists were ambling about and staring at things that were normally part of the background, such as pubs and second-hand bookshops; and Londoners found themselves staring too, struck by the curious notion of their city as a place to visit, to discover. I made little discoveries of my own, just as in the August when I walked out of the air terminal to look for a room. Five years ago. It seemed like an age.

John and I were glad to see each other, as usual. But there was a constraint in his manner that he'd never shown before, even when we had first met as strangers.

'When did you get to London?' I asked.

'Yesterday.'

'Where are you staying, then?'

'With some friends.'

'Your room's available, you know.'

'Well, you see, these people have invited me before, and I sort of promised them.'

He was avoiding my eyes. I realized that he didn't want to stay at the Manor House in Vernon's absence. It was ridiculous, but also sad. We had always been friends.

John knew – he had no talent for concealment – that all was not as it should be between Professor and Mrs Longuehaye. I didn't mind his knowing, but I'd have preferred him to know from me. It dawned on me that it was Vernon who had told John to ring me up and ask me to dinner: Vernon, probably, who was responsible for John's presence in London.

Why? Because he was puzzled about my state of mind and thought John could pick up some clues? Or because he wondered what sort of life I was leading, all on my lonesome? Or because he suspected me of staying in London to do a bit of screwing with all and sundry? A sad thought indeed. But anything was possible now.

John asked what I was doing with my time, and was I seeing any friends.

I said: 'Look, John, the reason I didn't go the the villa is that I'm fed up with the villa – it's as simple as that. But I didn't expect to enjoy staying at home, and I'm not.'

Rather awkwardly, he said that if he could help me to pass the time he was at my disposal. We decided to go to the theatre, at least if we could find any tickets that had been left over by the tourists. And two nights later we saw a play

219

which had been understandably overlooked by the culture-seekers from Pittsburgh, Wuppertal and Yokohama. Actually, we saw the first act and agreed that only the cast had an obligation to complete the experience.

'I'm sorry about that,' John said as we escaped into Shaftesbury Avenue. 'Shall we go and eat?'

I found that I wasn't hungry, though my lunch had been as scrappy as usual.

'If you don't mind, we could just go for a walk.'

It was a good night for walking: drizzling a bit, which discouraged the kind of people who stand on the pavement and make you circle round them, but warm and calm. We cut through to the Strand, and from there down to the Embankment. I set a brisk pace, which prevented conversation. We must have looked like a married couple with nothing to say to each other, heading for a parked car and home. John didn't take my arm, but gave it a controlling touch when we had to cross a street. I daresay he thought I was likely to walk in front of a car.

When we got to the Embankment, he asked: 'Where are we going?'

'Nowhere that I know of,' I said. 'I've got out of the habit of having an aim.'

'Pat,' he said anxiously, 'what's wrong?'

'Nothing.' But I owed him more than this, if we were friends. 'A bit of everything. My life. You know.'

We walked on, going eastward along the deserted pavement past the Temple. He took my arm and slowed me down.

'You were so happy when I first got to know you,' he said.

'I was, yes. Everything seemed to be so simple.'

'But now it isn't?'

'Now it isn't. I should have known better than to imagine that being married to Vernon could be a simple matter.'

'It was optimistic. But optimism is your great quality, I've always felt.'

'It's given out by this time,' I told him.

220

'I'm very sorry to hear that.'

We passed a couple standing by the railings and kissing; in the darkness, they made a single shape. We stopped talking until we had gone by. Then John asked: 'Does this mean . . . ?'

'I don't know what it means, John. I honestly don't. I keep telling myself I ought to be grateful for what I've got. I do realize I've got a lot. I mean, Vernon Longuehaye.'

'But you don't convince yourself?'

'I don't think I can cope.'

'With Vernon Longuehaye?'

'With Vernon Longeuhaye. I don't understand why he does . . . anything he does.'

We walked in silence for a while. Cars rushed by, splashing us with rain-water. It was a silly place for a walk.

'It's lonely here,' I said. 'We might as well be in bloody Plumstead.'

'We could cut up to Fleet Street.'

Fleet Street was better. It was comforting to see newspaper vans charging along, and an air of bustle. A photographer side-swiped me with his camera-bag as he hurried towards his office.

'Let's eat,' I said. 'I've worked up an appetite.'

We went into a grubby, crowded café and ordered steaks.

I said: 'I know what I want to do.'

He gave me a worried look, evidently fearing the worst.

'I want to have a talk with your mother.'

This astonished him. I was astonishing myself, too; the idea had come to me out of the blue.

'What for?' he asked.

'It seems to me that she's the only person who could help me to understand Vernon. I can't talk to Laura — she's dead. And I don't suppose she had the problem, or probably didn't feel the necessity. But if Vernon opened himself to anyone, wouldn't it have been to your mother? I mean, he was young then.'

John didn't answer, so I pressed him: 'Isn't that right?'

'I can't say. She's never talked about him to me. Not about

221

her life with him.'

'Perhaps you never wanted her to. I do.'

He looked more worried than ever.

'I don't think it's a good idea, Pat, I really don't.'

'Would it be painful for her?'

'No, that's not what I mean. She's very strong. But for you – isn't it a bit of a risk?'

'Because that marriage broke down?'

'Well, yes.'

'Do you think I'm looking for a justification for leaving Vernon? I'm not, John, truly I'm not. If I can find a way to get things right with him it'll be wonderful.'

'In that case it doesn't seem logical to talk to a woman who left him.'

'Did she? It was that way, was it?'

John frowned; he hadn't meant to say this.

'I don't know. I'm guessing. They parted, at all events.'

'Well, talking to a woman who left Vernon is a risk, I agree. But also, I'd be talking to a woman who loved him. Or didn't she?'

'Yes, she did.'

'You're not guessing about that?'

'No. It's the one thing she made sure of my knowing.'

'All right then.'

'All right. I'll give you the address. She's called Dr Hewitt – it's her maiden name.'

'She's a doctor?'

'Yes, she's a doctor.'

Dr Hewitt lived in Sheffield, as John had once told me. He gave me two addresses, her home and the health centre where she worked. I considered ringing up, but it was too difficult to explain on the phone who I was and what I wanted. So I took a train to Sheffield and arrived at about five o'clock.

A woman who was waiting for a bus outside the station told me how to get to the health centre. In fact, she was going the same way and made sure that I got off the bus at the correct stop. She had a motherly manner and a strong

Yorkshire accent, which made me feel that I was in the right place and helped me along. I wasn't feeling confident; I had got out of the habit of finding my way in strange surroundings.

The waiting-room was packed. I almost backed out and went to take the next train back to London. Dr Hewitt was sure to be very busy. I was struck dauntingly by the intrusiveness, indeed the absurdity, of what I was doing. I stood in the doorway for a minute, feeling both frightened and depressed. The people here were a sad lot, or that was how I saw them. The old ones looked as though only the sunlight was keeping them alive; the children were fractious or else unnaturally silent.

However, I nerved myself to go up to the receptionist and ask if I could see Dr Hewitt.

'She's not on today. You can see Dr Ahmed.'

The receptionist didn't have a Yorkshire accent or (being younger than me) a motherly manner. I said I'd come back another day.

'Suit yourself,' the receptionist said sharply. She probably thought I was making a point of seeing a woman doctor, to get birth-control advice or else to find out whether I was pregnant. Or, perhaps, that I was refusing to see the Pakistani doctor. I found myself worrying about what this girl thought, but afraid of making matters worse by explaining that I didn't want to see Dr Hewitt as a patient.

I stopped a man in the street and asked the way to where Dr Hewitt lived. It involved changing buses and sounded too complicated for my present capacities, so I went back to the station and got a taxi. Going in the opposite direction, and steeply uphill, I reached a district which looked as though the rich had lived there a couple of generations ago. The houses were built of stone, with small windows, giving the impression that they'd been designed to resist an attack by the mob.

I paid off the taxi. The street was deserted, and it occurred to me that I'd be stuck if Dr Hewitt wasn't at home. The

223

house I was going to was enormous – practically a castle – but it was divided into five flats. I went up eight steps to the big double front door, and pressed the bell labelled 'Hewitt' quickly, allowing myself no time to hesitate. I was really frightened by now. The whole expedition seemed doomed to disaster. Besides, I hadn't the faintest idea what I was going to say. I had travelled by train instead of driving to Sheffield in order to do some planning, but I'd been quite unable to think to any purpose.

The door was opened by a woman in a green trouser-suit, the sort that makes a 'good buy' and can be worn for work, going out, or an evening at home. I was wearing a green trouser-suit myself. Vernon liked it. I almost burst into idiotic laughter at the idea that we were both in a Longuehaye wife uniform.

'Dr Hewitt?' I managed to ask.

'That's right.'

I said: 'You don't know me, but I know your son.'

She gave me a warm, welcoming smile and said: 'Do come in.' I followed her miserably. Obviously she thought that John had found a suitable girl-friend at last. It seemed to be my fate to create false impressions.

She had the back half of the first floor, overlooking a garden with some gloomy-looking shrubs and laurel bushes. The flat, however, was cheerful. The walls were done in a bright yellow and there were three big paintings of Yorkshire landscapes – the work of a friend, no doubt, but good paintings too.

'Well, sit down,' Dr Hewitt said, and cleared some medical journals out of a big comfortable chair. I sat down. She stood leaning against a table, looking at me with frank and friendly interest.

'How's John?' she asked.

'He's fine,' I said. 'I'd better explain who I am. I'm Vernon's wife.'

She looked surprised, of course. Not taken aback, however; intrigued was more like it.

224

'Well, well,' she said. 'This is one for the book.'

'I was going to phone you before coming,' I said. 'I ought to have done. I'm sorry.'

'Oh, that doesn't matter.' She smiled, almost mischievously. 'You haven't by any chance brought Vernon with you, have you?'

'No, he's in Italy.'

'Is he? Well, it's nice to make your acquaintance . . . Mrs Longuehaye.' We both laughed. 'No, it sounds funny for me to call you that, don't you think? It's Pat, isn't it?'

'Yes.'

'I'm Ruth. Would you like a cup of tea, Pat? Or a drink?'

'It's late for tea, isn't it?'

'Right you are, it's late for tea. Will Scotch do? I'll just get some ice.'

When she came back, she said: 'You never know, do you? I was just resigning myself to an evening with the telly. My chap's away – also in Italy, oddly enough. Cheers.'

'Cheers. Cigarette?'

'I don't, thanks.'

'Doctor. I forgot. You don't mind if I do?'

'I'm used to it. I'll find you an ashtray.'

She did this, then sat down and looked at me reflectively, I suppose revising her first impression.

'I never saw Laura,' she said. 'I was curious about her, naturally, but I never saw her. Did you?'

'No, I didn't meet Vernon until after she'd died.'

'I know she was a good-looker. So are you. Trust Vernon.'

'Well, Ruth, you set the standard.'

'Oh, aye.' I noticed the north-country intonation now. I didn't know whether she came from Yorkshire originally or had picked it up from living there.

'Wait a minute,' she said, got up to rummage in a desk, and handed me a photograph of herself and Vernon. They were sitting on a park bench; the photographer, maybe one of Ruth's family, had clearly been an amateur and Vernon had a rather cross expression, presumably because he was bored

225

with holding his pose. He wasn't much like my Vernon, this clean-shaven and short-haired young man in Army uniform. But he was one in a million, like my Vernon, and I felt a sharp stab of jealousy at what Ruth had had of him. I tried to look at her rather than at him. She had been, if not beautiful in Laura's fashion, a tremendously attractive girl. (And she was still, as John had said, an attractive woman, and fortunate in certain durable assets – notably her eyes, which were an extraordinarily clear and luminous grey.) In the photo, she was smiling at Vernon with a contentment, a delighted absorption, that made her entirely oblivious of the camera. She was utterly happy, you saw, in the mere fact of being with him. She had loved him – there was no doubt of that.

I said: 'Yes, I see.'

Ruth laughed – a brisk, common-sense sort of laugh. 'I wouldn't want to put that picture on the wall. But I wouldn't want to throw it away, either.'

'Of course not.'

'I've kept his letters, too. Somebody might write a biography of him one day, d'you think?'

'I daresay. Anyway, I'm sure they're very good letters.'

She gave me a shrewd look, and I said quickly: 'I wasn't asking to see them.'

'I wouldn't mind. They're not love-letters, except for bits here and there. He was having a fascinating time, I mean just after we were married. The war, working with the French Resistance, then the Dutch, then being in Germany after the collapse. I didn't imagine he had much time to miss me. But the letters were terrific – he described things so well. He could have been a writer, or a historian, if he hadn't gone for philosophy. It was amazing to me – a man with so many abilities.' Again the brisk laugh, the dismissal of nostalgia. 'I went through the letters with John when he was about seventeen. It's the only time I've looked at them.'

'And you've never seen Vernon, all this time.'

'No.'

She was thoughtful for a moment, a little unsure of herself

226

for the first time, or at least unsure of how much she would say to me. I gave her back the photograph, and her fingers smoothed its edges with a caressing movement of which she may have been unconscious.

'It seems silly to you, I expect,' she said. 'These sociable meetings between people who've been divorced, they weren't the custom when I was younger. And besides ...' She hesitated, then took the plunge. 'I'll tell you, Pat, I'm not so tough as I may look.'

She did look tough, in the sense of being well able to take care of herself. There was intelligence, humour, and a cool realism in the grey eyes. I was aware, too, of a core of determination, an irreducible independence, within the tolerant friendliness. It would have taken firmer shape during the years of making her own life, but something of it had surely been there all along. Yet 'tough' wasn't the word that I'd have chosen. There was no armour, no immunity from feeling. And she had loved Vernon.

She was saying: 'I was afraid I couldn't manage a sociable meeting. And afraid that I'd be hurt if it turned out that Vernon could manage it quite easily. Because you can do something you think is right ... I mean, I broke it up, in case you don't know. For various reasons. Well, you can do something you think is right, and still feel a tremendous sense of loss. So if I'd seen him it would have been – I won't say unbearable, nothing's unbearable, but I didn't choose to inflict it on myself. I hope you can understand that.'

I said nothing. She stood up suddenly and put the photograph on the mantelpiece, face downwards.

'How's your glass?'

'Thanks.'

'You'll have something to eat, won't you? Pot luck, but no problem.'

'Thanks very much.'

'Where are you staying?'

'I'm not. I mean, I haven't done anything about it.'

'You weren't thinking of going back to London tonight,

were you?'

'I just hadn't thought at all.'

Ruth looked at me very keenly. Then she said: 'Don't tell me you've come up here without any things. You won't get into a hotel without a suitcase, not in Sheffield. Well, you'd better stay here.'

'I couldn't possibly . . .'

'Oh, nonsense. There's the spare room empty, the bed's even made up. After all, we are related, sort of. There ought to be a word for it, oughtn't there?'

I said: 'I wasn't expecting . . . I just haven't been very efficient.'

She didn't reassure me; doubtless she was thinking that I was capable of being reasonably efficient and there must be some reason why, just now, I wasn't.

The phone rang. Ruth took the call and said to me: 'I'm afraid I've got to go out. I don't think I'll be long. Could you start the food? There's some beef — do it how you like. I've got potatoes and onions, carrots I think. Look, I'll show you where everything is.'

When she'd gone, I started the meal with the slight uncertainty and extra care caused by cooking in someone else's kitchen. This kitchen was small, with small gas stove and a small refrigerator; it was right for someone who didn't cook for more than two people. I thought about how Ruth lived, making a home-like atmosphere when 'her chap' was with her, but not allowing herself to let things slide when he wasn't. He had gone to Italy, most likely, for a holiday with his wife and children. I wondered how that felt, for Ruth.

The living-room was well stocked with books, and I thumbed through a few, but couldn't settle to reading. I picked up the old photograph and stared at it for a long time; then, with a vague feeling of guilt, I replaced it exactly as Ruth had put it down. After that, I just sat and smoked. I was still uneasy about being here, but feeling better than before.

'Well, that's done,' Ruth said when she came back. 'Couldn't be another call tonight, I shouldn't think. How's the food, love? I bought a bottle of wine.'

'We could eat now, if you like.'

'Let's. I don't know about you, I'm good and ready.'

We ate in the kitchen. There was just room for the table and two chairs.

'What was your call?' I asked.

'One of my old women – she fell downstairs. It's lucky the neighbours heard her and went out to phone me. She hadn't broken anything, though. I put her to bed and tucked her up.'

Ruth gave her brisk, unsentimental laugh. 'Silly old cow. They make more work for doctors than anything else, you know, these old women living alone. Steep narrow stairs, it's suicidal, but d'you think she'd sleep on the ground floor? Not likely. And the Council's got a free scheme for phones, but she's never had one and she's not going to have one now. She ought to have gone into a Home years ago, really. But there you are, if she didn't have her own bit of pavement to sweep, what would she have? It's the house she came to as a bride, she told me. It stands for her life.'

'It's hard to imagine,' I said. And wished I hadn't; Ruth's life had twenty years on to mine.

She took it easily, however, and said: 'Yes, that attachment to a house, it's not for me. I've had this flat six years. I like it, but I'll probably make a move before long.'

'You never married again, did you? You could have, of course.'

'Yes, I could have. I really meant to. It wasn't easy, bringing up a child alone and working. And I haven't spent my whole life lamenting for Vernon, don't worry. But when it came to the point, I always found myself thinking: who's this fellow, to have more of me than Vernon had?'

'And meanwhile you're a doctor,' I said. 'And a very good doctor, I'm sure.'

'Yes,' she said without any false modesty. 'And you're a photographer. What's that like? I don't think I know any.'

I told her, at some length. She was the kind of person who can take a genuine interest in another kind of life, and she led me on with questions that flattered my much-weakened self-esteem. I was describing the life I'd led before marrying Vernon – or, at all events, before giving up my job – so my use of the present tense was a deception. But, while in full flood, I didn't admit this either to myself or to Ruth. We were on equal terms, two busy and capable professionals.

We finished the meal, and I washed up and she dried, and we went on talking. It was cosy there in the little kitchen, smoking and drinking coffee, and then going on to the Scotch again. We talked about living in Sheffield (which was in fact her home town) and living in Northern Ireland and living in London; about John and his adventure with the Persian princess; about Aethra and the oddities of comprehensive schools. We laughed a good deal. It was as entertaining as an evening with Gabrielle, but more relaxed and comfortable. I had made a new friend; I completely forgot how tense and frightened I'd been when I rang Ruth's bell. Nor did I notice, at the time, that I'd drunk more than my share of the wine and the Scotch.

Then – I'd been talking about the villa and why I found it boring – Ruth suddenly asked: 'Does Vernon know you've come up here to see me?'

'No. At least, he may know from John. But I didn't tell him I was coming.'

'He won't be pleased.'

'I suppose not.' I lit another cigarette.

'You smoke too much, Pat,' Ruth said.

'I know.'

I stubbed out the cigarette. We stared at each other. I suddenly felt cold sober, and frightened again, and aware that Ruth had been observing me and drawing her conclusions all along.

'You didn't come just for fun, did you?' she asked.

I said: 'You've been very kind. I can understand it's not fun for you.'

'It's you we're talking about, Pat.'

'I hope you don't think it's just curiosity. I'm trying . . . I think I'm trying to understand something about Vernon. It's not exactly easy, coming into a man's life at the point where I did.'

'You want to know why I left Vernon, don't you?'

'No ... well ... I've no right to ask you that. Oh, this is terrible. I'll go to bed. I'd go away if I could.'

'Take it easy, love. I don't think it's terrible, and I'm the one to say. I'll make some more coffee.'

She made it, and said firmly: 'Right, you'd best just sit and listen.'

In the spring of 1944, Ruth was a first-year student at Oxford. Winning an open scholarship had been a triumph for her – so much of a triumph as to feel like a fluke. No such thing had ever happened to a girl from her undistinguished grammar school, nor to anyone in her family. (Her father had a butcher's shop, now swept away by redevelopment.) Oxford was very strange. She wasn't confident of passing her first-year exams, nor of coping with Oxford in any way. She was – as she described herself – badly in need of someone to rescue her from loneliness.

'And love, of course. I'd shut that out, working for the scholarship. Never had a boy-friend. And I'd been snooty about girls who fell for uniforms – deliberately snooty, secretly envious. So when it hit me, I boiled over like a pressure-cooker.'

Vernon had gone into the Army after taking a notable First; had fought, or whatever Intelligence officers do, in North Africa and Italy; was waiting for the invasion of Europe; came to Oxford on leave, staying with his old tutor. They met in a crowd – Saturday afternoon on the river. Someone had asked Ruth to make up the numbers, as Gabrielle had asked me. By the end of his leave they were in love, ecstatically happy, and engaged.

Stationed not far away, he was with her at weekends. They were married as soon as possible. He went to Normandy: she passed her exams. Then she found that she was pregnant.

'I'd been taking precautions. I had to get my degree, and we

231

hadn't a home, and of course there was the war. I said all that, and he agreed. There'd been just one time – he wangled a day off when I didn't expect it, and we went out into the country on his motor-bike, and walked in the woods, and . . . oh, you know, we went wild. I thought afterwards: it's just once, it'll probably be OK. But it wasn't.'

'What did you feel?'

'Oh well, with my parents being delighted, and all the rest of it, I convinced myself I was delighted too. And there's an instinctive joy, a biological response, especially when it's with the man you love. I did wonder whether he'd gone wild like me or whether he'd known what he was doing. I didn't see him again until after John was born, and then there was no point in asking him. Or rather, it was impossible.'

Ruth went back to Sheffield, to live with her parents. 'Nowadays, of course, you'd find a flat and make various arrangements and go on studying. But one just didn't then. There was nowhere I could have lived at Oxford except in college.' However, she kept up with the course, through books, as best she could. She had set her sights, in her schooldays, on becoming a doctor.

'I reckoned I'd start again after missing a year – that is, in autumn 1945. But I didn't.'

'How old would John be then? I'm trying to work out . . .'

'The problem wasn't John,' Ruth said tersely. 'The problem was Vernon.'

A lorry trundling along the road made a surprising noise. It had become very quiet; it was late.

'When we got married,' Ruth said, 'I had a definite idea of what Vernon was like. The same idea that everyone's had about him, no doubt, all through his life. Perfectly sure of himself, knowing exactly where he was going, headed straight for success. I said to you before, his gifts amazed me. Well, you know him as he is now. Success is part of him, I can well believe. But at that time, he was lost. It's a fact, really lost.'

He tried, she said, to be a candidate in the 1945 election. For a young officer, with a command of words, a pleasing personality and a good war record, it wasn't difficult to be selected either by the Tories or – as Vernon wanted – by Labour. Two of his friends brought it off and became MPs (one of them, later, a minister). But, by bad luck or bad advice, Vernon tried a constituency where the electors weren't swept off their feet and chose a local man who had been a councillor for twenty years.

I said: 'I never knew that Vernon wanted to go into politics.'

'He wanted to be famous,' Ruth answered.

Not being an MP, he had to stay in the Army. He was posted to a headquarters in Scotland. Ruth was happy to be with him – they had a home of sorts, in lodgings – but she'd lost another year. She understood that, whereas he hadn't missed her much during the excitement of the war, he now needed her. He had no serious duties; he was bored and restless. She was bored and restless too, but had to conceal it.

In the long monotonous evenings, there was one subject of conversation: what was he to do in civilian life? He thought of the law, the BBC, journalism. Each of these threatened years of what he called 'drudgery' – subordination, routine work without achievement or fame. With his First and his Oxford connections, he could always find a niche in the academic world; but this, which was eventually to make him a celebrity, then seemed to him a dead end, a last resource. He had black moods in which he told Ruth that he had no future – the best of his life was over. He was bitter about men who had snapped up good jobs before getting out of uniform, jobs which he was too far from London to hear about. Dismayed and baffled, she exclaimed: 'But it's ridiculous – you haven't even tried yet!' He sat hunched over the fire (their rooms were always cold, Ruth said) and repeated: 'What's the use?'

'And I came to see,' she said, 'that, after I'd given myself to him trusting him to help me along, now I was the one who was sustaining him.'

'That must have hurt.'

'Yes and no. It was a shock all right. I was very young, I knew nothing about men, I thought they were always stronger than women. But being needed gave me a new kind of pride. I was able to love him more deeply now that he wasn't simply a hero. No, that wasn't when things went wrong.'

When he was demobilized, Vernon still hadn't made any decisions. He took a fellowship at his old college, to tide him over for a while.

'So,' Ruth continued, 'when he said we were going to live at Oxford, I said fine, I could start again on my degree, couldn't I? He looked startled – that's all, startled. All that year, you see, we hadn't talked once about my becoming a doctor. I'd assumed it was agreed on. He had problems, I didn't. Now I realized, in a flash, that he'd forgotten all about it. That did hurt.

'He began to raise difficulties.' Ruth listed them, and I could hear Vernon's logical, persuasive manner of speech. 'Our future was uncertain. He might get a job in a year's time where I couldn't do a pre-med course. And how could I study, not to mention being an interne, with John to look after? And it was to be hoped that John wouldn't be an only child. I didn't argue. I don't think I listened properly. Everything had changed.'

'And that's when you left him?'

'Well, I gave Oxford a try. A few months – I forget exactly. It was a bad time, much worse than in Scotland. Not for him, far from it. He had plenty of good company and stimulating evenings – all men, of course – and he began to publish papers, and almost right away he could see himself going ahead the way he has gone. So he didn't need me any more. He wanted me with him – you know, by his side – and I knew he loved me; but his life was on course, and mine was stranded. I watched the dons' wives. The educated ones helped their husbands with research – looked up references, actually – and the others were just dons' wives. They were perfectly happy. I was tempted, or menaced, whichever you like, by their kind of happiness. It was necessary for Vernon

234

that I should depend on him, to cancel out the time when he'd depended on me. He would never have seen anything wrong with that.

'So one day I said to him: "Vernon, you don't want me to be a doctor, do you?" He started again on the difficulties. I said: "Look here – you, Vernon, don't want me, Ruth, to be a doctor. Ever. Isn't that true?" He didn't answer. He produced thousands of words, naturally, but no answer. That was the end, really.'

It was the end, but Ruth gave me the sequel. Leaving Vernon didn't automatically enable her to resume her studies. Her parents didn't sympathize – blamed her, indeed – so she got no help with looking after John. As she refused to take money from Vernon, she had to work and save for years. She was over thirty by the time she qualified. But it was her victory, her very own.

'Well, now you know,' she said at last. 'It could have been different if Vernon had made his way before he married me. If he'd been more sure of himself, able to let me compete a bit. Sometimes I wish I'd stuck it out. But as things were then – as he was then – I didn't think I had any choice.'

I lit a cigarette, despite myself, and said: 'I want to tell you something now, Ruth.'

The grey eyes settled on me. 'Go ahead.'

'What I told you before – about being a photographer – wasn't true. I mean, it was like that, but it's all finished. I don't work now. I'm supposed to be a freelance, but actually I don't do anything at all.'

She said gently: 'I see. That does explain why you're here, doesn't it?'

'I've been alone, wondering what to do. I keep thinking, there must be some way. I love him. But then, you loved him too, didn't you?'

'Yes.'

I thought, for fully a minute, that she would say nothing more. Then she gave me a slow, rueful smile and said: 'Loving him is the trouble, isn't it?'

235

I nodded.

'I've had time to think a lot about Vernon. I think of him often, even now. When I'm alone, and when I'm with other men, which is worse. It's what I meant by a sense of loss. Or it's part of what I meant . . .' Here, I think she decided not to attempt something that was beyond words. She went on in a firmer tone: 'The thing is this. I know what he should have been, for our marriage to last. Balanced, reasonable, unselfish, prepared to compromise. But if he'd been like that, I shouldn't have loved him as I did. I hate to admit it, Pat. But it's the truth.'

'I know,' I said. 'It is the truth.'

'Well, think on, as we say in Yorkshire. It's not easy to be a woman, and that's the truth too.'

'But you did say that what you did was right. And you still think it's right. You did say that, didn't you?'

'Yes, and that's the truth again. Only . . . nothing's simple, and the truth isn't all of one piece. Doing what's right – is it what matters most? I made my decision; to stand on my own feet, to carve out my own achievement. And yet, there's thousands of doctors. One more or less doesn't make so much difference. Most of what I do, someone else could do. Giving my chap what his wife doesn't give him – someone else could do that too. But a life with Vernon Longuehaye, loving him and being loved by him – that's rare. I don't need to tell you, Pat.'

'Please, Ruth,' I said. 'If you'd made that choice, if you'd never done what you have done, you'd always have been sorry.'

'Oh yes, I'd have been sorry, and bitter too. That's what I saw at the time, clearly enough. What I didn't see was that I'd be missing him the rest of my life.'

She gave her brisk laugh; I understood now how it helped her.

'I've got you all confused, love, haven't I? But if I tried to make it easy for you – take your problem to Auntie, get your answer – I'd give you no kind of truth at all. Because it's never easy.'

'Ruth,' I said, 'You're the most honest person I've ever met.'

'I don't know. I'm not so sure of myself as I used to be, that's a fact. Not sure enough to say: do the same as I did and you'll be all right. Each of us is different, and each of us is alone. Think on, Pat.'

'I'll think on.'

'All right. I'll let you go to bed now. It's very late.'

She looked suddenly tired, but like someone who has fulfilled her task. She yawned comfortably.

'Come on. D'you wear pyjamas? Mine'll hang on you, but never mind.'

I slept peacefully and woke late. When I got up, I found a note from Ruth: she'd gone to work, and I was to help myself to breakfast, there was a pan of coffee. I noticed that the old photograph had been put away.

I found a bus stop, reached the station, and took a train to London. In the dining-car, I shared a table with a man: good-looking, smartly dressed, probably a middle-rank executive in a Sheffield firm going to London for a conference. He chatted me up and asked me to have dinner with him. Two years ago, when I was happily married, I should have been amused and pleased. Now I was irritated. Vernon mattered, only Vernon, even if I was leaving him; how could a man like this presume to distract me? I was too irritated even to pretend that my evening was taken up. I just said: 'No thanks.'

'But you are free?' he asked, puzzled.

'Yes.'

'That's fine then. I'll be in the small bar at the Piccadilly Hotel at half past seven.'

'I shan't turn up.'

'Oh, I daresay you will,' he said cheerfully.

I went home. There was a letter from Vernon; he was extremely concerned because I hadn't written and begged me to reassure him that I was all right. Conscience-stricken, I picked up the phone and dictated a wire: 'Terribly sorry never have been good at letters love Pat.' When the operator read it back, I changed Pat to Patricia. I read through some of his other letters; yes, he wrote beautifully. I had left them scattered about the house, but now I bound them up neatly with a rubber band – maybe for his biographer.

Then I was overcome by tiredness, as though I hadn't slept at all. I curled up on the couch and dozed, surfacing and sinking again at intervals. At last I came sharply awake, knowing that I'd had a dream but unable to recall it. It was seven o'clock, and it struck me that if I took my car I could meet the man at the Piccadilly Hotel. I decided against giving that kind of man that kind of satisfaction. So I ate some biscuits and cheese – there was nothing else in the house – drank a certain amount of Scotch, and watched television.

The next morning I said to myself: today I really have to think about whether I'm leaving Vernon or not. However, I put it off. I read the papers thoroughly, as usual. I went out and bought some food and cigarettes and so forth. And it dawned on me, while I was putting the food away in the kitchen, that there was nothing to think about – or, more precisely, that the thinking would be a pretence. I was going to leave him. I knew it. I had no more need to weigh up the arguments than when I'd started to live with him.

For you don't, in real life, think over the big decisions. You reach them, in an almost literal sense of the word, where they're waiting for you. Ruth had advised me to 'think on', but she hadn't done so herself. She had come to know what I knew now, at a moment which she had described to me. When people leave their husbands or wives – and for that matter when they leave the Catholic Church or the Communist Party – it simply means that what was once impossible has become inevitable.

Now that it had happened – and of this I was certain, although it had happened only within me – what I felt above all was a great sadness. I remembered, as Ruth too still remembered, the joy and pride of being Vernon Longuehaye's wife. A real joy, more real than anything else in my life; a rare joy indeed; a joy more precious in memory than in easy possession. Now it was gone, quite gone.

Yet this sadness was altogether different from the fretting pain, the blind and desperate misery, of the last year. It was a tranquil grief, like grief after a death. I felt myself to be a survivor : the survivor of my marriage.

I thought again, with gratitude but also with a perception of irony, about the talk with Ruth. If she had brought me to the point of recognizing the inevitable, it wasn't by encouragement so much as by her final caution. She had given a value, a dignity to what had to be done. She had warned me that I should suffer: that my choice, like hers, was a choice of deprivation. It was wise of her to warn me – there had been no one to warn her. It was honest of her to say that her choice need not be mine. She didn't know me; she didn't despise Laura's way, and nor did I. Yet she must have guessed that, in the ultimate division among women, I was with her and not with Laura. To be myself – to survive – I knew what I had to do.

What was it exactly – I thought hard about this, because it was important – that Ruth had warned me of? Uncertainty, yes; it would recur at all the hard moments of my life. Regret – no, in the deep truth of myself, I believed that I should never regret what I was doing. But a sense of loss: yes, for ever, in some part of me, even if I won through to future happiness, there would be that.

I hoped, very much indeed, that Vernon would suffer less than me. It was quite possible, I thought, once he got over the shock. Much that was important to him would remain undiminished – his work, his fame, his accumulated rewards and satisfactions. He would be hurt and mortified to find that he had twice given his love mistakenly, but he would erase me from the record, like Ruth. Most likely, he would marry again; he was a marrying man, and not yet old. If I was right about all this, so much the better. If I was wrong, I must bear guilt as well as loss. But that too I had to face. I was leaving

239

him, not with a light and callous heart, but from necessity: not to reject or punish him, but to free myself.

The sense of loss began from this moment, as I wandered about the silent rooms. The house, which I had sometimes laughed at and sometimes hated, seemed purely beautiful and gracious. It had been a prison for me, but now it was ... I don't know what, more like a luxury liner in which my journey was coming to an end. But really – I couldn't deny it – a home, the only home I had. Everything that met my eyes reminded me of the life I had shared with Vernon: our two big breakfast cups, a painting we'd bought together, books we'd both read, a mock-orange which I'd planted in the garden and which had flowered this year for the first time.

I remembered our dinner-parties: opening the door in a warm rush of excitement, and the house suddenly alive with greetings and news, and hours of good talk and laughter, and Vernon's summing-up as we yawned and undressed. I remembered the delight of going out with him, of being part of the enrichment that he spread. I remembered the homes of our friends, and the flat at Norwich crowded with students, and the circles that had formed round us in lecture-halls and theatre foyers and TV hospitality rooms. The friends had liked me – a good wife for Vernon – but it wasn't to be expected that these rare and brilliant people would have any use for me apart from him. I was leaving the splendid scene, the delectable world, to which I had gained the brief privilege of belonging.

But I thought most of all of Vernon himself. I loved the man, all of him: his body and his mind, his voice and his words. There was the true, the irreparable loss. In a strange way, I felt myself to be more in love with him now – more deeply, more purely, more completely – than ever before. He had made me terribly unhappy; he had come near to destroying what I valued most in myself. I was leaving him because to stay with him was in an absolute sense intolerable. All that was true, and yet it didn't touch my love for him.

There was another week before he came home. I stayed in

240

the house most of the time, just as I had before. John rang up and asked me to dinner; I said I was down with a stomach upset.

'Did you see my mother?' he asked.

'Yes, she's a wonderful person. We got on awfully well.'

There was a pause; he must have realized that I didn't intend to say any more.

'Well, see you some time,' he said. 'I ought to go up to Cambridge, really.'

'All right. I'm so sorry I can't manage dinner.'

Now that I'd reached my decision, I went through what I can best describe as a convalescence. I felt that I was emerging from a long period of weakness, so uncharacteristic of me that I could scarcely believe that I'd succumbed to it for such a length of time. I had to test out my ability to make plans and act independently, as one might test out the ability to walk upstairs or lift weights.

Still, I felt more of my energy coming back almost by the hour, and with it my natural cheerfulness. The sense of loss would always remain, but I could see myself living with it, controlling it. I began, in fact, to look on the bright side. I was certainly better placed to start out on my own than Ruth had been. I could plunge into my chosen work at once, I could earn good money, and I hadn't got a child to care for.

I was quite clear about what to do. I would join Eileen's co-op, if there was still a place for me; failing this, I'd apply for a job with some agency or other. And I would find a flat – a small flat for myself, because sharing with other girls didn't seem like a good idea. I began to feel impatient to get active and set everything up. But I felt that there was something callous about doing this while Vernon was unaware of it, so I restrained myself from ringing up Eileen.

I made up my mind to tell Vernon face to face that I was leaving him. It seemed cowardly, and unworthy of what we'd meant to each other, to walk out before his return and leave a letter. If I did that, I'd always feel afterwards that I'd been afraid of his talking me round and regaining his ascendancy

241

over me; and really, by this time, I wasn't afraid of that in the least. In any case, he wouldn't believe what I was telling him unless he heard it in my voice and saw it in my eyes.

On the other hand, it would be right to tell him as soon as he got home, and it would be embarrassing to stay in the same house with him – not to mention Aethra – even for a few days. Even for a night, indeed. I was, I found, afraid of one thing: going to bed with Vernon, or alternatively having to refuse to go to bed with him. So I decided to find a flat. I got a letter from him about his flight to London, and to my relief it was due to land at two-thirty in the afternoon. I'd have plenty of time to get the necessary scene over and be out of the Manor House by the evening.

With three days to go, I started doing the rounds of estate agents. It's never easy finding a flat in London, and everything in a 'desirable' neighbourhood seemed to be either on a short let to tourists or wildly expensive – I didn't realize how much furnished rents had soared in the last three years. I felt justified in taking some money out of our joint account, to be repaid later, but there were limits. After a lot of chasing about, I managed to strike lucky with the basement of a house in Pimlico. A young couple had taken it, and had got a phone put in, which was important to me, and then they'd suddenly cancelled – maybe they'd split up, I thought wryly. Living in a basement might be a bit gloomy in winter, I reflected, but I could move before then. At the moment, being newly decorated in bright colours, it looked remarkably cheerful.

I moved my things in two trips, using Vernon's car which was bigger than mine. I didn't want to take anything except my clothes and oddments, and of course my cameras; I abandoned various things, such as books and records, which were strictly mine but had got mixed in with Vernon's. Still, I found that I wasn't travelling so light as when I'd moved into the Manor House. It's amazing what you accumulate when you have a house to put things in – and when you're married, I suppose.

The crucial day came – a Sunday. I packed my few

remaining possessions in a suitcase, left it at the flat, and drove on to the airport. It was an unpleasant day, sunless but hot and sticky. There was a lot of traffic and people drove in a bad-tempered way, perhaps because of the weather, perhaps because they were going to visit relatives whom they didn't like.

I saw from the notice-board that the flight from Milan was going to be an hour late. The airport was very crowded and I had to search for a place to sit down, on a bench with two fat men who told each other funny stories in, I think, Arabic. I got bored, went to buy a paperback, and found that my place had been taken. I queued in the self-service for some foul coffee and sat at a filthy table, getting butter on my book. A further delay of forty minutes was announced.

They always do this at airports, announcing the delay in bits so that you can't go back to town or do anything useful with your time. I got more and more impatient, more and more on edge. While I was sharing another bench with some appalling American children, an announcement came to say that people who were meeting the Milan flight were to call at the information desk.

That was it, then – the plane had crashed. I felt myself freezing and sweating. I was sick with love for Vernon.

I ran all the way to the information desk, charging into people and pushing them aside. The plane hadn't crashed, though. It had developed some kind of trouble and landed at Paris. The passengers were being brought to London on other flights.

I waited and waited. I had to meet all the flights from Paris – which came in a steady stream, it being a Sunday evening in August – because I didn't know which one Vernon and Aethra were on. It occurred to me that they might have decided to stay a night in Paris, as a treat for Aethra. I might as well go home. Home . . . where? the Manor House or the flat? I couldn't take the risk; probably they would arrive. They did, at nine o'clock.

Vernon, looking tanned and healthy, kissed me fondly and

243

told me: 'You should have gone home, darling. We could have taken a taxi.'

The traffic was now monstrous. there was barely a gap between the jams from the west and the jams from the south-east. Vernon chatted for a while, telling me things about the villa which he'd put in his letters, and asking how I'd spent my time, to which I replied: 'I don't know.' Then, crawling on, we sat in weary silence.

'Home at last,' Vernon said jauntily as he put the suitcases down in the hall. I avoided his eyes. I was wondering whether I felt equal to the scene that I must go through before I reached the haven of my flat, and whether I shouldn't put it off to the morning after all. No, I decided, better to get it over.

Aethra then announced that she didn't feel like going to bed, because she'd slept in the plane and wasn't tired now. No, I thought, oh no. But we no longer treated her as a child and imposed a fixed bedtime on her.

'I think you'd better turn in, Aethra,' I said, trying to achieve a relaxed tone. 'You've had a long day.'

'I haven't done anything today. Only sitting around.'

'You must be tired, even if you don't realize it.'

'I said, I slept on the plane.'

'Go upstairs, Aethra,' I said sharply. 'If I've got to spell it out, I want to be with my husband.'

Vernon gave me an affectionate smile. After elaborately selecting a book to read, Aethra departed.

'I'll just glance at my letters, darling,' Vernon said.

I gulped. My throat felt dry; speaking to him would be even a physical effort.

'I've got something to tell you,' I said.

And I told him. It all came out clumsily and awkwardly, not in the least as I'd hoped. The phrases – 'we can't go on any longer', 'it hasn't worked out' – sounded in my ears like lines from a bad play, unconvincing, remote from what was really happening to us. I talked on and on, unable to round off my speech; I realized that I'd expected him to interrupt. But

244

he stood and stared at me, holding the bundle of letters which he'd picked up from the table in the hall.

'I don't believe it,' he said at last.

'You must believe it, Vernon.'

'How can I? I look at you, knowing you with the certainty of love, and I hear these words which contradict everything I know. Words that don't belong to you, Patricia, my Patricia.'

'It's not my fault if I can't express myself very well. Especially — well, this isn't easy.'

'You don't express yourself — your true self — at all.'

'That's just the trouble, don't you see? My true self — it's what you don't know about, you don't want to know.'

'I can't accept that. I recognize that, if this destructive idea has entered your head — this destructive impulse, I may call it . . .'

'It isn't an impulse. I've done nothing but think about it all the time you've been away.'

'My poor darling, I should have made you come with me. But I was about to say: if this wild idea of breaking up our marriage can be so much as a possibility for you, it means that we have something serious to talk about. You've never found me unwilling to discuss whatever is troubling you, I think.'

'We're beyond that now, I'm afraid.'

'No, Patricia. Two people who are bound together as we are can never be beyond speaking frankly and grappling with their problems. We've a lot to talk about, I see that. Shall we leave it until tomorrow? I'm tired, if Aethra isn't.'

'I'm leaving you. You've got to face that. I'm leaving tonight.'

'This is ridiculous — hysterical. Where do you imagine you're going?'

'I've taken a flat.'

This shook him, though not too gravely. 'I really shouldn't have left you alone,' he said.

'I want to go now, Vernon. It's the best way.'

'You don't expect me to agree to that, do you? Very well, we'll talk tonight. Sit down, Patricia.'

245

I sat down; he sat down too, settling himself comfortably and crossing his legs. It looked as though he was all set to enjoy himself. Discussion was his element; he had the air of a man starting to play chess with an opponent who can give him a game, but not threaten him.

'My dear,' he said, 'I'm aware that a marriage involves a continual process of readjustment. There's a tension that doesn't exist in a mere friendship, nor in a purely physical affair, I suppose. It's the tension of emotional intimacy, the tension of love itself. The need for readjustment can arise unexpectedly – I admit you sensed it earlier than I did on this occasion. It can be painful. We've had disagreement before now, though let's remember that we've survived them. You've said things that have hurt me keenly, things that I've felt to be unjust. I don't recall that in order to reproach you, believe me. When the tension rises, you feel that you can't stand being with me – isn't that so? You feel an anger, directed against me, that you couldn't feel against someone who mattered less. This time, apparently, you've made youself imagine that you want to leave me. I didn't see that coming, I confess. But I understand, and I beg you to understand too, that this is the ultimate proof of how much we mean to each other. It's the sensitive, throbbing nerve of what is most vital to us. It's the cry for the ideal, because an endless quest for the ideal is what we are linked together to pursue.'

'But you don't imagine, do you,' I asked, 'that the way we live is anything like ideal? I've been very unhappy, Vernon. Not tense or angry – unhappy. If you don't know that, you ought to.'

'That's what we have to talk about, surely.'

So we talked, for about two hours. I could see perfectly well how this suited him; we were talking about the readjustment, about the terms on which we were to live together in future, as if my threat to leave him were just that – a threat which had served its purpose. But I couldn't help it, so far as I could make out. To dodge this discussion would be to reveal myself as lacking in confidence, and therefore in serious purpose. I sat and listened – he did most of the talking, of course – guarding within myself the calm determination which I had achieved a week ago and fingering the key to the flat, which was in my pocket, as a kind of talisman.

We talked for quite a time about how he'd made me give up my work. He disputed this way of putting it, but I insisted on it.

'I'll admit you didn't mind my taking a few pictures now and then,' I said. 'But it doesn't work like that. You're in the business or you're not.'

'Should I have known how it worked? As I recall, it was only by degrees that this became clear to you.'

'But when it was clear, you didn't take any notice.'

'If you felt that, then I was at fault. Very well, let's tackle this problem. What sort of arrangement would you suggest?'

'Can I have a job?' I asked.

I thought I'd caught him, but I hadn't.

'That's open to you, as it has always been open. But if you take a job next week, what will it mean? Not that we've found the right solution, I'm afraid; merely that it's assumed a symbolic significance for you.'

This phrase really got my goat. I said: 'I bloody well am getting a job next week. But I'll have left you by then, shan't I? So it won't concern you.'

He looked at me incredulously.

'What have we been talking about all this time, may I ask? We've been dealing with your problems, trying to set right what has gone wrong, and I've admitted to being at fault – and now we're back with this talk of leaving me, as if it were impossible for us to resolve our disagreements.'

'It is impossible, Vernon. It's just papering over the cracks, all this. You'll give me what I want if you're forced to. But to want it for me – that's what you'll never do.'

'I want your happiness, my dearest. I love you. I thought until now that you loved me.'

'I wish that was enough. But it isn't. That's what I've

247

learned in the last three years.'

He didn't answer. It had got through to him at last; he understood that I had really made up my mind to leave him. I took advantage of the pause and stood up.

'I'm going,' I said. 'It's late. And it's useless, going on like this.'

He stood up too and moved quickly. Was he literally going to bar my way, I wondered?

'I've been a fool,' he said. 'It has indeed been beside the point, all this talk, hasn't it? But then, if you'd told me the truth you could have saved a lot of time.'

'I've tried, haven't I? There are some things you don't want to know. Let me say it again: I have to be someone in my own right, it's what I'm like, I . . .'

'Please, Patricia, stop this farce!'

'What d'you mean?'

It began to dawn on me, but I didn't want to believe it.

'It's conventional enough, no doubt,' he said. 'One takes a risk, marrying at my age. Well, it isn't surprising that you refused to come to the villa. Nor could you find time to write to me – a tactical error, I think. At least you must admit that I've never spied on you.' He was staring at me, his face contorted with pain – or wounded pride, I wasn't sure. 'Patricia – I've loved and trusted you.'

'You're just being silly,' I said.

'Am I? Am I? How is it that you're so impatient to hurry to that flat of yours? Do you expect me to believe that no one is waiting for you?'

'I'm not answering.'

'I see no reason why you shouldn't tell me who it is, if only to satisfy my curiosity. An old lover, or a new one? Shall I try to guess? Perhaps it's your footballer?'

I started to laugh. 'Football reporter,' I corrected.

'I beg your pardon. And his.'

'Look, Vernon, this is absolute fantasy. Of course if you want to believe it – if it's easier for you – I can't stop you.'

He stumbled to a chair and dropped into it. This sounds

248

melodramatic – still in the vein of that absurd, bad play – but I think he actually felt dizzy. Sitting there, he looked defeated, exhausted, years older.

'I don't know what to believe,' he said. 'I don't understand anything that's happening. Patricia – I don't understand.'

'No, you don't, do you? That's what's so sad.'

'Don't go, please. I can't bear it.'

'It's the best way, honestly.'

'Don't go tonight, at least. It's so cruel – such a sudden blow. You've caught me off balance. It's not fair, indeed it's not fair. Stay here tonight, please, please.'

I wavered. 'It can't do any good.'

'It can't cost you much, surely.'

'It's a mistake. I know it's a mistake. But all right, I'll stay.'

He reached out one hand. I took it, and he looked at me gratefully as he got up. We went upstairs, as we had so many times.

'I'll sleep in John's room,' I said.

'That isn't what I meant, Patricia. I meant, stay with me.'

'No, Vernon. That can't possibly do any good.'

'You're still my wife.'

'Vernon, honestly . . .'

'Our love is still alive. You haven't denied that. You can't deny it.'

So we went to bed, and we made love. I thought that perhaps he wouldn't be able to make it, and that would be all to the good. But no, I reproached myself, this was a cruel thought. Anyway, it was like one of the many nights we'd enjoyed so richly when all was well with us. And I thought, why not? For it was indeed one of many nights, although it was the last; it belonged to our life together.

I didn't try to hold myself apart from him. I moved with him as I always had, and gave myself freely to him. To leave him while I loved him, and to feel the sharpness of it, was a test I had to pass, a point of honour. Besides, the body has its own commands and its own memories. Yet in the depths of myself I was calm, and sure of my courage. I had regained myself, and I knew it even now. I was proud that I hadn't taken the easy way out by pretending, to Vernon or to myself, that I was leaving him because I no longer loved him.

Afterwards, he kissed my breasts and murmured: 'My own darling.' I could see that he was perfectly contented; he believed, for the second time in a couple of hours, that he had disposed of my threat, or my impulse, or my wild idea. Love, securing the territory softened up by rational discussion, had triumphed. I wondered if I had the heart – or the energy – to convince him that he was deceiving himself again. However, he fell asleep. I disengaged myself from him, went to wash, and climbed in at the edge of the bed; he didn't stir. He was very tired, certainly.

I slept in fits and starts, and woke finally at eight o'clock. Vernon was sleeping like a log as he had all night. It struck me that I could get out of the house without disturbing him. I dressed very quietly and went downstairs. I was dying for a cup of coffee, but I decided to stop at a café. My throat was parched, all the same, so I went into the kitchen and drank a glass of orange-juice.

Aethra appeared.

'Are you off now?' she asked.

I had to think fast. I'd forgotten all about Aethra since sending her to bed. Was it my duty to explain things to her, I wondered, or was I justified in leaving that to Vernon?

She said with a sly smile: 'I heard everything you said last night, if you want to know.'

'I see. In that case there's nothing for me to add, is there? I hope you'll look after your father.'

'Oh yes,' she said. 'We'll manage without you, don't worry. Actually, I always thought you wouldn't do.'

I slapped her face hard. It was something I'd wanted to do for a long time. She gave me one brief glare of hatred, and scurried upstairs.

I went into the living-room to find my handbag. For the life of me, I couldn't remember where I'd put it down. Or had I taken it up to the bedroom? – I hoped not. Getting a bit panicky, I considered going off without it, but I remembered that the keys to my car were in it. Also, my pills. Eventually, I spotted it on the window-ledge.

Vernon was at the door of the room wearing his dressing-gown.

I said: 'I'm just going.'

He sighed, as one sighs when someone persists in a course of sheer obstinacy, or fails to see the point of an argument.

'You really are?' he asked. 'Despite everything?'

'Don't try discussing it any more, Vernon, please.'

He looked at me thoughtfully.

'It doesn't seem to help much, does it?' he said. 'Probably we're too close to it. It may be wise for us to live apart for a while. Think over what I've said, Patricia. That's all I ask.'

'Yes, I will,' I said dutifully.

'I love you. I shall miss you. I know you'll come back.'

I said nothing. There was no point. And I felt that I was going to cry, though whether out of real sorrow or exasperation I wasn't sure.

'You see how I trust you,' he said.

'Yes, Vernon.'

He kissed me. It was a firm and affectionate kiss, but curiously unemotional, as though to diminish its significance.

I drove away without looking back at the Manor House. When I got to the main road, the traffic was dense. I'd forgotten what going into town in the rush hour was like. But I didn't care; I was only doing the journey one way, after all. I listened to the radio as I inched along. After a while I remembered that I was in need of coffee, but it no longer seemed so urgent. I decided to do a bit of shopping, and make coffee for the first time in my new home.

The flat still pleased me, though it needed dusting. I made the coffee, and sat near the window listening happily to the sounds of London: cars a few yards away from me, the tube somewhere underneath me, boys yelling in a school playground not far away. I'd chosen an exceptionally noisy place to live, and this pleased me too. I rummaged in my bag for cigarettes, and realized that I hadn't taken my pill. This made me laugh. The laughter turned into tears, which didn't surprise me; I lay down on the divan-bed and had a good, unrestrained, therapeutic cry.

I was yanked out of this by the phone. It was a wrong number, obviously – it couldn't be anything else – but it was nice to talk to somebody and to know that the phone worked. I hunted for my address book, found the number of Eileen's co-op, and dialled it.

Eileen answered.

'It's Pat. Pat Bell.' I spoke my name loud and clear, glad to have it back.

'Pat! Hello there! How's everything?'

'Pretty good. Fine, I'd say. Listen, you know you once asked me if I'd join your co-op? I'm wondering if you could still have me.'

'Could we! You bet your life we could. We're run off our feet. It's gone like a bomb, you know.'

'Oh, that's good.'

'When could you start, Pat? I don't want to rush you, but Sam's on holiday. I mean, like next Monday, is that a possibility?'

'Why next Monday? Today's Monday, isn't it?'

Eileen laughed. 'Oh, this is great. Well, we'd better talk about money and so forth. Could you get along for some lunch? Where are speaking from?'

'My flat. I've got a flat. It's near Victoria.'

Eileen said: 'It's like that, is it?'

'Yes, it's like that. There've been a few changes.'

'OK, let's have lunch and you tell me all.'

I took my camera-bag. As Eileen had said, there was plenty of work lined up. I spent the afternoon at a theatre, taking rehearsal pictures. The old trick came back to me, of concentrating on my job while at the same time taking in everything else that was going on and even enjoying bits of the play. It was marvellous to be surrounded by all these people – the actors, the director, the costume and design and

252

make-up people – intent on their work, arguing, picking up and discarding ideas, grabbing cups of tea and puffing at quick smokes. Eileen rang me at the theatre and asked if I could fit in a street scene for a poster campaign before it got dark – 'I know it's a bit much, Pat, but they're screaming for it.' After that, she and Peter took me out to dinner to elebrate my first day. By the time I got back to my flat, I was exultantly weary. I hadn't dusted the place, nor even unpacked. That would have to wait, I decided. I asked for an alarm-call, flopped into bed, and fell asleep.

It went on like that. The pressure eased up a bit after the holidays, but more work kept pouring in. I'd brought good luck, I said to Eileen. No, she said, I was doing good work and raising the reputation of the outfit and the word was getting around. I certainly did my best, just as I had at the old agency, taking extra trouble in spite of the endless rush, and repeating a job whenever the pictures weren't absolutely right. In my free time, such as it was, I took on jobs on my own account, which came my way easily enough. I wanted to be busy, busy without a break. Besides, I needed money. I'd never had a flat of my own before, and I'd reckoned without having to buy a vacuum and cooking things and what have you. My car started letting me down; it was six years old, since I'd bought it second-hand in the first place, and it didn't seem to like being forced into constant activity after the easy life it had led in Plumstead. So I traded it in for a new one, borrowing an advance on my salary.

I wrote to my parents explaining what had happened, and also to Ruth. My mother rang up at midnight, when I'd just come in from a job at a City banquet.

'Pat? For God's sake, girl, I've been trying to get an answer on this phone ever since your letter came.'

'I'm working, Mummy. I'm never in.'

'Oh, is that what it is?'

'Yes, that's what it is.'

'Is it a flat you've got? What sort of a flat?'

'It's very nice.'

My mother then said my letter was a bolt from the blue, and I ought to have told them that things were going wrong, and come over to talk about it, or she would have come to London any time. 'After all, dear, that's what mothers are for.'

'I had to work it out for myself, Mummy.'

'Well, you've worked it out and no mistake. I hope you won't be sorry, that's all. You don't find men like that at every street corner.'

'I'm well aware of that.'

'Is there any chance you can make it up? Concessions on both sides, you know. It's worth the effort.'

'No, that's out of the question.'

'I don't know, Pat, you were always the sensible one of the family. I wouldn't have expected you to be the one to make a mistake.'

'It hasn't been a mistake, Mummy. Just a part of my life.'

'I'm glad you say that. There's not too much bitterness, I hope.'

'Not so far as I'm concerned.'

'Ah well, I suppose it could be worse. It's lucky you didn't have any children, as it's turned out. Now what about this flat, it's furnished, is it? Is there anything you want from here? We've got two of everything, mind.'

'I can't think of anything just now. I'll tell you if there is.'

'Would you like me to come over at all, Pat? It's hard to talk properly on the phone.'

'Not now. I'm working very hard. It's what I need. I'll come to you for Christmas, I expect.'

Ruth wrote: 'Your letter didn't surprise me, though it came sooner than I'd have guessed, which makes me wonder about my responsibility. But you're equal to making up your own mind, or else I shouldn't have spoken to you as I did. I admire you for telling Vernon you were going. I left a note – I don't think I admitted that to you. Well, we're two of a kind, aren't we? I hope we'll stay friends. Come and see me again and stay a bit longer when you have time on your hands. But that, I'm sure, is just what you're taking steps not to have.'

I heard nothing from Vernon. I hadn't given him my address, but it isn't impossible to trace people especially when you know the kind of work they do. I wondered how long he would go on persuading himself that we were 'living apart for a while'. He would prefer the move toward reconciliation to come from me, naturally. But I was more and more convinced, as the weeks passed, that he knew I'd gone for good. And he had several good reasons for not pursuing me: fear of failure, concern for his dignity, Aethra's attitude and perhaps Cressida's, a certain philosophical stoicism which he could summon at need : and to close the wound, to cover the pain in silence, as he had with Ruth. He was on TV and in the papers as usual, I noticed. It was good, I thought, that he and I were both busy.

I knew quite well why I was keeping busy. It wasn't only because I loved my work and needed money. I too had a wound to close. The thought of Vernon, the aching loss of Vernon, struck at me again and again at the lonely times: returning to my empty flat, going to bed alone, having breakfast alone. I reached out for him in my sleep or half-awake; I dreamed of him. It was natural, I told myself. I had reckoned with it. But going through it was something else.

I counted over what I had gained, or regained. I was free – that simple word held a supreme, a precious value. I was, truly, in control of my life. I was working, and finding satisfaction in my work. I'd lost none of my skill, none of my quickness and accuracy of eye. I was assured of this by my own demanding self-scrutiny, as well as by my partners and by customers. I was out and about in my cherished London, constantly meeting new people, challenged and stimulated and amused a dozen times a day.

Was I happy? I took that for granted at first, in a bound of release, an outburst of cheerfulness. After a few weeks, I wasn't so sure. I didn't give myself time to think about it, certainly not time to be unhappy as I'd been in the

255

dragging days at the Manor House. Yet it irked me not to be sure; it seemed to me that I deserved happiness, having sacrificed love for it. Wasn't I capable of it any more? There was an alarming thought. Then I understood that I must wait for happiness, and achieve it by degrees. I was still convalescent.

I noticed that I was always talking – talking while I worked, talking in pubs and cafés, talking on the phone. The kind of talk available to me was far from being as rich and fascinating as in the world I had renounced, but it was light and easy most of the time, and I reached out for it eagerly. I noticed, too, that I was usually the one who suggested going to the pub, or bought another round of drinks when the other photographers were ready to go home. I was shielding myself from silence. In the flat, I kept the radio by my bed and switched it on as soon as I woke in the morning.

I was doubtful, now, whether I'd been right to live alone. It had seemed to me that sharing would be a false attempt to revive my Kensington life; a chasm of experience divided me from single girls, and I mustn't pretend to be twenty-one again. Also, presumably I'd want to live with a man again sooner or later, and I fancied the idea of bringing him on to my territory. Above all, I'd had some notion of being alone to sort myself out. I was getting nowhere with that, I had to admit. The flat wasn't, in practice, any more use to me than a single room would have been. I liked it, but I wasn't in it much except to sleep. I didn't invite anyone to it. I was always glad to work in the evenings and on Sundays. I went to parties whenever I was asked, I lingered in pubs, I went to the movies, if necessary by myself.

As to men, particularly, I didn't know what I wanted. It was fine, in principle, to be in a position to attract men and be attracted by them, without guilt and without being unfaithful to anyone. It was an essential aspect of my regained freedom. I was meeting men all the time, in much the same way as before my marriage – that is, partly through friends or at parties, partly in the course of my work – and quite a few of them

256

showed a keen interest in me. I had, compared with the Pat of three years ago, a certain assurance and sharpness which men often find challenging (they were unaware of the uncertainties that it covered) as well as a range of talk and a sophistication of manner derived from my sojourn in intellectual high society. If they knew anything about me, they were all the more intrigued. Nothing excites a man more than a woman whose marriage has just broken up, always on condition that she's not the deserted party. And a woman who had in the first place snapped up Vernon Longuehaye, and in the second place had the careless insolence to discard him, was a unique attraction.

I went out, not with everyone who asked me – work came first, and moreover I could afford to be choosy – but at all events with six or eight men in about a month. I didn't sleep with any of them, and I avoided a repeat dinner date with the same man when the implication was obvious. They were surprised, and I was surprised at myself. I was in a high state of sexual alertness, responding automatically to the smile across the dinner-table, the arm round my waist, the hand on my thigh in a car. Yet I suspected that this mood wasn't genuinely sexual at all. I was demonstrating my freedom, and to demonstrate it was enough. My pleasure in being with men, and being wanted by them, was only an aspect of my need to have my time filled, to be distracted – not to be alone. I went over my evenings out, and admitted to myself that I'd never stopped talking.

I hadn't freed myself from Vernon so much as I'd imagined. Perhaps work and independence were all I could take at this stage, without coping with men as well. Trying to figure myself out, I felt that I could just about handle a very simple affair. Plenty of affection and understanding; no danger of deep emotional demands on either side; a good dash of fun and laughter, going with the right kind of uncomplicated enjoyment in bed; and a cut-off point when we'd given each other all we set out to give – that was the recipe. I wasn't ready for a man who wanted more. I'd be ready in time, I

257

hoped with some confidence, but not yet. I thought of the two men I'd liked most among those who had taken me out. One was divorced, the other was keeping up his marrriage for the sake of the kids. I didn't want to solve their problems or fill the void in their lives. They were men of integrity, I could see, capable of devotion – aiming at devotion. Either of them would make, at the least, a lover's commitment; might want to marry me; would fall in love with me, more likely than not, because he needed love. I trembled. I couldn't face it.

I came to see that leaving myself no time to think had been my big mistake. It was no use turning my back on what I'd lived through, hoping to snap out of it by a change of scene. No: I must recollect it in whatever I could achieve of tranquillity, seek its logic and its meaning, set it in order through the understanding that was granted by its completeness. Only then would it become the past, and release me to create a future.

One Sunday, when I had no work arranged and was kept indoors by pouring rain, I began to think in this way more seriously than before. I got confused over some details, over the order of events; so I started jotting down dates and incidents on the back of my appointment-pad. Suddenly I had an idea. I would write it all down, just as it had happened – all of it.

I went out, running through the rain, to the newsagent's shop on the corner and asked for a writing-pad.

'Like this, love?'

'No, a big one.'

'Well, we've got these.'

'Haven't you got a really big one?'

The man disappeared into a sort of cave at the back of the shop, and after an interval returned with a fair-sized pad called 'Ruled Air Mail'.

'Don't get much call for these,' he remarked. 'People mostly don't write long letters nowadays, do they?'

'It isn't for letters. I'm writing a book.'

He looked at me as much as to say: 'We've got all sorts in

this neighbourhood.' What he did say, however, was : 'Better take two of them, hadn't you?'

'Yes, I will . . . '

I thought of it from the start as a book – my book, Pat Bell's book. Not to be published, course, for obvious reasons. But with shape of a book, the fullness of a book, the ambition of a book.

I wrote all day, while the rain pattered in the yard ouside my window. I felt hungry at about four o'clock, made myself scrambled eggs and coffee, and gulped it down, grudging the time. Then I went on writing. A man rang up in the evening, and I said: 'Oh I'm busy now, could you call me at the office tomorrow?' I stopped writing at two in the morning, because my fingers were hurting.

From then on, the book filled all of my life that wasn't given to my work. I stopped going out with men, I stopped going to parties, I stopped going to the pub with Eileen and the others. I didn't chatter so much – my thoughts and my words were being saved for the book. As soon as I'd finished work I hurried home, threw my coat on the bed, and took up my writing.

The book grew at a tremendous pace. I could scarcely believe that I was getting on with it so fast and, in terms of my own purpose, so well; it ought to be more difficult, surely, to do something that wasn't in my line. I had talked with enough writers in the past three years to know how often they were toiling, driven back, blocked. Completing a novel in a year, I remembered, was considered as proof of great – even suspicious – facility. But then, I wasn't concerned with style, even with good English, nor with achieving any kind of effect. I wrote as I talked, telling my story as Ruth had told me hers. And I was spared the task of invention. Telling the truth was the whole point, and the only point.

One afternoon, when I'd dashed into the office to dump my films and collect my messages, Eileen said: 'Join us for a drink, Pat?'

'Oh, I can't, I'm sorry. I've got to rush.'

Eileen smiled. 'Well,' she said, 'it's good to see you so happy.'

'Do I look happy?'

'Oh, come on Pat, it sticks out a mile. Peter was saying just this morning, you're a changed girl. You were rather on edge when you started here. Very naturally, of course.'

'I'm glad I've changed, then. It must be nice for all concerned.'

'OK, get along,' Eileen said. 'If you're going to rush, rush.'

We both laughed, though not for the same reason. I realized how much I must have looked, then and on other days, like a girl who can't wait to be with her man. I hadn't told anyone about the book.

When I got home, I didn't start writing at once. I really must be happy, I decided, since I've stopped wondering whether I am or not. But it wasn't the same kind of happiness as when I first came to London, nor the same as in the good time of my marriage. Then, I had been constantly aware of happiness and of enjoying it. This new happiness was calm and quiet, created within myself, my very own.

It was the book that had brought it about, I knew. Day by day, I had worked toward understanding: toward the acceptance of myself, away from the counting of gain and loss, into wholeness and serenity. I felt that I was near to the end of a long journey. In its course, I had been helped by many people – by my parents, by the girls in Kensington, by Mrs Baldwin and Eileen, by men who had desired and pleased me, by Vernon most of all. But for these final strides, I need rely on no one but myself.

I drew the curtains against the autumn darkness, and settled down to write.

A few days later, the phone rang soon after I got home. It was a Friday, which was always busy, and I'd worked until seven o'clock. I was just trying to make up my mind whether to make a snack or a real meal, and inclining toward the latter. It wasn't necessary any longer for me to give every spare minute to the book.

An Irish voice asked: 'Is it you, Pat?'

'Yes?'

'This is Bob Curran.'

He was in London for an exhibition of building equipment. My mother had given him my number and asked him to see how I was getting on.

'Oh, Bob, d'you mean you wouldn't have rung me up except for my mother?'

'Now don't make fun of me, Pat. It'll be great to see you. I was hoping I could take you out this evening, but I don't expect you're free.'

'Sure I'm free.'

'That's fine, then. Could we go to a show? It's a bit late perhaps – I phoned before, but you weren't there.'

'Oh, never mind about going to a show. Let's just talk. Listen, I'll tell you how to get here.'

He arrived, after inevitably getting lost, and greeted me with a mixture of pleasure and wariness. I could see that he was wondering how far I had travelled from the Pat he knew. Anyway, he wasn't used to visiting independent women in basement flats.

On my side, there was nothing but pleasure. I had always found being with Bob warm and easy; and to welcome him now – in the room where I wrote my book, the room where I was becoming fully myself – seemed to be a summing-up and a vindication of that process.

'Why, you're a picture,' he said. 'Your mother thought you mightn't be well, for some reason.'

'I'm fine. Never better.'

'She says be sure and come for Christmas. It's a long time since the old home saw you. Oh, and Mary sends her love.'

'How's Mary? And the kids?'

'Thriving, the whole brood of them, thriving.'

He offered to take me out to dinner, but he was pleased when I said I'd make a meal. I hadn't yet cooked for a man in my own place, and I felt it was the right time for that too. Bob ambled about while I got the food going, looking at my cameras and my photos, which reminded me of what had first made us friends. The flat seemed smaller with him in it; he'd always been the kind of man who takes up space, and he had put on weight. But it seemed warmer and cosier, too. A man was what it needed.

'What's all this?' he asked, referring to my pads. There were eight of them by now.

'Oh, I'm writing a book,' I told him.

'Ah, you were always the clever one.'

'Nonsense. Anyone can write a book. Maybe everyone ought to.'

I sent him out for a bottle of wine, and got the food on the table. Bob ate heartily, cutting himself three thick slices of bread and finishing all the cheese I had in stock. I made tea afterwards; he'd never got to like coffee. I felt lazy and comfortable as I kicked off my shoes and sprawled on the divan.

'Now there was a meal for a hungry man,' Bob said.

'D'you want anything else? Just help yourself. There's a tin of fruit salad in the fridge.'

'No, I've done well. I'll wash up.'

'Oh, let's do it in the morning,' I said without thinking.

He put down his cup of tea and asked: 'Do you know what you just said, Pat?'

'What? Oh, I see. It slipped out. Don't you want to stay the night with me, though? It would seem to me very natural. We're old friends.'

'It's not whether I want to. You're more attractive than ever, I've been thinking that. There's ... you know, complications.'

'No, I don't think there are any complications. Mary's my friend too. You don't imagine it would make any difference to what Mary and you have got going together, or do you?'

'Well, no. Nothing would make any difference to that.'

'That's what I thought.'

'How do you mean, that's what you thought?'

'Oh, come on, Bob, are you telling me you live like a monk

262

while Mary's having all those babies?'

He burst out laughing. 'Aren't you the sharp one then, Pat?'

However, we didn't go to bed in any hurry. He lay beside me, and we kissed and cuddled as we used to at the beginning of my book, and talked in quiet voices.

'Is it all finished with you and the Professor?' he asked.

'Yes, it's all finished.'

'You're getting a divorce?'

'I expect so. I haven't got time just now to mess about with lawyers.'

'Was it you that had the roving eye, or was it himself?'

'It wasn't like that. I was the wrong sort of wife for him.'

'It's his misfortune, then. What could the man want?'

'Oh, I don't know, Bob, I wouldn't be the right sort of wife for you either.'

'We won't argue about that. You're a great girl for weekends, that's certain.'

'Can you stay all the weekend?'

'It's expected of me. "You're not often in London," Mary said to me, "so make the most of it." '

'You've got a good wife, Bob.'

'Ah, I know it.'

Late in the night, after we had made love and slept and made love again, he asked: 'What are you thinking of, Pat?'

'I'm thinking I'll stay in this flat. I wasn't sure about it, but it's just right. What were you thinking of, Bob?'

'I was remembering what you said, that it's natural for us to be . . . like this, because we're old friends. I wouldn't have understood that once, but I do now.'

In the morning he made breakfast, and washed up the dinner things as he'd promised. Then he went to his hotel, from which he returned freshly shaved and in a clean white shirt, carrying his suitcase. I had some fashion pictures to do in the little park by the Houses of Parliament, so he came with me. The model was a girl I'd known for years and liked using a camera herself; she photographed me with Bob, and then I photographed her with Bob (which delighted him – she was

263

very glamorous) and then we all went back to my flat for lunch. When the girl left, we discussed various plans – a drive in the country, maybe a trip on a river-boat – but eventually we went to bed again, as we'd really known that we would. The cars swished by, the tube rumbled, kids rattled sticks on the railings, and Bob said I lived in the noisiest place on earth, and if I wasn't so lovely he'd never be able to keep his mind on the job. But when we rested and I lay with my face on his chest, it seemed to me that it was peaceful. And it had all been simple and friendly and the best of fun, like the afternoons in his room years ago.

I didn't want to dress and get up, much less go out again. But Bob insisted on taking me to a show; he said he hadn't spent a penny on me, which was shameful, and anyway Mary would want to know what show he'd seen. So we went to a musical whose fame had reached County Tyrone. It was dreadful, but the tunes were catchy and the girls were nice, and Bob enjoyed it so much that I found myself enjoying it too, or at least enjoying being there with him. Finally we had a meal at a kebab place, which he liked too; and kissed in a taxi, and of course went to bed together again.

He had to leave soon after lunch the next day, because it took ages to get home from Belfast on a Sunday. I went to the air terminal with him.

'Pat, it's been wonderful,' he said. 'Short but wonderful.'

'It was enough, Bob, wasn't it?'

'Yes, you're right. It was enough.'

'But thank you, Bob.'

'You're thanking me?'

'Oh yes. It was such a stroke of luck. You see, you'd have enjoyed it any time. But for me, it happened just when it should have happened.'

'Does that mean it won't happen again?'

'I don't know. No promises, no plans. Leave it like this.'

'You're right again.'

'You must go,' I said.

We kissed.

'See you at Christmas, Pat.'

'Yes, see you at Christmas. Give my love to Mary.'

'I will.'

'And tell my mother I'm fine.'

'I will. So long, Pat.'

'So long, Bob.'

I went home, and remembered that I hadn't done any writing for two days, for the first time since I started my book. So I settled down to it. It wouldn't be long now before I finished it, and I wondered whether I'd feel lost without it. But I didn't think so. When it was done, I wouldn't need it any more.

I decided that I would finish the book with this time I'd had with Bob; and end, surely, on the right note.